MW01181559

The Legionnaire: Mask of the Pharaoh

For Janice,
Thank You for
Everything!
~ Sim

SJ PARKINSON

ISBN: 0985789921
ISBN-13: 978-0-9857899-2-3

The Legionnaire: Mask of the Pharaoh

A novel by SJ Parkinson

Edited by: Misti Wolanski (Red Adept Publishing)
Cover art by: Christine DeMaio-Rice (Flip City Author Services)
Formatted by: Jason G. Anderson

DEDICATION

For Celyn.
A better friend could never be dreamed of.

AUTHORS NOTE

The events in this novel were imagined to have taken place in 2008 as that is when the majority of this novel was written. Any references within the story should be taken in this context.

CHAPTER 1 – A SIMPLE ACT OF VIOLENCE

Nicky Kavanagh drove a short tire iron into the man's gut. The man doubled over, the wind driven from his lungs. Running had only delayed the inevitable. After a short chase, Kavanagh had caught up to him in an alley behind a grimy deli.

"No—No—" echoed weakly off the graffiti-covered red brick walls. Several nearby people heard; a few glanced over instinctively, but they did nothing to help. The pragmatic people in the North End knew those who didn't get involved lived to see another day.

No one knew who Kavanagh was, but they easily recognized what he was. His jeans, T-shirt, and leather jacket were commonplace, but the black snakeskin boots, bulky Rolex watch, and oversized gold chain around his neck advertised his occupation: street thug.

"Roy wants his money." Kavanagh radiated arrogance with his body language. He struck his victim on the cheek, stunning him temporarily and loosening several of his teeth. The man fell into a pile of garbage bags beside an overflowing rusty Dumpster. The thin black plastic burst open and covered the flailing man's shoulders with a pile of decomposing kitchen refuse. The smell was horrid; Kavanagh ignored it. The man

1

uttered something unintelligible, his voice throttled by pain, and instinctively raised an arm to ward off further blows.

Kavanagh batted the arm aside. "Three thousand was due yesterday at four o'clock."

The metal bar struck his victim's shoulder. Kavanagh ignored the screams and cries for mercy. He had done this too many times for it to bother or interest him.

"Now you owe thirty-three hundred. When you borrow money from the Nealy Street Boys, we expect you to pay it back."

His next blow landed just above the elbow, causing his victim to grab his arm and scream pitifully.

"If it's not paid by this time tomorrow, I'll be back."

With the message delivered and his job done, Kavanagh casually strolled away. The tire iron disappeared under the back of his dark leather jacket. No one met his eyes as he left the alley; they never did. As he strode down the sidewalk, people instinctively moved out of his way.

Kavanagh had walked a half-block down the street when his cell phone rang. "Yeah."

"Mr. Kavanagh?" an unfamiliar male voice asked.

"Who's this?"

"I have a client who wants to employ your services. Can you meet me in the parking lot at the Carlisle strip mall tomorrow morning at eleven? I assure you I will make it worth your while." The voice was smooth and spoke calmly.

"What's the job?"

"Not on the phone. Tomorrow, eleven o'clock at the Carlisle strip mall. Good-bye."

"Hey, how will I know you?" Kavanagh asked, but the call had already ended.

* * *

Kavanagh went to the strip mall the next day, arriving an hour before the appointed time. Suspecting a setup, Kavanagh checked out the few parked cars in the lot and on the adjoining streets, but he saw nothing suspicious. It was quiet for a Tuesday, and early enough that there was little traffic. He didn't notice any covert surveillance. He bought a black coffee from the 7-11 on the corner and stood outside the Play Now arcade, suspiciously watching everyone who passed.

At eleven o'clock, a spotless white Lincoln stretch limo pulled into the mall parking lot. Contrary to his expectations, the chauffeur never left the driver's seat. When the passenger stepped out from the rear door, Kavanagh noted a gray pinstripe Armani suit, shiny black leather shoes, and a folded portfolio under his arm. Kavanagh's instinct told him the guy couldn't be a cop. He looked too comfortable in the expensive clothes.

Kavanagh ditched the remnants of the coffee in the garbage and walked over to the man. "You the guy who called me?"

"Good morning, Mr. Kavanagh. You are right on time, I see. Punctuality is something my client appreciates." The man had a slight accent, but Kavanagh couldn't place it. It certainly wasn't local.

"Client?" Kavanagh asked suspiciously. That was the second time the man had mentioned a 'client.'

"Yes, I'm an attorney. I've been hired to do some business in the city. However, we have an obstacle that needs removing, and you were recommended."

"Where'd you get my name?"

"We originally approached Brandan Duggan, but he was unable to take the job, so he gave us your number. He said to mention the twenty-three dollars you owe him."

Kavanagh nodded slightly. Duggan had just begun a three-year stretch in the state penitentiary for aggravated assault. A core member of the Nealy Street Boys, he was one of their enforcers. The 'twenty-three dollar' reference was an old private joke between the two of them, and it proved Duggan had referred the man.

"All right. What's the job?"

"There's a man in town. To finish up some business deals, we need him out of the way." The lawyer's voice was emotionless.

Kavanagh's pulse quickened. He knew he would never be a core member of the 'Boys' until he killed someone. He had only participated in thefts, hard beatings, and the odd arson—the same as a half-dozen others in the group. He wanted to establish a name for himself, and he recognized the opportunity standing in front of him. "So, what's in it for me?"

"Twenty thousand. Two thousand up front, the balance on completion."

Double the usual fee. Kavanagh frowned, immediately suspicious. "Why so much? This guy a cop or something?"

"No. We need this to look accidental. His death cannot draw any unusual attention. So, are you interested?"

Kavanagh paused for a moment. While he was sure he wasn't talking to a policeman, he didn't want to risk having his voice agreeing to a murder for hire on a hidden tape recorder. Instead he looked the lawyer in the eyes and nodded very slightly.

The lawyer accepted the nod as assent and gave Kavanagh a small piece of paper with two phone numbers on it. "The man's name is Stephen Anderson. The first number is his home, so you can arrange a meeting. You call the second only when the job is done."

He unzipped his folio case and handed Kavanagh an envelope with the down payment: two thousand dollars cash. The hundred-dollar bills were well-used and had non-sequential serial numbers.

Kavanagh, feeling the satisfactory weight of the money in his hand, asked, "So how do I get this Anderson guy to meet me?"

The lawyer reached into the portfolio and produced a small but thick transparent plastic sleeve, with a white cardboard insert and round stamp inside. He handed it over.

Kavanagh noticed that the lawyer was wearing thin latex gloves that were almost transparent. He hadn't noticed them before. The stamp looked woefully unimpressive, with simple printing and faded handwriting over a signature. It had a value of one penny. *It costs a lot more than that to post a letter today.*

"This is a Bermuda Perot Provisional stamp dated 1848. It is written on the back of the cardboard in case you forget. It was

4

stolen with several others eighteen months ago from a private vault in Augusta, Georgia. Just call him up, tell him you have the stamp and are looking for a small reward. Set up the meeting and do the job."

Kavanagh flipped over the stamp and saw the green writing on the rear of the protective white cardboard. He read aloud, "Bermuda Perot Provisional… 1848… Okay… Simple enough. So what did this mook do to deserve a bullet?"

"That is none of your concern."

"No prob. As long as the money is good. Anything else I need to know?" he asked. *Why would a crappy piece of old round paper like this interest anyone?*

The lawyer leaned forward, his blue eyes steadily looking into Kavanagh's. He spoke calmly, but with menacing undertones. "This must look accidental. My employer was quite specific on that. I leave the details up to you. We'll also want that stamp back when you are done. Don't misunderstand the importance of this, Mr. Kavanagh."

"Yeah, yeah. Back off, man. No problem. It'll be done by the end of the week," Kavanagh said dismissively, ignoring the underlying threat that he normally wouldn't overlook. The promise of twenty grand and higher status bought some short-term restraint.

The lawyer stared hard into Kavanagh's eyes for several seconds, then simply nodded, got into the back of the limo, and drove away. Kavanagh realized the lawyer had never given his name.

* * *

Kavanagh spent a thousand dollars that night. He went to one of his usual haunts, an unlicensed gambling parlor run by an associate of the Nealy Street Boys. Once there, he bought a few rounds, then lost the rest of the money playing poker. Afterward, sitting in a private booth, he talked to the club owner. He was a trusted friend who had a private pilot's license. One thing led to another, and the pilot arranged to supply a handgun and a plane for a 'terrible airplane accident.' When the pilot said that, they both started giggling.

Kavanagh lowered his voice so only the pilot could hear. "Yeah, Officer, we went up with a friend for a sightseeing tour of the city, and then he goes and falls right out of the plane as we were showing him downtown. Just like that." He mimed a falling body with his hands, fingers flailing wildly until his palm slammed loudly into the table. The many empty glasses and bottles on the round table jumped up slightly and added to the noise. They both laughed riotously and ordered another round.

* * *

The pilot booked an aircraft for two days later. The next afternoon, Kavanagh placed the call to Anderson from a bus station pay phone. The call was picked up on the fourth ring.

"Anderson."

"Yeah, my name is Kavanagh. I've got a stamp here I won in a poker game last weekend, and I'm told you might be interested in buying it."

"What kind of stamp?" Anderson asked calmly.

Well, it's round, in a white cardboard liner with a plastic cover. On the back it says 'Perot Provisional–1848.' Look, I'll be straight up with you. I took this in exchange for a five hundred dollar marker. To me, it ain't worth crap, but I need to get at least that much for it. You interested?"

"Perhaps. I need to ask a few questions first."

"Shoot."

"Is the plastic cover open on the back?" Anderson asked.

Kavanagh pulled the stamp out so he could describe it. "No, it's taped closed with a small piece of thin masking tape."

"The stamp description—is it typewritten?"

"No. It's hand printed in green ink."

"Green ink?" Anderson's voice rose slightly in excitement. Kavanagh could hear him scribbling furiously over the line. A cute redhead in tight black shorts boarded a nearby bus.

Kavanagh watched her while waiting for Anderson to stop making notes.

"Yeah… So you interested?"

"Last question, who did you get it from?"

"The guy's name was 'Buddy.' He said he was up from Atlanta, Georgia. Never saw him before or since." There was a pause in the conversation. Kavanagh heard him making more notes.

"Okay, Mr. Kavanagh. It sounds like something I would be interested in looking at. Where can I see it?"

"I work over at Belleview Airport, so how about I meet you there tomorrow at 2 PM? That's my break. Hangar 7F."

"Okay. Belleview Airport, hangar 7F, 2 PM. I will see you then," Anderson replied.

"Listen, man—I don't need any more tax issues. Make sure you bring cash."

"No problem. See you tomorrow."

"Right."

Click.

* * *

Anderson showed up the next day promptly at 2 PM in a sand-colored Land Rover 4X4. He had decided to dress casually, wearing blue jeans, a simple black hoodie, and a pair of hikers.

He parked the car beside the hangar and, finding the side doors to the building locked, walked around to one end. The end doors of the hangar were wide open. The airfield was still and quiet except for a slight breeze. No one was in sight.

Anderson saw a Douglas DC-3 parked in the hangar. *That aircraft is almost twice as old as I am.* He stared at the large balloon tires under each engine, with a much smaller tail wheel just under the empennage, and noted the lack of chocks under the wheels. No one was in sight, so he walked around the aircraft under the end of the left wing.

As Anderson passed under the wingtip, a man emerged into sight from the cargo door on the side of the DC-3. He flashed the stamp quickly and waved him up inside the aircraft while smiling genially. "Hey, come on up. I'll be finished in a few minutes."

That must be Kavanagh. Right place, right time, and he has the stamp. The man was not what Anderson had expected for an aircraft mechanic. He wore faded blue jeans and a loose-fitting Harley Davidson sweatshirt with long black sleeves. The thick gold chain around his neck seemed out of place for an airport employee as well.

That didn't cause Anderson undue concern. Many of the people he dealt with had rough backgrounds, and the man did have the stamp in his hand. There were no stairs to climb, but the bottom of the cargo hatch was at waist height, so Anderson easily pulled himself up into the plane.

As Anderson climbed aboard, the man pulled out a snub-nosed revolver, pointing it at Anderson's face. The weapon had not been well-cared for—small rust spots all over the weapon, the handle thickly wrapped in black electrical tape—but it looked functional.

The man's friendly demeanor disappeared, and he waved Anderson over to one of the wooden slat benches with his free hand.

He scanned the interior of the aircraft, looking at the layout. No one else was present. "Are you Kavanagh?" Anderson asked quickly.

"Get your ass on the bench, and don't even think about moving." Kavanagh sneered.

"What's going on? Why the gun?" Anderson asked, raising his hands slightly and awkwardly backing away from the gunman, up the incline toward the cockpit. Anderson had to stoop slightly to avoid hitting his head on the metal ceiling. *What the hell is this about?* The weapon pointed in his face and the ease he had been duped set off a primal reaction in him. Recognizing the anger, Anderson started to breathe deeply, calming his mind.

"It looks like you pissed off the wrong lawyer, pal. Sit down. Right there."

Anderson sat on the indicated bench and watched as Kavanagh slipped the stamp into the back pocket of his jeans before sitting himself opposite. Anderson cringed—the Perot Provisional was worth over $100,000.

The unseen pilot wasted no time starting the Pratt & Whitney engines. The three-bladed propellers began to spin, the engines to roar, the metal airframe to shake. They sat for a few minutes while the engine oil temperature rose. After receiving clearance from the tower, the pilot taxied the aircraft out of the hangar. It only took a few minutes to get down the taxiway and onto the runway. Theirs was the only airplane in the circuit, so they were able to depart immediately.

Anderson studied the aircraft interior. The DC-3 cargo plane had been rigged for use by weekend sport parachutists. The exposed internal ribs of the aircraft and their thin lateral reinforcing supports had all been painted khaki green many years before. Two benches of lacquered wooden slats ran the entire length of the interior on both sides, supported by sturdy metal brackets every three feet.

Anger clawed Anderson behind the eyes, threatening to overcome his reason. His clenched fists began shaking. *Losing control won't help.* Anderson knew that from experience.

He willed his mind back to calm with controlled breathing and meditation techniques as the aircraft climbed. With the anger reined in, Anderson casually looked around. *Leverage. I need leverage.*

The wooden bench slats were solidly attached. Nothing in sight to use as a club or distraction. The cabin was sparsely decorated, and everything seemed firmly attached to the airframe. He'd be dead twice over before he got halfway to the cockpit to see if he could use anything there.

Anderson turned his attention to the gunman and studied his face. *I've never met this guy. I'm sure of it.*

Even with the powerful twin engines of the Douglas aircraft and the light load, it took a long time to climb to altitude. Anderson tried to engage the gunman in conversation. "So what's this all about?"

No response.

"Do I know you?" Anderson tried again.

Kavanagh simply sat with a slight smirk on his lips, the gun barrel never wavering until the aircraft leveled off. Then Kavanagh used the gun barrel to indicate Anderson should stand.

"You're going for a walk, mister!" Kavanagh yelled over the noise of the aircraft engines and air rushing past the open cargo door.

"Look, let's talk about this," Anderson called back while standing to face him. "Here, I brought your reward, plus an extra thousand." He reached behind his back for his wallet. It was the only potential distraction he had. He had brought the extra money intending to solicit additional information on 'Buddy' in Atlanta.

His fingers never got to the wallet. Anderson saw Kavanagh tense up at his sudden movement, and the weapon went off rapidly three times.

The second bullet hurt a lot more than the first. The first hit his stomach and the second struck higher, directly on the bone in his right shoulder. The impact knocked Anderson off his feet.

As he went down, the third round passed over his shot shoulder, missing his head by inches from the sound of it. Anderson landed hard on the cold aircraft decking with his head toward the cockpit. The metal floor of the airplane had been polished smooth from many rubber-soled feet over the years, but it was just as hard as the day it was made, as Anderson's back discovered.

Anderson was winded from the impact to his stomach, and the strike in the shoulder added to the discomfort. *God, that hurts. I should have worn a full vest instead of just a flimsy Kevlar hoodie.* As he lay recovering, the nose of the airplane began to rise up. Anderson glanced up into the cockpit. The pilot was slumped over to the right-hand side of his seat, the back of his head bloody, and the back of the dividing wall behind the cockpit had a bullet hole. The third round must have missed him, punched through the thin metal wall and hit the pilot.

As the nose went steadily up, Anderson began sliding down the smooth metal floor, toward the back of the aircraft cabin. He splayed his legs wide and braced his feet between two opposite metal supports under the benches. He looked down; Kavanagh lay with his side against the rear cargo compartment door. He still held the gun, but limply, pointing it at the deck. He was motionless, shoulders hunched, looking at the decking and ignoring him completely.

Strange. Kavanagh obviously wanted him dead, but the shooting appeared to set off a deep reverie in the man.

Something soft slid into Anderson's left shoulder; he instinctively grabbed at it: a standard sport parachute harness with black nylon casing. *Probably the pilot's.*

Anderson had no idea how to fly a plane, but he knew how to skydive. *Time to leave.*

The nose of the aircraft exceeded forty degrees and kept rising. Still holding the parachute firmly, Anderson released his footholds and quickly slid along the smooth metal decking toward Kavanagh. Kavanagh didn't see him until it was too late, and both rugged soles of Anderson's hikers hit him square in the gut. Kavanagh collapsed against the back wall, gasping for breath and the loosely-held weapon flew out the open cargo hatch after a single bounce.

Anderson grabbed the stamp from Kavanagh's back pocket and slipped it into his own. He turned to put on the parachute harness when Kavanagh roughly grabbed him by the shoulders screaming almost incoherently, "It was supposed to be an accident! It was supposed to be an accident!" over and over.

The plane suddenly stalled and lurched to the port side. Gravity took over; Kavanagh's grip on Anderson failed as his shoulder hit the hard frame of the metal cargo door. They both fell out of the open cargo hatch and plummeted toward the earth. The wind ripped away Kavanagh's scream.

Panic hit Anderson for a few seconds as he began falling. He had parachuted several hundred times, but never without wearing an actual harness. The wind began screaming past him as gravity pulled his falling body toward the ground.

Anderson glanced down, squinting. *I'm at least 10,000 feet up.* From his skydiving experience, he knew he had no more than seventy or eighty seconds before hitting the ground. Putting on a parachute harness on the ground took twenty to thirty seconds. He'd never heard of anyone putting one on in freefall.

Anderson kept a tight grip on the harness so the violent slipstream of air wouldn't knock it out of his hands. He had to squint to keep the fast-moving air off his eyes.

The fabric straps whipped around wildly in the air. Anderson oriented himself so his head and shoulders were slanted down, though he knew it would make him fall faster, so he could use the air stream to keep the harness above him. He guided his feet through the leg loops in the harness and pulled them up to his thighs, tumbling a few times while positioning the webbing. Once his legs were through the loops, he flipped over so he faced up, the nylon casing of the parachute pressed against his back by the air stream. He got his arms through one shoulder strap, then the other. A chest strap went between the two shoulder straps, and once he got that secure, he was able to use both hands freely, untwisting material and tightening the harness at the same time.

When Anderson was secure, he flipped over to face the ground. He arched his back and spread his arms and legs wide to adopt the traditional skydiver pose. A quick check showed he was roughly three thousand feet up, so Anderson knew he had time to spare. Falling at terminal velocity—roughly a hundred and twenty-five miles per hour—he could see that he was heading toward a large mall complex, surrounded by a blacktop parking lot.

With the harness on, Anderson began to relax. He saw an open field in behind the mall and planned on maneuvering for that.

Without warning, something hit him hard on his legs. Against all odds, the panicking Kavanagh had somehow made it to him and now desperately had his arms pinned around Anderson's thighs. Kavanagh screamed desperately at Anderson, but the words went unheard, whipped away by the hurricane speed of the rushing air. The pair tumbled wildly for a few moments, and Anderson knew that he had to get rid of him or they would both die; the light sport parachute would never take their combined weight.

The logical side of Anderson's brain knew he needed to keep the man alive for questioning. Someone wanted him dead, and he needed to know who and why.

The knowledge that Kavanagh had put them in this situation, combined with the close proximity of the ground, overpowered Anderson's self-control. Fury exploded inside him. Anderson hit and kicked Kavanagh furiously to get rid of him. The desperate man took the abuse; his eyes clenched shut in fear as he screamed incoherently. The struggle caused them to rotate in the buffeting air, and they dropped together in an uncontrolled fall.

With the altitude rapidly diminishing, Anderson ran out of time. He rolled over to face the earth and pulled the ripcord. The small pilot chute deployed first, which in turn tugged the bridle line attached to the main canopy. As the rectangular canopy deployed, the individual cells filled with air, causing a deceleration so rapid that no human could possibly hold on, and Kavanagh was ripped away by inertia. Anderson winced as Kavanagh's fingernails raked his thighs. Several of the cells in the light chute material ruptured from the unexpectedly hard jolt caused by the momentary weight of the two men. Kavanagh fell through a large square glass skylight fifty feet below. Anderson had no time to deploy the steering handles on the risers to direct the parachute. With no wind to affect his course and several damaged cells in the canopy, he headed straight down into the hole created by Kavanagh. Anderson crossed his legs at the ankles, folded his arms in front of his chest, and braced himself for the impact.

* * *

The large area beside the food court of the Fairfield Mall was sparsely filled with shoppers either taking a break or having a late lunch.

Kavanagh came through the skylights. The high-speed impact of his body shattered the aluminum framing and released a shower of glass. The body hit the edge of one of the rectangular Formica tables, and the impact bent the thick steel support tubing, leaving the tabletop sticking up at a forty-five degree angle. The angle shunted Kavanagh's lifeless body under a table in the next row, where it stopped, wrapped around another heavy tubular table support.

The glass from the skylights was tempered, so there were no shards, just small pebble-sized fragments that fell on empty tables and scattered on the floor like hail.

Luckily, no one in the area was hurt. Young mothers pulled their children away from the falling glass. Some elderly people sat frozen in shock, while others ran from the scene, dodging falling pieces of the skylight.

Seconds later, the food court got a lot darker as Anderson's parachute cast a broad shadow from above, and he dropped through the hole in the skylight. The tough nylon ripped as the parachute canopy got caught in the skylight's aluminum frame for the shattered windows. Anderson slowed, then jerked to a firm stop a few feet over the floor. He hung between two rows of tables, where he swayed back and forth slightly. Anderson could feel his heart rate was much higher than normal, but he was otherwise uninjured.

He raised his hands to the parachute risers. His hands shook with the adrenaline in his system. Anderson expertly grabbed the releases on the risers and pulled sharply, instantly separating the canopy from the harness, and he dropped. He landed lightly on the ground, knees slightly bent with a crunch of glass under his feet. Anderson undid his chest strap, pulled the harness over his shoulders, and let it drop around his ankles. Many in the crowd looked him over. Several were too busy, as they were dialing their cell phones.

Anderson looked around, but he only saw Kavanagh's body on the ground. No one else was injured, he was glad to see. He'd been lucky. Despite the adrenaline making his body shake, he smiled at his good fortune.

To his surprise, two uniformed policemen came running to the scene, each with one hand on a pistol holster and the other holding a foam coffee cup. Anderson stepped out from under the damaged skylights and waited for them to arrive.

CHAPTER 2 – THE COSTARICAN TRADER

A commercial dockyard in any part of the world is always busy. In Alexandria, a city inhabited by four million Egyptians and a major African cargo hub, it was typically chaos. That day, it was anarchy. A long convoy of army vehicles had rolled into town unannounced during the midmorning, and traffic was backed up in all directions.

Twelve sand-colored jeeps led the procession. Each vehicle had a driver with a radio and at least one other soldier standing in the rear deck, holding the handles of a loaded .50 caliber machine gun mounted on a metal support. The men wore desert camouflage fatigues. Armbands and red berets on their heads denoted them as members of the Egyptian Military Police.

Behind the jeeps were eighteen ZIL-131 general-purpose trucks painted in a sand-colored camouflage. Originally made in the Soviet Union, each weighed three and a half tons and had six wheels. Inside the truck cabs were an army driver and a Military Policeman carrying an MISR assault weapon. Each truck bed carried cargo in wooden crates, civilian workers from the Cairo Museum, a few mechanics and more armed MPs.

A command jeep with several long radio antennas came next. This vehicle carried three MPs, one of whom was a colonel, and a harried-looking civilian in a light suit, tie, and large-brimmed white hat. The civilian had his left hand on top of his hat to stop it from being carried off in the slipstream. Finally at the rear of the column, four more jeeps with MPs and mounted machine guns brought up the rear.

After six hours of slow and methodical hand-loading of the wooden crates, the convoy had left the Cairo museum at midnight. The slow enforced speed limit of the convoy and two trucks breaking down en route destroyed the overly ambitious schedule. Instead of the planned seven hours, it had taken eleven hours to traverse the 220-kilometer route from Cairo to the departure dock in Alexandria.

The heat of the day was starting to emerge, and Alexandria was bustling with activity. The blue skies contrasted with the thick layer of smog that eternally hung over the city. The choking fumes were quite oppressive. The only distraction from the vehicle exhaust was the whiff from the odd sewer grate.

Between the buildings, four lanes of traffic ran down roads designed for only two. The mass of pedestrians crossed the road wherever they wanted. Buses and tramcars were whales among the fish, using their size to intimidate their way through the smaller vehicles. One in every three cars was a private taxi. Many drivers felt using their horns helped the situation, though it simply added another dimension to the chaos.

The front elements of the convoy arrived at the docks just after 11 AM. The departure berth was known well in advance to the officer in charge of the convoy. He had driven the entire route with his senior officers two days previously. The first four jeeps in the column halted at the dock entrance, let the rest of the convoy pass, and then blocked all other traffic in or out. The lead vehicles pulled onto the reinforced concrete dock followed by the cargo trucks.

The concrete of the decades-old dock had cracked over the years from the strong sun and saltwater spray. Chunks had fallen from the edge in many places, and rusty trails showed where rebar met salt water. Haphazard repairs through the years had rusted and rotted. Though the rusted crane mounts bolted to the concrete were perfectly serviceable, the crane motors and cabs themselves had been removed many years before and never been replaced. As a result, the ships on that dock had to use their own booms or manual labor to load and unload cargo.

Downtown traffic had been backed up significantly as the convoy progressed through the city, but around the dock it had been frozen in place. Civilian cargo trucks and vehicles sought to get into or out of the dockyard from adjacent berths but were stopped by the armed jeeps. Egyptian drivers used their car horns freely in displeasure, despite the sight of heavily armed MPs.

The cacophony grew, and crowds surged into the area to see what was happening. Then the reporters arrived. Word of the journey had been leaked, and several Egyptian, European, and American reporters surged through the crowds to get video of the event. Both the reporters and public were easily stopped by the line of MPs blocking the end of the dock with their jeeps and weapons. After half a century of military rule, a military policeman with a loaded weapon received considerable respect in Egypt.

Dr. Mohammed Al Dhabit was the man primarily responsible for the convoy and its cargo. Negotiating and organizing the movement of several hundred valuable and irreplaceable Egyptian artifacts for overseas exhibition had occupied the last year of his life, but the last twenty-four hours had brought him to the breaking point.

Much of the stress was self-imposed. Despite the several talented people under him, he was a micro-manager and still felt the need to check every detail and supervise as much as possible himself. At the end of the day, even if someone else made a mistake, it would be his head on the proverbial platter.

The smell of the harbor distracted him from those thoughts for several minutes. Multi-colored floating refuse and plastic bottles covered the water. It reeked of sewage, oil, and all manner of discarded garbage. Every visible surface on the docks was covered in seagull guano, yet there were no birds in sight.

Dr. Al Dhabit stepped out of the command jeep the second it stopped. He released his grip on his hat, and his arm felt considerable relief. He had broken the hat chin cord many weeks ago and had not thought to replace it before he had started on the journey from Cairo in the open jeep. During the night he had stowed the hat under the seat, but in the harsh morning sun, covering his balding head was no longer optional. Colonel Urabi, the commanding officer of the convoy, had been beside Al Dhabit for the journey, and the doctor had seen Urabi use considerable self-control to not laugh at his predicament.

Urabi also dismounted. Al Dhabit watched the colonel adjust his red beret, the thick braided gold rope under his epaulette, and pistol belt to perfection before heading up the line of vehicles. The colonel imperiously carried a short rattan swagger stick under his left arm, exactly parallel to the ground.

Dr. Al Dhabit stood still and shook his hand to help the blood flow return to normal. His arm muscles tingled. He glanced up the line of trucks; Urabi was gesturing to his troops yelling orders while making sweeping motions with his swagger stick.

Several heavy truck tailgates slammed open, and the people in the trucks began to descend to the concrete platform to stretch their legs. Dr. Al Dhabit turned his attention to the ship he had hired to carry his precious cargo.

The freighter was moored with her starboard side hard against the quay, with her bow pointing into the port. The Liberian flag flew listlessly off the stern of the single-deck general cargo carrier. Several thick hemp lines ran from various points on the ship to the dock davits. Two gangways were in place, both off the starboard side.

Al Dhabit was even with the stern of the vessel and could see her entire length of several hundred feet. The name of the vessel was painted in white on the dark blue hull. It said *Costarican Trader*, with *LIBERIA* centered under the name in smaller block letters. There was a single large lifeboat on either side of the vessel. Both had bright orange hulls, and they were located just to the rear of the superstructure.

The only movement on the ship was a single man, standing on the starboard flying bridge. He had a white short-sleeved shirt with white peaked cap and was looking out over the military convoy with binoculars pressed to his eyes.

The ship may have looked rough to the uneducated eye, but compared to the many other dilapidated vessels in Alexandria's harbor, it was a stellar example. In any event, Al Dhabit had not chosen the vessel for her looks, but for her performance record. It was not the number of successful ocean crossings she had made that impressed him; it was the fact that the ship arrived on schedule more often than not. Al Dhabit needed reliability over all else for this voyage.

A painfully thin man, Hisham bin Dhaen al-Hamli, appeared at Al Dhabit's elbow, wearing a white long-sleeved shirt and tan slacks. The trousers did not have a belt, and he wore his well-worn black loafers without socks. Hisham was short, only coming up to Al Dhabit's shoulders, had dark hair, and was in his early thirties. He offered the doctor a plastic bottle of water dripping with heavy condensation droplets on the outside.

Al Dhabit took the water without acknowledgement. It was cold in his hand, and he flicked away the external droplets, twisted off the cap, and drained a third of the bottle immediately.

Hisham was Al Dhabit's assistant on this trip. He was always underfoot, trying to be helpful but always getting in the way. Hisham always had an expectant smile on his face, as if delivering this bottle of water would result in an instant promotion. When learning English at the American University in Cairo, Al Dhabit had come across the word *sycophant*, and that described Hisham perfectly. Hisham was there only because the time to get ready for the exhibition shipment had been severely limited and a successful replacement could not be found—rather, one had been found, an eager young man from Aswan, but he had never shown up after accepting the post. At least Hisham did not know they were looking for a replacement for him. Al Dhabit was weary of seeing his face and doubted Hisham's services would be retained once the exhibition had returned to Egypt.

"I found the water stored in an ice cooler in one of the jeeps, Doctor," Hisham said in Arabic. "I gave the rest to the staff."

Al Dhabit ignored Hisham's words from long habit and pointed in the general direction of the ship's bridge. "Find the captain and set up a meeting with me as soon as possible. Then get everyone organized, and we'll load the cargo. Remember, we need to keep the letter and number crates separate. I'll be back in ten minutes."

"What will you be doing, Doctor? May I help?" Hisham asked, smiling just a little too eagerly.

"I need to make a statement to the press. You have your instructions. Now go." Al Dhabit answered tersely, waving Hisham away.

Dr. Al Dhabit removed his hat, dropped it onto the seat, and combed his graying hair quickly. He needed to look presentable for the reporters. Part of his job was public relations, and Dr. Al Dhabit wanted to be the Secretary General of the Supreme Council of Antiquities when the venerable Zahi Hawass inevitably retired. He would certainly be on the short list of nominees, and positive public exposure from the international exhibit would not harm his chances.

Al Dhabit reached under the rear seat of the jeep and grabbed a thick yellow envelope held closed by a red cord, as well as a brown attaché case. He tucked the envelope under the arm, holding the case and walked up the dock passing the trucks on his way. Members of his team smiled at him as he passed, most of them sincerely. Colonel Urabi was poking an army mechanic in the chest with his swagger stick as Al Dhabit passed. The doctor did not listen to what was being said. He was busy mentally composing a brief speech for the camera crews—a 'sound bite,' the American media called it.

The doctor walked toward the knot of reporters where he saw the most cameras. He put a genial smile on his face as he approached. They turned on him immediately and began shouting out his name and questions in both Arabic and English, which he ignored.

Al Dhabit had learned a long time ago how to handle the press. He walked past the line of MPs and stopped just beyond them so that the reporters were within an arc to his front with the dock and ship framed behind him. The doctor knew the military police uniforms behind him would give the moment more visual impact. He paused just long enough for the cameramen to adjust their focus onto him before he spoke in English.

"Good morning. I'm Dr. Mohammed Al Dhabit, deputy administrator of the Cairo Museum." He paused a second time to let the photographers take a few still pictures. He gestured grandly toward the ship and convoy of vehicles behind him, and he forced as much kindly grandfather into his smile as he could. He had cultivated the persona in front of the cameras for many years. He paused between sentences so they could edit them into their news stories.

"Today we embark on a historic journey, taking the glory of the 18th Dynasty to foreign shores. This is the first time in almost forty years that some of these New Kingdom antiquities have left Egypt. We hope this series of North American exhibitions will generate goodwill for the country and people of Egypt. I'm told advance ticket sales are breaking all previous records, and this will truly be the event of the decade for the seventeen cities involved. We hope this tour will encourage many to come to Egypt and see the thousands of other wonders we offer. My staff and I are very much looking forward to this tour. Now if you'll forgive me, I have many duties to perform and do not have time for questions. Thank you."

Al Dhabit turned just as the first questions were howled after him in both English and Arabic. He ignored them and passed back through the line of MPs. The reporters surged forward and were physically blocked by the soldiers wearing the red berets. The smile vanished from the doctor's face the instant he turned away from the cameras. Feeling the heat of the day, Al Dhabit drained another third of the water bottle.

Colonel Urabi intercepted Al Dhabit as he returned to the line of vehicles. "I've never been able to tolerate reporters," he said in Arabic. "You continue to amaze me, Doctor."

Al Dhabit nodded at the compliment. "It is a necessary evil, Colonel. I'm sure you have done many things you did not like in order to get to your current position."

"True." The colonel changed the subject quickly. "I have my men posted around the perimeter, with at least one guard on each truck. No one will be allowed in or out of the dock area until loading operations have finished. As each truck is emptied, I would like one of your people to double-check it and ensure nothing is left behind. I'll have my men check, as well. The truck will be driven to the far side of the dock and parked under guard until we are done with all of them. Do you have any other needs?"

"Not at this time. I'll be talking to the captain soon to coordinate the loading. I'm glad for your company, Colonel. The value of these artifacts is a temptation to many."

"I can guarantee their safety as long as they are in my care, Doctor. Although I must admit, I'm most uncomfortable with our national treasures leaving the country."

"As am I, Colonel. I brought the same objection to the Antiquities Council myself. However, since those fool Saudis flew those airplanes into New York and Washington, tourism has dropped too rapidly. Egypt needs the money. Our past exhibitions have always resulted in increased tourism. So it was argued that the only way we could rekindle interest is to 'take Mount Safa to Mohammed,' as it were."

The colonel appeared to think about Al Dhabit's words for a moment. The rattan stick was twisting slowly in his hand. "When my father took me on boating trips as a child, he would say to bait our hooks with something shiny to catch the big fish."

This mental image amused Al Dhabit, and he laughed. "Exactly, Colonel. Now, if you will excuse me, I need to go speak with the captain."

"Of course," said the colonel, informally saluting the doctor with his rattan stick.

Hisham met Al Dhabit at the base of the forward gangway. "Doctor, the captain awaits you in his cabin. I know the way, if you'll follow me, please."

Hisham walked quickly up the sloped surface. Al Dhabit noticed a series of metal mesh panels between wooden slats on the gangway surface to stop slipping. He tested the tread, found it secure, and followed Hisham up the gangway to the main deck.

A section of the ship's railing had been folded back, allowing them to walk on board. Al Dhabit noticed a vibration under his feet as soon as he stepped on the deck, as if powerful machinery was in operation below decks.

As Hisham led him, Al Dhabit noted the ship felt solid and appeared to be well constructed. There was the odd rust spot, but most of the ship was freshly painted. It looked up to the task of an ocean crossing, and he felt better about his choice.

Hisham reached the flying bridge ahead of the doctor. Al Dhabit observed that the ship's officer with the binoculars was gone. Hisham pushed open the heavy metal bridge door, then stepped inside, holding the door open for the doctor. Al Dhabit entered, felt the cool air conditioning, and paused to take in his surroundings.

The bridge was well-lit. Sunlight streamed into the seven front windows arranged in a subtly arched row. Three main consoles with white enamel finish stood just behind the windows with essential steering and navigation gear. Both sides of the back wall had a short corridor leading to cabins.

"This way, Doctor." Hisham closed the hatch and led Al Dhabit down the closest corridor to the rear of the bridge. An interior stairwell was immediately to their right, and a cabin door marked CAPTAIN was straight ahead. Hisham knocked politely on the door.

"Come!" was heard clearly through the door and Hisham opened it.

The captain's cabin was underwhelming to the doctor. Small and compact, it was certainly a utilitarian accommodation, with off-white fiber walls and what was best described as a modified bunk bed against the left wall. The top bunk held a neatly made bed, with curtains drawn back, and the bottom was a small desk and alcove.

There was a chest of drawers and a wall safe in back of the room. Near the middle of the room were a small round table and four chairs. The door to a private bathroom was open immediately to the right of the cabin door.

The captain stood from his small desk and spoke in unaccented English. "Good morning, Dr. Al Dhabit. I'm Captain Kincaid, at your service. Welcome aboard. Please have a seat."

Captain Kincaid reached out and gave the doctor a firm handshake. They were of equal height, but the captain had a much thicker torso. He wore a creased short-sleeved white shirt and matching uniform pants with a black belt. Black epaulettes with four thick gold bars indicated his rank. The shine on his shoes was brilliant and almost as shiny as the gold Citizen wristwatch he had on his right arm.

"Thank you, Captain. Hisham, wait outside."

Hisham was inside the cabin and in the process of closing the door when Al Dhabit spoke. Looking like a whipped puppy, Hisham slipped out. The remaining pair sat at the round table. There was a pause as Al Dhabit opened his bag and withdrew a yellow notepad with many pages of notes. He readied a pen to make more.

"What's the condition of the ship, Captain?"

"Excellent. We topped up the bunkers this morning. The crew's clearing up a few minor issues, and I see no reason why we can't make our planned departure time. Do you have a copy of the cargo manifest, passenger list, and customs information I requested?"

"Yes, here." The doctor undid the red cord on the envelope and handed over a thick series of forms and paperwork. "We have two separate shipments in the crates. Their labels contain only either two numbers or two letters, so only museum staff know what items are in which crate. I ask you protect these documents to that end.

"Lettered crates are destined for the Carnegie Museum in Pittsburgh and will be dropped off at our first port of call. The numbered crates will stay on board and are going to the Jensen Museum in Norfolk, Virginia. Each crate is sealed with wire and red wax to reveal any tampering. Our tour schedule will be seventeen cities total, with the lettered crates going to six major museums. The numbered ones will go to ten smaller venues. Both will eventually end up in Vancouver for a last combined show in Canada, and we will return through the Panama Canal on another vessel."

The captain looked methodically through the paperwork for a few moments before pausing at the cargo declaration. "We usually carry rice, corn, and other bulk commodities. Looking at your cargo contents, I've no idea what a 'Pigment Djed' or 'Naos with gold lamina' is. No, sir—please don't explain. I probably wouldn't understand it, and we haven't the time." The captain held up his hand to stop Al Dhabit's explanation.

He continued, "The crate labels will smooth things along no doubt. I'll talk to the stevedores and will endeavor to keep the crates separated as much as possible. We'll be putting your cargo in the forward hold, for the rear hold is already full of Egyptian cotton bales."

Al Dhabit looked flustered, "Only one hold? Captain, the amount and weight of cargo we have is staggering! That is one of the reasons why we didn't use aircraft."

Captain Kincaid held up the cargo list and asked patiently, "Doctor, have you seen the holds?"

The doctor shook his head briefly. "No, this is my first journey on a ship."

The captain held the paperwork in his hand for emphasis. "Rest assured, this amount of material will take up no more than a third of the space in the forward hold, and that's the smaller of the two. The cotton will be needed for the crossing; it'll keep us more stable if the weather turns rough. Plus, transporting ballast doesn't generate us any income. The payment from the museum was generous, but not enough to take the entire vessel. There will be lots of room for your goods, and you'll have exclusive use of the forward hold."

"I see," replied Al Dhabit, doubtfully. He would have to see for himself and squeezed in more text on the already crowded page.

The captain continued, "Your guards came aboard this morning, and I put them down near the crew quarters. There are six men, but I understand at least two of them will be in the hold at all times, so they only have four bunks assigned to them, since space is limited. We were able to give each a separate locker, though. I saw them carrying pistols, and I must insist that those weapons be kept secured in the forward hold. I don't want them elsewhere on the ship for everyone's safety. Once the cargo is loaded, I've arranged to have a small table and a few chairs placed there for their use. Your staff will be placed in the transit cabins on the 02 and 03 deck."

The captain noticed the doctor's confused look. He reached over to his desk and grabbed a laminated map of the ship showing a side cutaway view of the vessel. Pointing at it, he continued, "Forgive me; the decks are numbered from top to bottom. The bridge level is 01. Below us is 02 with the radio room and stores. Main deck is 03 with the mess, library, galley, laundry, additional staterooms, and crew quarters. Last, engineering and cargo holds are on the 04 and 05 decks. With the exception of you and your guards in the forward hold, the 04 and 05 decks will be off-limits during the voyage to all but crew. We'll give a full safety and orientation briefing to all hands before the ship sails. I've placed you next door in the chief engineer's cabin. He'll be bunking aft of the engine room for this voyage. It's roughly the same layout as my cabin and has a private head."

"Sorry, a what? Head?" asked Al Dhabit leaning forward, concerned.

"Nautical term for *bathroom*. Single shower, sink, and toilet. It's the only other private head apart from my own," Captain Kincaid explained while pointing to the open door.

"Ah, I see. Thank you."

"Everyone else will have shared heads and showers. We have reverse osmosis filters on board for fresh water, but it is limited, so we enforce water rationing. Don't worry, Doctor—it's not bad; it just takes time to get used to. Once we get everyone on board, I'll need to collect passports and any other travel documents to clear Egyptian checks on this end and US customs and immigration when we dock. Once I've confirmed their information matches the customs paperwork you gave me, I'll return them. Did you have any other questions, Doctor?"

"No, I don't think so, Captain. Our needs should be few during the voyage, and it sounds as if you are organized. When will you begin loading?"

"In just under an hour. We can bring your people's luggage aboard in the meantime and get them situated. My crew is eating their lunch at the moment, and I want to wait until *Dhuhr* prayers finish so the loading process will be uninterrupted."

Al Dhabit nodded. "Respecting the religious needs of the local workers is commendable, Captain. Many westerners know little of Islam."

"I have considerable experience in the Middle East, Doctor. It's a small thing to accommodate. We have reviewed the menu and our cook Giuseppe has reflected his choices to be acceptable to Islamic tenants. Incidentally, my navigator has entered a waypoint for Mecca in the navigation system. If anyone needs to know what direction to face for their prayers, they just need to call the bridge. We will also make an announcement five minutes prior to prayer times on the PA system in Arabic."

The captain's attention to those details truly impressed Al Dhabit. While not a deeply religious man himself, he knew some of his staff were and would appreciate the effort the captain had made. "Thank you. That will be most helpful."

"Several members of my crew follow Islam, and this is routine for us. We hope to be accommodating hosts for your journey, Doctor." The captain stood, and Al Dhabit did, as well. "While your people are loading their baggage, I can conduct you around the ship for a quick tour, if you like. I don't take over the watch until 12:30."

This confused the doctor. "The ship is tied to a dock. What needs to be watched?"

"A ship always has a standing watch, Doctor. Whether at sea or not, there is always someone monitoring the various alarms and sensors throughout the ship. The crew also walks the vessel regularly looking for issues. In case of problems, they can raise the alarm quickly and hopefully avoid costly damages."

Captain Kincaid saw the description was getting the doctor concerned and continued, "This will be our forty-third Atlantic crossing, Doctor. My crew is seasoned and professional. We will see that every one of your people and every stick of cargo arrive safely."

"I am sure you are capable, Captain. Please remember, I have a considerable burden with these artifacts, and it will not be lifted for another seven months. I thank you for your professional and courteous planning," Al Dhabit said sincerely, putting away the notepad.

"This way, Doctor. I'm very proud of the *Trader* and enjoy showing her off."

"Before we go, I have one last thing to discuss. I see you have a safe in your quarters. Is there one in the chief engineer's cabin?"

"No, sir. This is the only one on board. Why do you ask?"

The doctor unsnapped the attaché case and reached inside. He produced a small canvas bag, a dirty beige color about eight inches long, with a lock on the zipper similar to what banks used for transporting small amounts of money. He handed the bag to the captain, lowering his voice to a conspiratorial level. "Could you secure this package for me until we dock? I would rather not tell you what it is for security reasons. It is not dangerous, but it should not be accessible. Only I should have access to it, and I will come to you in the unlikely event that I should need it. I have the key for the bag, and no one else on board except one person knows I have it. I would like to have it in a safe place for the voyage."

Captain Kincaid felt something like small metal tools inside the lightweight bag. "Of course, Doctor. This should fit easily. If you would step outside, I'll place it in the safe and join you outside momentarily."

"Thank you, Captain," Al Dhabit said at normal volume. He snapped the case closed. He picked it and the envelope up. He went to the door and opened it without warning, only to be greeted by the nervous smile of Hisham right outside the door. The doctor stepped outside and closed the door quickly so Hisham could not see into the cabin.

Al Dhabit passed the instructions onto Hisham that he had discussed with the captain.

"Yes, Doctor."

Al Dhabit continued, "Also, as long as we are docked, I'll want one of our guards at the bottom of each gangway. We should be loaded well before departure time, and I would like to give the staff a chance to see Alexandria before we leave. They may only take personal items, which are to be searched whether leaving or coming on board. Colonel Urabi and his MPs will be on the dock, providing security until the ship clears the outer seawall. They will also ensure nothing is removed or brought on board without being searched. Ensure the staff has their IDs on them, and tell them to be back on board no later than 5:30 PM, no exceptions."

"Yes, Doctor."

The door to the captain's cabin opened, and Captain Kincaid emerged, placing his gold-braided white officer's hat on his head as he spoke. "Ready, Doctor?"

"Lead the way, Captain. Off with you, Hisham."

* * *

From loudspeakers mounted on the minarets of mosques throughout Alexandria, the voice of the muezzin issued the call to prayer in a lilting voice, marking the start of *Dhuhr*, the second of the five Islamic prayers of the day. During the prayers, all work on the docks stopped. Tools were laid down, loaded cargo booms stopped in midair, and vehicles halted wherever they were. Traffic noise reduced to a minor din, and the crowds thinned noticeably. Many traveled to local mosques, but just as many remained in place.

The prayers were done in relative silence while they stood, bowed, knelt, and prostrated themselves in the prescribed sequence. Eight minutes later, they were finished; the rugs were rolled up and hidden away. Then, as if someone had flipped a giant hidden switch, the docks became alive once more. The noise levels rose, traffic began moving again, and people reappeared at the end of the dock.

Heavy hydraulic motors on the *Costarican Trader* whined into life, and the forward cargo doors cracked open, letting bright sunshine into the empty forward hold. A few military policemen posted on the main deck to watch the port side of the ship stepped back several paces, not sure what was happening. The doors folded into quarters and smoothly retracted against the port side.

Al Dhabit watched from the starboard flying bridge and could see the huge space below. His doubt about the ship's ability to handle his cargo disappeared. The hold was monstrous at seventy feet long and forty-five feet wide. He couldn't see it all from his vantage point, but it was at least twenty feet deep. *The captain was correct*, the doctor thought. *This is much more space than what was needed.*

The exposed inner bulkheads of the cargo hold showed a heavy series of corrugated metal supports that gave the ship rigidity and strength.

A crewman in blue coveralls on the main deck took the opportunity to begin greasing the now exposed hinges of the cargo doors with a grease gun, reinforcing the doctor's earlier observations of a well-maintained ship. Al Dhabit decided this was the right ship and crew for the journey.

Because of the hold's depth, Al Dhabit could not see Hisham and the others he'd sent to the forward hold, but Hisham would do as instructed. The man had little imagination and could be counted on to follow simple orders, though the doctor would be sure to check up on him later.

Al Dhabit looked over the dock and the loading process. Museum employees milled about the loading area to supervise and make sure the crates were handled with great care. Military policemen formed a security perimeter around the civilians and oversaw the whole process. Everything went smoothly as the two booms handled load after load. When empty, each truck was inspected inside and out by a member of the museum staff and an MP before driving to the opposite side of the quay to park.

In just under three hours, all the trucks were emptied, and the last of them retreated across the quay. Al Dhabit made his way down to the cargo hold, where he was glad to see that a pair of guards in his employ was already on duty. Al Dhabit had contracted with a well-established Egyptian security firm and had them supply six men to guard the shipment in transit.

Each man had been cleared by a thorough background check by the Egyptian state security police, and each spoke English reasonably well. They wore gray long-sleeved shirts with forest green epaulettes. Their trousers were the same gray color, with black leather belts and sturdy patent leather shoes with thick soles. On their belts were Glock 17 pistols in shiny black leather holsters. On the epaulettes, in gold thread, was embroidered 'El Rashim Security' in flowing Arabic script, with English below. Each guard stood in opposite corners of the cargo bay to keep an eye on everyone in the hold.

The guards appeared alert and professional, Al Dhabit noted with satisfaction. Just as he was turning away, he noticed an obvious dark area on the side of one guard's gray shirt, like a tea or coffee stain.

Hisham was supervising the others. Crates had been stacked with lots of deck space between them. Several low piles had already been secured to the deck, with cargo netting pulled over the crates to make sure the cargo did not shift or move in transit. The nets and straps attached to stainless steel rings in the deck designed for that purpose.

Stevedores and museum personnel were in the process of securing the last three crate stacks. Al Dhabit saw with satisfaction that all of the forward crates were lettered and the crates further aft were numbered. None of the lettered or numbered crates were together in any one pile.

The doctor tested several of the stacks at random and found the cargo netting as taut as guitar string. Reassured that all had been competently secured, he went back to every single stack and checked the crate seals. Each crate had a loop of thick wire through a locking hasp, wire that twisted and embedded in a thick, circular disk of red wax. Each wax seal depicted the same hieroglyphics, embedded deeply in the wax.

No crate could be opened without first destroying the seal. If opened, no one could re-seal the crate without one of the seal molds that were currently in the captain's safe locked in a canvas bag with spare wax. The molds had been custom-made for the exhibition.

All of the seals were intact. The crate labeled *AJ* was even placed where it should have been, on top of another larger box. Al Dhabit carefully avoided showing too much interest in that particular box, but he was glad to see it was there with an intact seal.

Hisham sidled up to the doctor. "I checked all of the seals as the crates were put in place, Doctor. There were no problems. The shipments have been divided by destination, and the guards are on duty as you prescribed. The crew delivered a small table, chairs, and some magazines and books. They also sent down a large thermos of coffee and mugs from the galley. The crew said it gets cool in the hold, so I made sure the guards had warm clothes and sweaters. They will change shifts every eight hours at 8 AM, 4 PM, and midnight, Eastern Standard Time, to avoid complications of the time zones as we cross them. They will keep the same shift throughout the trip. They will bring sandwiches with them for meals when they come on duty and lock the doors behind them for their entire shift. If anyone wants access to the hold, they have to call down to the telephone over there to be let in by the guards. The crew also put a small chemical toilet in the far corner behind the curtain."

The doctor was impressed. Hisham had covered all of the major points, and even the doctor had not considered how time zone changes could upset the shifts.

"Good. Hisham, I see one of the guards on duty has a stained shirt. This is not acceptable. Each guard was to receive four shirts, two pairs of trousers, and two pairs of shoes. They are to maintain a professional appearance, and you'll check that each guard has those items prior to sailing. There is a laundry on board, and there's no excuse for an unprofessional turnout at the start of their shifts. Remind each guard of his obligations."

The doctor checked his watch. "Once the last crates are secured, you, the staff, and off-duty guards will have some personal time to spend on shore. If the guards need to purchase any items to maintain their uniforms, they should do so then. Remember to remind everyone to be back on board no later than 5:30 PM."

A loud hydraulic scream interrupted. Inside the hold, the noise of the motors was a lot louder than it was on deck. The overhead cargo doors folded down slowly, blocking the outside light until only the artificial lighting remained. The noise stopped and was soon followed by hammering noises above. Al Dhabit assumed the crew was dogging the cargo doors. The doctor had to wait a minute until his eyes adjusted to the lower light level. Hisham had already gone to check on the last crate stack.

The doctor decided he needed to talk to Colonel Urabi again and left the hold by way of the open hatch. He made his way up several stairways until he emerged from the starboard side into the bright daylight.

CHAPTER 3 – HOME

Yellow crime scene tape had gone up almost immediately, cordoning off the area around Kavanagh's body and the fallen glass. Following that, several rounds of pointed questions had been asked of all present.

A plainclothes detective had shown up during Anderson's second recounting of the day's events. The detective intentionally looked disinterested in being there, but he listened intently and made copious notes on everything he saw and heard, including the sergeant's interrogation of Anderson. Anderson's observation about the pilot being shot in the head would help clear up the mystery of why the plane crashed just outside city limits.

Murphy's first impressions of him were neither positive nor negative. *Clean-cut and well spoken, but dressed very casually. Seems reasonably intelligent, but just came through a skylight on a parachute with a body preceding him. Six feet, two inches; decent shape and mid-thirties. Trace of an accent.*

However, the detective had his own questions that needed to be answered. The uniformed sergeant took a half-step back as the detective spoke up. "Mr. Anderson, I'm Detective Murphy, Robbery-Homicide. Let's start again, shall we? You say you didn't know the deceased." Murphy's pen hovered over the small notepad in his hand, ready to take immediate notes.

"Right. He called me yesterday for the first time. Never heard of him before that."

"What was the purpose of the call?" Murphy asked.

"He said he had something I would be interested in buying off him. He wouldn't go into details over the phone and wanted a face-to-face meeting to talk about it."

"Okay. Do strangers call you often with these kinds of offers?"

"Not often, but in my line of work I get leads from all sorts of sources."

"And what do you do, sir?" The detective poised his pen over the notepad, ready for the answer.

Anderson reached back for his wallet and pulled out a business card. He handed it to the detective, and Murphy studied it intently. The card was embossed and on good quality card stock. The background was a light sky-blue with a stylized Worthor Insurance logo in gold leaf at the top left corner. The center of the card said simply in black ink: *Stephen Anderson, Special Investigator.* Left-justified below the text was his e-mail address on the worthor.com domain, and to the right was a telephone number with a local area code.

"Worthor. There is a Worthor Tower downtown."

"Yes, the head office is there," Anderson clarified.

"May I keep this?" asked the detective, holding the card out slightly by the corner.

"Certainly."

Murphy tucked the card into his shirt pocket. "So what does being a 'Special Investigator' entail, Mr. Anderson?" the detective asked, with his pen back in place over his notebook.

"Simply put, I investigate lost, damaged, or stolen items covered by Worthor Insurance policies." Anderson unconsciously rubbed his stomach as he talked and winced.

"Are you okay?"

"I will be. This Kevlar hoodie stopped the bullets, but it has no padding beneath. I will be sore for a week." His hand continued to move across his stomach.

"It seems strange that I've never heard of you before. We handle all robbery cases in the city, and I've been on the job for over ten years." The detective knew it wasn't a question, but he waited patiently for Anderson's response.

"Well, I only get involved if we carry coverage on the items in question, so by default, the majority of crimes don't concern me. Worthor is also an international company, so I often end up out of state or overseas. Between that and the high-profile and high-value thefts I tend to work with, I deal more with the FBI rather than local police."

"Oh. Who do you deal with there?" Murphy asked nonchalantly.

"Special Agent William Bryant was my local contact on the last investigation."

Murphy wrote the name even though he knew Bill Bryant very well. Their kids played soccer together. "Can you tell me about that incident?" *If I am going to talk to Bill to check out this guy, I might as well have something to discuss.*

"That would have been just over two months ago. The Churchill Hotel." Anderson didn't say any more. He didn't have to. All the local papers had splashed sensational headlines for a week over that caper.

"I see," Murphy said flatly, making a few notes. He had been on vacation during the Churchill robbery, and none of his counterparts had mentioned Anderson. He'd read the newspaper stories upon his return, but the press had given the FBI full credit for resolving the robbery, not mentioning anyone else. *I have got to check this guy out.*

In the end, the detective questioned Anderson for another forty-five minutes and let him go. Murphy's last act was to take several color images of the gunshot bruises on Anderson's torso for evidence of the assault.

* * *

Anderson left the mall and hailed a cab. While waiting for it to pull up, he transferred the stamp to the hoodie pocket to keep it from getting damaged. Anderson had not mentioned the stamp for good reason: it would have ended up in a police evidence locker for years.

He got in the taxi and went back out to the airport to pick up his Land Rover. The drive took fifteen minutes, which he spent musing on the day's events.

As the cab entered the airport gates to go to the hangar, he saw a couple of uniformed police officers milling around the main administration building. Their vehicles' lights flashed red and blue, but they ignored him, and he didn't make himself known. Anderson paid the cab, grabbed a receipt, and jumped into the Land Rover.

He pulled away from the hangar, driving slowly around the edge of the tarmac to avoid garnering attention. Once past the inattentive police, he went through the gates and then back onto the access road. He was on the interstate in minutes and drove downtown.

Anderson saw the Worthor Tower well before he got there. It stood twenty-three floors high, with a reflective series of windows.

After parking in the concrete garage, Anderson called for an express elevator. The doors opened to reveal speck-free mahogany wood and gleaming brass trim with a pristine white marble floor beneath. The typical series of numbers above the door showed the floor designation, *G1*. The doors closed, and the elevator began to move up automatically to the only other floor it visited. The floor numbers showed in sequence as the elevator rose, passing them, and skipping the nonexistent 13th floor.

When the elevator reached *20*, the elevator slowed smoothly, then stopped. The doors opened, revealing a cherubic blonde with a brilliant smile sitting behind a dark cherrywood desk.

"Well hi, stranger. Did you finally miss me enough to actually come see me, or are you looking for the address to a decent men's shop?" she asked impishly, her blue eyes sparkling as she eyed the disheveled clothing he wore, and her left hand absentmindedly sweeping through her shoulder-length Champagne blonde hair.

The receptionist for the executive floor was smiling, as always. Her own clothes were her standard: stylish without being name brand. She was a foot shorter than Anderson and truly vivacious. Anderson knew a hidden closed-circuit camera had shown her who was coming up in the express elevator, and he suspected she had hurriedly preened herself for him with a hairbrush. She usually did.

Anderson smiled honestly. "Hi, Gillian. Of course I missed you. I just popped in to see the boss. Is he around?"

"Oddly enough, he is. He got back from Singapore late last night. One sec." She picked up her multi-line phone and called down the hall.

While he waited, Anderson studied a glass sculpture with the Worthor Corporation logo etched in the back side. It began with a nine-by-four–foot free-standing sheet of solid textured glass, to the side of the elevators. Water ran continuously over the front face of the glass, making the logo undulate. With no visible motor, pump, or plumbing, he was mystified how it worked.

Gillian put the phone down and spoke to him. Her smile was gone. "'Natasha says you can go down," she said blandly.

"That is not very nice, Gillian." Anderson turned away from the glass and water sculpture to face her.

"Well, she may speak six languages, but she's never sociable or open to any conversation or office activity. She didn't even want to sign Mary's card for her baby shower. Oh, don't get me started." Gillian sounded frustrated. She held up her hand, both stopping any response and dismissing him simultaneously.

Anderson walked down the corridor to the executive wing. He passed a couple of offices, a small discreet kitchenette, and an empty conference room.

The last office Anderson passed held a bear of a man leaning way back in his chair, with his feet up on the edge of the desk as he talked on his multi-line phone. His jacket was hung on the broad-back chair behind him, and his shirt and tie were undone, hanging loosely around his neck. The few hairs on his head were arranged in an unsubtle comb-over. He must have been over fifty. As soon as he saw Anderson through the open door, his hand shot up in an over-the-top wave and a huge smile broke out on his face.

Anderson could not help but smile back, and he waved before passing. He didn't stop.

At the end of the corridor, he reached a pair of closed wooden doors made of deep-grain mahogany. He went through the right-hand door without pausing and entered the outer office of the man he had come to see.

Anderson stopped when he beheld the goddess. At least, that was the only word that came even close to describing her. Tall, slender as a reed and carrying herself with a liquid femininity, Galina Ivanovna Tarasov was a truly unique beauty. When he entered, she stood at a filing cabinet putting away several thin folders into the second lowest drawer.

Clothes, body, hair, jewelry. Everything was in the proper proportion. Physical attributes aside, she did indeed speak six languages and needed that talent often. Galina was executive assistant to Warren Worthor, Founder, Chairman, and CEO of the Worthor Corporation. She was efficient and intelligent, and she had earned her position through talent and ability.

Galina raised her head as Anderson closed the door behind him.

"Good afternoon, Galina."

Their eyes met momentarily and Anderson once more appreciated her deep hazel eyes. She stood, closed the door of the filing cabinet and moved back behind her desk. She was graceful in her movement, gliding more than walking before sitting down behind her desk. She deliberately looked at her appointment book before responding. When she spoke, it was in her usual flat business tone with neutral expression. Anderson had never seen her smile and her stern visage remained locked in stone.

"Good afternoon, Mr. Anderson. Mr. Worthor can see you. Please limit your time to fifteen minutes. He has a conference call scheduled."

"Of course. Thank you for fitting me in." Anderson walked to the inner pair of doors. He knocked twice, paused momentarily, and then walked into the office.

The large corner office with two glass walls overlooking the ocean was impressive, yet it was the man in the room who caught Anderson's attention. Warren Worthor was almost as tall as he was, with salt-and-pepper hair, a closely-trimmed beard, and silver-rimmed glasses with round lenses. Slender and approaching retirement age for most, he was in the best shape of his life.

Warren Worthor cared about results and the people who worked for him. How much a suit cost or how fancy a car was meant nothing to him—which was why Anderson had not changed before coming here. Whether he had been in a tuxedo or just a Speedo, he would have been greeted just as warmly. Worthor rose from his desk and met Anderson halfway across the carpet with a firm handshake.

"Stephen, it has been too long. How are you?" The smile on Worthor's face radiated warmth.

"Fine, Warren. Thank you. It looks like you got some sun since I saw you last."

"Yes, I was in Singapore for three days without seeing a single cloud. Janet and I stayed on the *Mary Rose*, and I caught one or two rays too many sitting on the pool deck. Janet escaped the sun by staying inside various stores shopping. Sit, please. Can I get you anything to drink?" Worthor indicated they should sit at a small table. He took a chair at the end of the table, and Anderson sat to his right.

"No, thank you. I wanted to show you something right away, as I knew you would be interested." Anderson pulled the recovered stamp from his pocket and handed it over.

"My word, the Perot Provisional. Did you recover the other four from the collection?" Worthor asked looking over the small stamp.

"No, just this one. There is no doubt this came from the Augusta robbery. Strange thing is they used it to draw me into a trap and tried to toss me out of a plane at altitude."

"The plane crash this afternoon?" Worthor asked, and Anderson nodded. "I just heard that story on the news. I had no idea you were involved." Worthor pressed a stud on an intercom. "Galina, ask Bill to step in, please."

"Yes, sir," she replied professionally.

"So what happened?" Worthor asked with obvious concern.

Anderson gave him the true, albeit condensed, version of what had gone down on the aircraft. Just as he finished, a polite knock sounded on the door, and the balding man who had given Anderson the exuberant greeting walked in.

Anderson stood up, and they shook hands. Bill Collins had done up his shirt and tie before entering the office, making him look more like the Executive Vice President and Chief Operating Officer that he was, second in the company only to Worthor himself.

"Well, Bill, what do you think?" Worthor asked, indicating the stamp.

Collins looked over and whistled softly. "I think Her Majesty will be pleased." He looked at the table. "Just this one was recovered?"

"Yes, no sign of the others, and the men who could help us are dead ends. Literally," Anderson replied dryly. "I will follow up on this, but doubt any strong leads will come from it."

"Well, I'll leave it in your capable hands, Stephen. Bill, will you start the paperwork for Stephen's usual commission and make arrangements to return this? I think we should send it straight back to the palace instead of returning it to her cousin, given his security lapses of the past." They all chuckled, and Worthor concluded the meeting by standing up.

Collins collected the stamp and reached for Anderson's hand. "Stephen, there is a corporate golf tournament on the 23rd at

Sunny Brook. No excuses this time; I want you there." Collins shook his hand vigorously, nodded at Worthor, and left. Anderson started to leave as well.

"Stephen, one moment. I can detail a couple of men from Executive Protection to watch your place." Executive Protection, another Worthor-owned business, provided bodyguard services to celebrities and the wealthy under threat. It was low-key and never advertised publicly.

Anderson held up his hand. "No, thank you. I appreciate your concern, but I'll be fine. That plane crash will bring a lot of attention on whoever did this. People like that prefer the shadows, and I doubt they'll be back for some time, if ever."

"Very well. The offer stands, though. Thanks for coming in to see me. Do try to make the golf tournament. Don't make me send my driver to pick you up."

"I will try. Thank you. Have a nice evening," Anderson said.

"You too, Stephen. You too." Worthor escorted him out of the office and closed the door behind him.

Galina was behind her desk, making notes. Anderson checked the time on his white-faced Bulova. "Thank you, Galina. Looks like I made it out with four minutes to spare," he joked as he walked out. "Have a nice evening."

"Good afternoon, Mr. Anderson," she said in a disinterested voice and turned back to her desk.

* * *

The thick case files on Detective Murphy's desk were stacked two deep and five wide. He hadn't seen the wooden desktop in months. It took him a few minutes of rummaging before he found the number for the local FBI office.

The phone rang twice before someone picked up. "FBI, Agent Maru."

Murphy fiddled with his pen. "This is Detective Murphy looking for Special Agent Bryant."

"One moment, please." Murphy was put on hold and forced to listen to tinny-sounding blues music. He started doodling while waiting.

A minute later, a strong voice came on the line. "Special Agent Bryant."

"Afternoon, Bill. It's Mike Murphy."

"Mike, good to hear from you! Peter's looking forward to the start of the playoffs next week."

"Elliot has been talking about nothing else for the last month. I think they'll go all the way with this year's coach. Listen, Bill, sorry to bother you, but I have an official inquiry for you. Did you hear about the plane crash this afternoon?"

Bryant's voice shifted into 'cop' mode, abruptly serious. "The DC-3 that went down today?"

"Yes. It involved a guy named Stephen Anderson who said he works at Worthor Insurance. You know him?"

"Yes, I have worked with him a few times. He really helped us out on the Churchill Hotel thing. He located the perps in New York while we were still following up on some dead-end inquiries. He let us have all the credit, too. When you say 'involved,' what do you mean? Is he in trouble?"

Murphy recounted the events on the plane as he understood them, only relating the facts he knew and avoiding speculation. "... so I am just following up, since he mentioned your name."

"Well, Mike, what can I say? If life were a cowboy film, he would definitely wear a white hat. I did a cursory background check on him when we first met, and he's clean. Normal background; born and grew up in the Midwest. Went to the University of Maryland for a bachelor's degree in geology. After school, he worked nine years for Global Oil Explorations in North Africa as a surveyor before starting on with Worthor.

"He has a valid state P.I. license and concealed carry permit. No record of any kind, pays his taxes, and he has references so high up that they would make you lightheaded.

"Personally, I like him. Straight-up guy. If he says something, take it to the bank. When he got back from New York, he had to come in to the office to give a statement. We ended up down on the range, and he held his own against me. He said he'd never handled a 10mm before, but put everything in the bull's-eye.

"He is smart, too. I'd offer to make him an agent, but we can't afford him."

"What do you mean, 'can't afford him'?" Murphy asked.

"Well, he told me his deal with Worthor. He makes twelve percent of the value of anything he recovers."

Murphy pulled a desk calculator from under a case file and tapped numbers as he spoke, "So for the three mil in diamonds from the Churchill, he made..."

"Three hundred sixty thousand dollars," Bryant interrupted, just as the figure popped up on Murphy's calculator.

"Geez..."

"Not bad for two days' work, huh?" Bryant laughed.

"Not bad at all. Okay, Bill. Thanks for the background. I'll get back to you if I find anything else. The NTSB are going over the wreckage now. If this is an airborne shooting, I suspect your guys will be taking over before long. I'll see you in a few nights when the boys play the 'Lucy's Pizza' team."

"Thanks, Mike. Bye."

* * *

Anderson headed out of the office. Gillian wasn't at the reception desk. He pressed the call button, and the express elevator doors popped open instantly. On the ride down, Anderson once more thought about the day's events, but he could not come up with any reason why he had been targeted. Anderson had been an investigator at Worthor for three years. In that time, he'd had some notable successes recovering several highly valued items. No doubt he had irritated a few within the criminal world, but who would hate him enough to want him dead? What had Kavanagh said? *"It looks like you pissed off the wrong lawyer, pal."* Anderson seldom dealt with lawyers, and the few he had investigated had no reason to kill him.

Anderson used his key fob to deactivate the car alarm and locks before climbing into the driver's seat. He pulled into the rush hour traffic and headed toward the northeast side of town. He decided to pull off the crowded interstate and head through the dock area. Anderson kept on the coast road and eventually turned back inland, passing under the interstate and into a light industrial area well north of the main city. After the morning he'd had, Anderson made sure to check for a tail at regular intervals. He saw nothing untoward.

Anderson drove through what had once been the city's industrial center. He turned the Land Rover onto Watson Street and passed several red brick buildings that had survived the centuries and been reborn. Anderson pulled up to a three-story structure of red brick. Over the door, the number *1863* was chiseled into an off-white arched keystone. The building had been renovated; the lack of graffiti said that much.

Anderson tooted his horn to warn anyone inside and drove in slowly. The narrow entrance had originally been built for horse-drawn wagons, and Anderson entered carefully. 1863 Watson had originally been built to house the Cranston Bottling Company in the year 1890. That year was inscribed on a white granite cornerstone at the base of one exterior wall.

The main floor had been converted into a combination garage and workshop. A half-dozen oversized parking spots were outlined by yellow paint on the floor, three of which were occupied. A nondescript white Ford E-Series van was first, followed by a dark green BMW M6, then a midnight black BMW 750i, four-door.

Two sets of stairs—one going up, the other going down—had translucent plastic strips hanging from the ceiling to keep vehicle exhaust fumes from traveling through the rest of the building. Overhead, fluorescent lights illuminated the entire space and the several workbenches opposite the cars. Even with the cars and assorted equipment, the building was still roomy and open.

Anderson pulled to the right and backed into an empty space. He killed the engine to minimize the exhaust fumes. As soon as the car door was opened, he could hear the muted strains of opera coming over several ceiling-mounted speakers. Having heard it many times before, he instantly recognized it as Giuseppe Verdi's "Aida."

A thirty-year-old man with jet-black hair emerged from the plastic strips around the basement stairs. His slender build belied the strength on his tall frame. His white coveralls sported only a few dirty spots, and they emphasized his heavy tan. He wrung his hands in a spotted rag as he approached Anderson. Vincenzo "Vinnie" Scarlatti had worked for Anderson for two years.

"Hey, boss," Vinnie said in cordial greeting as he approached. His voice still had a strong accent from his native Italy. "I got the rough pipe work done for the hydrogen tanks. We can fill them directly from the alley now. I have to drill through several feet of concrete to get lines up here, and I will start that tomorrow. I took the Alfa into the basement so I could work on the wiring. I have been having strange issues and decided to replace the whole electrical system from bumper to bumper. It's gonna cost about twelve hundred more, so I hope that is okay?"

"Not a problem, Vinnie. You do what you think is needed. I can give you a hand with the drilling tomorrow. Is Masumi in?" Anderson asked.

"She left about an hour ago in a taxi. She said she would be back late. You need me for anything?"

"I don't think so. You are off the clock." Anderson smiled.

"I'm gonna strip out the rest of the wiring before I go home. I called the missus. Her and her sisters are playing cards again, so I hafta do something." He laughed. Anderson knew Vinnie loved his wife dearly, but he could not stand being around most of her family for long. He let Vinnie use the garage as a refuge from that storm.

"No problem. Have a good night, Vinnie." Anderson knew Vinnie would have the car cleaned, checked, serviced, and gassed before he left, with the gate closed and alarm set behind him. Anderson didn't need to remind him.

Anderson passed through the hanging plastic strips and walked up the staircase. At the top was a smaller landing, with industrial metal sliding door on rollers and counterweights. A flashing red LED told him the alarm and door lock were active.

47

He keyed in his access code, entered, and the electric lock engaged with another 'thunk' as the door closed behind him.

Anderson removed his shoes before walking through the great room and into the modern kitchen. Hidden sensors detected his presence and turned on overhead lights automatically. He pulled open the refrigerator and poured himself a tall glass of pineapple juice. With that in hand, he walked to the three large couches in the center of the great room. He grabbed the large remote control off the coffee table and pressed a few buttons; several components in the entertainment system lit up, and "Beautiful Day" by U2 began playing at a low volume. He walked toward one of the opposite doors. Behind him, the kitchen lights turned off of their own accord.

Anderson opened the door and walked in. The lights came on, revealing a large open-concept office with a huge desk, a multi-line phone, and a large computer monitor. Four eight-inch monitors, mounted two by two in the desk cabinetry, turned on. They showed several areas of the building from hidden video cameras. Concealed speakers brought the soft music from the living room into the space.

Anderson sat in the chair and rolled it over to his desk. He sipped his juice as his free hand moved the trackball. Anderson started a spreadsheet program and opened a file containing a blank expense form with his name, address, and employee number already filled in. He began to fill in his expenses for the day.

The only company connection Anderson had was the logo on his business cards. The e-mail address on the card was automatically routed from company servers to his home account. The phone and fax numbers went directly to his desk at home. He had no office space or even a desk in the Worthor building, and he mostly communicated with company personnel by phone or e-mail. Anderson set his own hours, came and went as he saw fit, and when not actively on an investigation, he could travel or do whatever projects interested him. Anderson was given latitude because he got results, and that was all that mattered in the mind of Warren Worthor.

Anderson briefly considered checking some online news sites, but he decided he'd had enough for the day. His shoulder and stomach ached, and he needed some aspirin, a hot shower, and a few hours' sleep. He locked the computer screen, got up from his desk, drained the rest of the pineapple juice, and left the empty glass behind on the coaster. The computer, like the lights, would power down automatically, so he just walked away. Anderson went to the circular staircase and went upstairs into his master suite.

* * *

The lawyer knew Dallas was seven time zones behind him, making it early morning, but he had been given strict instructions to call. He dialed and then listened to the phone ring a dozen times.

"Yeah," the strong voice answered over the cell phone with a thick Texan drawl. He was breathing hard, as if the walk to the phone was almost too much for him to tolerate.

"Good morning, sir. The shipment is loaded. I just met with the principals, the necessary materials are aboard, and all preparations have been made as we discussed. There were no complications."

A grunt of satisfied acknowledgement was all that came over the cell.

The lawyer continued, "I also thought you would want to know about the other matter. The courier we hired was not up to the task. The package you wanted was picked up successfully but not delivered."

The voice on the other end of the line grunted between ragged breaths. He didn't like hearing about failure. "What about the postage?"

"Non-refundable, I am afraid."

"… and the courier?" The growing irritation was evident in the accented voice.

"Out of business. Would you like me to arrange for a second delivery attempt?"

"Hell no! I never piss into the wind a second time and it's getting too close to the main event. I want y'all here as soon you can. When is your flight?"

"I will be in the air in three hours and am scheduled into DFW at 8:30 PM tomorrow."

"Right. I'll be out at the south ranch. Y'all be there by ten. We need to arrange insurance options for the main delivery," the voice demanded.

"Yes, sir. Goodbye." The lawyer hung up and casually tossed the cell phone off the concrete breakwater into the brackish salt water of the harbor. The lawyer did not think of the phone again; he had three more prepaid GSM cell phones in the trunk of his black Mercedes Benz limousine. The lawyer cast one last long look at the distant blue-hulled freighter across the harbor. He swept his fingers through his short blond hair as he stepped past the local driver holding the rear door of the limo open for him. He got into the limo, and the air conditioning took the edge off his brief exposure to the North African air. The chauffeur slipped into the driver's seat.

"Sofitel Cecil Hotel," said the man in the back seat. He was glad he had chosen a tropical weight Gianni Vironi suit.

"Yes, sir," the Egyptian driver enthusiastically replied.

* * *

The man had hired the limousine for the day to drive him around to various locations. The driver assumed his passenger was some sort of businessman, because his destinations were hardly the usual tourist ones. Not that it was any of his business, of course. He wanted to ask why he had thrown a perfectly good phone into the water, but he restrained himself. Everything about his passenger reeked of money, and he was looking forward to making some decent *baksheesh* for his day's work. He hoped his discretion would earn him a little more at the end of the day. The driver pulled into the busy Alexandria traffic and joined in the symphony of car horns.

CHAPTER 4 – DEPARTURE

The *Costarican Trader* departed the Alexandria docks within a minute of its expected departure time. Both the harbor pilot on the bridge and the tug alongside were in place early, something almost unheard-of for an Egyptian port. Captain Kincaid wondered if the notoriety of the special cargo had anything to do with this unexpected outbreak of efficiency. He stood patiently to one side as the pilot set up his navigation gear.

"Captain, you may depart the dock at your discretion." The Egyptian pilot spoke in an old school English accent.

"Thank you, sir."

The gangways had been removed along with all mooring lines except two. There remained one line off the bow and one off the stern, both on the starboard side. The captain turned to his first officer and commanded him to cast off all lines. He then keyed his walkie-talkie to speak to the captain of the tugboat. "*Rozi— Costarican Trader*. Our engines are standing by. We are casting off lines now." There was a burst of static as the captain released the talk switch.

"Roger, *Trader*. We ready," came the terse and heavily accented reply from the tug captain.

Slowly, the bow moved further and further away from the dock. The stern came away at a slower pace, as planned. As soon as he judged the stern was far enough away from the dock, Captain Kincaid spoke to the pilot beside him. "Pilot, we are clear of the dock." Then he turned to the bridge crew. "Pilot has the helm."

The helmsman acknowledged the order, "Pilot has the helm—aye, sir."

The Egyptian pilot checked his GPS display before giving his orders. The ship began turning in a very tight circle to the left. With the tug hauling the bow around, the ship could turn on a much smaller radius than it could alone. Kincaid stood silently, watching the activity. Even though the pilot was giving helm commands and evidently saw nothing amiss, the vessel was still the captain's responsibility. He did not relax one iota.

The ship had passed through ninety degrees of turn before the pilot spoke again. "Captain, you may cast off the tug."

Captain Kincaid wasted no time. He keyed his walkie-talkie and said, "*Rozi—Costarican Trader.* We are in position. Cast off tow lines."

"Cast off tow lines, aye," acknowledged the *Rozi*'s captain. The tug crew swarmed over the deck to release the lines running to the bow of the cargo ship. This took a few minutes, and as soon as they had been dropped into the water, the tug moved back slowly to give the *Trader* sea room.

Captain Kincaid keyed his radio one last time. "*Rozi—Costarican Trader.* We are clear. Thank you and fair winds."

"Safe journey, *Trader. Rozi* out." The tug tooted her steam whistle twice, and Captain Kincaid responded with the *Trader*'s own horn, which was much louder and deeper in tone. Passengers standing by the rails on the 03 deck jumped unexpectedly at the sudden noise.

After several minutes of leisurely cruising, the pilot turned to the captain. "Sir, we are clear of the harbor. The helm is yours."

"Thank you, sir. The helm is mine," said Captain Kincaid. The pilot turned to pack up his GPS unit.

"Captain. Pilot boat approaching off the port side," the first officer called out.

"Thank you. Engines to standby. Helm, keep her so. Lower the sea stairs and prepare to disembark the pilot." His crew all moved in response to his orders.

The ship now coasted, slowing to allow the pilot's boat to come alongside to take the harbor pilot back to Alexandria. The only pause in the procedure was caused by the captain and pilot shaking hands. They exchanged a few words of cordial Arabic before the pilot left the flying bridge. The pilot walked down the port side on steps that had been winched down. He stepped off onto the deck of the smaller boat with a practiced hop. As soon as he was on board, the pilot's vessel roared off and headed further out to sea to meet an incoming oil tanker. The cargo ship crew raised the sea stairs with the motorized winch.

The first officer called out, "Pilot boat is clear. Sea stairs are raised and secure."

"Thank you. Secure all lines and equipment. Make ship ready for sea," Captain Kincaid responded.

"Secure all lines and equipment. Make ready for sea, aye, sir." The first officer relayed the orders into his walkie-talkie.

"All ahead two thirds," the captain told the helmsman.

"All ahead two thirds, aye, sir." The bells rang out once more as the telegraph handles were shifted. "Sir, engines are answering, two thirds ahead."

The vibration in the deck picked up noticeably, and the *Costarican Trader* surged into the Mediterranean Sea.

* * *

Dr. Al Dhabit had observed the departure from the starboard side of the main deck, surrounded by his staff. Just after the ship had left the dock, he'd looked back in time to see Colonel Urabi saluting the vessel with his cane.

Al Dhabit was impressed how smoothly the departure process had gone. He knew that moving a large ship was no small task, and it had only looked easy because of the professionalism of the captain and crew. Dr. Al Dhabit was now confident in his choice of this vessel. His trust had to be earned, and Captain Kincaid was doing an admirable job so far.

Before departing, the captain had personally performed the ship's briefing to the museum staff and off-duty guards. He spoke clearly about the various areas of the ship, what they should do in case of problems, and where to muster. He outlined the daily life on board his vessel, meals, water usage restrictions, the procedures for smoking, garbage, and call to prayer, and what was expected of everyone aboard. The captain was a lot more personable than his initial meeting with the doctor. Kincaid answered all the staff's questions with professionalism. He even added a little humor at times to put them at ease.

Now that they were underway, Al Dhabit's staff left the deck in ones and twos. Some lingered to take pictures, but the further from land they got, the less there was to see. Al Dhabit really had nothing to do except wait until they docked. He had to attend to a few administrative chores—like checking on the guards in the forward hold at odd hours to ensure they stayed alert. There were also letters to write, and progress reports to the Museum Administrator and the Antiquities Council, but they would take hours to complete, not days. The ship's radio room had a satellite uplink for phone conversations, slow Internet access, and even a fax machine, which would ease things. After several months of hectic activity, he could now relax before the continuous stress of the exhibition began. *A wonderfully long relaxing sea voyage*, he thought.

The doctor watched the land slowly retreat into the distance. With each lungful of the salty sea air, he felt himself actually start to relax. The sparsely populated sandy shores of northern Africa held few settlements for the ship to pass as they traveled west. After a time, he no longer saw anything to keep his attention, so he went for a walk around the forward cargo hold.

Al Dhabit had only made it past the superstructure when Hisham came running around the corner, wide-eyed and screaming for him. "Doctor! *Doctor!* There's a warship closing in on us!"

"What? Show me!" Al Dhabit demanded, alarmed.

They both ran to the starboard side railing, where Al Dhabit could indeed see a warship approaching from an oblique angle, traveling much faster than the cargo ship. White water was hurled up high on either side of the angled knife-edged bow. A single large-barrel cannon was mounted in a cylindrical turret, and multiple missile boxes were located just below the low, sleek superstructure behind the bridge. At two-thirds the length of the *Costarican Trader*, the incoming vessel was leaner and much, much meaner. The deck was dark gray or black in places, and Al Dhabit could see multiple radar antenna rotating. Very little smoke came from the warship's stack. As it came closer, the doctor squinted and could just make out the faint gray letters on their bow: *F946*. The warship looked to be on a collision course with the *Trader*.

On the incoming ship, a light started blinking irregularly. Al Dhabit looked up at the starboard flying bridge and saw the captain standing with a crewman. Al Dhabit turned and ran up the outer stairs on the outside of the superstructure. On the last section of stairs, he began calling the captain's name aloud.

"Captain Kincaid! Captain Kincaid!"

But Kincaid simply raised his hand in a *stop* gesture, and Al Dhabit stopped on the last stair, breathless and bewildered. The captain turned his attention back to the crewman, who was speaking in a low voice. The captain spoke to the younger man with a small signal lamp. "Send: What are your intentions?"

The younger man clicked the lamp for a minute and a half. Everyone on the flying bridge silently awaited the response. Soon, the warship began to flash a message of its own. Dr. Al Dhabit was beside himself with anxiety as it arrived. He had visions of trying to repel boarders with nothing but chairs and soup ladles. Six guards with pistols suddenly seemed woefully inadequate.

Al Dhabit was shocked back to reality when the captain and light operator both laughed at the incoming message.

"Send: Understood. Thanks for the company." The captain waved the doctor to come up the stairs. "Doctor, it seems we have an escort to Gibraltar. Do you recognize the flag on the ship?" asked the captain.

Al Dhabit looked over and saw the ship was turning to parallel the freighter's course. A flag flew from the central radio mast. The top third of the flag was red, the center third was white, and the lower third was black. In the center of the white bar was a golden eagle with long wings. "It is an Egyptian ship!" the doctor said in total surprise. Though not a religious man, he also added in Arabic, "Praise Allah in all his glory," before leaning heavily against the flying bridge guard rail to cuff the sweat from his brow.

"It is the frigate *Aboukir*. They have been detailed to escort us as long as we are in the Mediterranean," said the captain.

"I do not know what to say, Captain. I was not informed of a naval escort, but I should have expected it." Al Dhabit recovered a little of his composure. "Captain, why did you laugh? What did they say when you asked what their intentions were?"

"Oh, they said they were here to discourage your 'Libyan neighbors' from dropping by and conducting a 'customs inspection.'"

"I see." Al Dhabit did not smile, but he was greatly relieved nonetheless. He took out a handkerchief and mopped his forehead again. "That is indeed fortunate. If you will forgive me, Captain, I will retire to my cabin."

"Of course, Doctor." Kincaid checked his watch. "We will be serving a late dinner in twenty minutes. My apologies for the delay, but I needed the galley crew for handling lines in port."

"Perfectly understandable, Captain. The delay will just result in bigger appetites, I suspect." The doctor turned and entered the bridge through an open hatch. He felt cooler immediately out of the sun. He turned right, nodding to the helmsman. The navigator was working at the chart table with his back to him and did not notice him passing by. Al Dhabit walked past a wall containing an electrical panel to his left. Beyond the panel was a cabin door with *CHIEF ENGINEER* in white lettering on the door. The door was unlocked, and he let himself in.

Closing the door behind him, Al Dhabit removed his jacket and dropped it over the back of a chair. He unbuttoned his shirt, entered the head, and washed his hands and face in the sink with cold water. He dried off with a clean towel and stared at himself in the mirror. He composed a mental checklist of the necessary tasks he needed to accomplish for the voyage. *A wonderfully long relaxing sea voyage*, he thought to himself again, only this time with just a little doubt attached.

* * *

Hisham had stood at the railing, watching the approaching warship so intently he had not heard the doctor leave. He did hear the doctor screaming the captain's name out as he had ascended up the stairs, and Hisham turned to look up at the flying bridge. He could hear nothing but the faint clacking of the signal lamp, and he had no idea what was being said. The rushing air from the ship's movement took many of the words away from his ears. He did hear the laughter a few minutes later, which confused him all the more until he turned back to the warship and saw the Egyptian flag for himself. Even so, it took a few moments for everything to sink in.

For a horrible moment, Hisham had panicked, thinking everything was going to come undone in a blaze of naval gunnery. However, now that the ship was abeam of the cargo ship and both ships were maintaining speed, his fears were slowly disappearing. It was an escort, nothing more. He dismissed it from his thoughts and returned to his biggest problem.

Hisham resented the doctor's dismissive treatment. He had spared no effort in being helpful and willing to act on Al Dhabit's merest whim. What did the man expect of Hisham, that he could not give him the slightest amount of respect? Could the doctor not see that he was hardworking and dedicated, that he was worthy of more responsibility, promotion, and a larger income?

When the North American exhibition had been announced, Hisham had been tasked with crating up over eight hundred and fifty items from the New Kingdom era. The artifacts ranged in size from a two-centimeter obsidian statue of Anubis to the wooden coffin lid of Ramses II. Plus, Hisham had to crate up the acrylic display cases to be used for certain items. Each crate needed to be custom designed and built to cushion the items on their journey. Every piece had to be hermetically sealed in plastic to avoid humidity changes or seawater corrosion. Doctor Al Dhabit had also insisted that each crate be positively buoyant so they would float in case the ship sank. So a thick outer border of rigid insulating foam had to be accommodated, as well. Then wooden crates were built around each case.

All those tasks needed to be performed many times over, and Hisham had been the right person to supervise the job. He directed a couple of able carpenters and younger laborers and even pitched in himself where needed. It had involved long hours and a few setbacks, but in the end, they were ready before the deadline. Even the head administrator at the museum had been impressed by the effort and brought tea and sweet cakes for all to show his gratitude.

Hisham made his way westward on the freighter. He would stay with the main exhibition to ensure the material was unpacked properly and keep the packaging safe for their many scheduled destinations. While the exhibitions were being seen by the public, Hisham would act as Dr. Al Dhabit's assistant.

Hisham realized dinner would be soon, and he walked to his cabin to wash up. The day's activities had left him dusty and dirty.

* * *

The first meal on board was a boisterous affair. Everyone felt a sense of accomplishment at getting everything on board without incident. Now their workload would be dramatically reduced for several days, and they could relax. None of them had ever been on a freighter before, and the change of scenery excited many of them. Doctor Al Dhabit did not squelch their enthusiasm. In fact, he participated in the excitement to a small degree, so they'd know they had his permission to have a little fun.

By tradition, the men and women of the museum sat separately, but all enjoyed the moment. The men told humorous stories of their trip from Cairo, and they illustrated their experiences with wild hand gestures. It became a competition of who could tell the best story, and before long, unbelievable embellishments were being added, to great laughter. The women in the group talked more quietly about the excitement of shopping opportunities in America and the bittersweet emotions of leaving their friends, families, and partners behind.

Hisham sat near the far end of the table, away from Al Dhabit—it had been the only spot available by the time he arrived.

Two off-duty private security guards ate with the staff, as well; the others were either in the hold or sleeping. The guards did not mix as freely, but the light atmosphere of the gathering did not exclude them. The team had all worked exceptionally long hours to get to this point and needed to blow off a little steam. They were on a rare adventure that would probably not be repeated in their careers, and everyone in the mess felt it. Their boss's presence helped keep things in check. A few members of the ship's crew talked quietly at one end of the tables.

The ship's mess and attached galley were designed for the rough Atlantic weather. The tables had a slight rim raised from the edges to catch dishes and cutlery in rolling seas. Rubber mats under the dishes and cups minimized any movement in all but the fiercest of seas.

On the end of the mess, a small but efficient galley could be seen, filled with steel appliances, cabinets, and counters. The two double sinks had all shape and manner of dirty pots piled high in them. Giuseppe, the ship's cook, and a Pakistani assistant were in the kitchen, putting the finishing touches on a few lemon meringue pies for dessert. A small shortwave radio was tuned into RAI short wave. Popular music and news came over the speakers in Italian, barely audible, but the music and odd burst of static added to the atmosphere nonetheless.

The tables held the remains of a meal that had consisted of green salad, vegetable soup, and shish taouk, a marinated chicken breast skewered with vegetables and spices. Al Dhabit thought the captain had not exaggerated when he'd called Giuseppe a good cook. The food was exceptionally well prepared and presented.

A large stainless steel bowl of Basmati rice, with steamed carrots mixed in, was passed down the table. One of the office staff fumbled as he passed it, but he caught it before anything spilt.

"Everyone, make sure Ibrahim does not help unpack the crates!" Al Dhabit pointed at the embarrassed man, and everyone laughed. The man beside Ibrahim good-naturedly slapped the bowl holder's back.

"Doctor, perhaps we should turn around and put him back on the dock before he does real damage!" said one of the assistants, to even more laughter and backslapping. Ibrahim's face took on a rosy red glow, and he smiled uncomfortably, doubtless trying to think of some way to get out of the spotlight.

The Pakistani galley assistant—he had been introduced earlier as Wadud—left the kitchen to distribute small piles of plates and forks. He retreated back into the kitchen and returned with a pie in each hand. He slid one pie on each table and walked back into the galley. The mess got a lot quieter as everyone ate dessert. Wadud brought out a tray of insulated carafes of coffee and tea, which he placed on the tables. He picked up several empty serving bowls and used cutlery before returning.

Al Dhabit skipped the pie. He had overindulged with a second portion of chicken, and he would get nothing but grief from his wife of twenty-two years if he came home any heavier. Instead, he poured himself a cup of tea and stirred in a small dollop of honey. He sipped the tea, mentally retreating from the mess while he ran several things through his mind. When he wrapped up his thoughts, he saw the meal was done. Wadud was clearing the dessert dishes, and everyone was quieter. Doctor Al Dhabit rose and held his tea in his right hand. The little conversation that was going on died within moments. All eyes turned to the administrator.

"Well… We've certainly had a long and busy day," Al Dhabit said genially. Everyone chuckled and nodded. "I would like to thank you for all your hard work over the last few months. I know it has taken you away from your families, but in the end, this trip will raise Egypt's profile on the world stage and advertise the glories that we see every day. We'll certainly be busy when we get to the United States, and so I encourage you to use the time onboard to rest and relax. It may be the only break we get until the long return voyage from Vancouver." Everyone nodded slightly in agreement.

"Tomorrow there will be a lifeboat drill at 10 AM, and everyone except the guards in the hold are expected to be there. Other than that, there will be no other organized activities except for meals and prayers. I hope you use this time productively. I'm available to any of you if you have any questions. Have a good voyage." He raised his tea mug, and everyone smiled with pride.

Al Dhabit sat and finished the rest of his tea. Small numbers of people left the galley, and the doctor could see the men in the kitchen starting to scour the pots. One of the off-duty crew walked over to the television that was securely braced to the wall and slipped in a DVD. In seconds, the speakers were blaring with a Jean-Claude Van Damme action film. Al Dhabit watched the first ten minutes of the implausible story. After the third oversized explosion, Al Dhabit drained the last of his tea, left the cup on the table, and went back to his cabin to write some reports.

* * *

Al Dhabit pulled away from his stack of papers and decided he'd had enough. He glanced at his watch. *1 AM?* He hadn't realized it was so late. The guard shift had just changed; it would be a good time for an unannounced inspection of the forward hold.

Al Dhabit ran a comb through his hair before leaving his cabin. As he entered the bridge area, he had to slow down; the only illumination was a dim red coming from the panels. The backlights had been dimmed as well, to improve night vision. As his eyes adjusted, he saw the first officer in front of the radar panel, to the right of the helmsman. Al Dhabit walked over to him.

"Good evening," the doctor said simply.

The officer turned and straightened. He offered his hand to the doctor. "Good evening, Doctor. We have not met. I am Theodore Antonious, first officer. It's nice to meet you." It was light enough to see that the officer was tall, over six feet with dark hair and brown eyes. His name confirmed his Greek ancestry, but he spoke English with a mild British accent.

"Mohammed Al Dhabit. It is nice to meet you. I would like to go and check on my people in the forward hold."

"Certainly. I'll call ahead. Will you require an escort?" Antonious asked.

"No, thank you. I know the way. I just wanted you to be informed, and I wanted to see how things are going."

"Very well. All's quiet at the moment, and we are making good progress. We still have our escort to starboard and little traffic on radar. Nothing to be concerned about. The captain is off watch for now and will be back on the bridge at 6 AM. When you go below, please watch your step. The corridor and stairwell lights are dimmed at night, and it can be treacherous until you get familiar with them," the officer cautioned.

"I shall. Thank you. Have a good... watch, is it?" Al Dhabit asked.

"Yes, thank you, Doctor." Antonious smiled.

Al Dhabit went down through the ship via the internal staircase. The dim lights caused dark shadows, and he took his time. When he got to the 05 deck, he walked to the port side, turning right to head down a short corridor to a watertight hatch. Al Dhabit tried the hatch wheel and was glad to see it was locked. He pulled a twenty-five Piastre coin out of his pocket and rapped on the hatch three times. In well under ten seconds, the hatch opened, and brilliant white light streamed into the hallway, making the doctor blink as his eyes adjusted. The forward hold had all of the lights on.

One of the uniformed guards appeared, looking serious; then, recognizing the doctor, he threw the hatch open all the way. Al Dhabit nodded his appreciation, passed through the hatchway, and saw the other guard standing a few feet back with his hand on his pistol holster, ready to draw in case of trouble. As soon as he saw the doctor, his hand relaxed, but did not leave the weapon until the hatch was closed and secured behind him by the first guard.

Al Dhabit had taken the time to learn all of the guards' names. He greeted them in Arabic. "Good evening, Farhaan, Kareem." He nodded to them each in turn. "How is your shift going so far?"

Kareem spoke first. "We just came on duty, Doctor, but the outgoing shift reports no issues. They said a member of the crew came through earlier to check that the crates were secured, but all was well, and he left quickly. You are the first person to come in since he left."

Al Dhabit nodded and walked over to the portable card table and two chairs that the crew had set up. A half deck of cards was stacked on the table, and the two sets of cards fanned out and face down showed the doctor that he had interrupted a game in progress. On the wall above the table, a folded stretcher was lashed to a supporting rib, and a first aid kit with both the Red Cross and Red Crescent symbol. A small pile of periodicals and newspapers from several countries were on the deck beside the table.

The doctor turned and spoke to Kareem. "Is there anything you need?"

"I don't think so, Doctor. We brought food and drinks for the night, and the weather has been quite calm. So far it has been a pleasant journey."

The doctor nodded and walked around the periphery of the hold. Everything appeared the way he had left it earlier in the day. The ship rocked slightly every few seconds, but as Kareem had said, it was minor. The crates didn't move.

Everything appeared to be in order, so the doctor moved back to the hatch. "If you do need anything, just call the bridge on the telephone. Good night."

Kareem opened the hatch, "Good night, Doctor."

Al Dhabit stepped through the hatch, and it closed behind him, plunging him back into a red-tinged darkness.

* * *

As soon as the door was closed, Farhaan ran over to the table and pulled a shiny bag out from under a newspaper. He held it up to his face and retched violently into it several times. A low moan was all that emerged afterwards. The ship's ventilation system struggled to clear the smell of vomit.

"Farhaan, I can't believe you are sick this soon. It is very calm tonight." Kareem shook his head. He poured water into a mug and handed it to his partner.

Farhaan pulled the bag away and took the water eagerly, quickly drinking half. "*Oh.* I thought he would never leave. I should've skipped dinner."

"Why in the name of all that is holy did you volunteer for a trip when you knew you would get sick?" asked Kareem.

"This is a small price to pay to see America. Besides, I've never been on a boat before. I had no idea it would be like this." Farhaan cuffed the sweat from his brow onto his sleeve. "Please don't say anything to Doctor Al Dhabit, Kareem. This will pass."

"Relax, my friend. I will not tell the doctor anything he does not need to know. Perhaps you should speak to the crew and see if they have anything to help?"

"No, the Koran does not allow drugs unless a medical doctor approves, and there is no doctor on board. I will have to suffer and hope that it gets better with time." Farhaan drained the last of the water and handed the mug back to Kareem. "Thank you, Kareem. You are a good man."

"Sit down, Farhaan. Perhaps I can take your mind off it by beating you at a few more hands of cards."

* * *

Al Dhabit made it back to his cabin without incident. He was satisfied that the cargo was secure and in professional hands. With the harsh white lights in the cargo hold, it would be hard to sleep in there, and he wanted the guards alert. He stripped off his clothes and hung them over the desk chair. He decided the pants were clean enough to wear one more day, but he tossed his shirt into the floor of the locker. The ship had a washer and dryer, and when the pile was large enough he would do a load. Al Dhabit pulled himself between the cool sheets and switched off the light. The day had been a long one, and he was asleep in seconds.

CHAPTER 5 – SIDI BEL ABBÈS

Anderson woke up at 7:34 AM. Soft illumination streamed into his master suite after diffusing through the five-foot border of glass block near the ceiling. The light touched the cedar furniture and flooring, giving the room a warm glow. He rolled onto his back and looked at the ceiling. His shoulder was mottled and bruised from the previous day's activities. Anderson was no stranger to injury and had been shot before, but that had literally been in another life.

'Stephen Anderson' was a lie and a well-maintained secret. Thirty-seven years previously, he'd been born Étienne Martin in Paris, France. His adult life had rotated around a small two-room apartment and the grueling and unrewarding job as a laborer on the Marseilles docks. Constantly angry at the world, he spent his days in mind-numbing labor and most of his nights drinking with his co-workers until he was numb. The liquor combined with his temper triggered many fights. His mother's death was a wake-up call for him, and he had looked for an alternative to his destructive lifestyle. Eventually, he ended up in a recruiting office for the French Foreign Legion.

Signing up for the standard five-year contract, Martin was assigned to the 2e REP (*Régiment Étranger de Parachutistes*) airborne regiment in Calvi, Corsica. Wanting to challenge himself even more, he gained all of the qualifications for marksmanship that were available, along with several heavy weapons qualifications. His instructors recognized he was a natural shot. After four years, Martin had been posted to the embattled city of Sarajevo as part of the United Nations Peacekeeping force. The Legion was tasked to hold the airport that was directly between the Serb and Muslim combatants who exchanged fire often. One summer day, Martin was in the rear of an armored car parked on a taxiway when an anonymous Serbian opened up with a heavy machine gun. A *commandant* from another French unit had been hit and fell on the tarmac. Martin had scrambled out of the safety of the armored car. He was able to reach the fallen officer and began to drag him back. Just before they reached the safety of the armored car, a heavy-caliber ricochet bounced off an armored door and hit him in the shoulder, driving him forward onto the concrete. He had been in a hospital for several weeks to recover. That encounter earned Martin medals and a promotion to *sergent*. As his unit already had too many NCO's of his rank, he was posted to the 3e REP, which was the Legion's only other airborne regiment based in Sidi Bel Abbès, Algeria.

When Martin had reported for duty in Algeria, the nightmare began. *Colonel* Rochon ruled the regiment and camp with an iron fist. Punishments were harsh and meted out to the men almost on a whim. More serious offenses were met with draconian brutality. As a *sergent*, Martin was insulated to a small degree, but he saw the after-effects firsthand.

One of the senior enlisted men in the camp did not help matters. *Adjudant Chef* Rodin was a former Corsican thug, and his story was well-known by all. He had enlisted with the Legion to escape prosecution for stabbing an undercover police officer in a bar fight. Rumors that several 'deserters' had actually been victims to Rodin's blade and buried in the desert gave him a notoriety that few wanted to challenge. An oppressive atmosphere ruled the regiment.

After six months in the 3e REP, Martin joined the elite Deep Reconnaissance Commando (*Groupement des Commandos*

Parachutistes or GCP) unit. The 3e REP GCP only had positions for thirty men, and due to the high standards, they were never at full strength. He ended up as a section commander who was respected by both his troops and the GCP *capitaine* in charge. The *capitaine* leading the GCP recognized the oppressive nature of the camp and took his men on regular extended field marches away from Sidi Bel Abbès whenever possible. Those training exercises had exposed the men to temperatures of one hundred twenty-plus Fahrenheit, constant sandstorms, spiders, scorpions, and harsh freezing nights. However, not one man in the GCP complained, knowing the environment in camp was worse in many ways.

One day, a pay clerk from the headquarters staff had been flown back to France for an emergency appendectomy. One of Martin's *caporals* had a finance background and temporarily replaced the evacuated clerk. Legionnaires were paid in cash, every two weeks, and were not allowed to have independent bank accounts. The soldiers had the option of placing money back into a Legion-maintained account at no interest for safekeeping, and many took this option. However, the *caporal* had found a series of small discrepancies on the regimental accounts and investigated. In the end, he discovered that someone—the *caporal* heavily suspected Rodin—had taken most of the money in the regiment's accounts and placed them into various unauthorized investments that were generating huge profits. On paper, the Legion accounts said the money was there, but in reality, eighty percent of it was being invested secretly, generating annual profits of several hundreds of thousands of Euros.

The *caporal* went to *Sergent* Martin, who instantly saw the seriousness of the problem. By chance, the GCP *capitaine* was on leave, and the regiment's *adjudant* was away on a staff course. So *Sergent* Martin took the *caporal* directly to the next level in the chain of command, *Colonel* Rochon.

Sergent Martin informed the *colonel* of what was going on, and the *caporal* presented the documentation, which was conclusive, highlighting the scheme. Rochon had looked at the figures and listened in shocked silence to the tale. After several moments of thought, he told the men to say nothing to anyone, as the *Gendarmerie Nationale* would need to thoroughly investigate the matter, behind the scenes. That night, the young pay clerk was lured out into a remote part of the camp by Rochon. Working with Rodin, Rochon interrogated the *caporal* harshly and determined only he and Martin knew of the embezzlement. Martin, arriving unseen at the last minute, saw Rodin kill the *caporal* and was unable to prevent it. He then overheard the pair planning his own demise.

Martin had fled into the desert. After navigating through almost two hundred kilometers of barren terrain, he had come across the corpse of an American oil surveyor who had died days before. Documents on the body were made out in the name of Stephen Anderson. Martin found they were very close in age and physical characteristics. Martin placed his uniform and identity papers on the body and took Anderson's clothes, passport, and other papers for himself. From that day forward, he had become Stephen Anderson.

Two more days of tortuous walking in the desert finally brought him to a road, where he was able to catch a ride and make his way through Morocco. He spent some time in London recuperating and taking English lessons to reduce his accent. Eventually, Anderson traveled to the United States. Stepping into a dead man's life had its challenges, but it gave him the opportunity to start again in relative safety.

* * *

Anderson's eyes snapped open when he realized he was falling asleep again. The red digits on the ceiling said 8:01. He yanked back the comforter and got out of bed naked. He pulled out a pair of black gym shorts from the red cedar dresser and slipped them on. Anderson quickly made the bed.

He went to the small padded cushion in a corner and sat on it, cross-legged in a half lotus position. Placing his palms on his knees and straightening his back, he closed his eyes and began slow, rhythmic breathing, feeling the tight skin on his back where he was injured. He relaxed, dropping his pulse and breathing to a third of their usual rates. Anderson meditated on the previous day's events for twenty minutes, controlling his negative emotions with the meditation. He then opened his eyes and stood to start his day.

He walked toward the kitchen, pausing to press a couple of buttons on the remote controls. The television came on with some sort of garden show, and he changed the channel to cable news. He was just in time to hear the overused "This just in…" preface concerning something to do with the upcoming federal elections. He ignored it. They were still seventeen months away.

Anderson walked to the television and swiveled the screen so that it faced the exercise area. He watched the news while he jogged on the treadmill. A weather reporter—or *Severe Weather Expert*, as the banner below the man stated—began discussing the heavy rains in the southwest of Texas, displaying a time-lapse satellite view of the United States for emphasis.

Anderson tuned out most of what was said. He had long ago learned that cable news said the same few things over and over again, with frequent breaks for commercials showcasing new breakfast cereals, heart clinics, and personal injury attorneys. Anderson mused that the lawyers probably ended up suing the cereal companies for their high sugar content after their clients ended up in cardiac wards.

After the commercial break, there was a forty-five second spot that grabbed his attention: the DC-3 had gone down in a farmer's field. They showed video of the impact crater just past the standard yellow crime scene tape flapping in the breeze. The tail of the aircraft was the only recognizable piece remaining. It had been blackened from the fire after the crash, but not by much. Faceless men were walking around the wreck, wearing zippered jackets with yellow *NTSB* on the back.

A lone man with *FBI* on the back of his jacket was visible for only a half second before they cut to the reporter standing just outside the cordoned-off area for her 'live' report. "… and so the investigation continues," the woman summed up. "… Rumors that the crash was a hijacking gone wrong are unconfirmed at this time. This is Gail Nakamura reporting. Back to you, Colin."

Colin's face with perfectly coiffed hair appeared on the television in a split screen with the reporter. He wore a navy-colored jacket with dark red tie over a white shirt. He had his 'serious' look in place. Anderson had only seen three different looks on this particular announcer.

"Gail, has the crash been linked to any terrorist activity?" Colin asked, leaning forward and looking quite concerned.

"We have seen several members of the FBI and NTSB around the crash site, but so far they have not issued an official statement. The National Terror Alert level is set to 'Elevated,' and we will have to see if it gets raised to 'High' because of this incident. Colin..."

"Thank you, Gail." Colin's half of the split screen grew, pushing her off the screen, and he continued, "Meanwhile in Texas, heavy rains continue to take their toll..."

Anderson tuned the rest out. He was shaking his head slightly. *No confirmed rumors of a hijacking, and no links to terrorist activity... yet.* Plus, as far as he could remember, the Terror Alert level had been at 'Elevated' for nine months now. Of course, they didn't mention that little fact, either. He wondered once more why he watched this same show every morning. *Does scaring people generate more revenue from commercials?* he wondered.

The treadmill wound down over the last minute and then stopped. The control panel blinked the distance traveled and number of theoretical calories burned, but Anderson ignored it, as he always did. He disconnected the safety lanyard and went to the heavy bag. Anderson always saved this until the end. Randomly, he would whirl quickly and drive his foot, knee, elbow, or hand into the opposite side of the bag. Full of fine sawdust, the heavy bag weighed two hundred and fifty pounds, but it was soon swinging on the linked chain from the impacts. Anderson used different strikes with his hands: open hand, fist, side, forearm, and elbow.

When he was done, he was dripping with sweat. Anderson grabbed his towel and wiped off most of the sweat from his neck, face and torso. He swiveled the TV screen so it faced the kitchen, then walked up one of the circular staircases to the second floor walkway. He went to the door of his bedroom and entered the bathroom to shave and shower.

* * *

Anderson dressed in a yellow polo shirt and tan Dockers slacks. He swiped his wallet, keys, and coins off the top of the dresser, pocketing them. He paused in front of the tilted floor mirror for a quick zipper check, and he headed out the bedroom door, emerging on the walkway.

Anderson went down the circular staircase and to the coffee table. Out of habit, he picked up the remote for the television on his way to the kitchen—but he dropped the remote onto the dining table and entered the kitchen. He poured himself a half glass of pineapple juice. He sipped that while he made coffee and a toasted English muffin, with butter and strawberry jam. The television droned on about elections and heavy rain in Texas, but there was nothing else of significance being reported.

He flipped the channel to the weather network and waited for the local forecast as he ate. By the time Anderson learned that it would be cloudy with scattered sunshine in the afternoon, he had finished eating. He turned off the TV and walked the dishes into the kitchen, leaving them in the dishwasher.

He selected a pair of black leather shoes from the hall closet and put them on. He closed the heavy door behind him and headed downstairs.

As he went through the plastic barrier at the bottom of the stairs, the door buzzer sounded. Anderson walked over and cracked open the access door built into the larger sliding gate.

"Good morning," said Detective Murphy.

"Morning, detective." Anderson slid the door fully open and invited him in. "It looks like you have had a sleepless night." Anderson observed Murphy's rumpled appearance. He looked to be in his mid-forties, had thinning brown hair. His pants were heavily creased from too much sitting. His shirt had been dulled by many washes and was moderately ironed—probably in his clothes dryer—and his tie was undone slightly at his throat. He wore his gold detective shield in a tan leather holder, on a silver ball chain around his neck. The detective's emerging pot belly would take a few more years and several dozen cases of beer to mature.

"Yes, I was at the morgue until 2 AM last night." Murphy stopped just inside the doorway and saw the row of shiny cars. "Wow. Yours?"

"Yes. They get me around."

Murphy took a quick look around the cars and high-ceilinged workshop and then turned his attention back to Anderson while pulling out his notepad. "They identified the man on the DC-3. Ever hear the name of Nicky or Nicolas Kavanagh?"

Anderson thought quickly and replied honestly. "No. He called himself 'Kavanagh' on the phone, as I said earlier, but I have never heard that name before then. What's his background?"

Murphy opened his notebook. After Bryant's positive evaluation of Anderson, he was willing to be a little freer with his information than he usually would be. "Irish descent. Petty thug. Couple of assault and stolen goods charges. A long string of misdemeanors for being under the influence. Minor drug possession. Nothing too serious. I have informants with worse records. He was associated with the Nealy Street Boys, but they're known for protection rackets and loan sharking, not contract killings."

"Contract killing? You think I have an enemy," Anderson said with concern.

"It is the only thing that tracks, given the facts. He didn't try to rob you. If he wanted to do that, he certainly didn't need an aircraft. He asked you to bring cash, but never asked for it when you got there. You said that when you reached for your wallet to give him money, he shot you, so I'm fairly sure greed was not the motivator. For that matter, he could have shot you at the hangar if he just wanted you dead; it's isolated enough. Then they could've wrapped you up in chains, flown your body out to sea, and dumped it way offshore, never to be seen again. Instead, he tried to toss you out of an airplane at altitude, well back from the ocean, which tells me he wanted it to look like an accident."

"What about the pilot?" Anderson asked. He leaned up against the hood of the BMW.

"No ID yet. He was crushed in the cockpit, and his remains were badly burned. The flight plan he filed was bogus, and we are assuming the name he used was fake, as well. Might be his real name; stranger things have happened. We are still looking into it, but my gut tells me he's another minor player like Kavanagh, tied in with the Nealy Street Boys. We'll have to rely on dental records for an ID, unless he was a convict at some point and we have his DNA in the system. However, both of those options will take weeks to confirm or deny. Having the second person involved smells of a contract scenario as well," Murphy concluded.

"Wish I could help. The only 'Irish' person in my past was an Aer Lingus stewardess several years ago, and we departed on amiable terms."

"All right. Well, I wanted to see if you recognized the name. I'll be back later with your formal statement for your review and signature. Just getting it typed up at the office now. Keep an eye open for anything out of place. If there's a contract out on you, we will eventually hear of it. It wouldn't hurt to vary your routine, and if you remember anything, here is my card." Murphy handed over a business card.

"Thanks. I'll be in touch if I have anything for you." Anderson shook his hand and walked him out through the smaller door.

Anderson watched the detective get into a nondescript blue four-door Ford. As Murphy was leaving, Vinnie arrived in his white Ford panel van. Anderson dragged open the large door for him so he could drive in without pausing.

"*Grazie*, boss," said Vinnie, waving through the open driver's window as he passed. Vinnie pulled to the right, then backed into his usual spot. Anderson left the door open to let the air circulate through the garage.

As Vinnie climbed out of the van with his lunch pail, Anderson spoke to him in passing. "I'll be down in the range if you need me."

"Right, boss. Have fun."

Anderson passed through the plastic dividing screen and walked down the stairs into the basement. His way was illuminated by a few bulbs in the stairway, but he had to flip on the lights in the basement proper to see anything past the foot of the stairs.

The area had been converted into a work area with several rugged benches. Racked SCUBA gear and various pieces of diving equipment were laid out neatly on shelves and peg board. Four tall yellow tanks were hooked up in series beside a heavy duty air compressor.

The area in front of the elevator had Vinnie's project, the carcass of a stripped-down 1971 Spider Veloce sports car. All the body panels, carpeting, and seats had been removed, leaving only the bare frame, steering, engine, and mechanical systems, suspended on brand new Pirelli tires.

Anderson didn't touch the vehicle. The parts that had been repaired were lovingly restored. The frame had new metal welded in place, which was ground down evenly with the rest of the metal. New parts showed where Vinnie had removed rusted or broken pieces. An exposed suspension system looked like it had just come out of the box. Not a single thing had been overlooked.

A dividing wall and pair of doors was behind the sports car. Anderson headed to the farthest door and pressed a combination into the door lock. It clicked open, and he entered the room.

Anderson walked into a four-position forty-foot-long shooting range. He approached a green metal cabinet, which opened with a key code combo lock. Inside was a small but respectable arsenal of weapons. At the top of the cabinet were a pair of semi-automatic MP5A3 machine pistols with tritium sights, below them were two Browning BDM 9MM pistols, and last was a Beretta 92. All of them were legally purchased and registered. Anderson used a key to open the lower part of the cabinet, which had several boxes of 9 x 19 mm hollow-point ammunition and several magazines for the weapons.

Shooting came instinctively to Anderson. Over his lifetime, he had put thousands of rounds downrange. An accomplished marksman, he had a natural gift for guns, and that allowed him to fire while letting his thoughts wander. Based on the little he knew, Kavanagh had been hired by a 'lawyer' with no name or description. That man had wanted him dead, and he'd wanted it to look like an accident. Anderson had racked his brains looking for reasons. Sure, there were people he had put behind bars, but they were generally light sentences. The longest punishment was only twenty-four months, but Anderson had been a minor player in that affair. None of them had the motivation for retribution, at least not on that scale. Even if they did, they would not need the charade and additional expense of an aircraft accident. They would just have him shot. No, there was no one in his immediate past who would have suitable reason to want him killed, and without more data, he had hit a dead end.

When all six mags were empty, the 'head' and 'chest' of the paper profile target had many holes, with only a couple of stray rounds outside of those areas. Satisfied, he brought the target in closer for a better look. Only one round had gone beyond what he would consider acceptable. The rest were accurate enough to stop the imagined assailant.

Taking out a cleaning kit, he stripped down the weapon and removed all powder residue from the metal parts of the weapon, barrel, and magazines. He then put a thin film of weapon oil on the surface for protection. By the time everything was done, he had spent more time cleaning than actually shooting.

Anderson reassembled the Beretta and made sure the safety was on before replacing it in the storage cabinet. The unused ammo was stored away, and he swept up the spent casings from the floor of the booth, dropping them into a white bucket in a corner to join several hundred other casings.

Anderson snapped off the ventilation fans, locked the ammunition and weapon cabinets, and then left the room.

CHAPTER 6 – ATLANTIC TRANSIT

Life aboard the *Costarican Trader* fell into a steady routine. After the lifeboat drills on the first full day on the water, nothing more was expected of the passengers. Day in and day out, the only things that varied were the menu, the weather, and the state of the sea. As the freighter passed the Rock of Gibraltar, their escort, the frigate *Aboukir*, turned back after flashing *Good wishes*.

The water had turned a dark blue as soon as they passed through the congested shipping lanes near the Spanish port city of Tarifa. When they left the protection of the land, white-capped water became the norm in the full force of the North Atlantic winds. The wind and rolling waves rocked the freighter from port to starboard with a slow regularity as they entered the Atlantic proper.

The wind tore salty mist from the waves and drenched all exposed surfaces. Anyone standing on deck without rain gear would be soaked in minutes. The water made temperatures drop, especially at night. The captain ordered warm air to be pumped into the living spaces to compensate, but hatches would let the cold in whenever they were opened.

The passengers stayed inside, pulling on sweaters or wrapping blankets around their shoulders to keep warm. Only the crew in the engine room went without additional layers. Heat from the continuously-operating diesel engines kept them toasty warm. Tea and coffee consumption rose sharply, and Giuseppe began making regular pots of hot chocolate to keep the passengers warm. The mini marshmallows startled the museum staff, who had never seen them before. The first course of any lunch or dinner started with a bowl of hearty soup or stew.

When the last view of land disappeared over the horizon behind them, everyone onboard felt a sense of loss, crew and passengers alike. Surrounded by nothing but open water, with no other ships in sight, many felt isolated. Everyone grew more introspective, some more than others. As the *Trader* pulled away from the Gibraltar Strait, the bridge crew could see smoke trails on the horizon, indicating that other ships were nearby, but none approached close enough to be seen.

The frigate's departure made Doctor Al Dhabit very nervous. He would fret and pace on the forward part of the 03 deck for hours at a time. Only Hisham tried to talk to him, only to be curtly dismissed. Hisham retreated and went to make sure the next pair of guards was ready for their upcoming shift.

Without warning, a Royal Air Force Nimrod MR2 patrol aircraft appeared. It flew low, only three hundred feet up, and approached from the stern to fly parallel up the ship's port side. The thunderous noise of the four Rolls-Royce jet engines grabbed everyone's attention. Anyone not sleeping or on duty below decks lined the windows of the ship to wave to the RAF crew as they passed. A few brave souls journeyed outside, but they quickly retreated from the wet decks.

Up on the bridge, the VHF radio came to life, and a woman spoke with Scottish accent. "*Costarican Trader*, this is Strawberry Five. We are the RAF Nimrod currently off your port side, over."

Captain Kincaid grabbed the handset for the radio. "Strawberry Five, *Costarican Trader*. Good afternoon."

"*Costarican Trader*, Strawberry Five. Be advised we are your escort. Per an official request from the Egyptian government, we have been tasked to maintain a continuous radar watch on you until 40° west longitude. US-based P-3s will take over at that point. We will be out of sight but monitoring this frequency if you require assistance. We will check in every six hours, over."

"Strawberry Five, *Costarican Trader*. Understood. Good to have you in the neighborhood. Over and out." Kincaid turned to Al Dhabit, who was on the bridge. "Did you hear the conversation, Doctor?"

"Yes, but what does 'forty degrees' mean?"

Kincaid pointed at the chart on the navigation table. "That is the position for the middle of the North Atlantic. Here, you can see it here on this chart, just past the Azores island chain. At that point, the RAF will turn back, and we should have an escort of American P-3 maritime patrol aircraft."

"Excellent news. Thank you, Captain."

Satisfied, Doctor Al Dhabit withdrew down to the mess for some tea. Someone had put on a movie, an old 1930s western with white-hat heroes and black-hat cattle rustlers. To his surprise, he found himself enjoying the film—not for the simplistic plot or acting, but for the wild and untamed scenery in the background. The rugged landscape with little vegetation reminded him of home. He was looking forward to seeing America, and the film reminded him that each passing day brought him closer to those shores.

The film ended; the credits said the film had been shot in Death Valley. The name did not offend Al Dhabit in the slightest. He had read the *Book of the Dead*, and he worked with entombed mummies and death-related artifacts every day. The TV screen turned blue as the video stopped. No one in the galley stood to change the DVD.

Enjoying the sudden silence, Al Dhabit took out a writing pad and began to write his dear wife Ghayda a long letter as he sipped his honey-sweetened tea.

* * *

Several days later, Farhaan felt queasy as he came onto his shift, as he'd felt on every shift. The rolling of the Atlantic Ocean was making him miserable. When not eating or on guard duty,

Farhaan lay in his bunk, trying to get a few moments of rest. There was no extra manpower to take his place, and not wanting to impose on the other guards, Farhaan forced himself to hide the symptoms, restricting his diet to soups and light beverages. He had already lost several pounds from the vomiting. His stomach ached from continuous convulsions, and his inability to sleep left him with a gray pallor and large bags under his eyes. Many of the crew recognized the symptoms for what they were, but no one said anything. Al Dhabit had left the organization of the guards to Hisham and had other things to worry about.

The crewmember on watch checked the forward hold as part of his regular rounds. As soon as the hatchway closed behind him, Farhaan grabbed another shiny seasickness bag. He did not use it, but he came close. He dropped the empty bag on the card table and slunk in his chair, moaning pitifully and holding his stomach.

Kareem looked at Farhaan with sympathy. "We are alone here, and no one can see. Let us set some blankets on the collapsible stretcher so you can rest."

"I cannot sleep on duty! I must stay alert," Farhaan replied, looking deathly gray.

"You don't need to sleep. You can just lay down. You told me last night that it feels better if you are horizontal. The door is locked; if anyone calls for us to unlock the door, we can get it put away in seconds. Here, I'll do it for you." Without pause, Kareem unfolded the green stretcher with wooden handles. He arranged a blanket to form a crude mattress.

Farhaan could not resist. He told himself it would just be for a few moments, and lay down. Kareem took another blanket and folded it into a crude pillow, which he put under Farhaan's head. A second blanket went over his prone body.

The nausea retreated slightly. "Yes. This does feel good. Thank you, my friend."

"It's a small thing. Simply lie there until you feel better. Would you like a book?" Kareem asked.

"No, I am fine. This does feel better... Talk to me, Kareem. Tell me of your family."

Kareem sat at the card table while Farhaan lay on the stretcher. They reminisced of home, family, and their respective towns. They discovered they had the same favorite soccer team as well, and the discussion got lively at that point.

As the conversation paused, Kareem opened a small travel bag and produced a medium-sized thermos. He unscrewed the cup lid, followed by the insulated threaded plug and a few wisps of steam emerged. Kareem slowly poured the orange and yellow contents into the cup until it was three-quarters full. The pungent smell of curry quickly filled the large space, and Farhaan's nose twitched.

Kareem stood and walked over to him with the cup in hand. "Here, my friend. I have a surprise for you. I spoke with the cook and told him I was feeling seasick. He made this carrot and coriander potato soup, with nutmeg and several spices that he says will calm your belly. Here, try some."

"… But the Koran—"

Kareem interrupted patiently. "There are a hundred and fourteen *sura* in the Koran, and none have a prohibition against nutmeg. Indeed, it is listed favorably several times, and the rest of the soup is natural spice and ingredients that would not offend even the most rigid Imam."

Farhaan paused, but the smell overrode his hesitation, and he looked at the thick orange-colored soup. All the ingredients had been ground down no larger than the size of rice kernels; shreds of carrot, potato and various peppers and spices were visible. The combination mixed to form a heady aroma. Farhaan took a small experimental sip, and his eyes widened. "Oh, Kareem! I've never tasted anything as wonderful as this. It reminds me of my mother's cooking!" He swallowed several mouthfuls.

Kareem reached over, grabbed the open thermos, and topped up the soup in the cup. "I am glad you like it. The cook, Giuseppe, said this was a traditional meal for rough weather. It is easy to digest and should help your stomach."

"It does. I can feel it working. Thank you, my good and dear friend. This is truly thoughtful of you. Will you have some?" Farhaan pointed at the thermos with the cup in his hand.

"I have my own thermos to enjoy. Giuseppe insisted I have enough for both of us, since we needed to bring a meal with us anyway. I'll have mine later with my sandwiches. You may have as much as you like."

Farhaan drained three cups of soup over his shift. His stomach felt immediately at ease, and his body started to relax for the first time since he had stepped aboard. It was the first meal that did not threaten to immediately come back up.

Kareem spoke as Farhaan finished the last cup. "So do you think El Zamalek will make it through the finals this year?"

"I do not know. They still have talent on the field, but are they good enough to get to the World Cup? Their forwards are not playing as well as could be expected, and many players have left or retired in the last two years," Farhaan replied.

Kareem reached down and took the empty cup back from his ill friend. He put the thermos plug in and screwed on the cup lid. "Ahhh, this is true. To have El-Horeya Emam back in goal would be a wonderful thing. Still, the team has an enviable record of accomplishment, which I'm sure will inspire the new members to perform well. That's why I support the team. They'll live up to that legacy." Kareem's voice trailed off and he looked introspective. He took his lunch bag and began to rummage around in it. Farhaan took a moment and closed his eyes to shut out the harsh overhead lighting.

The next thing Farhaan knew, someone was vigorously shaking his shoulder. His eyes popped open.

"Farhaan! Wake up! You drifted off."

"What?" Farhaan asked, confused. "How long was I...?" He sat bolt upright.

"Only a few minutes. We were talking about soccer. I started to eat my lunch and realized you were asleep. I thought about letting you get some rest, but I knew you would not want that," Kareem explained.

"I must have drifted off. I am sorry. Yes, you were right to wake me." Farhaan sat up on the makeshift bed. He could see

Kareem had opened up his thermos of soup and eaten several sandwiches. "I feel like a fool."

"No harm was done, my friend. No one came by, and it was only for a few minutes. With your lack of sleep, it is not surprising." Kareem smiled.

Farhaan began to get off the stretcher, but he paused when his nose twitched at something. "What is that smell? A cigarette?"

Kareem looked embarrassed, and he fussed with a magazine. "Yes, I had one with my lunch. Being stuck in here and not being able to smoke for eight hours at a time is rough. I only had the one, and the ventilation system will get rid of the smoke soon enough. It was the only one I could find before we came aboard. It was a momentary lapse, and I'll not do it again. You have my word."

Farhaan got up off the stretcher and folded the blanket on top of it quickly. "What if the doctor came through?"

"It is almost four in the morning. I doubt he will leave his warm bed for several more hours." He finished off his last sandwich fragment.

"Four o'clock? I did not realize we had spoken that much. We can get in trouble if he learns of this," Farhaan warned.

"Then let's make a deal. I will not mention your falling asleep if you do not mention my cigarette. That way we are both safe."

Farhaan thought for several seconds. It was true that both of them had made mistakes, but they were minor. Kareem had been a good friend in not letting him sleep, and Farhaan felt obligated to settle things amicably. He was still nervous. "Very well. Here, help me put this stretcher away, just in case he does come through before shift change."

"You're feeling better then?"

Farhaan stood up straight and realized he was no longer feeling the ill effects of being seasick. "Yes! That soup was remarkable. I feel fine. Well, I am quite tired, but I am sure I will sleep better when we get off shift."

The pair stowed away the stretcher and passed the rest of their shift with a few dozen hands of cards. A friendly debate on the worth of the various players on the El Zamalek soccer team filled in the gaps.

* * *

"Hello?" asked Doctor Victoria Wade, her voice light and feminine. The white towel wrapped around her hair had to be pushed up out of the way to accommodate the phone receiver. She had just finished a post-workout shower. She was just starting to relax in her white bathrobe when the hotel room phone rang.

"Dr. Wade," an unfamiliar man's voice said flatly.

"Speaking."

"Peter Cahill. I am on the organizing committee for the exhibition at the Carnegie."

"Good evening, Mr. Cahill." Victoria recognized his name immediately, but she had never spoken to the man before. He was a long-term member of the Carnegie Museum of Natural History supervising committee, and he was generally known as a self-promoter. "How are you today, sir?"

"Good, thank you," he said reflexively. "I know Sid would normally handle this, but his daughter broke her foot last night, and he is running her around to see specialists today."

"Oh, no." Her boss, Sid, had one daughter, Vanessa, who was daddy's little girl. Sid would be sick with worry. "I'll give him a call later."

Cahill ignored her comment and went on with his business. "I just got an update from the *Costarican Trader*. It was faxed to me a few minutes ago by Sid's assistant, Clara. They'll be docking tomorrow at Pier 23D about 4:30 PM. You'll be there to meet the ship, of course."

Victoria paused to write down the information on a notepad near the phone. Both the small pad and dark blue plastic pen had a Westin Hotel logo. The ink ran unevenly, and as she was left handed she took care not to smudge the writing with the side of her palm. She repeated the information as she wrote it to ensure she had heard correctly. "Pier 23D, 4:30 PM tomorrow. Yes, I'll be there."

Cahill continued, sounding very serious. "Good. Dr. Wade, as you may already know, your choice as liaison between the exhibition and the Carnegie was not a popular one with some committee members. Other more prestigious names were floated before yours, even though their Egypt experience was limited. I must admit I was initially leery of your participation given your age and lack of experience with these types of things.

"To be fair, no one has experience on an exhibit this large. The preparations and groundwork you have done to date have been satisfactory. Sid's regular presentations to the committee have clearly given you the credit you deserve. However, I wanted you to be aware that the committee is still divided by a close margin on your selection, and any issues the exhibit suffers will not reflect kindly on you. I don't say this to be spiteful or mean; I simply feel that you should know exactly what is going on here."

Victoria was unsurprised. She knew the committee had several members who either saw themselves deserving the job or knew colleagues who they would like to see in her place. Sid had told her that Cahill was one of the former. She already knew that she'd be blamed for any problems, and that even if things went well, the committee would take most of the credit. "Thank you, Mr. Cahill. I'll ensure that any problems are kept in the small scale. Was there anything else?"

"Security. Have you checked on the arrangements?" Cahill asked.

"Yes, I've done that over the last few days. I had a final meeting with the operations director at the Credence Security offices this afternoon. We have seven eighteen-wheel transport trucks with armored cabs and protected containers ready to go. The containers are bulletproof and can be hermetically sealed. They're the same ones used to transport large diplomatic shipments. Once the cargo is loaded aboard, a convoy will form.

"There'll be sixteen armed guards from Credence on-site and with the convoy to Pittsburgh at all times, plus the Egyptian Museum's small contingent of guards. We had a bit of union trouble over the presence of Egyptian private security guards, but we made it clear their participation did not take away any jobs we were providing. They insisted on having their people in those positions until I told them the Egyptian guard presence was a condition of the exhibition, and if they were not allowed, the exhibition would be canceled, with no one getting any work."

"I see. All right, Dr. Wade. I suspect Sid will be back at his desk tomorrow. Good night."

"Good night."

Click.

Victoria returned to the bathroom. As she walked, she pulled the towel from her shoulder-length black hair and rubbed it vigorously to dry it as much as she could. At age thirty-two, her hair was dark, shiny, and healthy, without a lick of gray.

She finished drying her hair with a hair dryer set on *low*, brushing her hair as it dried. Once done, she collected it at the back of her head using a black scrunchie. She was not overly particular about how it looked at that time of night, as long as it was out of the way. Her amber eyes looked at her face critically, as she did every night. Still no major flaws, but the start of crow's feet had been visible for a few weeks. *Arrrggghh.*

After her trying day full of dull meetings and endless phone calls handling the minutia of the exhibit arrangements, it felt later than it was. Victoria ran through her nightly ritual of using a facial scrub cream followed by moisturizer. She then grabbed her toothbrush, but she immediately replaced it in her travel bag with a smile when she remembered her plans. She snapped out the light to the bathroom and walked out into the hotel suite. She undid the robe and tossed it over the back of a chair.

She pulled a worn blue T-shirt out of her bag. It was long and two sizes too big for her, but to her 'Ol Bluey' was a dear friend. She slipped into it, and it came down to just below her mid-thigh. She enjoyed the warm and familiar feeling it gave her.

She turned around and went to the mini-fridge, pulling out a recently purchased pint-sized Ben & Jerry's Cherry Garcia ice cream carton. She smiled. She popped off the top of the container and started to walk to the bed when she realized she had no spoon.

Victoria feared she'd have to postpone her plan, but then she spotted a coffee maker on the side table, with two small teaspoons by the sweetener and two mugs. She took one of the spoons, lay on her bed, and turned on the TV with the remote control. She grabbed her fashionable black-rimmed cat's eye glasses from the side table and put them on to look at the screen. A spoonful of ice cream melted on her tongue as she slowly channel-surfed.

She put the remote down when she came across a redecorating show. After her long day, she needed something mindless, and she ate her ice cream and watched as the obviously gay host transformed a one-bedroom apartment into an open 'living space.' The show host used the lisped word *super* far too often for her tastes, and she went back to channel surfing. Victoria ended up on the Discovery Channel, watching a shark exploding out of the water in slow motion—a commercial for Shark Week that instantly intimidated her.

She nearly changed the channel, but an announcer said, "Coming up on the second half of *MythBusters*..." She instantly dropped the remote beside her with a grin. Watching crash test dummies being dropped, struck, and exploded sang to her sense of humor. Another mouthful of Cherry Garcia muted her chuckles as they set up another experiment, something to do with flaming gasoline. She wondered if one of the hosts would lose another eyebrow. Her students at the university would never imagine the publicly stoic professor of Egyptology watching and enjoying the quirky show.

The *MythBusters* segment finished with a huge explosion and cackling laughter just before the credits rolled. Victoria turned off the television and put the remote and her eyeglasses on the side table next to her watch and jewelry. She stood up and placed the lid back on the ice cream, then returned the container to the bar fridge. She went to the bathroom, brushed her teeth, and then slid into bed. She adjusted the alarm on the LCD clock. With the ship coming late in the afternoon and no other meetings until 2 PM, she could afford to sleep in a few extra hours. Victoria turned off the light, rolled over on her side, and pulled the cool sheets over her shoulder.

CHAPTER 7 – NEBKHEPRURE

The *Costarican Trader* motored along on a sea of glass under wispy altocumulus clouds. No fog, unlimited visibility, and a calm ocean that was only disturbed by the wake of the freighter formed a rare day of weather. Several oil tankers paralleled the coast further out to sea. A few pleasure craft were on the water, but widely separated and close to the green city park past the harbor breakwater. The sailboats had a hard time making any progress in the calm conditions.

Every one of the passengers on the *Costarican Trader* and any crew not on duty were on deck as the United States came into view on the horizon. An announcement from the bridge over the PA pre-warned everyone on board. After more than a week of not seeing land, their gazes hungrily devoured the landscape before them.

On the portside flying bridge, the harbor pilot carefully steered the ship. He had come aboard a half hour before to guide the ship into harbor and barely looked at the LCD color map display on his GPS. Instead, he kept his binoculars at his eyes, watching the surface of the water for the little tells. A small branch floating on the surface could tell him which way the currents were flowing; a small oil slick showed him where dead water was located. The flags flying all along the breakwater could be examined to gauge wind speed and direction. Though slight, the wind would still make the long freighter drift, so the pilot made sure to compensate.

The calm conditions made the pilot's job easier, but it did not remove the responsibility from his shoulders, and he was no less vigilant. The captain stood at his side also scanning with binoculars, while the first officer stood on the opposite flying bridge, watching for any navigation hazards on that side of the ship. The *Costarican Trader* slipped past the channel buoys at a slow but steady rate.

On the 03 main deck below, Dr. Al Dhabit stood at the rail, apart from his staff. He was glad to see the US finally, but he wanted to get the exhibition on the road. They had a lot to do: clear customs and immigration, unload the cargo onto the trucks, spend at least eight hours in a convoy to Pittsburgh, unload the crates at the Carnegie, sleep, unpack them, and then prepare the exhibition for the first public showing in nine days. While things had been well planned, unforeseen issues always happened. He worried about what would happen.

The freighter slowly approached pier 23D, a construction of solid concrete pillars and lateral support beams. Thick wooden decking the size of railroad ties ran over the top. Al Dhabit could see several 18-wheeler trucks with container trailers parked side by side. A charter bus sat almost as high as the trucks, and several bulky black SUV-type vehicles with large tires were interspersed amongst the larger vehicles. Each of the SUVs had a small gold crest on the doors. At least a dozen men dressed in identical long-sleeved sky-blue shirts and dark blue trousers stood in various places around the pier. Shiny white badges clipped to their left shirt pockets reflected the sunlight occasionally as they moved. They wore holstered pistols on their hips, and a couple of men standing on top of an adjoining building were holding what looked like Vietnam era M-16 rifles in the crooks of their arms.

Several obvious dockworkers in various colors of hard hats were milling about ready to receive the ship. A dockside crane swung lazily over the area as the operator moved the boom into position.

Yellow barricades were erected just back from the entrance to the pier, and two city police vehicles sat behind them at an angle, with their red and blue lights rotating. Beyond the barricades were the usual assortment of press reporters, TV camera operators, and several dozen members of the public. Behind them were a half-dozen satellite news trucks with garish logos of various colors, their transceiver dishes raised high into the air on masts.

"Hisham!" Al Dhabit called loudly. The slight man appeared in seconds with the usual expectant smile on his face.

"Yes, Doctor?"

"The captain has told us to be in the mess after we dock, so that we can start the customs process. Ensure everyone has their passport, declarations, and papers with them—including the guards in the cargo hold, who should have taken them on their duty shift. I do not want any delays in getting the cargo off-loaded. Once we get a pair of guards cleared, we will rotate them to the hold and bring the last two up to the mess for clearance."

"Yes, Doctor."

"Also, I will want you in the cargo hold for the unloading. Only the lettered crates are to be removed. The numbered crates will be left on board to be shipped to Norfolk as we discussed."

Al Dhabit had told Hisham the same thing at least a dozen times during the voyage.

"Yes, Doctor. I'll do as you ask."

"Right. Off with you, then."

Hisham disappeared to speak with the museum staff. Al Dhabit began mentally composing his speech to be delivered to the press on the dock later in the day.

* * *

Standing on the concrete pier, Victoria stood apart from a small group of government officials and security personnel. Knowing she was going to be on board a ship with angled gangways and stairs she had opted to wear a dark blue pinstripe pantsuit, coral blouse with wide lapel. Black flat-heel leather shoes with small silver side buckles and a solid grip sole were on her feet. At her height, she didn't often wear heels, anyway. Her single row of artificial pearls rode high on her neck. A simple black Yves Saint Laurent Hobo-style purse was slung over her left shoulder.

Lengthy meetings had taken place over the last two weeks with everyone in the group, to plan out the day in detail. Regardless, watching the massive steel ship dock distracted everyone. Only the customs and immigration officials looked bored. They had seen the same scene many times over and joked amongst themselves to kill the time. Infrequent bursts of radio static could be heard as dockworkers and the security force communicated with each other.

One of Victoria's favorite catalogs was J. Peterman, but even their upbeat writers would have a tough time describing the smell from the water. *Exotic* would be the closest anyone could come to being kind. *Eclectic* would be Victoria's choice. She smelled diesel fuel, saltwater, dead fish, decomposing seagulls, wet driftwood, and garbage. Then there were the half-dozen foul things she didn't recognize, nor did she want to know what they were.

Victoria spotted Dr. Al Dhabit along the rail of the *Trader*. She didn't wave; they had only ever communicated by e-mail and telephone, so he would have no idea what she looked like. His picture had been displayed in many Egyptology publications and Web sites, so she had the advantage.

She saw *him* looking at her again. He was off to her side, and she caught his glance in her peripheral vision. She did not know his name, nor did she want to. He was some sort of dock supervisor wearing a high-visibility jacket and yellow hard hat. He had tried to flirt with her when she arrived, but seeing the gold wedding band on his fingers, she had treated him like a student who had been caught cheating on a major exam. He had retreated quickly, but he still shot her the odd hopeful glance.

What, does he think I am going to suddenly change my mind? What a creep...

There had been several men in her life, but nobody she considered serious. There were a few good lovers and considerate men she still thought of occasionally, plus a few she had never thought twice about, but no one she would ever consider 'The One.'

Victoria had three failings in the eyes of many men. She was intelligent, an introvert, and independent. Most wanted her to be dependent on them, and that would never happen, given her upbringing. Many did not have the patience to coax her out of her shell. She could spend weeks in a library basement, engrossed in a research project, without talking to anyone in the outside world. A lot of men could not take that. She had a few affairs through the years, even fell in love a couple of times, but they always faded away because of her work, which isolated her. Her best friend Katherine would simply say 'Their loss...' or 'It wasn't meant to be...' with a smile, but now that she was thirty-two years old, her lack of male company was starting to be noticed more and more often. She had her brother Michael, of course. However, he would be married soon and had his own career with the Marine Corps. It was just not the same. There were nights when she was alone and just wanted someone to hold her. She might be a tomboy on occasion, but under it all, she was a woman who desired someone she could trust and talk to in her life. *But certainly not you, Jack,* she thought toward the leering man off to her side.

Victoria kept her gaze on the ship as it approached the pier. It slowed and twisted, gliding into position with the starboard side a few feet from the dock. Victoria wondered how heavy the ship was. *Several thousand tons, at least.*

When the vessel was a few dozen feet from the dock, a maelstrom of foamy water was kicked up by the propellers indicating that someone was applying a lot of engine power. *A problem?* She instinctively took a half-step back. Yet the hull of the ship was maneuvered against the pier gracefully and the propellers slowed. Lines were thrown from the bow and stern sections of the ship, and the ends were made fast. On direction from the bridge, several crew members used motorized winches in the deck to put tension on the lines, and the ship edged sideways until it rested on massive bumpers against the pier. The lines were tied off, the propellers stopped, and the *Costarican Trader* officially arrived in the United States.

The overhead crane lifted a gangway with welded metal railings over the heads of the officials. The crane operator slowly dropped it down over the side of the starboard deck amidships. Two deckhands on the side of the *Trader* grabbed the sides of the gangway and guided it into place as it lowered. It clunked down solidly, and the opposite end lowered down until it came to rest on rollers built into the end. The crew lashed the top of the gangway into position with copious amounts of rope. The rollers on the opposite end of the gangway rested on the pier and moved slightly with the slight motion of the ship.

The officials gathered at the base of the gangway. The harbor pilot came down first, with his GPS unit carried in a slender backpack. By law, the pilot was supposed to be cleared through customs like everyone else coming from a foreign vessel, but it was a law seldom practiced.

"Afternoon, Harv," greeted the customs official, waving him through.

"Hey, Jeff. Long time no see," he joked as he passed. They had seen each other an hour and a half before.

As soon as the pilot had cleared the gangway, several men and women with identical navy blue zip jackets ascended to the top. The jacket backs had large yellow letters saying *POLICE*, followed by *ICE*, which she knew stood for Immigration and Customs Enforcement. Everyone else, including Victoria, waited on the pier. They could not board the vessel until it had been cleared by customs. The first officer greeted the group at the top of the gangway and guided them to the mess.

* * *

The captain was there with Al Dhabit and everyone not on duty. Two immigration officials began inspecting passports, while a customs inspector looked over the ship's manifest, crew list, and other paperwork. They spotted no problems, since all names had been pre-submitted prior to their arrival for background checks, and all the paperwork was in order. Despite the officials' adeptness at their jobs, it took two hours to review everything. Only one incident took Al Dhabit by surprise.

"Doctor Al Dhabit, my name is Robertson. I am an agent with the ATF."

Al Dhabit looked confused. "Pardon? ATF?"

"Yes, sir. I am with the Bureau of Alcohol, Tobacco, Firearms and Explosives. I understand you are importing weapons into the country."

The statement threw the doctor into total confusion. He had no weapons beyond several three thousand-year-old hunting bows packed away in the forward hold. Then he remembered that several months before he had submitted a request to have the guards import their pistols. "Of course, forgive me. We have six pistols belonging to the private security force. They are stored in the forward cargo hold." Al Dhabit flipped through his wad of paperwork and produced the papers he had prepared long ago. "This is a list of the makes, models, and serial numbers of all of the weapons."

"Thank you." Robertson compared the doctor's list with the one he had received ahead of time through his office. "I will need to see the weapons, Doctor."

"Certainly. Hisham!" Al Dhabit looked around.

Hisham had been one of the first to be cleared by the immigration agents. He appeared quickly. "Yes, Doctor."

In English, Al Dhabit said, "Escort Agent Robertson to the forward hold. Instruct the guards to allow him to inspect the pistols."

"Yes, Doctor. This way." Hisham also responded in English, and the pair disappeared down the internal stairs.

Meanwhile, three customs personnel with large black flashlights, one with a German Shepherd drug dog, began a cursory inspection of the entire ship from stem to stern. The *Costarican Trader* was not on their list of suspicious ships, nor had it been randomly selected for a thorough search. A thorough search could involve up to twenty-five ICE agents, several dog teams, and many days' work. For this search, they briskly but methodically went through the ship, letting the dog sniff items and containers at random as they looked in the different cabins and rooms on board.

Al Dhabit paced pensively in the mess, waiting for the officials to do their job. It had been a long cruise across the Atlantic. Too long, in his opinion, and he was eager to get on with his work. The bureaucratic delays were necessary, and he knew they were accommodating him in many ways to ease the process. Egyptian customs would certainly not be as efficient when he returned to his own country. However, it did not stop him from pacing. It was his way to deal with the nervous energy within him.

After twenty minutes, Agent Robertson returned, with Hisham in tow. Robertson sat at a table and methodically filled in several blocks on a preprinted form. Robertson signed it, separated the three-part form, and stamped an official seal on all three copies. He placed one copy in his folder and handed two copies to Al Dhabit. "Doctor, I found no problems with the weapons or ammunition. All of the serial numbers match the declared form. I've issued you with a temporary weapons permit. It's good for no more than one year. These weapons must be exported out of the country prior to this date next year, or they will be subject to seizure. If you need to extend this period, apply to a local ATF office for assistance. The pink copy is yours, and the blue copy should be given to the customs office at your port of departure. They'll check that the weapons are being exported and will close the file. If any weapons are lost or stolen, you are obligated to contact any office of the ATF within twenty-four hours of the loss to report it. You will need to give them the permit number on the form. Do you understand?"

"Yes. That's very clear. Thank you." Al Dhabit placed his copy of the form into his growing paperwork stack. Robertson nodded, walked over to the head customs agent, and spoke quietly to him before leaving.

Another half hour passed before the customs and immigration agents finished their paperwork. The three-man search team with the dog had found nothing of consequence, and the head agent simply turned to the doctor, saying "Welcome to America" before leaving with his people.

With a huge sigh of satisfaction, Al Dhabit began barking orders to his group to assemble their luggage on the main deck and prepare to begin unloading procedures. The captain and Hisham disappeared into the crowd.

* * *

After the customs officials descended down the gangway, the remainder of the group waiting on the dock ascended, including Victoria. A pair of intimidating Credence security guards took post at the base of the gangway. They were instructed that nothing was to enter or leave the ship without being thoroughly inspected. The light outside was getting softer as the day began to end. However, there were still several more hours of daylight left.

Victoria met the first officer at the top of the gangway. The walk up the metal tread was welcome after such a long period of inactivity. "Good evening. Can you tell me where Dr. Al Dhabit is, please?"

The first officer looked her in the eye as he responded. "In the mess, adjacent to the galley. Right through there." He pointed toward the rear of the vessel.

"Thank you." She smiled politely and moved to the indicated hatch.

Victoria spotted Al Dhabit quickly. He spoke to three Egyptian staff in concise Arabic. His speech was far too rapid for her to follow everything with her limited knowledge of Arabic. He seemed to be talking about the unloading operation, and she waited patiently until the group moved off before walking in toward him.

"Dr. Al Dhabit? Dr. Victoria Wade. We have spoken several times." She did not try to shake his hand. Traditionally, Islamic men were not supposed to touch women outside of their families. She was glad when he extended his hand, though, and she shook it.

His face, however, was stern. "Dr. Wade. I have followed your recent work closely. You've upset quite a few of my esteemed colleagues' theories concerning the New Kingdom."

His words took her aback, and she was unsure what to say. She needed his cooperation to make the exhibit a success, and it sounded like he had developed some sort of grudge with her.

He released her hand and smiled warmly before continuing, "Of course, their theories were archaic to begin with, and they needed updating. It's nice to meet you."

The feeling of relief swept through her as she returned the smile. "Thank you, Doctor. May I introduce Jonathan Merridew of Credence Security? He'll be the security coordinator for the Pittsburgh portion of the exhibition."

"Mr. Merridew," said Al Dhabit pleasantly as they shook hands.

"Good evening, Doctor." Merridew placed his briefcase on the table and opened it. He produced a stack of laminated identity badges. They had both metal clips for attachment to clothing and broad lanyards to go around the neck. "We used the photographs you sent to us to prepare these identity credentials. Yours is on top. The cards are unique, with holograms embedded in the background, as you can see. They were produced for the exhibit, and you and your staff will have to wear them at all times when with the exhibit. They'll be needed to pass through our checkpoints.

"We'll conduct full searches of bags or anything else coming in or out of the secure area. Anyone who does not have a badge will be held until you or one of your delegates can confirm their identity. We are not police, so we cannot arrest anyone, but under state and federal laws, we can perform what is called a 'citizen's arrest' and hold someone until police arrive. My men are armed with pistols and trained in their use for self defense, but honestly I expect no trouble."

"Yes. I saw the men with M-16s on the rooftop. Is that really necessary?"

"Actually, the rifles you saw are semi-automatic AR-15s, and yes, they are needed. The docks have several active underworld operations, and violence is not unknown here. By putting up a show of force, we immediately discourage any small-scale efforts. However, the danger of a large armed force trying to steal your exhibit is a real one we cannot ignore. We will have a small police presence with us as long as we are in the city. Once in the convoy, we will be responsible for security. When you have the time, I can give you a brief overview of what will happen from here to Pittsburgh."

Al Dhabit indicated that Victoria and Merridew should sit. "I have a few minutes now while they are preparing to off-load."

All of them sat down, and Merridew continued. "As the cargo is unloaded, the crates will be secured on pallets. Forklifts will then load the cargo into the truck containers. We calculated the space required from your manifest and then added twenty percent for safety, so we'll have enough space. Once filled, the back doors will be padlocked and numbered anti-tamper plastic seals applied. We have a bus for your people, their luggage, and yourself. Plus, we have six SUVs for our guard force. They're bullet and bomb-resistant, as are the containers on the trucks themselves. We will form a convoy and move as one, with the bus behind the trucks. There will be an SUV behind each truck. If any truck or the bus breaks down, then the convoy stops together until it is fixed. If an SUV is the issue, we will leave it behind and continue on. All of the truck drivers are armed as well. We subcontracted them from another security firm and have worked with them in the past."

"I see. It sounds like you have made thorough preparations," Al Dhabit observed.

"Once in Pittsburgh, we have arranged for a secure area just off Forbes Avenue in a parking lot adjacent to the loading bays where we can unload. Once inside the museum, there is a dedicated area already set aside for you and your staff to unpack the items and set up the displays. We'll be in the museum from that point on. There is one area where we may have issues, however." Merridew paused.

"Yes?" prompted Al Dhabit.

"The Egyptian guards you have with you. I understand some will be staying on board to go to Norfolk while the rest come with us. You may or may not know that we had some union issues, with our people insisting that the Egyptians were taking jobs from them, and while we settled that point prior to your arrival, there is still some animosity. Unions here take a dim view of outside workers, and there may be some friction. Once we have the cargo out of the holds, I ask that you put the Egypt guards on the bus until we arrive in Pittsburgh. If we can get the local guards slowly used to their presence, then we may be able to avert *tension*. If you follow me?" Merridew carefully emphasized the word.

Victoria saw Al Dhabit looked like he was about to object. "Doctor, the goods will be in the trucks at that point, anyway. It is a small matter, but it will certainly help."

Al Dhabit paused for a long time before conceding. "Very well. I will instruct them to do just that."

"Thank you, Doctor. It'll significantly smooth over ruffled union feathers. Did you have any questions?" Merridew asked.

"No, Mr. Merridew. You seem to have things well in hand."

"Thank you. Dr. Wade and I have been working through the arrangements over the last week, and we foresee no issues. I need to make preparations for the journey. I will be on the dock if you need me. Here is my card. My cell phone number is written on the back. Please call me at any time, day or night, if you have any questions or issues." Merridew shook the doctor's hand and departed, leaving him with Victoria.

"Your preparations are quite thorough, Dr. Wade. I'm impressed. Shall we watch the unloading?"

"Thank you. Yes, please."

They both rose and went out on the deck on the starboard side. The scream of hydraulic motors stopped as they emerged on deck, and they could see the forward cargo hold doors had been opened. A boom from a dockside crane swung lazily over the ship. The huge boom arm moved slowly, driven by large hydraulic motors. Victoria watched as a block with heavy hook and cargo netting stopped over the open hold. It swung there slightly for a few seconds. Al Dhabit began to say something, but Victoria did not hear it because without warning, the block dropped into the forward hold—far too quickly.

The sound of the impact combined with the noise of shattering wood. Several screams from inside the hold plus multiple loud radio calls added to the din.

Doctor Al Dhabit ran over to the edge of the hold and looked down, beating Victoria by a few paces. Victoria saw Hisham beside the Egyptian guards and stevedore. Hisham's fingers were clutched in his hair, and he was looking in horror at the fallen block, which had struck the top of a wooden crate.

Al Dhabit cupped his hands and yelled down trying to get his attention, "Hisham. Hisham! Which crate is that?"

His hands still in his hair, Hisham yelled back, "AJ!" before his horrified gaze returned to the crate.

Al Dhabit's face grew ashen. He said, "Blessed be Allah, the Lord of the Worlds!" in Arabic. He ran for the hatchway with Victoria in tow. She was glad she wore the flat shoes, since they were moving quickly along the sometimes slick decking. Once inside the superstructure, they descended down to the cargo deck. The cargo hatch was open, and they entered without delay.

* * *

The closer Al Dhabit got to the damaged crate, the more he slowed. The deformation in the top was much deeper now that he was looking at the box from the side. The hook and block were deeply embedded in the top of the box. The wood had been shattered, and the hook had penetrated at least six to eight inches.

Al Dhabit never heard the captain and head stevedore come in the hold behind him. Both men had clipboards in their hands, with a thick wad of paperwork on each. "Is everyone all right?" Captain Kincaid asked.

He got no answer; everyone was staring at the damaged crate. He tapped Al Dhabit on the shoulder. "Doctor, is anyone injured?"

"Captain, we must inspect the contents for damage immediately!" Al Dhabit's eyes never left the crushed lid.

Kincaid surveyed the hold and could see no injuries, which was his first priority. He then turned to the stevedore at his side. "Take it up, slowly."

The head stevedore used his hand held radio to talk to the crane operator. "Take it up slow, Ralph."

After a few seconds, the heavy gauge wire moved through the block above the hook, and it rose up slowly. The box went up with it for a couple of inches, the broken wooden lid clinging to the metal hook.

Without warning, the crate let go and fell heavily onto the lower crate. Al Dhabit jerked back as the box slammed down. He moved in closer and found Hisham in his way, speaking in Arabic. "Doctor, we should wait until we get to the museum to inspect for damages. We do not have the facilities here."

Al Dhabit was too shocked to speak and simply pushed the younger man aside. Taking the unbroken seal between his fingers, Al Dhabit twisted it free of the wires embedded within, and the wax crumbled onto the deck. Pulling the wire through the locking hasp, the doctor dropped that on the floor as well. He put his hand on the lid, paused only long enough to mutter an unheard prayer, and pressed the lid back on its hinge. He then used his other hand to grab the inner layer of solid foam insulation, which had been badly broken, and moved that up out of the way as well. Al Dhabit then tentatively peered inside the box.

* * *

Captain Kincaid and the others started toward the box, but Al Dhabit dropped the lid and it slammed shut before they could see inside. Al Dhabit turned, collapsed on the decking and leaned heavily against the lower crate. Kincaid saw Victoria move to his side instantly. She touched his forearm lightly and tried to get his attention. "Doctor, what is wrong?"

"Gone. It is gone," was all he said, over and over again. Tears started, and his breathing got more and more ragged. He repeated "Gone... Gone..." until he was close to hysterics.

Captain Kincaid did not understand what was going on. He saw the crate was labeled with the letters *AJ*, and he looked it up on the cargo manifest on his clipboard. He ran his finger down the list. Beside *AJ* on the manifest it simply said *Funerary mask of Nebkheprure*, followed by the weight and physical dimensions of the box. It meant nothing to him.

"What is a *Neb-ke-pru-re*?" Captain Kincaid asked himself, pronouncing the unfamiliar word by each syllable as he read it off the paperwork.

Victoria immediately stood and walked over to the captain. She read where he was pointing. Her mouth opened, and she covered it with her hand.

"Oh no" was all she said, softly. She turned to look at the broken lid with a horrified look. "Oh no!"

The captain was losing patience at not understanding what seemed to be obvious to everyone else in the room. "Miss. Miss! For the love of God, would you please tell me what is going on? What is missing?"

Victoria gathered her wits and explained. "In ancient Egypt, when an Egyptian royal was born, he was given a birth name. When he ascended to the position of Pharaoh, he took a different one, called a throne name. *Nebkheprure* was the throne name of a famous Pharaoh."

"Okay. I have never heard of him," said Kincaid. He was just as confused.

"That is because most people refer to him by his birth name." Victoria bleakly stared at the crate.

"Okay. So what is his birth name?"

"Tutankhamun," she said quietly. "And that box contained his gold burial mask."

CHAPTER 8 – INTERVIEWS

Anderson peeled through the streets at a speed just shy of reckless. The V10 engine of the BMW M6 was pressed to its limit as he took corners at speed. He had never pressed the car this hard, but the car responded like a champion.

The stick shift responded smoothly as Anderson kept the RPMs near the top end. It nudged into the red zone on the tachometer a few times, but there was no hesitation in the German-engineered vehicle. He made it to the interstate in record time. Thankfully the bulk of the rush hour was over, and he did not have to worry about heavy traffic congestion. There was a chance of an unmarked police car catching him speeding, but it was a risk he had to take.

Captain Kincaid had called the Worthor Insurance agent immediately to notify them of the loss of Tutankhamun's burial mask. Anderson's private line had rung eight minutes later. Warren Worthor told him to get down to Pier 23D as fast as humanly possible. Once Anderson heard why, he needed no further inducement.

He passed slower traffic with ease, and everyone was slower. He cut off a station wagon to get to the right exit off the interstate and was halfway down the ramp before the irritated horn sounded behind him. If not for the seriousness of the situation, he would be enjoying himself, but he focused on the task at hand.

Nearly two weeks after the aircraft shooting, his bruises had healed, and no fresh leads had emerged.

The streets around the docks were agreeably empty. Anderson had to slow down as he approached the pier. The line of news satellite trucks had too many people walking around them to risk speeding. Anderson found a clear parking spot near a warehouse and jumped out, setting the car alarm with the electronic fob as he jogged toward Pier 23D.

Making his way through the crowd, Anderson could hear the television reporters making their segments or talking to their producers. They were calm, talking about the upcoming exhibit starting in Pittsburgh, so chances were no one knew about the theft yet. He hoped that held for as long as possible, because it would be a circus when the news leaked.

Anderson walked up to the barricade and flashed his wallet interior to the uniformed police officer standing behind it. His state private investigator card was on top, and a second more impressive laminated ID below it identified him as a *Special Investigator.*

"My name is Anderson. I am here to see the ship's captain," he explained.

It didn't impress the cop one bit. "Sorry, bud. No one gets in or out without a real badge," he retorted sardonically.

"Is Detective Murphy from Robbery-Homicide here?" Anderson tried name-dropping.

The policeman shook his head, that time hesitantly. People did not typically bandy the names of homicide detectives about in daily conversation. "Just us four. Why, what's going on?"

Before he could respond, a female reporter behind him in the crowd asked, "Hey, what is the FBI doing here?"

Anderson turned and saw Bill Bryant getting out of the front seat of a huge black GMC Yukon. His government sourced navy blue zip jacket had *FBI* on the front and back in yellow letters. He ignored the shouted questions from the reporters.

The two men and the woman with Bryant all wore the same style jacket. Two of the agents carried thick black plastic briefcases. Bryant was a toned man who towered over the rest of his group. Anderson left the cop behind the barricade and wove through the crowd to get to Bryant. All of the agents turned as he approached.

"Evening, Bill."

Bryant was startled to see him, but he recovered quickly. A white smile appeared on his deep brown face, and he shook Anderson's hand with a firm grip. "Hey, Stephen. What brings you out here?"

"Same thing as you, I suspect. I got a call about ten minutes ago. We cover the cargo on board." Anderson kept the conversation generic, mindful of the many cameras and microphones around them.

"Well, there is not a lot I can do for you, right now. We need to get in there and see what is going on." Bryant had to follow procedure and keep the crime scene secure. Anderson was not a credentialed law enforcement officer, so Bryant wouldn't be able to let him in until they were done.

"Look, Bill, I know what the rules say, but—"

The sharp trill of a cell phone interrupted Anderson. Bryant pulled a slim Samsung Android out of a belt holster.

Anderson could only hear one side of the conversation, and there were long pauses in between as Bryant listened. "Special Agent Bryant... Good evening, sir!... Yes, sir... Yes, sir... He is here now... Yes, sir... Very good, sir... Good-bye."

Bryant returned the phone to his belt and looked at Anderson. There was a definite pause and hard stare before he spoke in a low voice. "Want to hear a remarkable coincidence?"

"Sure," Anderson said, puzzled.

"In the last twenty minutes, at least half the members of the Senate Judiciary Oversight Committee have called the director, who by the way is on vacation in Aruba. The director called my

SAC[1], who just called me. Seems I am to provide you with any cooperation necessary, without compromising my investigation."

Thank you, Warren, was all Anderson could think. *Worthor must have pulled in some strong favors from his buddies in Washington.* "Does this mean I get an FBI jacket like yours?" Anderson joked to try to break the mood.

Bryant looked slightly irritated, and the joke fell flat. Bryant jerked his head for Anderson to follow him, and they passed the police barricade. Once clear of the crowd and out of range of the microphones, the group stopped. "Okay, look, Stephen. You are a decent guy, but I won't allow anyone to compromise this investigation. The scale of this is simply unheard of, and I'm including the Gardner[2] robbery in that.

"So here are the ground rules," Bryant continued. "You have your foot in the door. However, if you do anything I don't like and jeopardize this investigation, then you are gone, and I don't care if the Archangel Gabriel vouches for you in person. Understood?"

"No problem. Okay. Let's go." Anderson turned to walk to the gangway.

"Wait. Second, if you learn anything, I want to know it. Got me?"

"As long as that goes both ways, no problem. Look, Bill, we are on the same side, and we have worked together before."

"Right, but it had to be said. Agreed?" Bryant held out his right hand.

"Agreed," said Anderson, shaking the offered hand.

"Right. Let's roll." The group ascended up the gangway past the guards at the foot of the gangway.

---

[1] Each field office of the FBI is run by a Special Agent-in-Charge, the SAC.

[2] On Saint Patrick's Day, March 18th, 1990, two men dressed as policemen entered the Isabella Stewart Gardner Museum in Boston. They handcuffed the guards and made off with 13 paintings by Manet, Rembrandt, and Vermeer. The total value of that art was over $300 million dollars. It is considered to be the largest theft of art in US history, and the crime is still unsolved.

Captain Kincaid met the small group at the top of the gangway. Introductions were made and hands were shaken all around. Anderson's lack of a blue jacket made him stand out.

The captain addressed Bryant, because he was the senior agent. "Thank you for coming so quickly. I have all passengers and crew in the mess except for the bridge watch and the two Egyptian guards on duty in the forward hold. Nothing has been touched since we discovered the artifact was missing."

"Thank you, Captain. Agents Montoya and Islington will need to get down to the hold. Could you have someone escort them, please?"

"Yes. Carl!" Kincaid yelled up to the bridge.

"Sir?" came a voice from above.

"Come down here."

Someone clumped down the external metal stairs, and a pudgy man in lightly stained blue coveralls appeared.

"Take these two agents down to the forward hold," Kincaid ordered.

"Yes, sir. This way, please." Carl indicated the proper hatchway with his hand. The trio disappeared.

"Which way to the mess, Captain?" Bryant asked.

"This way." The captain began to lead them down the side of the superstructure.

"Captain, a forensics team will be coming soon. Could you see they are met and escorted down to the hold as well?" Bryant said as they walked.

"Certainly. Here we are." Kincaid turned the handle on the hatch and pulled. The door opened outward. The subtle smell of roast beef came through the door before they entered.

Bryant entered first, Anderson close behind. The group had a scattering of emotions on their faces. Some looked shocked, some upset, a few angry. Most of them wore laminated ID cards around their necks. An older man at the end of one of the tables sat unmoving, with his face buried in his hands. He did not look up.

Bryant briefly held up his badge. "Ladies and gentlemen, I'm Special Agent Bryant of the FBI. I need to ask that—"

The man at the end of the table exploded, advancing toward Bryant with a wild look in his eye. Anderson thought Bryant would draw his sidearm, but the man stopped well short of him. His hands were empty and open toward Bryant in a pleading gesture. "You must find it—you have to find it—the greatest treasure my country owns, and it is gone! *Gone!*" The man saw two people behind Bryant. "You need more men! Many more. We have to fill this area with police and find it. By Allah, how could this have happened?" His face contorted in grief, as if a close family member had died.

Anderson saw a striking woman in a dark pantsuit appear at the distraught man's elbow and gently pull him, unresisting, back into his seat. "Be calm, Doctor. Shhh... Here, sit down. They will find it. You need to start thinking clearly so you can help them."

The man slumped back down onto the bench, his head low. She crouched down beside him and patted the back of his hand, reassuring him.

Bryant continued to the room at large, "We will need to start interviewing all of you. I want to start with those people who were in the hold at the time the object was discovered missing. Could you please hold up your hand if you were there?" The captain, the head stevedore, an Egyptian man, and the young woman all raised their hands.

The woman indicated the upset man, who remained immobile. "Dr. Al Dhabit was there, as well."

"Very well." Bryant turned to Kincaid. "Captain, is there a place we can use for interviews?"

"The library is down the hall on the port side. It's small, with a table and few chairs, but should serve. You can also use the crew quarters further down starboard."

"Thank you, sir." Bryant turned to the lone agent with him. "John, can you separate those witnesses and make sure they don't talk. Once you get more agents, you can take over the crew quarters and start interviewing the remainder of the crew. We will need to begin a search, as well." The other FBI agent moved along the room. Bryant turned to the captain. "Captain, let's start with you, if you don't mind."

Bryant and the captain began to move to the library, and Anderson followed down the passageway. Bryant stopped short. "Where are you going?"

"With you. It'll save us valuable time if we only have to listen to the stories once. Otherwise, we'll be duplicating effort. This is your investigation, and you ask the questions. I just want to hear what he has to say."

Bryant paused briefly, thinking, but finally nodded and turned to follow the captain.

The library was cozy, three walls of bookshelves with many soft and hard cover books, periodicals, videos, and magazines in eight different languages. There seemed to be hundreds of *National Geographic* magazines, as if a crewmember had a longstanding subscription. The square table had a folded newspaper on it. The table top had the usual raised edge to stop things from rolling off in rough seas and was bolted solidly to the floor. Four chairs surrounded the table, with a stuffed red leather easy chair under the sole window. The captain sat down after putting his open can of soda on the table, and Bryant took the chair to the captain's left. Anderson stood behind Bryant and off to the right, near the wall. Bryant pulled out a wide notepad and small Sony digital recorder, which he propped on the desk, using two small metal stands that pulled out from the side of the recorder. "Do you mind if I record this interview, Captain?"

"No."

Bryant flipped on the recorder and stated the time and date before continuing, "For the record, this is Special Agent Bryant speaking with Captain Kincaid of the *Costarican Trader*. In attendance is Stephen Anderson, Worthor Insurance. May I have your full name please, Captain?"

"David Allen Kincaid."

"Your citizenship?"

"Canadian. I was born in Port Coquitlam and raised in various places in British Columbia before joining the merchant marine."

"How long have you been master of this vessel?"

"I was first officer for four years and have been captain for three."

"Can you describe the incidents that led to the discovery of the theft, please?"

"I was standing on the starboard flying bridge when offloading operations commenced. I was speaking to the head stevedore—I am sorry, but I don't remember his name. I gave him a copy of the manifest and instructions on which crates were to be unloaded. Only some of the crates were to be offloaded here. They were labeled with letters. The rest, with numbered markings, were bound for Norfolk.

"After the stevedore radioed for the crane to begin unloading, a crane boom was swung over the forward cargo bay with a hoist hook and netting slung on it. It let go and fell into the forward hold out of sight. I heard the impact and screams, so I ran down to the forward hold as fast as possible, along with the head stevedore. I was worried about injuries more than damage to cargo at that point. However, the crane luckily missed everyone and stuck in the top of a heavy crate. We arrived to see Dr. Al Dhabit break the seal and after looking inside he collapsed on the deck, repeating, 'It is gone.'" Kincaid paused to take a sip of soda.

"I looked on the manifest and saw it was a 'Funerary mask' for a Pharaoh I'd never heard of before. Dr. Wade—she is the young lady who was consoling Dr. Al Dhabit—explained it was Tut's gold burial mask. I suspended the unloading immediately, called our insurance agent, and then gathered everyone in the mess. The agent said to contact the local FBI office, which I did immediately."

Bryant took notes as the captain spoke, and he finished writing before continuing, "You're sure you saw the doctor break the seal?"

"Yes, each box has a unique red wax seal on the locking hasp to show if it has been opened or not. I saw it clearly before the doctor broke it off. It looked intact to me before he grabbed it."

"Since you docked, has anything been taken off the ship? Garbage, luggage, anything at all?" Bryant asked.

Kincaid shook his head slightly. "Nothing except paperwork from customs, immigration, and the ATF when they departed. No packages or luggage left the vessel, and most garbage is incinerated on board. There were private security guards placed at the base of the gangway as soon as we docked to stop anyone or anything leaving."

"Okay, so Captain, you're fairly confident that it could not have left the ship since it docked?" Bryant placed his forearms on the table and assumed a more conversational tone.

"I don't see how anything could have been taken off without someone seeing it."

"Did you search the boat for the mask?"

"No, sir. The insurance agent told me to gather everyone together until law enforcement arrived, and I did just that. We had to assist Dr. Al Dhabit up the stairs. He was distraught and unresponsive until you arrived," Kincaid stated firmly.

"Who had access to the manifest?" Bryant asked, again making notes.

"Myself and Dr. Al Dhabit. The head stevedore was given a copy just before the accident. Dr. Al Dhabit asked me to keep it to myself, which I respected. It was locked in my cabin for the entire voyage until this afternoon. I've had it with me continuously since. It is here." Kincaid patted the clipboard on the table.

"May I see that please, sir?"

The captain unclipped the paperwork and handed it over. "The stevedore had his copy in his hands less than a minute before the incident. Even so, the contents were listed cryptically. I didn't know it was the gold mask of Tut until Dr. Wade told me."

"Did you ever see the mask?" Bryant asked.

Kincaid shook his head again. "No. I had no idea it was even on board. All of the cargo arrived in a guarded military convoy that came right to the dock in Alexandria. Heavy machine guns mounted on jeeps and lots of troops. The boxes were all sealed when they arrived and have been guarded continuously by at least two guards since being placed in the hold. I only saw the inside of that one box briefly when the doctor opened it."

Bryant finished scribbling a line in his notebook. He glanced back at Anderson. "Stephen, do you have any questions?"

Anderson surged forward, then checked his eagerness by stopping beside Bryant. "Just a couple. Captain, did the Egyptian military stay in position until you left the dock in Alexandria?"

"Yes. Military police were there for the entire loading operation and until we pulled out of sight. They kept perimeter security, and they checked all people and packages coming and going from the ship. I am confident nothing left the ship at that time."

"You said, 'people and packages coming and going.' Who do you mean?" Anderson asked.

"After loading operations were completed, Dr. Al Dhabit allowed his people to go ashore for a couple of hours before we left. Pick up personal supplies, buy a meal, whatever. There were no issues, and everyone was back in time. I believe most of the museum staff and off duty security guards took advantage of the shore leave. They were searched going and coming by the MPs."

"Did the doctor go ashore?"

"Yes, several times. He was talking to the officer in charge of the convoy, and at one point just before we sailed said he was going to phone his wife. He was gone no more than fifteen or twenty minutes," the captain replied.

Anderson seemed to choose his words carefully. "From the time you left the dock in Alexandria until you arrived here, did any other vessels approach you?"

"For the initial part of the voyage, an Egyptian naval vessel escorted us, but they were never closer than two ship lengths abeam. They turned back at Gibraltar. From there, we saw only aircraft, RAF Nimrods and American P-3 patrol aircraft. No other traffic came within five nautical miles on radar at any point. So no, there were no other ships near us. Well, apart from the pilot boats at both harbors," Kincaid clarified.

"Pilot boats," Anderson repeated. "Did they bring any gear on board?"

"Just the usual GPS navigation box. They were escorted by either the first officer or myself from the time they boarded until they departed, as is our custom. They went to and from the flying bridge directly back to their vessels, and they took nothing else with them when they left."

"How big were the navigation boxes?"

Kincaid demonstrated with his hands. "About ten by ten inches and eight inches thick or so."

"Last question: Did anything major happen on board while you were underway? Fires, smoke, man overboard, anything like that?" Anderson thought it could not hurt to ask.

"Nothing of consequence. The fresh water filters broke for the better part of a day in the mid-Atlantic, and we had to strictly ration fresh water until we got them back up and running, but that was temporary and handled as a routine fix. That was it. Everything worked very well on this voyage."

"Thanks, Captain. That's all I had, Bill."

"Okay, I have no more questions, although we will probably want to talk to you later, Captain. This is Special Agent Bryant concluding the interview. The time is 7:17 PM."

Bryant snapped off the recorder and rose up with the captain. "I'll be on the bridge or in my cabin if you need me," Kincaid said before leaving the library.

Anderson looked out of the rectangular window. He watched the setting sun in the distance as he considered the possibilities.

"So what're you thinking? Any theories?"

Anderson never turned his gaze from the window; the tops of the clouds were a brilliant red color as the sun sank lower. "Eight at the moment, but it is too early. We need to talk to the others."

"We agreed to share info, Stephen," Bryant prodded.

Anderson turned from the setting sun to look his friend in the eye. He said warmly, "We agreed to share when we knew something. Right now we know nothing except a general timeline of events. We need a lot more information before we can start drawing conclusions. Offering theories prior to knowing the facts is a great way to confuse things."

"Yeah. You are right there. Okay. Who next? Al Dhabit?"

Anderson shook his head. "Let's let him recover a while longer. From what I can see, he was with the shipment for the entire duration. We need his input, but it would be nice to have an overall picture of what happened from the others. The doctor certainly had the access to pull this off, and right now I have to consider him a prime suspect. The captain mentioned Dr. Wade several times. Let's see what she knows. We can corroborate what the captain told us and build up a general timeline of events."

"Right. I'll go get her."

* * *

Anderson observed Victoria sitting in the library chair, relaxed with her forearms on the table and slender fingers intertwined. Bryant turned on the digital recorder and stated the time, date, and location of the interview. "For the record, this is Special Agent Bryant speaking with Dr. Victoria Wade. In attendance is Stephen Anderson, Worthor Insurance. Could you state your full name and occupation, please, Doctor?"

As Victoria focused on Bryant, Anderson let his eyes wander over her face. Behind the black cat-rimmed glasses she had soulful eyes. He'd noticed the amber color the moment he saw her. Her stoic exterior could not take away from the long oval face and shiny healthy hair that surrounded it. She was in her early to mid-thirties and wore stylish clothes that weren't too trendy. Her watch and jewelry were subtle and complemented her features without distracting from them.

Independent was his first impression. *Intelligent* was the second—though that second one was hardly difficult to deduce, since she did have a doctorate. Anderson was sure she had a dazzling smile hidden away, but he got the impression she didn't smile much. She had no rings on her long slender fingers.

Anderson returned to observing her eyes. They had a familiar quality.

"Victoria Dorothy Wade. I am a professor of Egyptology at the University of Pittsburgh, currently acting as a representative of the Carnegie Museum of Natural History to coordinate the Egypt Exhibition. May I ask why this other gentleman is here?" She nodded toward Anderson as she spoke, without looking away from Bryant.

Anderson knew Bryant well enough to detect his surprise at the question, though he doubted Victoria would notice it.

"Mr. Anderson is a representative of Worthor Insurance. Their policy covers the cargo being shipped on the *Costarican Trader*, and he is here to investigate its disappearance. He has been involved in several other successful FBI investigations and is here by direct authorization of the director of the FBI. Why, is that a problem, Doctor?"

"No," she responded flatly. "I just wondered why he was here. Thank you."

"Doctor, can you please tell me about your actions after stepping on board today?"

"I came on board with Jonathan Merridew, the head of the Credence Security detail, just after the customs people left. We went into the mess to see Dr. Al Dhabit. Jonathan gave him a stack of laminated ID badges for the staff, and we discussed the arrangements for transporting the exhibit items to the first show in Pittsburgh. After that discussion, Mr. Merridew left, and Dr. Al Dhabit and I walked outside to watch the unloading operation. I saw the crane drop into the forward hold with a loud crash, and we both ran down to the hold." She pulled her hands off the table and into her lap.

From there, her story followed the captain's, point for point. She described what she saw from her perspective, and Bryant took copious notes.

"Dr. Al Dhabit fell on the deck after looking inside, mumbling 'It is gone' over and over. I didn't know why he would react in that way. As soon as I heard the captain say the name 'Nebkheprure,' I knew it was a serious loss, because anything related to the boy king is essentially unique and irreplaceable. When the captain showed me the cargo list, I saw it was the gold burial mask, and I knew why it affected the doctor so badly. The burial mask is arguably the single most important archeological find of at least the last hundred years. It is over 3,300 years old and absolutely unique. I told the captain who the mask belonged to, and that was when he ordered everyone to the mess. Dr. Al Dhabit was so stricken with the loss that both the captain and the other man—I don't know who he was, the foreman with the radio—had to help him up the stairs." She shrugged to indicate her lack of knowledge.

"So you definitely saw the doctor take the red wax seal off the box. You are certain of this?" Bryant asked .

"Yes, it looked the same as the one on the crate directly underneath. It was whole and intact until Dr. Al Dhabit broke it," Victoria insisted.

"Very well. Stephen. Any questions?" Bryant turned to Anderson.

* * *

Victoria took the opportunity to check the insurance man's left hand. *No ring... muscular hands...* She raised her glance and met Anderson's eyes. She had noticed Anderson the second he had stepped into the mess earlier, and again when she went into the library. There was something about him that unsettled her, though she couldn't quite place what or why. Maybe it was the slight accent he had. It was well hidden but unmistakable. He spoke precisely without using many contractions, like some of the foreign archeologists she had worked with in the desert.

"Dr. Wade, has any further examination of the cargo been made since the loss was discovered? What I am wondering is if anything else has been stolen."

"No. We were ordered out of the cargo hold by the captain, and only the guards have been there since. It's conceivable more items have been taken, but nothing else looked out of place to me." Victoria looked him straight in his steel-gray eyes.

"Assuming the incident with the crane had not taken place, when would the crate have normally been unpacked?" Anderson continued.

She thought about this carefully. Her gaze drifted as she thought. "It would've been an eight or nine hour drive to Pittsburgh. Once there, we would've off-loaded everything and put it under lock and key for the night. Then everyone would've gone to the hotel for some rest before doing anything. They would not get to bed until the early hours, and I doubt anything of consequence would happen before noon the next day. So we wouldn't have noticed the loss of the mask for another twenty-four to forty-eight hours if the accident had not occurred. Maybe longer, if nothing else had been taken and depending on where we started with the unpacking."

"Yes. That sounds about right. Thank you." Anderson nodded.

"Mr. Anderson, how much is the insurance coverage?" Victoria asked. She felt the interview coming to an end and impulsively wanted an excuse to keep his eyes locked on hers.

"Eighty million US dollars," Anderson replied.

Bryant appeared surprised. "The cargo is insured for eighty million dollars?"

"Well, to be specific, the general cargo is insured for $270 million. The mask carries a separate rider and is insured at eighty million dollars," Anderson clarified, his gaze transferring to the FBI agent.

"So the total insured value of the entire cargo is $350 million?" Bryant asked.

"A little higher. Some of the smaller jeweled pendants and a miniature gold coffin are also covered by separate multimillion dollar riders. The total coverage is just under $400 million. That's not public knowledge, so I would appreciate your discretion as far as the press is concerned."

"I see." Bryant looked back at Victoria, while Anderson looked out the window again, lost in thought. "I have no further questions, Dr. Wade, but we may need to ask further questions at a later time. This is Special Agent Bryant ending the interview at 7:46 PM."

Victoria left the room with a last backwards glance at the insurance man as he stared out at the distant horizon. He was tall, over six feet, and had broad shoulders. She found herself studying his profile before turning the corner.

Then she realized what nagged her about him: his bearing reminded her of her brother.

* * *

Anderson spotted an FBI agent as he popped his head around the corner. "Bill, forensics just arrived. I sent them down to the hold. Anywhere else you need them?"

"No. Just the hold for the moment, thanks." The agent disappeared, closing the door behind him. Bryant turned to Anderson. "So what are you thinking?"

"All the statements are more or less identical to this point and don't give us anything actionable. All we know for sure is the time of discovery of the theft. If we can find when it disappeared, we can define who, what, and where… In fact, I am wondering…" Anderson let his words trail off. Something was starting to nibble at his subconscious. He'd had the feeling before, an unconscious ability that had saved his life on a few occasions, and now it was trying to tell him something. *But what?*

"What?" said Bryant, confused.

"I'm not sure. We need to get more information. Who is next?" Anderson asked.

"The stevedore. I'll get him."

* * *

Victoria sat down in the mess under the television, away from everyone else. She could do nothing else until the FBI finished their interviews and hopefully located the mask. She rebuked herself for looking at Anderson while a tragedy of monumental proportions threatened her career. *Why did I look to see if he had a ring? He certainly didn't pay me any special attention.*

The thin Pakistani kitchen assistant dropped a mug of coffee in front of her without warning. He pointed at it and smiled with perfect white teeth and said "De-caff-in-ate" with a little difficulty followed by another smile before retreating. She was too surprised to say anything before he had gone. There was a small packet of sugar and a mini cream container on the side saucer, which she added to the coffee. She needed something in her stomach; she had not eaten anything for some time.

The coffee didn't last long. As she put the empty mug on the table, Victoria wondered if anyone at the Carnegie knew what was going on. She decided to use the prepaid cell phone she had picked up that morning to call Sid and see. Victoria could also check on his daughter's foot at the same time. She walked the length of the mess to the outside hatch.

* * *

The stevedore was named Steve Kerrigan. He had worked the dock for twenty-two years and been the supervisor of the crew for almost eight years. He was shown into the library, and Bryant ran through the same procedure to establish the evidence chain. He stated the time, date, and place of the interview into the recorder before asking Kerrigan to describe the events as he'd seen them.

Again, the recounting of what happened was more or less identical to what the captain had said. Hardly surprising, as they had been side by side the whole time. Unlike the others, Kerrigan moved his arms as he spoke, emphasizing his statement with a series of continuous hand gestures. However, it was toward the end that the stevedore said something in passing that got a physical reaction from the two other men in the room. "... So the hook starts to come up, and the crate fell back hard—like *wham*, you know? So the older fella is coming up to the busted crate and the little gypo fella tries to stop him, yammering

THE LEGIONNAIRE: MASK OF THE PHARAOH

something real fast like in A-rab. The older guy just pushes him aside and opens the box—"

Bryant interrupted, "Just so I understand you, the younger man stepped between the doctor and the crate?"

"Yeah. He was right worked up about something, but the older guy just blew past him and opened the lid." His hands waved furiously.

"Thanks. Please go on." Bryant made a few notes. The stevedore continued talking and matched the others' statements from that point on. There were no further revelations.

Kerrigan finished his story. Bryant wound up the interview like the others and Kerrigan left. As soon as the door closed, Bryant turned to Anderson. "Okay, that was something no one else mentioned. The younger man, Hisham, tried to stop Al Dhabit from opening the box."

"Definitely, but that could be for any one of a hundred reasons. No one else said anything, so it was probably a minor thing to them. He spoke in Arabic, so no one else understood what he was saying. We can note that for now, and we can ask Al Dhabit, if he does not mention it up front. We can talk to him next and leave Hisham until the end and see how his story holds up," Anderson replied.

"Right. I'll go get the doctor," said Bryant.

* * *

Doctor Al Dhabit looked somewhat recovered as he sat down at the table, though his eyes darted back and forth nervously. Both Bryant and Anderson interpreted it as evasive behavior, but in his country, being questioned by a federal policeman was neither routine nor pleasant. The CIA flew Al Qaeda detainees specifically to Egypt for interrogation for just that reason. Al Dhabit said nothing, wringing his hands together in front of him.

Bryant started the recorder and stated the usual preamble of time and location along with who was present in the room. "Doctor, we have a good understanding of what happened in the hold. What we need from you is to start at the beginning and fill us in on what took place, starting in Egypt. Begin with the last time you saw the burial mask."

"If I may begin by apologizing for my behavior earlier? I was not myself. Discovering the loss unnerved me to a degree I did not think possible. There will be a national uproar for this act, and as the one responsible, it will fall on me in its entirety." His hands fidgeted more as he spoke, and he clasped them together tightly to stop it. "To answer your question, I last saw the mask as we sealed it in its crate about twelve hours before the convoy left the Cairo museum. All of the higher value or fragile items were done last for obvious reasons." The rubbing of his hands continued.

"And what security was in place at the time, Doctor?" Bryant queried.

"The room was guarded by tourist police for over a week as the items were packed away. There were four policemen on duty in the packing room at all times, plus two in the corridor and two more on the basement elevator and stairs, restricting access to just myself and the other staff involved with the exhibition. No other members of the museum staff were allowed in there as long as we were packing." Al Dhabit was calming down as he tried to recall helpful details.

Bryant had a thought. "Doctor, who knew the contents of the crates?"

"Only myself and Hisham. The crates were custom designed by Hisham and a few carpenters to accommodate the individual items. That is his specialty. The crates were placed on one side of the room and loaded with items by staff. When filled, they were moved to a second area and marked with spray paint and stencils. Letters for Pittsburgh, numbers for Norfolk. Hisham did this. He wrote the contents onto a list that eventually became the cargo manifest. No one else saw the list. I made several checks to make sure it was safe. I definitely saw the mask as we sealed the box. I watched as it was taken to the paint area and saw Hisham mark the box with *AJ*. No one else knew of this—" The doctor pressed himself back in his chair to get comfortable.

Bryant interrupted, "You said there were museum staff and tourist police there. Could they not see the box contents and labels?"

"None of the packing staff or policemen could see both areas. They were separated by a curtain wall. So the people in the packing area did not know what markings the box ended up with, and the police watching Hisham in the label area did not know what was in the box when he marked it. They were then stored in an area by the loading doors. Once everything was packaged and sealed, the military police arrived to take over the security for the convoy. We loaded the trucks and made our way to Alexandria under heavy guard, with MPs on every truck. Once the cargo was on the ship, I kept at least two private security guards in the hold at all times, and I am unaware of any issues on the voyage. I made several surprise visits on all shifts, and they were always alert."

"That brings us to the unloading and your discovery of the mask being missing. Can you describe those events?" Bryant prompted.

Al Dhabit did so. His version was very close to Victoria's. The meeting in the mess, the falling crane, his yelling into the hold, the shock of discovering which crate had been damaged. Toward the end of the story, he leaned forward. "... And when the crane went up, the box went with it, and it fell back a short distance onto the lower crate. I thought my heart stopped! I walked over and opened the lid to find it gone! The rest I do not remember until you arrived." His hand gestures indicated his inability to remember.

Bryant did not look at Anderson, but he wanted to. Al Dhabit had not mentioned Hisham trying to stop him from opening the box. "Doctor, we understand someone talked to you before you opened the lid. Is this correct?"

"Hmmm? Oh yes, before I got to the crate, Hisham stopped me, saying we did not have the facilities to open the box there. This was absurd. I only wanted to see if there was damage, and I went around him. Hisham is a decent worker when supervised, but he has difficulties with clear thought sometimes. He comes from Marsa Alam on the Red Sea. It is a small town, and he is not very..." Al Dhabit touched his temple with his forefinger. "You know?"

Bryant recognized the 'not very smart' gesture. "I see. So from the time you last saw the mask, until you opened the box and saw it missing, there was no time where the crate was unsupervised?"

"Correct. We spent a great deal of money on security so that could simply not happen. Impossible," Al Dhabit firmly concluded.

"Doctor, why was the manifest entry for crate *AJ* falsified?" Bryant asked.

Al Dhabit almost came out of his chair in protest. "This is not true! The manifest was fully declared. What do you mean by this—?"

Bryant took the manifest and showed it to the doctor. "Here on the line for crate *AJ* it says *Funerary mask of Nebkheprure*, but in other places there are references to Tutankhamun. The mask belongs to Tut, does it not?"

"The Pharaoh Tutankhamun used both names, and this is not incorrect! To provide additional security, we used the throne name on the mask and higher-priced jewels, for Nebkheprure is unknown outside of a small circle of experts. If anyone did see the manifest, it would mean nothing to them. There was no deception here!" Al Dhabit replied vigorously.

"Thank you, Doctor. I had to ask. Stephen?" Bryant prompted Anderson to take over.

* * *

Anderson asked his first question immediately. "Doctor, when and how were the crates sealed?"

Al Dhabit no longer sounded nervous. His tirade had purged his nervous energy and seemed to bring him back to normal. Al Dhabit's finger lightly tapped the tabletop. "Hisham did this, just after checking the contents for the manifest list. He placed a wire through the locking hasp and sealed the ends in red wax. I had two custom molds created with the royal seal of Tutankhamun embedded in it. In this way, we could see if any tampering had been done."

"Why two molds?" Anderson asked.

"As I said, the cargo was to be separated, with some crates going to Norfolk, Virginia. The second mold was to go with the staff to reseal the crates between stops," Al Dhabit explained.

"Did you notice if the seal on the crate was intact after the accident?" Anderson pushed a little harder.

"Yes, the seal was good before I broke it. It was just as I had seen it many times before." The doctor leaned back in his chair.

"And where are the molds now?"

"I asked the captain to lock them in his safe for the voyage. We would need to reseal the crates in between each exhibit, so we had to bring them with us. I did not tell him what it was. I was going to ask for it back after the unloading was done, but I did not get a chance. It is still there. They are locked in a secure bag, and I have the only key to open it."

"Who created the molds?" The question was a long shot, but Anderson thought there could be a copy out there.

"My brother by marriage," Al Dhabit said without hesitation.

"Your brother-in-law?" Anderson interpreted.

"Yes, I believe this term is correct. My wife's brother is a metal worker of good quality items. I told him we needed them for making decorations for advertising the exhibit. He had no idea what the real use was. No one else knew of this arrangement, only he and I." Al Dhabit sounded normal now. He did not seem as nervous as he'd been when he began.

"Did the guards report directly to you?" Anderson asked.

"No. Hisham was their contact. I had too much to do. It was a simple task, and so I let him do it. He made sure they were comfortable and had proper food in the hold. He arranged the guard schedule to Eastern Standard Time for consistency during the transit. He made sure they were ready for their shifts. There were no problems in this area." He waved his finger for emphasis.

"Doctor, why did you engage a private security firm? I would have thought national treasures would be guarded by regular police."

"This was proposed initially, but there were many reasons we went with private security. Involving the police would have meant bringing the Interior Ministry into the process, along with their formidable bureaucracy and overhead cost. The Interior Ministry is known to want total control over projects, and it would have complicated matters if we had involved them. There were also concerns about liability. If there was an incident between a US citizen and one of our police, the government of Egypt could be directly sued. The private force gives us a layer of protection against that. Many of the guards are former policemen in any event. Each guard underwent a thorough background check, has reasonable English skills, and was randomly chosen for this duty."

Anderson nodded as if he had no more questions, but he wanted to see how the doctor would react to something. He turned to Bryant. "We should open the remaining crates and see if anything else is missing."

"No," said Al Dhabit flatly before Bryant could comment.

Bryant turned to face Al Dhabit. "Doctor, those crates are within my crime scene, and I can have a search warrant in under twenty minutes without your cooperation. We need to see if any other items have been taken."

Al Dhabit simply reached inside his suit jacket and pulled out his passport. It had the square-shaped eagle symbol of Egypt at the center, with Arabic script on top and bottom, with the words *'Passeport Diplomatique'* under the eagle. Instead of being the usual blue, the cover was deep red. "These are my formal credentials as a diplomatic member of the Egyptian Embassy to the United States. I hold full diplomatic immunity for myself and the items under my care. As noted in the manifest, all the artifacts are listed under my name and therefore are not subject to search or seizure under international law. No one will open those crates except my staff under my direction and supervision. Those items are the property of the government of Egypt and are very fragile. I will not allow untrained foreigners to handle and potentially damage those goods."

Anderson watched Bryant study the passport with care. It appeared authentic to him, and he saw Bryant make a note of the passport number. Bryant would have to check with the State Department to ensure its validity, but for the moment they were stuck, and they both knew it.

Al Dhabit continued, "I am willing to cooperate with you for the recovery of the mask, but I cannot risk further damages. If pressed, I will simply insist the cargo return to Cairo. I am sorry, gentlemen, but the care of the remaining artifacts must be my prime consideration." No doubt colored his voice.

Bryant handed the passport back after double-checking that the passport number matched his notes. "Very well, Doctor. I cannot force you, but I appreciate your offer of cooperation. Anything else, Stephen?"

"Does anyone else on your staff have diplomatic protection, Doctor?" Anderson asked.

"No. The government only gave this passport to me so I could protect the artifacts. No one else has a special passport."

"We will need to make sure the molds are indeed in the captain's safe. Do you have any objections to us studying the molds for forensic purposes, Doctor?" Anderson spoke a little more respectfully than before. He would need the man's cooperation.

"That is acceptable, as long as they are returned to me for safekeeping," Al Dhabit responded.

Bryant interjected, "Of course, Doctor. We'll respect your wishes. Thank you. This is Special Agent Bryant terminating the interview." He summarized the end of the interview and shut off the recorder.

Al Dhabit rose to leave. He paused briefly as if to say something, but then just nodded and left the room. Bryant closed the door after him. "Impressions?"

"Security was tight on the surface. Isolating the packing room from the labeling area was smart. Keeping the cops separated in pairs was a good idea. Egyptian police are not paid much and bribing them is not unknown. Nothing personal, Bill, but we have crooked cops here, too. I doubt the military convoy could be corrupted. They probably did not know what they were shipping until the orders came down, but as of now I cannot discount it. The doctor seems to have done a good job of oversight here. I did not find any flaws in his arrangements. Of course, there must be a flaw, since the mask is missing. Making sure people were watched by others at all stages makes it a lot harder. A conspiracy is always tougher to coordinate than a single man acting alone. He didn't mention Hisham stopping him initially, but of course no one else except Kerrigan did, either. His explanation for the incident was smooth, so I doubt he is lying. Overall, what he says sounds plausible, but I think it is time for us to talk to Hisham and get confirmation for what the doctor said. What do you think?"

* * *

Bryant agreed fully with Anderson's assessment. On the surface, the security for the artifacts looked solid, and he was actually glad Anderson had come into the investigation. *He would have made a decent agent.* Bryant then realized Anderson had no notepad. The agent had filled thirty pages in closely written notes so far, but Anderson had not committed a single thing to paper. "Right. I will get Hisham."

* * *

Anderson pegged Hisham as nervous the second he saw him. When Bryant reached for the recorder *on* switch, Hisham gave a visible start. "I sorry; I not used to the police men," he gushed in badly accented English.

"It's all right, Hisham," said Bryant, with a warm smile to put him at ease. "This will just record your statement. We just need to clear up a few things. It will not take long, and then you will be free to go."

Bryant stated the usual preamble to the recorder and then asked Hisham to tell them what he had experienced.

Hisham spoke hesitantly. His English was passable, but not anywhere near the same level as the doctor's. He stumbled over several words and said them in Arabic when he got stuck. Anderson understood the Arabic from his time in Algeria, but he didn't admit it, wanting to keep that ability hidden for the moment.

Hisham described the packing room with tourist police presence. He told of the crate marking and sealing behind the curtain wall. Then he described how the manifest was locked in a drawer when he was not actually making notes. Finally, Hisham told of the military convoy and ship loading in much the same terms as the doctor. It then came to his description of the crane accident. "... I was stand in the open area by side of ship. Yes? Guards with me and one other man. Loading man from dock. Yes? The crane head came over with net and fell. Boom into crate!

"Doctor Al Dhabit call from open door above which crate? ... And I call back *AJ*. Doctor Al Dhabit disappear. Loader man with me in hold whistle and say lucky no one kill. Yes? Doctor Al Dhabit appear with woman, follow by captain and loader chief. Yes? Doctor Al Dhabit open lid of *AJ* to see mask gone. He fall to floor with a great... anguish. Yes? Men take Doctor Al Dhabit to ship mess, and we follow." Hisham was trying to smile and relax, but his eyes darted continuously around the room.

Bryant spoke calmly. "Others tell us you tried to stop the doctor from opening crate *AJ*. Is this right?"

"The doctor Al Dhabit say this?" Hisham asked, but Bryant stayed silent, and the nervous man continued talking while nodding. "This is true. Yes, this is true... I say to Doctor Al Dhabit that ship hold not correct place to open artifact. Yes? That damage may have occur and museum better for assess. I not understand that Doctor Al Dhabit only look for damages. Yes? I make wrong think... Yes?"

"So you thought the doctor was going to open the artifact in the hold. You misunderstood," Bryant summarized.

"Yes, I misunder-tud," Hisham said, trying to parrot the word and failing. He smiled broadly, still nervous.

Bryant turned and nodded to Anderson, giving him the opportunity to speak.

* * *

"Hisham, how many times have you traveled outside of Egypt?" Anderson began.

"None. This first trip I take outside of country. I have no passport until three week past. Yes?"

"So you got your passport three weeks ago and have never used it," Anderson prompted.

"Doctor Al Dhabit hold passport for trip. Doctor Al Dhabit give to me on ship first time," Hisham replied.

Anderson continued, "Hisham, how many wax seals did you have to redo?"

"Re-doo?" Hisham asked, looking rapidly back and forth between the two men.

Anderson was tempted to use Arabic, but he restrained himself. "Yes, how many wax seals had to be done a second time?"

"Ah... *Sittah, sabba'ah*..." Hisham held up six and seven fingers, respectively. "Wire break and some wax stick inside bowl to break. Yes?"

"And what happened to the old seals?"

"I melt second time to re-doo? Yes?" Hisham seemed pleased that he had learned a new word.

"You did not throw any of the seals away?"

"No. Doctor Al Dhabit take all lefted wax to himself when last crate done. Bad seal is melt. We use again in America for exhibit between city. Yes? He take bowl," Hisham explained.

"Did anyone else touch the 'bowl' for the wax seals." Anderson used Hisham's word for the mold.

"No. Doctor Al Dhabit very clear. He give to me to use, and I give to Doctor Al Dhabit when end. Yes?"

"Thank you, Hisham. You have been most helpful," concluded Anderson. He nodded to Bryant.

"This is Special Agent Bryant ending the interview." Bryant ended the recording in the standard way.

Hisham shook both their hands before leaving. His palms were sweaty and his grip feeble.

Anderson sat down beside Bryant, "So?" asked the FBI agent.

"If he is acting, he deserves an Oscar. His reason for stopping the doctor is plausible. However, did you notice that he wanted to wait until they got to the museum before the box was opened? The doctor did not say that; Hisham prompted it. However, perhaps the doctor is right." Anderson wordlessly tapped his forehead with his forefinger.

"Maybe, but he strikes me as being uncommonly nervous. He almost ran out of here at the end," Bryant countered.

"Yes, but suspicions are not evidence, and I doubt Hisham could pull this off. Between him and the doctor, Al Dhabit had more access and control of events. I still have to lean toward him, and he has immunity. Those are the major witnesses to the events, except the two Egyptian guards and the stevedore with Hisham in the hold when the crane fell. However, I don't expect anything of consequence coming from them."

"Right, the other agents are interviewing them. So. Back to square one." Bryant sighed.

"Looks like. Shall we go into the hold and take a gander for ourselves?" Anderson asked.

"Absolutely not. No. Not even I am going to go in there until the forensic people are done. The chances of a contaminated crime scene are simply too great. No. No way."

"I need to get in there and investigate the scene myself, how long will they be?" Anderson asked impatiently.

"At least twelve hours."

"Twelve hours? Why? If the boxes are diplomatically protected, then all that is left is the walls and deck."

Bryant answered patiently, "This is reality, not *CSI*. On the cases we've worked together in the past, you were not called in until after the lab boys were gone. It takes a hell of a lot of work and a hell of lot of time to document and develop evidence properly over that large a space. The lab folks progress in inches, so yes, twelve hours, minimum. In the meantime, we will continue interviews with the rest of the crew and staff. Someone saw something. They always do. We just need to dig for it. We will button up the ship for the night while they do their thing. No one who is under suspicion gets on or off. Then we will see what the morning brings."

"Okay, Bill. Sorry." The pair rose from the table. Bryant grabbed his notepad and recorder before they left the library.

* * *

Victoria saw Anderson emerge from the corridor behind the black FBI agent who seemed to be in charge. *He must be ex-military. He carries himself just like my brother Michael.* Their eyes met immediately. She turned away, looking up seconds later to see Anderson approaching. She ran her fingers through her hair and turned to face him. She faced him with her stoic 'class' face and spoke politely. "Any luck, Mr. Anderson?"

"Stephen, please. And no. Nothing of consequence at this point," Anderson responded, looking slightly down into her eyes. "How are you holding up, Dr. Wade?"

"Victoria. As well as can be expected, I suppose. I just broke the news to Sid, my boss at the Carnegie. His daughter Vanessa broke her foot yesterday, and this didn't help things. At least she'll be fine."

A loud rumble issued from her stomach. She felt her cheeks burn with mortification as she put her hands on her stomach. "Oh my God. I am so sorry."

"Nothing to be sorry about. When did you eat last?" Anderson asked.

"I had a muffin at 2 PM." she was embarrassed to admit.

Anderson checked his watch. "It is too late for anything decent to be open. May I offer you a home-cooked meal? It will not be fancy, but I am a fairly decent cook."

Victoria paused and looked up at him, conflicted. Her initial reaction was to say no, but her hotel was not known for its menu. Victoria barely knew him, but he appeared to be on good terms with the FBI agent, so he was probably a decent man. He reminded her of Michael, so that counted for something, too. She liked when his gray eyes looked at her. Still, she was unsure.

He didn't wait for an answer and continued, "Truth be told, we are both outsiders here, and I am completely ignorant about the artifact I am supposed to be looking for. I would not mind trading food for conversation and a quick education on the subject. I assure you, it would only be dinner."

She was certainly out of her depth as far as the investigation was concerned, but relating facts about the mask was well within her abilities. Then she realized Anderson might be able to help her recover the artifact and save the exhibition. Her stomach rumbled again, that time silently, spurring her to speak. "Give me your address, and I will meet you there in an hour. I need to go back to my hotel and check my messages first." The words rushed out, taking even her by surprise.

Anderson pulled out one of his business cards. On the back, he wrote his street address. He handed it to her. "See you in an hour."

CHAPTER 9 – KAISEKI

There were three e-mail messages waiting for Victoria on her laptop at the hotel, all of them from Carnegie committee members wanting information she could not possibly have: *Where is the mask? Who took it? Why?*

How the hell would I know? I am not psychic. She threw up her hands in frustration, sighed loudly, and walked away from her laptop. *They should be talking to Sid.* They were probably sending him the same questions. The e-mails could wait until she had answers, she decided.

She walked into the bathroom and examined herself critically in the mirror. She pondered whether she should put in contacts, shower, and change. She could put her hair up, and she did have her little black dress and designer heels in the closet.

She wondered why she was thinking of dressing up. *It is a simple dinner, not a date. We are colleagues and are just going to sit, eat, and have a polite conversation. Changing might give the wrong signal. No, change nothing. The pantsuit is fine.*

In the end, she just brushed out her hair and briefly touched up her makeup. With a final mirror check, she snapped off the bathroom light, grabbed her purse, and left the suite.

Victoria was in the lobby in moments. She asked the concierge to call her a cab, and one was at the main door within two minutes. She got in the back seat, grabbed the business card from her purse, and read off the address: "1863 Watson Street, please."

The Persian cabby nodded and began driving without talking to her. She watched the unfamiliar skyline of the city as they drove. Soon they got out of the downtown core, and they drove on the interstate for a short time. As they crossed over a green metal arched bridge, she could see the ocean was very calm. A container ship was passing many miles offshore, its navigation lights plainly visible.

The cab pulled off the interstate and entered an area with sparse street lighting. They made a few turns, and the buildings got a lot shabbier. *Red brick, old and dilapidated for the most part.* She was about to query the driver if he was sure of where he was going when he made a right turn and she saw *WATSON ST* on a street sign. The cab passed a disco, and even with the windows up, she could clearly hear the deep bass *dub-dub-dub* beat.

The cab pulled up to a red brick building with an old industrial feel to it. She saw the number *1863* above the sliding doors. She checked the business card twice; it matched.

"Sixteen dollar," said the cabbie flatly as he threw the automatic transmission into *park.*

Victoria reached into her purse and handed over a twenty. "Keep the change. Can I have a receipt?"

The driver grabbed a pad of pre-printed receipts off the dash and made a few quick scribbles, then tore the page off to hand it to her. She saw it was written up for $20.

The main door was closed, although she could see bright light leaking from the high windows. "Could you wait a few minutes, please?" she asked, before she got out.

"Okay." The cabbie didn't look up.

Victoria exited the cab and walked up to the main door, which was illuminated by the headlights of the cab. She could see a smaller entry door with a buzzer beside it, which she pressed. A minute passed, and she was about to buzz again when the door opened inwards.

A man emerged wearing his white coveralls, wringing his hands in a stained red and white-checkered cloth. He gave her a welcoming smile. "Dr. Wade?"

"Yes," Victoria said with relief.

"I am Vinnie. Please come in." Vinnie stood back from the door to let her walk in. "The boss is waiting for you upstairs." He pointed to the stairs.

Victoria stepped in while waving off the cab, which immediately drove away. Vinnie closed the door behind her. The lights of the garage were all on, and she could see the vehicles, workbenches, and other equipment. Everything was clean and in its place, from what she could see. She recognized a familiar tune. "Is that 'The Barber of Seville'?"

Vinnie grinned, "*Sì*, it is Rossini's most popular work. You have a good ear for the classics, miss."

"I know it from a Bugs Bunny cartoon." Victoria smiled slightly at the memory. She looked at her watch. "You are working late?"

"My wife is staying with one of her sisters tonight, so I get to spend some extra time with my girlfriend."

He is married and has a girlfriend? She faced him again, raising her eyebrows. "Girlfriend?"

"*Sì*, a 1971 Alfa Romero Spider Veloce. It is downstairs, and I am working on the wiring. My wife says it must be my girlfriend, as I spend so much time with her."

"Oh, I see," she said with amusement. Vinnie appeared to be open and friendly. "Do I just go up?" she asked, pointing to the stairs.

"*Sì*, miss. You are expected." He smiled warmly.

Victoria hesitantly walked through the heavy plastic strips surrounding the stairs, taking her time to part them before going through. *What are these for?* She tried the stair treads before putting her weight on them, but she found them to be solid. The treads had open metal mesh, and she was glad she hadn't worn heels.

As she walked up the stairs, she saw that a lot of work had been put into the old building. The walls had all been recently painted, and the stairwell was well-lit. At the top of the stairs was a large sliding metal door. She pressed the buzzer and waited about thirty seconds.

The door slid open to reveal a geisha. At least, that was the first word Victoria could think of to describe the small Japanese woman with a white powdered face who was a full head shorter than Victoria. Dressed in a traditional kimono, the woman shuffled forward and deeply bowed at the waist. Her black hair was up, and when she bowed, Victoria could see it was held in place with long pieces of cherrywood with decorative jade tips. The woman's makeup around her eyes and mouth was rich in contrast with the whiter skin. The silken material of her kimono was snow white with small birds and cherry blossoms, and it was cinched to her waist with a flawless red sash.

The white-faced woman spoke demurely in rapid Japanese as she held the bow, then straightened and backed up, allowing Victoria to enter.

Victoria did not understand the woman and hesitantly stepped forward, caught off-guard by the unexpected sight. The woman in the kimono slid the door closed behind her and indicated a shoe rack near the hall closet in front of the doors.

Victoria knew enough of Japanese culture to know to remove her shoes. She slipped off her black leather pumps and placed them on the wooden shoe rack before facing the kimono-wearing woman, who led the way into the main room. Victoria expected the wooden floor to be cool on her bare feet, but it was warm. *Some sort of in-floor heating.*

She saw a huge room with thousands of books lining the periphery of the room. A glint of light from above caught her attention, and she beheld the most intricate mobile she had ever seen before. Breathtaking crystal birds, detailed to the point of having individual feather patterns, positioned at various stages of flight. Some were suspended from the main arms in pairs off smaller suspension arms, with a few triples here and there. They hung suspended on thin metal rods from wires that were the same off-white as the ceiling.

Victoria gaped. As she advanced into the room, she could see more and more of the piece. The scale of it was staggering and quite unexpected.

After several seconds, Victoria saw the Japanese lady standing by the closer of the two circular staircases. Victoria followed her, and the Japanese woman walked up the stairs. She had to walk slowly, due to the kimono restricting her legs.

When they got to the top of the stairs, the geisha led Victoria down the walkway to an open door and stopped, indicating Victoria should enter.

A king-sized bed, covered with a patchwork quilt made up of hundreds of hexagons, was in the middle of one wall. The matching stained red cedar headboard, chest of drawers, night tables and armoire all had the same decorative scrollwork on each piece. A wide closet with double louvered doors was at the foot of the bed. The room had to be at least twenty feet square, and the huge bed looked small in it.

What was on the bed caught Victoria's attention: three separate articles of clothing. Obviously of fine quality, the kimono set had a rich custard yellow color that reminded Victoria of her yellow Egyptian scarf she used to wear daily.

She looked at the Japanese woman who stood at the door, waiting patiently. "Do you want me to wear this?" Victoria asked slowly.

The woman responded by bowing slightly and speaking in more soft Japanese while indicating the yellow kimono. Victoria got the impression that she was supposed to change into the clothing. *Why did he invite me over for dinner, then go through this rigmarole? Okay, it isn't lingerie and stockings, but it's almost as strange.*

Victoria considered leaving, but she turned back to the bed, reached down, and felt the yellow silk with her fingertips. Cool to the touch, it was the finest quality fabric she had ever experienced. There were small white chrysanthemums stitched into the fabric. She looked closer and suspected that the entire garment had been hand-stitched by an artisan. It must have cost thousands of dollars and was the most luxuriously beautiful outfit she had ever seen. The second she touched it, she wanted to wear it.

Victoria turned to the white-faced woman at the door, speaking slowly and clearly. "My name is Victoria," she said, pointing to herself. She then pointed at the Japanese woman. "What is your name?"

"Masumi," she said, bowing again, following her name with more Japanese that Victoria couldn't understand.

Victoria pointed at the outfit on the bed. "Masumi, can you help me put this on, please?"

The woman bowed again, with another long string of Japanese. She closed the bedroom door when she was finished speaking.

* * *

Victoria emerged from the bedroom wrapped from neck to ankles in yellow silk.

She had never felt so feminine, and her only negative observation was that she should have shaved her legs, for the inner silk garment caught slightly on the stubble below her knees. The three-layered outfit wrapped tightly around her curves while making her breasts look a few sizes smaller. Her hair was up, and luckily she'd had her contact lenses in her purse. The cat-rimmed glasses looked wrong with the traditional outfit, so she had put her contacts in. She did not have any white face powder or special makeup, and she was glad she had touched hers up before leaving the hotel.

Masumi had done a professional job of dressing her and quickly doing her hair. Once more, Victoria was happy she had kept her hair long. Long hair might be a pain to care for, from day to day, but it looked wonderful when worn up.

As she emerged from the bedroom, she looked over the railing and saw Anderson standing below, dressed in a solid black matte silk kimono. Five hollyhock symbols were embroidered on his chest in subtle green thread. The trousers were light gray, and his slippers were black like the kimono.

The women descended down the circular stairs, and Victoria found that the material around her legs had enough give to allow her to go down stairs safely.

They arrived at the main floor, and Anderson bowed to Masumi, who returned it, then bowed to Victoria. "Good evening." His eyes wandered over her body for a moment before returning to her eyes. "You look wonderful."

She flushed slightly, bowed gently in what she hoped was an acceptable bow. "Thank you." She was still not sure what was going on, but she did feel feminine and was enjoying that a lot.

"This way, please." He indicated a closed door across the room.

Masumi led the way. She opened the door and entered, then stood aside to let the others enter. Anderson deferred to Western tradition and let Victoria enter first.

The room Victoria entered was about the same size as the guest bedroom she had dressed in upstairs, but this one's theme was completely Japanese. Several closely-woven tatami mats covered the floor. The remainder of the room was sparsely decorated. The walls were a light bamboo color, and a slightly raised shelf was in the far corner, with a small blue and white ceramic vase that held several bright sprigs of fresh cut flowers. Above the shelf was a tall, thin scroll with kanji running from top to bottom. To the immediate right of the shelf, faux paper doors with square framing contributed to the room's distinctly Oriental feel. A black hearth was at the center of the room, where water boiled gently. Two small tables rested on the matting before a larger table that was slightly higher and full of bowls and empty dishes. The ceiling had warm lighting hidden behind square paper covers that mimicked the door decoration.

The material of Victoria's kimono looked all the brighter contrasted with the décor of the room. The smell made her stomach growl in anticipation.

"Victoria, if you can sit here, please. You get the place of honor." He indicated for her to sit on the right, and Anderson sat to her left. He crouched down on his knees and sat on his ankles with an ease that bespoke practice. He continued, "By tradition, people usually sit in this pose, which is called *seiza*. It does take some getting used to, and we don't want you to be uncomfortable, so please sit as you prefer."

Victoria tried sitting the same way as Anderson and found it quite comfortable. Masumi took her place behind the large table. The Japanese woman bowed to Victoria, then to Anderson—who bowed back—and she began moving dishes, lids, and other items around the table to prepare to serve the meal.

The black lacquered table in front of Victoria had a bamboo mat on top. On the mat was a napkin rolled around a pair of chopsticks. Victoria was happy to see a second napkin beside the first, with a traditional fork and spoon. She had never gotten the hang of chopsticks.

Anderson began talking as Masumi prepared the servings. "Masumi is performing a variation of the Japanese tea ceremony called *kaiseki*. Instead of just serving tea, she will be serving several courses of soup and fish. This will not be a traditional ceremony, as both you as the guest and I as your host would normally have specific duties to perform. Because you do not know them, we shall skip over them for this evening and just let Masumi present the meal."

The Japanese woman moved her hands in prescribed, somewhat rhythmic motions, always purposeful. Removing a lid, taking food from the pot and putting it into a bowl—all was smooth and practiced, without wasted movement.

Victoria had never before seen the ceremony, and the professor in her watched closely. All she knew about Japanese food was to avoid *wasabi*, which had once burned her tongue.

Masumi took a tall white ceramic container and filled the shallow cups on their tables with clear liquid.

"This is *honjozo-shu sake*. It is usually served at room temperature and was chosen to complement the meal," Anderson explained.

Masumi produced a small black bowl of soup with a slight fish smell and placed it in front of Victoria, then put an identical bowl in front of Anderson.

"This is a fish broth called *niban-dashi*. It is made with dorado."

Victoria took her spoon out of the napkin and laid the linen cloth across her lap to protect the fine yellow material of the kimono. She stirred the soup, which was a simple broth with small white fish pieces and sliced leeks in it. She took a small spoonful for a taste test and smelled ginger as she brought it to her lips.

As the soup rolled over her tongue, Victoria almost shuddered. The soup was hot, but the flavor had more of an impact than the temperature. *Sublime! This could fetch $25 a bowl in any decent restaurant.* She devoured the soup.

When Victoria finished, Masumi removed the empty bowl and the used spoon. She then served a second bowl from another pot and replaced the used spoon with a clean one.

In between the servings, Victoria tried the sake. She wondered briefly if he was trying to get her drunk, but obviously the drink had limited alcohol. It had a rich aroma and flavor, and she sipped the contents.

The second black bowl had spinach leaves floating atop salmon-colored broth. Anderson explained, "This is an egg custard and shrimp soup. In Japanese it is called *chawanmushi*."

Victoria dragged her spoon through the mix and found sliced water chestnuts, scallions, and shrimp. She filled the spoon only halfway to minimize spillage, raised it to her lips, and sipped it. She tasted beef broth stock, to her surprise, along with wine, eggs, and mushrooms in there. The taste was exotic and yet familiar. No heavy spices, no sharp taste. *Subtle and elegant.* She took spoon after spoon, grabbing the odd piece of mushroom or shrimp on occasion. She was hungrier than she'd thought and the bowl's contents disappeared quickly.

There was little conversation while they ate. Both Anderson and Victoria politely watched Masumi as she prepared the food. When Victoria finished her soup, Masumi took the empty bowl and spoon, then began placing small portions of food from serving trays and pots onto a rectangular plate. It took a while to assemble the dishes, which apparently had a formal layout.

The plate was placed in front of her, and Anderson explained what they were. "The smaller white bowl is green beans with sesame *miso* dressing, the green bowl is a *kohaku* red and white appetizer and the plate holds sliced duck breast with a strawberry vinegar sauce. For the dishes in the bowls, you should stir them with a chopstick before eating, to ensure the flavor is spread evenly."

Victoria followed his instructions and stirred the bowls. She used separate chopsticks to avoid crossing flavors. Whatever doubts she had vanished with her hunger, and she found herself eating the best meal she had had in a long time.

She realized Masumi was refilling the sake cup whenever she emptied it. Victoria doubted she would get sloshed, but she saw no reason to press her luck with the unfamiliar drink, so she simply left a small amount in the cup to discourage refills.

They ate in relative silence, and Victoria had time to look Masumi and Anderson over. *They are a strange couple. Why such a formal meal? Did he make her do this? There is no way he could have whipped this meal up in an hour—or less than that, really, with the drive he had to make.* She wanted to ask, but the silence of the meal seemed part of the ceremony, and Victoria did not want to offend the obviously traditional Masumi. She seemed like a gentle woman. *Does he like his women that way, demure and inoffensive?*

Victoria glanced over at Anderson. Absorbed in his meal, he did not return the look. She looked at his hands again, his jawline and shoulders. She realized he had not touched his sake.

The duck breast was moist and tender and covered in a strawberry sauce. It was garnished with julienne carrots, cucumber, and endives, plus some rosy-colored buds she didn't recognize. She cleaned her plate. The portion sizes were perfect: enough to satisfy her hunger, while not enough to feel full. She let Masumi fill her sake glass one last time, and she felt contemplative for the rest of the meal.

After the last dish had been cleared, Victoria decided to break the silence. "This was an excellent meal, Stephen. Thank you. I don't know if I have ever had better."

"I am afraid I cannot take the credit for this. Masumi did the whole thing." Anderson turned to Masumi and spoke Japanese for a moment. Masumi responded while bowing, and Anderson translated, "She says that she is most pleased that you enjoyed her simple fare and regrets not having more time to prepare a more comprehensive meal."

"It was perfect. Thank you, Masumi," Victoria said, looking at the white-faced woman.

Masumi smiled subtly, bowed to her, and spoke more gentle words Victoria did not recognize. *She must speak some English.*

"If you would like to go and change, we can talk when you are ready," Anderson said.

Victoria didn't want to change out of the wonderful clothes, but knew she had to. She rose, and Anderson and Masumi did, as well. They all exchanged bows, and Victoria left, shuffling across the mats. She went across the living room, up the circular staircase, and went into the bedroom. The warm red cedar furniture welcomed her. She took off the yellow kimono and under-layers carefully and got back into her own clothes.

She took a moment to look at the quilt; it looked like every hexagonal panel was hand-stitched. *It must have taken months, if not years, for someone to do that.* A quick visit to the small bathroom came last, and with one last lingering look at the yellow kimono on the quilt, Victoria left the bedroom.

She found Anderson in the living room sitting on one of the couches. He had changed into tan Dockers slacks and a dark blue polo shirt. Gentle guitar music played over the stereo, and she recognized an Eric Clapton tune—no lyrics, only the music, and she thought it was a nice choice for such a late hour.

Full lights. Good. Dimmed lights would have indicated that Anderson had romantic intentions. There was no sign of Masumi, and as Victoria went down the circular staircase, she admired the mobile of crystal birds once more. *The Carnegie Museum of Natural History would pay serious money for that to hang in their lobby entrance.*

She approached the couch, studying Anderson's profile. If she had seen him on the street, insurance would have been the last thing she thought that he worked in. He was in good shape, well-muscled but not overly so, like a body builder. He seemed kind and thoughtful, but she sensed a rough edge hidden under that, and she was unsure why. She certainly had not seen anything negative to that point.

Anderson's home was wonderful. *All those books*—she could spend years reading them all. She wanted to take a closer look, but he was waiting on the couch. As Victoria neared him, she saw a small French press coffee pot and cups on a silver tray on the coffee table.

Anderson evidently heard her approach, for he stood and welcomed her. "I thought some decaffeinated coffee might be appropriate. Would you like some?" With his hand, he indicated she should sit.

"Please," she said, sitting before he did. "Will Masumi be joining us?"

Anderson began to pour the coffee from the press. "No, she went to bed. She had a long day and needs to get up early tomorrow. Sugar? Cream?"

So she sleeps here, they are a couple. "Just a half spoonful with cream." Victoria noted that Anderson sat a respectable distance away from her.

Anderson added the cream and sugar and stirred her cup. He placed the mug in front of her on the table, and she picked it up in both hands. The heat from the coffee nicely warmed up her fingers.

"So as I told you on the freighter, we don't have a lot to go on at the moment," Anderson began. "The initial interviews did not give us a major clue, and it is going to take time to develop the physical evidence, so I thought spending some time with an acknowledged expert in the field would be beneficial."

"What did you want to know?" Victoria asked. She took a sip of the coffee, and her eyes went wide. The flavor was subtle and mild, but it had a depth her usual cup of instant missed by a long shot. "Oh my. What is this? It's really good."

"It is a Brazilian Santos bean. I get a decaffeinated version from the city market. It is a nice coffee for evenings, and the

French press brings out the flavor nicely." Anderson sipped from his cup. "What can you tell me about the pharaoh and the mask?"

"We don't know much for certain about the boy king. A lot of what we do 'know' is based on findings in KV62, his tomb in the Valley of the Kings, and some ancillary evidence found in other sites."

She leaned back into the cushions of the couch, crossed her legs at the ankles, and relaxed. "The mystery starts at his birth. No one knows for sure who his parents were. Akhenaten and Queen Kiya have been theorized to have been the most probable couple, but there are almost as many arguments for Amenhotep III and Queen Tiye. A few contend he was the son of Smenkhkare. Records from the time are spotty. DNA has just started to be used in the last few years to try to clear up the mystery, but many key mummies have not been located, and it wasn't uncommon for a pharaoh to have multiple consorts bearing him children. Ramesses II—Ramesses the Great, as he is better known—had eight wives and was reputed to have had a hundred children.

"Tutankhamun became pharaoh when he was nine years old. He married Ankhesenpaaten, who may have been his half-sister, by some accounts. They had at least two children, both girls, who were stillborn and entombed with Tut in KV62.

"Twenty years before he was pharaoh, Egypt had many gods. Pharaoh Amenhotep IV changed that when he banned all religions in favor of Aten, the sun god. In fact, he even changed his name to Akhenaten, 'Agreeable to Aten,' and created a new capital city at Amarna on the east coast of the Nile. This established monotheism, which many Egyptians disagreed with, nobles and commoners alike."

She paused to sip more coffee. "So Tutankhamun took the throne during a time that was tumultuous, to say the least. He reversed the monotheistic policy soon after he took the throne and returned Egypt to their multiple gods. The capital was re-established in Thebes, and Tutankhamun probably became very popular with the people as a result. He certainly gained favor with the priests and nobles who followed the outlawed gods. Many Egyptians saw the brief period of monotheism as a crime, and Akhenaten's name was literally erased from many temples and monuments, including the one he had ordered built at Karnak. The erasure could have been done at Tutankhamun's command, but there is no proof." She paused to sip a little more coffee before continuing.

"Tutankhamun only ruled until he was eighteen or nineteen. His tomb in the Valley of the Kings was small, probably because his death was sudden and unexpected. Many have conjectured his death was actually murder, by his successor Ay, but his death was probably an accident when he fell off a chariot while hunting. We just found new evidence supporting the chariot accident, but it is still being hotly debated and argued. New theories take time to establish.

"In the end, we know he died, but the details are spotty, even contradictory. His tomb is unique, in that it is the only royal tomb found to be completely intact. There was evidence of at least two break-ins by thieves, but they must have been soon after the burial, for when found, the tomb was still sealed, and damage from those break-ins had been repaired.

"As time passed, debris from other tomb excavations covered Tutankhamun's resting place. Some worker huts were placed directly on top of the KV62 entrance, and he faded from thought."

She took another sip of the coffee. "Howard Carter found the tomb in November of 1922 and discovered many incredible pieces. Tutankhamun's granite sarcophagus had three separate coffins inside. One was made of two hundred and forty pounds of gold and is on display in the Cairo Museum today.

"Inside the inner coffin was Tutankhamun's mummy, wearing the golden funerary mask that was stolen. It is mostly gold, but it also has obsidian, lapis lazuli, carnelian, quartz, and turquoise. Not many people know that Carter's zeal to retrieve artifacts hidden inside the mummy's wrappings caused great damage to the mummy. The arms and legs were removed, the torso cut in half at the pelvis, and the head cut off. The funerary mask was sealed to the head of the mummy with resin, and Carter used hot knives to cut through the material to remove the mask." Victoria had another taste of the delicious coffee.

"The mask itself weighs twenty-five pounds and is primarily made of gold. I am sure you have seen pictures of it, so I won't bother going into detail. However, it is hollow gold, which makes it malleable and quite fragile." Victoria noted he had listened attentively and not interrupted her, and concluded, "...And that is the end of the Tutankhamun 101 lecture." She smiled slightly at her own joke and was glad to see him smile in return.

"So the mask is roughly the size of a man's head and shoulders, weighing about twenty-five pounds," he said thoughtfully. "It is also hollow and covered in precious stones and glass."

Victoria wondered if she had gone into too much historical detail, but she had enjoyed recalling the facts of the boy king's life, and he did seem interested. He had listened to her closely, and what woman didn't like that? She looked into those warm gray eyes of his and realized she wanted to talk to this man further, then mentally chastised herself. *He's with Masumi, you silly girl.* She was not a relationship predator and never would be. Her smile faded at the thought.

Anderson continued. "I saw on a recent documentary film that Ay was thought to have overthrown Tutankhamun. Is there any truth to this?"

"That was the common theory until quite recently. Ay was the prime benefactor in Tutankhamun's death, as he did take the throne and was suspected of murdering the pharaoh. After Tut died, his wife Ankhesenpaaten wrote a letter to Suppiluliuma I, the Hittite king, asking for one of his sons to marry her. The king dispatched his son Zannanza, who was murdered on the Egyptian border. It could have been at Ay's instruction, although Horemheb, who was general of the army and reputed heir to Tutankhamun, could have been the one responsible for—"

"Wait a moment. Horemheb was Tut's heir?" Anderson asked.

"Yes, we have evidence that he was designated the 'crown prince' by Tutankhamun and was therefore his heir apparent. Ay was royal vizier and evidently supplanted Horemheb in some unknown way, though Horemheb continued as general of the army under Ay's rule. Ay was Pharaoh for only four years before Horemheb came to the throne. I, among others, contend that he overthrew Ay forcefully. His position as general of the army would have made that remarkably easy, but why it took four years is another mystery."

Anderson looked thoughtful. "Do you speak Arabic, by chance?"

"Yes, but not fluently. I spent considerable time in Egypt. Why?" Victoria replied before sipping her coffee.

"After the crane raised up in the hold, Dr. Al Dhabit went to open the crate, and Hisham stopped him, saying something in Arabic. Do you know what it was?"

"Yes, Hisham said the ship's hold was not a good place to open the box. He suggested they wait until they got to the museum. Dr. Al Dhabit did not reply and just pushed past him. Why, is that significant?"

"I am not sure. It is the only thing that looks out of place at this point, so maybe I am making too much out of it."

Victoria stifled a subtle yawn, and Anderson checked his watch. "It is after midnight, and you have had a long day. Perhaps you should get some sleep."

Victoria agreed and finished the remnants of the coffee. "Yes, it has been a long day. I suspect I'll see you at the boat tomorrow?"

"Definitely. I want to get in the hold and see the crates for myself." They both stood and walked to the door. Anderson spoke as they walked. "Due to the late hour, I arranged for a ride for you. It is waiting downstairs."

Victoria slipped on her shoes and said, "Thank you. For that and the wonderful meal."

Anderson reached out and shook her hand firmly before sliding the door open. "Good night."

"Good night." Victoria descended the stairs.

Vinnie met her just past the plastic fume barrier. He had transformed himself out of the coveralls and was wearing a black single-breasted suit, white shirt, and black-and-green striped tie. "Good evening, miss. I have the car outside."

"You can just call me a cab. It's late, and I don't want to put you to any trouble," she protested.

"No trouble, miss. It is my job," he said, smiling, and he walked her to the door. He opened the access door, let her go through, and locked it behind them. A huge black 750i BMW was parked perpendicular to the door. The highly polished wax gleamed under the streetlights overhead.

Vinnie reached for the back door handle, and Victoria stopped him. "May I ride up front? I'm not royalty or anything."

"Of course, miss. Here." He opened the front passenger door for her. She entered the vehicle, and he closed the door behind her. The door gave a solid *thump*, and she found herself surrounded by black plastic moldings and soft wooden grains. The 750i was a true luxury vehicle with very comfortable leather seats. As Victoria did up her seatbelt, she found she had lots of leg room. Vinnie got in the driver's seat, fastened his seatbelt, and started the car. The lack of engine noise surprised her.

"Where to, miss?" he asked pleasantly.

"The Westin, downtown."

Vinnie pulled out onto the almost empty streets. As they passed the dance club, she noticed the *thump-thump* noise was dramatically reduced. "It's a very quiet car."

"*Sì*, miss. BMW layered sound insulation on the firewall, cabin, and inside the hood. The boss likes driving it on long trips. It is a very comfortable car. Lots of power with the V12 engine, as well."

"Yes. But it must use a terrible amount of gas. I never did like gas guzzlers." Victoria considered herself a bit of an environmentalist and drove a 4-cylinder Honda in Pittsburgh. *Typical male, going for an overpowered V12 that burns enough gas for three regular cars*, she thought but didn't say.

Vinnie smiled. "This BMW does not use gas, miss. It runs on hydrogen."

"What?" asked Victoria, shocked. "I didn't know there were any cars out that could do that."

"This model came direct from the factory able to burn hydrogen gas. The boss and I are piping it up from the basement so we can refuel the car easier. We eventually want to run all of the vehicles on hydrogen. The Europeans are a little further ahead in that technology. Iceland has even set up a series of hydrogen filling stations for their city buses. There are few stations operating in North America, but I suspect it won't be long until we see more. The price of gas keeps going up all the time. Hydrogen has no exhaust fumes and just a small trickle of water. A better long-term solution."

"You do mechanical work as well? So you are not his driver all the time, then?" Victoria fished for more information.

"Oh no, miss. I drive occasionally, but not always. It depends. I run the workshop, take care of the cars, and keep the house working. We have solar collectors on the roof that give a problem sometimes. I look after that and the machinery in the basement. Something always needs adjusting. The boss is a good man. He hired me when many would not because of my back."

The car turned up the same street she had arrived on. *It must be a main access road to the interstate.* "I'm sorry to hear that, Vinnie. Anything serious?"

He smiled disarmingly. "Well, sometimes. It comes and goes. I was an off-road racer for Fiat. I was in the last Paris-Dakar race just before it changed to the Arras-Madrid-Dakar route. It was my fault; I was in a hurry and jumped blind over a ridge. It was a lot higher than I thought and really bad terrain. The landing crushed several of my lower vertebrae. I should have stopped, but I wanted to win. I drove for four more hours and only placed second for my trouble. I lost by seven seconds and decided to retire then and there. The wife and I came to America so I could get surgery, and we ended up staying because she has a lot of family here. After the surgery I could not do regular work. The boss is the only one to give me a chance, and he hired me on for a two-week trial. That was two years ago, and it is the best job I could have asked for."

151

"I met Masumi tonight…" Victoria interjected suddenly, surprising herself, then trailed off to let Vinnie talk.

"Miss Masumi is a nice lady. She has been there for several months now."

"She is certainly a good cook. Her meal tonight was excellent," Victoria prompted.

"Miss Masumi cooks very well, but her food is so small. Now, if you like *real* food, you have to try the boss's pasta sauce and his garlic bread with a nice Cabernet. Last month, he invited my wife and me up for dinner, and the four of us had a huge meal of pasta. Big chunks of garlic, fresh Parmesan, zucchini, and eggplant. Ah, just like Mamma." He kissed his fingers in a typical Italian gesture.

Victoria smiled, but hearing Masumi and Anderson were hosting dinner parties together made her feel like frowning. *Why are the good men always taken—Why am I thinking that? I am not interested in him. Change the subject.* "The mobile in the main room is quite a piece of art. Do you know who did that?" she asked.

"The mobile was there before I arrived," he said flatly. However, the way he said it made it clear that there was more, which he was hesitant to discuss. Vinnie stopped smiling and paid more attention to the car's mirrors, so she did not press the subject. They pulled onto the interstate.

A few minutes later, Vinnie broke the silence. "Miss? Where are you from?"

"I work in Pittsburgh, at the university. I am a professor of Egyptology," she said.

"Do you enjoy that work?" he asked, with a little more enthusiasm.

"Yes, very much. It is a world where not a lot of hard facts are known. One mystery after another. You have to use logic and deduction to arrive at an answer, and you almost never know if you are right unless you find hard evidence to back it up."

"That sounds like the boss and his work," he said.

"Yes, it does," she said thoughtfully. "Looks like we have something in common. How long has he been doing insurance work?"

"Three years, I think. It was an accident, really. He got offered a job after saving Mr. Worthor's life," Vinnie said casually.

"Worthor?" She had seen the logo on Anderson's business card earlier. "The owner of Worthor Insurance?"

"*Sí*. Mr. Worthor was walking home from a party when a guy tried to rob him at gunpoint. The boss jumped him and took the gun. The boss was looking for a job, and Mr. Worthor offered him one the next day. Since then, he has recovered quite a few items, and I don't think Mr. Worthor ever regretted it."

"I didn't know that," she said simply.

"I know quite a few stories about the boss." Vinnie was smiling again.

"Really? Tell me some," she said plainly.

So he did.

* * *

They pulled up in front of the hotel ten minutes later. Vinnie hopped out and walked around to open Victoria's door. He grabbed the door handle and pulled it open smoothly. He offered her a hand to help her from the car. "There you go, miss."

"Thank you, Vinnie. Have a good night." She walked to the front doors.

"You too, miss."

She was well inside the lobby before she realized she had left her small purse with room key in Anderson's guest bedroom. She turned just in time to see the taillights of the BMW disappear onto the main road.

Victoria went to the clerk behind the counter. Luckily, it was the same lady who had checked her in a few days before. "Good morning," Victoria said as she approached the desk. It was almost one AM, according to the clock on the wall behind reception.

"Good morning, Doctor."

"I left my purse at a friend's house. Can I get a key for my room, please?"

"Of course. One moment," said the desk clerk.

Victoria looked at some tourist brochures while she waited. She did not wait long.

"Here you go, Doctor. I see you will be leaving us tomorrow." The clerk handed over a plastic electronic swipe card.

"Yes." Victoria said absently, then realized her departure would be delayed because of the theft. "I mean no. I will need to stay a couple of more days."

"That's going to be a problem, Doctor. The entire hotel is booked this weekend for a science fiction convention."

"Oh no." She could not imagine being surrounded by Trekkies. "Is there anything available?"

The desk clerk tapped her keyboard several times. "No. Nothing. All the surrounding hotels have been booked up for months. It is a huge event, and people fly in from all over the country for it. I am sorry."

"Very well. Surprising how Klingons know how to make reservations months in advance," she said lightly. "Can I keep my bags here until I find a place?"

"Of course. I will be here until 9 AM so just ask for me. I am June."

"Thank you, June. Good night."

"Good night, Doctor."

A few moments later, she had the electronic key in her hand and was going up in the elevator. It was too late to call Anderson for her purse, and she could survive without her glasses and ID for a night. She would just have to take a cab out in the morning to get them. Luckily, she kept an emergency $100 in twenties hidden in her luggage, so cab fare would not be a problem.

Victoria went into her room and did her usual nighttime routine as fast as possible. She set her travel alarm for 6:30 AM. After slipping into her favorite blue nightdress, she dropped her contacts into a spare holder with cleaning fluid, turned off the lights, and slipped in between the sheets.

She lay on her back in the dark and thought through her day. She had been hit on by a married man, the most famous ancient artifact in the world had been stolen, she had been interrogated by the FBI, her exhibit was now in danger of being turned into a complete media circus if not being cancelled completely, and her job with the Carnegie had possibly already been taken from her. To top that off, she would be homeless in the morning. *Not your best day, girl.*

Victoria tried to think of something positive that had happened, and she thought of a pair of steel gray eyes. *Yeah, and he has his strong arms wrapped around Masumi. That is no help. Not that I find him the slightest bit attractive anyway.* Victoria turned over on her side and tried to get to sleep.

CHAPTER 10 – MASUMI

Victoria awoke when her travel alarm clock sounded. She tapped the switch on the side of the unit, and it shut off. A quick phone call to room service ordered a pair of bran muffins with juice and coffee. The kitchen attendant told her it would be delivered in a half hour. She got out of bed, stripped out of her nightclothes, and jumped into the shower. Washing her hair was therapeutic for her, and she took her time.

When she emerged from the bathroom fifteen minutes later, she wore a white towel around her head and a hotel-supplied bathrobe. The hotel-laundered terrycloth of the robe was abrasive compared to the fine silk clothing Victoria had worn the night before. She packed her bags while her hair was drying inside the towel. She found a copy of her bill had been shoved under her door, along with a fast check-out form.

A discreet knock at the door announced breakfast, and she let in the white-coated waiter, who set up her meal on the small table. She spotted a crumpled five-dollar bill on the nightstand and gave that to him as a tip as he left. She ate quickly. Breakfast was average and the muffins dry, but it was food, and she knew she would need the energy that day. The coffee was bitter and a lot cooler than she normally liked it. Her memories of the meal the night before were like a dream. Once done eating, she returned to the bathroom to use the blow dryer, brush her teeth, do her makeup, and collect her things to pack.

She dressed quickly, again choosing pants over a dress in deference to her expected visit to the *Costarican Trader* later that day. She selected a simple open-necked blouse to go with the tan-colored pants. She wore the same black flat pumps as the day before.

Packing took a few minutes longer than usual. She had brought a small roller bag with a second bag that strapped on top, and it took her a while to get everything packed away properly. She had to fold her laundry to get everything back in. She made sure she pocketed two twenties from her hidden cache to cover cab fare.

A last-minute check of the suite revealed she had forgotten nothing, and she left the room at 7:35. She used the fast check-out form at the front desk and asked for June.

"Good morning, Doctor. You can put your bags in behind the concierge's desk, and he will give you a claim check," June said.

Victoria did just that and stuck the claim stub into her pocket. The concierge called her a cab. It arrived quickly, and she hopped into the back.

"Where to, lady?" said the driver with a Joisey type accent.

She realized the business card with the address was in her purse, but she remembered the address nonetheless. "1863 Watson Street."

"Right." He flipped the handle on the meter down, and they pulled into traffic. "So, you's a model, right?" the driver asked, the leer obvious on his face even from behind.

She looked into the rearview mirror, gave him her best professor 'This is the third assignment you have handed in late' look and flatly said, "No."

He took the hint, muttered something under his breath, and said nothing else for the rest of the trip.

Victoria looked out over the now-familiar route as they traveled. The city was just coming awake, and morning rush hour was underway. Luckily, there were no traffic slowdowns, and they made rapid progress.

Watson Street looked a little better in the daylight, but not by much. It was still a light industrial area with several abandoned lots. Things were obviously getting better, but it would take years before the abuses of the past were fully erased. She noted a SCUBA diving shop, rental car building, and a trucking warehouse.

The cab pulled up in front of Anderson's building, and she saw the front sliding door was open. She handed the cabbie a twenty and asked for a receipt. She waited for the driver to give her change; no tip. She didn't ask him to wait, since the front door was wide open, and if she did need another cab, she didn't want to go back with that driver.

She got out of the cab and slipped the change and receipt into her pocket. The cab drove away rapidly, and she was glad for it.

Victoria walked into the open door and could hear the now-familiar opera music, but she could not name the tune. There was no sign of Stephen or Vinnie, so she walked through the fume barrier, over to the stairs, and ascended.

At the landing, she pressed the call buzzer and waited just like the night before. After a short wait the door slid open. It took Victoria a full two seconds to realize that it was the same Masumi who had answered the door the evening before. The change was remarkable. Last night Masumi had been a translucent vision of white-clad feminine passivity. Now she was dressed in ripped jeans, rainbow socks with individual toes, and a tight form-fitting black T-shirt with a monochromatic picture of a rock band. The shirt had *Gabba Gabba Hey* along the top, and *Ramones* along the bottom, both in big red letters. Masumi had numerous solid silver bracelets around her left wrist and wore dangly silver earrings. Masumi's face lit up when she saw who was at the door.

"Victoria. *Hi!*" Masumi greeted her energetically. She lunged forward and grabbed Victoria gently by the forearms. Her smile could not have been wider or more sincere. "Thank you so much for last night. I had to beg Stephen to do the kaiseki. Come in. Come in.

"Do you want an espresso? I was just about to make one. Just kick off your shoes. Yes, right there's fine. Come in. Oh, last night was wonderful, and you looked darling in the kimono. Let's go to the kitchen, I'm just grinding the beans."

Masumi continued the animated, continuous chatter as they walked to the kitchen. Victoria wondered how many espressos Masumi had already had. Victoria couldn't imagine a greater change of personality from the previous evening.

Victoria walked after Masumi, and they entered the kitchen. It was spotless. Not a single dish or dirty utensil in sight. Masumi turned a bean grinder on and kept talking about the previous evening for several minutes.

"So how are you today?" Masumi asked, finally pausing.

Victoria didn't know where to begin. "Fine. I don't know what to say. I'm sorry, Masumi, but the difference between meeting you last night and now is a world apart."

Masumi laughed. "I suppose. Well, this is the real me now. Drink it in, girl." She raised her hands over her head and rotated in place dancing to some mental beat, her hips, head, and shoulders swiveling as she turned. Victoria saw her long straight black hair was down her back near her shoulder blades. When Masumi finished turning, she stopped and laughed. "Espresso?"

"Please," Victoria said, still reeling from the transition. Masumi expertly operated the espresso machine, and two cups were produced in under a minute.

"Come on. Let's sit on the couch. I've not had a good girl gab in almost a day."

"Sure," Victoria replied, her brain finally accepting the change. On the way to the couch, Victoria saw her purse on the pub-style dining table beside the flowers. "My purse!" She grabbed it on the way by.

"Yes, I found it this morning when I put the kimono away. It fell off the back side of the bed. I figured you would be back soon to grab it."

The women made it to the couch, and they sat with espressos in hand. Victoria sipped hers. "Thanks. So what did you mean about begging Stephen to do the kaiseki?"

"He called me from his car last night and said you were coming over for a late dinner. I was supposed to present to a professor last evening, but he came down with some light food poisoning from another student and had to cancel at the last minute. I had everything ready, and Stephen had phoned just before I began to pack it away. I didn't want the food to go to waste, and it was a good opportunity to practice, so I convinced Stephen to put on the kaiseki for you. I asked him how tall you were so I could choose an outfit that fit you.

"I really had to rush and had just barely gotten into my kimono and makeup when you rang the bell. You should have seen me, resplendent in my hand-stitched fifty-year-old white silk kimono butt-sliding down the circular staircase railing to get to the door in a respectable time. Ha ha ha! I was afraid you would not want to put your kimono on, but it is necessary for everyone to wear formal dress. I am glad you did, because I could not break character to convince you. Tradition."

Victoria frowned slightly, confused.

"Oh, sorry. I should have told you, I am in the Oriental Studies program at the university. I'm working on my Master's, and Japanese culture and tradition are the core of my workload."

"So you are Japanese?" Victoria asked, sipping the strong espresso.

"Yes, my father is a businessman in Osaka, and he gave me the option to come to the States to study if I got good grades. And here I am! So you know how that turned out." Masumi smiled and sipped her espresso.

"Why did you travel from Japan to study oriental studies here? That seems strange."

"Japan is modernizing so quickly that many traditions are being forgotten. Things like the tea ceremony are falling into disuse, and few practice it today in the pure form. Many of the old schools have closed and their practitioners retired, with no one willing to take their place. The few resources that remain in Japan are booked solid, and the schools that still teach the techniques have no spots open. I had to come here. There are practitioners of the art here, and hopefully with the training I get here I can return and take advanced classes, which are much more accessible once you have the experience. I want to document as much of it as possible for future generations. I really want to document the entire tea ceremony and variations on digital video."

"That sounds like an ambitious project. For a native Japanese speaker, your English is perfect," Victoria said.

"Thanks! Yours needs a bit of work, though." They both laughed again. "I had a series of English instructors before I came over. My father arranged for them, and I was lucky enough to find a Canadian tutor in Chiba who taught me much more than just pronunciation." She winked, and Victoria chuckled.

"I have been here for about nine months and love the open culture here. So much freer than Japan. Don't get me wrong. Japan is a wonderful country, and I love it dearly, but the culture is rather oppressive even with the modernizations. There is no way I could look this good over there. My father is quite traditional and would have a heart attack just from the rainbow socks." Masumi grinned; she held her feet up in the air and wiggled her toes.

"So how did you end up here?" Victoria looked up and around briefly, indicating Anderson's place.

"I was off-campus sharing a place with two other girls, but they were always partying, and my studies were going nowhere. One of my professors had been here for a dinner party. He saw Stephen's library and knew he had a series of out-of-print books on ancient tea ceremony practices, so I came over to see for myself. This place is a treasure trove for research. I was still visiting a week later, then Stephen commented that it would be easier if I just moved in. And I did!

"Hey, do you want to see something?" Masumi asked excitedly.

"Sure."

"Come with me." Masumi put her espresso on the table and walked over to the bookshelves, with Victoria close behind. She looked briefly and pulled several books from the shelves. "Here you go."

There were three books in Masumi's hands. *A Day in the Life of the New Kingdom, Hieroglyphic Translations from Karnak: The Precinct of Amun-Re,* and *The Campaigns of Thutmose III.* All of them were written by Dr. V. Wade.

"He has all of my books!" Victoria exclaimed, taking them from Masumi's hands in disbelief.

"As soon as he told me your name and what you did, I remembered these," Masumi said.

"It is remarkable. Only university libraries bought any copies from what I was told. None of them were best sellers by a long shot," Victoria gushed.

"I just wanted you to see: it's a comprehensive library. Stephen has thousands of works in several languages." Masumi swept her hand to indicate the shelves in front of her.

Victoria replaced the books on the shelves and saw many other interesting reference books. However, she didn't have the time to spend, so she reluctantly turned away. "Speaking of languages, you did a good job teaching Stephen Japanese. At least it sounded smooth last night."

"Oh, that was not me. He spoke the language very well before I came along. From what I have seen, his German, Arabic, and French are excellent, too. When I asked him where he learned them, he just says he 'picked them up along the way.' The Japanese room was there before I arrived as well. He said a friend decorated it for him."

"This place looks immaculate. Most single men don't live like this. He must be happy to have you here," Victoria observed as they moved back to the couch.

"Well, to his credit, this place was in pretty good shape before I arrived, but I'm a bit of a clean freak, so we got along." Masumi sipped her espresso as she sat down on the couch, tucking her legs under her.

"So when did you two get together?"

Masumi looked confused. "Sorry?"

"You know, you and Stephen. How long have you been...? You know."

"Stephen and I…?" Masumi looked puzzled until she got it. "*Eeeeeewwww!*" she exploded in protest, shaking her hands vigorously.

"What?" Victoria asked.

Masumi gestured madly. "We are not a couple. God, he is way too old! I am only twenty-five, and he is not my type. Don't get me wrong—he is a great guy, but… *Eeeeeewwww.*"

"I am sorry! I got the impression you two were… Sorry!" Victoria was flushing red. She had assumed incorrectly.

Masumi eyed Victoria and teased her a little more. "Oh, that's okay. Could be worse, I suppose. Besides I don't want my eyes scratched out. I know you are interested in him."

"N—No. What? No," Victoria stammered.

"One thing we tea ceremony gals get is a lot of time to look at the people when we are doing our thing. You were eyeing him throughout the meal."

Victoria looked around. "Is he here?" she asked quietly.

"Oh no, he went out earlier than normal. Don't worry; if he comes in, we will just do what all women do when a man comes by."

"What's that?" asked Victoria, perplexed.

"We just start talking about 'that cute little scarf,' where we got it, what we were wearing when we tried it on, how the clerk gave us a hard time because we tried to take four items into the change booth instead of three, and oh did you hear about Marion's baby getting colic—until they get bored and walk away. Then we can carry on with the real conversation."

There was a two-second pause, and both women roared with laughter. Victoria decided she liked Masumi. She was intelligent, funny, and expressive with a wanton love of life.

Victoria looked down into her espresso cup, searching for the right combination of words. It felt like she was confessing to murder. "Okay, I was looking," she quietly admitted. "I don't know why. There is something about him. It is familiar and warm, and when he looks at me I just… You know?"

"Yeah, I know. Don't worry, I won't say anything. Besides I am a little pissed at him at the moment."

"Really, why?" Victoria asked, concerned. She looked up at Masumi.

"Because during dinner last night he was looking at you more than the duck breast I made—and that was a damn fine duck breast!"

Feminine laughter pealed through the room once more.

"So is Stephen seeing anyone?" Victoria had assumed wrongly once; she would not do it again if she could help it.

"No, I think you are the first woman to come over for dinner in a long time. Certainly since I have been here. Some of his guy friends come over irregularly, and we have had a couple of parties for small groups, but he has never invited any single women over, and I don't know why.

"I meant what I said earlier: Stephen is a really great guy. He is generous, patient, and really smart. I just remembered: when I was moving in, I was unpacking some clothes in my room. I found a brand new Takuyo scarf in the top drawer of the dresser. It still had the tags on it, was in a gift box, and was gorgeous. Hand-painted white French silk with yellow and purple wildflowers. I took it to Stephen later and jokingly asked if it was a moving in gift for me. He took it off me and went silent for a long time, with a distant look in his eyes. He just walked off with it. He didn't say anything, and I have never felt comfortable asking about it since."

"And you have no idea who it was for?" asked Victoria.

"No. It must have been someone close to get that sort of reaction, and out of respect I left it alone. We are friends, but not to the level where I feel comfortable asking about that sort of thing. He is a very private person and really vague when it comes to his past, but I have no idea why."

Victoria absorbed everything Masumi had said. She finished her espresso and stood. "Well, thank you for my purse and the espresso. I should be going. I have to get to the boat and then find a new hotel."

"New hotel? Why?" Masumi looked puzzled.

"There is a big sci-fi convention in town this weekend, and all the downtown hotels are booked up. I was supposed to check out this morning, so I don't have reservations, and I am stuck here indefinitely until the cargo is released." Victoria sighed.

"So stay here." Masumi smiled. "You were in the guest room last night. I know Stephen won't mind. I've had girlfriends stay over before at the last minute, and I would enjoy the company."

"Are you sure? I don't want to impose—and besides, my bags are downtown," Victoria objected.

"Of course I'm sure. I exchange cleaning and laundry services for free rent with Stephen, so he does not mind—I take care of the guest room, anyway. Where are your bags?"

"With the concierge at the Westin," Victoria said.

"Okay. I will ask Vinnie to run down and get them. He is glad for any excuse to go into the city. There is an Italian ice cream shop he drops in on every time he is in the area. If we ask nice and slip him a few bucks, he will even bring us some back." Masumi grinned.

"You know, in offering me a room *and* ice cream, you are making it hard to say no." Victoria was glad to be invited to stay. It was much nicer there than in a bland hotel suite. *And they are not a couple,* she thought with satisfaction.

"That's the plan," said Masumi. "So what is the boat you needed to go to?"

Victoria explained. "Oh, it is called the *Costarican Trader*. It is the freighter that is transporting the Egypt exhibition I am coordinating. The artifacts were supposed to be unloaded and in Pittsburgh by now, but the theft has delayed everything because of the investigation."

"What theft was that?" Masumi asked simply.

"Stephen didn't tell you?" Victoria asked in answer.

"No. With the rush to get dinner ready last night and his leaving early this morning, we have not really spoken. So, what was taken?"

And so Victoria filled her in on the last twenty-four hours.

CHAPTER 11 – TWISTS AND TURNS

Anderson got up a lot earlier than normal, so early that he skipped his usual workout. He did not want to wake Masumi; her room was directly over the heavy bag. He dressed in khaki slacks and a navy blue Hard Rock Cafe polo shirt from Panama. He ate a quick breakfast and tuned into cable news—which had no mention of the theft, he was glad to see.

After finishing up his usual routine, he slipped on a tan leather bomber jacket from the closet and left. He went downstairs and jumped into the Land Rover Discovery. Turning toward the docks, he began to run the facts through his mind once more. Nothing had come from his late night re-examination of the facts as he lay in bed. There were no major leads, just one minor suspicion about Hisham's attempt to delay the opening of the box. Was that the act of a guilty man, or simply someone concerned about fragile artifacts acting in the best interest of the piece? Hisham was not the sharpest knife in the drawer, metaphorically speaking, but that did not mean he was any less conscientious about his job. Without further evidence, he could not proceed along that avenue.

Anderson pulled into a twenty-four-hour coffee place and picked up eight large black coffees in two trays, with extra packets of sugar and cream. He put the trays on the floorboard on the passenger side of the Discovery before driving to the pier.

A pair of police cars were at the end of the pier, along with four cops in uniform. There was no crowd. The members of the press were snug in their beds, and their vans off on other stories. He wondered what story Bryant had concocted to get rid of them so handily. He would've had to tell them something convincing about why the FBI was there. Anderson walked up to the closest cop and handed him a coffee without being asked. "Morning. Long night?"

"Thanks. Bit chilly with the fog, but that burned off a little while ago." His partner came by, and he got a coffee, too.

"Special Agent Bryant here yet?" Anderson asked.

"Never left. He's been burning the midnight oil. I came on shift at 8 PM, and he was out here just after 10 PM making a statement to the press. Turns out one of the ship's engineers has a warrant outstanding in Panama. They led him away in cuffs soon after, and the press disappeared."

Well, that explains that. "Okay. Mind if I go through?" Anderson asked.

"I know you're on the list, but it's gonna cost you two more of those coffees. The other guys are on the second half of an unexpected double shift." He nodded over to the other pair of uniformed cops.

"Deal. Here you go." With a smile, Anderson handed over the coffee, along with some cream and sugar packets, before walking toward the gangway. The transport trucks were gone, as was the bus.

A new truck with attached trailer had been parked against the warehouse doors. The cab and front end were shaped like a fire truck, though it was dark gray on the top half and light silver on the lower half. A dividing line of thin gold between the colors jogged upwards in a couple of places as it moved to the rear of the trailer. A decal of a flapping US flag was behind the entry door, and an FBI gold seal was on the door. A bold black strip with two smaller lines above and below ran the entire length of the vehicle just above the tire wells. It had ten wheels, eight of which were paired on double axles supporting the back end. The chrome decorative wheel covers shone brightly. On top of the trailer were several antennas and air conditioning units in sleek housings to minimize wind resistance, and a set of police lights were over the cab. The sides of the trailer had been expanded out a couple of feet to give more room inside. On the side of the expanded portion, he could see *Federal Bureau of Investigation* written in a slight arc with *Mobile Command Center* underneath.

Anderson saw several FBI agents milling around in and near the vehicle, but he did not approach it. The private security SUVs were still there, though, along with a few nondescript dark GMC Yukons that were probably FBI vehicles. The Credence Security guards at the foot of the gangway eyeballed him, but they didn't stop him from walking on board. The first thing he noticed was the cargo doors for the forward hold had been closed. *Probably to keep out the early morning fog.*

Anderson walked back toward the stern and into the mess. Almost every spot on the benches had been taken by FBI agents, who had turned the area into a workspace. Laptops, printers, radios, and cell phones were plugged into the few available outlets. Someone in the kitchen was making coffee, and the smell of breakfast was throughout the mess area.

Anderson spotted Bryant under the mounted television and walked over. He handed him a coffee, and the last few coffees went to the surrounding agents who had been with Bryant the night before.

"Thanks, and good morning, Stephen. Did you hear about the engineer?" Bryant asked.

"Panama, wasn't it?" Anderson responded.

"Right. His real name was Antonio Cesar Sanchez. He killed his wife and the guy she was banging fourteen years ago, skipped the country just before sentencing, and has been hiding at sea since then. We found his real passport when we searched the crew quarters and did a background check. No idea why the guy would keep an outdated passport with his real name. Dumb. We're questioning him now, but it looks unrelated to the theft. He was on the boat for five years. Captain says he was one of the better crew members he had. Hard worker, never had a single problem with him. Anyway, it gave us a cover story that the press seems to have bought for now. They disappeared last night after we gave them a statement and the fog rolled in." He took a tentative sip of the coffee.

"Any progress on the case?" asked Anderson.

"A little. For starters, the hook dropping into the hold was not an accident. An agent was interviewing the crane operator last night and got suspicious over something he said. He turned the screws a bit, and the operator told us one of the private security guys said there was non-union labor working in the hold. We are assuming he meant the Egyptian security guards. The crane operator is hard-nosed union, and he decided to put a little fear of God into them, so he purposely dropped the cable into the crate stack. Again, not related to the theft, at least on the surface. We are holding off on charging him for the moment, pending further questioning. No one was killed; otherwise it would be an involuntary manslaughter charge."

"Was the rest of the crew any help?" Anderson wondered.

"I had agents conduct interviews with all passengers and crew. There was no suspicious activity at any point. The only thing of consequence that happened on the voyage was the fresh water plant breaking down. That was caused by a seal that broke deep inside the filters. I talked to the chief engineer, and it takes two hours to disassemble the filters to the point where you can even get to the seal, and the system has to be completely shut down to access it, so doubtful it was sabotage." Bryant sipped his coffee.

"I see. How about the forensics?" asked Anderson.

"I got the lab boys to check the captain's safe. It was locked, and there was no evidence of tampering. Only his fingerprints were present on the door. There was a bag, just as Dr. Al Dhabit described. Inside were the seal molds and a small supply of wax in block form. So we are fairly confident that it was safe for the entire voyage. We checked them for prints and came up with Hisham's and Al Dhabit's. So that tracks. We returned the bag to the doctor when we were done, and he placed it back in the safe.

From the hold, we got tons of prints, fiber, and ancillary evidence. It is being processed now. We took a full series of digital pictures and video. That is also being reviewed. A lot of people and cargo have been through that hold just in the last month alone. It'll take time to develop. The hold is clear, and you can go down anytime, but I want an agent with you at all times to maintain the chain of evidence. I want this very clear. Touch nothing. Visual inspection only. You get one warning only, Stephen, and this is it."

"Right. Okay, Bill. I appreciate this. Thanks. Oh, I spoke with Dr. Wade last night. She speaks Arabic well enough to confirm what Hisham said."

"Thanks. Well, I have to call the SAC and give my report. John can take you down to the hold," Bryant said.

Anderson turned and found a medium-height agent standing beside him. *He must be right out of the FBI academy in Quantico, Virginia.* Black hair and rail thin, his field green jacket hung loosely around his chest. His FBI credentials were around his neck on a silver chain. He stuck out his hand and introduced himself. "Agent Walker."

Anderson shook the offered hand. The grip was firm. He was not as frail as he looked. "Stephen Anderson. John Walker?"

"Yep, like the spy and the whisky. Don't bother; I've heard them all." Walker gave a half smile.

"That's okay, Agent Walker. I don't drink, anyway. Let's go to the hold," Anderson said.

"Right. This way." Walker led Anderson through the mess, then down the internal staircase to the forward hold hatch.

The hatch to the hold was open. Walker entered first and stood aside so Anderson could review the layout of the hold. Inside were two Egyptian guards, sitting at a card table off to one side of the room. They looked up from their card game as the pair entered. The guards were in a narrow corridor marked off from the majority of the hold with yellow tape. Black block letters that said *CRIME SCENE—DO NOT CROSS* repeated along its length. The tape separated the guards from the crates.

Each stack of crates except one was covered in cargo netting, which was attached to rings in the floor. The uncovered stack was obviously the one involved in the incident. The top crate had a deep gash in the plywood top where the crane had struck it. Large stenciled letters spray painted on the side identified it as box *AJ*.

"Can we go in?" Anderson asked Walker.

"Yes, but as these are diplomatic goods, we can't touch or open anything without Dr. Al Dhabit being present. Okay?" Walker said.

"Right," agreed Anderson.

Walker went under the crime scene tape, and the guards dropped their cards and stood up to watch them better. The guards stayed on their side of the yellow tape. Walker held the tape up out of the way so Anderson could enter more easily.

Anderson spent a lot of time examining the closest crate stack, which still had the cargo netting in place. He studied the details, like the way the netting was affixed to the floor, the tightness of the net, and how it draped over the crates. Small things in and of themselves, but he wanted to see how the stevedores in Alexandria had done their job.

Under the netting, each crate had a metal lock hasp, with a piece of thick wire looped through the two hasps. One part of the hasp was located on the lid; the other hasp was screwed to the box, and they lined up when together. The wire ends ran through a red wax seal about an inch in diameter and 3/8" thick. *A simple but effective way of sealing the boxes. No one could open the lid more than a fraction of an inch without damaging or breaking the seal.* The red wax seal had a detailed series of hieroglyphics embedded in the surface. The seal was very good quality, with crisp, smooth edges; the craftsman had done a quality job. The seals on the other crates in the stack were more or less identical.

Anderson circled the box to check the hinges on the back side. They were mounted between the lid and rear of the box, so the screws were inaccessible unless the lid was fully open. The hinge pins were solid, with butt ends on the pins, so they could not be removed without serious effort.

Whoever built the boxes did so with security in mind. Very few screw heads could be seen on the outside of the box, most were inside. *Again, inaccessible unless you have the lid open.* Two of his theories—that the hinge pins had been removed or replaced, or that the side or bottom of the box had been unscrewed—lost credibility in his mind, but he would still check the *AJ* box to confirm.

Anderson moved to other stacks and found the same thing. The crates were all different sizes to accommodate the items within, but they were all sealed with the wax and constructed in a similar fashion. He lingered over each stack. Sometimes the netting interfered with his view of the hieroglyphics, but he saw the same red seal on every box. Walker followed him dutifully and said nothing, observing him closely.

It took Anderson forty-five minutes to go all the way around the crate stacks. Nothing obvious jumped out at him.

Literally leaving the best for last, Anderson finished all the other crates before he walked over to the *AJ* crate with the crushed top. He started at the back and worked forward. The hinges and screws were identical to the others. There was no damage to the hinge pins and no way the lid could have been removed from the outside. Anderson stooped down and looked at the bottom of the box. Most of it was hidden by the crate it was sitting on, but the slight fall had caused it to shift position slightly, but nothing except smooth wood was exposed. No screws or ways to get in, either. He wanted to lift the lid and look inside, but he stopped himself. *Perhaps asking Dr. Al Dhabit's permission might be worthwhile.*

While he was stooped down, Anderson checked the deck for wax seal fragments. He found nothing. The forensic team had done a thorough job in picking up the pieces.

He examined the crate for a long time. *Nothing; no evidence of tampering at all.* The crate looked the same as the rest: a solidly-locked box in a continuously guarded room. The mask had gone into it in the Cairo Museum and then disappeared into thin air. Anderson knew that would not fly on his written report to Worthor, but he had nothing else at the moment.

With a sigh, Anderson rose up and turned to Agent Walker. "Well, the box appears solid. Without a detailed internal exam, I have pretty much exhausted the possibilities."

Walker said, "Dr. Al Dhabit allowed the lab folks to check the inside of this box. As the mask was the only piece inside, there was no danger to any other artifact. They gave it a good going over with a portable X-Ray unit and said it's solid. No trap doors or hidden access points."

"Okay." Anderson stood there, running the rest of his theories through his mind. After a few minutes, he nodded and said, "Well, we are done for the moment. Let's go upstairs and see if the good doctor is up yet."

Walker went over to the yellow tape and raised it up again. Anderson followed. As he passed under the tape, Anderson saw the guards sitting back down. One reached for a sandwich and said to the other, "Time to eat," in Arabic.

Anderson paused, then turned and walked over to the chemical toilet and secured weapons locker in the corner. He had realized he had not even thought of looking at them. He gave them a critical examination for several minutes. Seeing nothing out of place, Anderson followed Walker from the hold, and they made their way to the deck above.

* * *

Anderson and Bryant met up in the mess and talked, but not for long. There was nothing new to discuss.

Bryant's cell phone rang, interrupting them. Anderson could only hear one side of the conversation. "Special Agent Bryant... Yes, Jim... When...? Who...? Lovely, thanks." Bryant snapped the phone shut. "Damn it! That was the duty agent. We just got informed that someone named Cahill has called for an immediate press conference at the Carnegie Museum of Natural History in Pittsburgh. They asked for the Pittsburgh FBI to supply a spokesperson to answer questions. Care to guess what they are going to discuss? Damn it. We had the press distracted and had some breathing room, but that is not going to last now."

Bryant turned to the female agent across the table from him. "Jill, I'll need more police on the barricade. Coordinate that with the local P.D. Inform the Coast Guard we need a presence on the water, and let Merridew at Credence know, as well. We're going to have a three-ring circus in under an hour." He delivered the last line loudly to the room at large.

Anderson wanted to call Victoria and try to get her to cancel the press conference, but he had no idea which hotel she was staying at. She had mentioned her boss at the Carnegie, Sid.

Anderson took his Motorola RAZR and called directory assistance. The operator had the number for the Carnegie Museum in seconds, and he paid the extra fee to have the operator dial it for him.

A young female voice answered the phone in an automated message. It warmly welcomed him to the Carnegie Museum. The message went on to give the street and Web site address before giving hours of operation. Anderson hit '0' to interrupt the message, and the phone rang through.

"Carnegie Museum. How may I direct your call?"

Anderson tried to sound like he had called there many times. "Can you put me through to Sid, please?"

It must have sounded correct because she said, "Sid Morgan? One moment please," and the phone rang again. *Thank God there is only one Sid.*

A woman's voice answered the phone. "Good morning. Sid Morgan's office."

"Good morning. My name is Anderson. I am working on the investigation team on the *Costarican Trader*. I need to speak with Mr. Morgan right away, please."

"I am sorry. Sid is not here. Can I give you his voice mail?" she asked reflexively.

"No, this is very important. I am working with Dr. Victoria Wade and need to speak with him immediately."

"Victoria? One moment." The phone went dead for ten seconds, and then it was ringing again.

"Hello?" said a voice, obviously tired. There were many other voices in the background.

"Sid, this is Stephen Anderson. I am a member of the investigation team on the *Costarican Trader* working with Victoria. I understand you have a press conference scheduled. We need you to stop it."

"Look, I'm sorry, but I don't know you, and—"

Anderson interrupted him. "We don't have a lot of time, Sid. Look, Victoria isn't here at the moment, but she told me your daughter Vanessa broke her foot. That is the only proof I can give you to show you I am working with her."

There was a pause when Sid must have considered what Anderson said, then he spoke more forcefully, "I've been trying to convince them to cancel this for the last half hour! Cahill has decided almost unilaterally to hold the press conference and declare that the loss of the... item was not the museum's fault. They just started. I'm there now."

Just as Anderson was about to say something else, he heard the room explode with shouted questions and the clacking of camera shutters. He did not need Sid to tell him what had just been announced. Anderson got Bryant's attention and gave him a thumb down and shook his head. Anderson could almost see the headache forming behind the FBI agent's forehead.

Anderson heard Sid say, "One sec," followed by more noise. The noise decreased suddenly, and Sid's voice came through. "Okay, I'm out of the room. I'm sorry, but I tried."

"Okay, thanks. While I have you, do you have a cell phone number for Victoria? She is not here yet, and I want to give her a heads-up."

"She doesn't carry one, but I know she's staying at the Westin," Sid responded.

"Right, thanks for trying. This is going to make our jobs a lot harder."

"Okay, you're welcome. Bye."

Anderson hit the *end call* button and turned to Bryant. "Bill, the cat is out of the bag. They just announced it." Anderson dialed local directory assistance and got the number for the Westin.

A pleasant female voice answered, "Westin Hotel, your five-star business and travel destination. How may I help you?"

"Dr. Victoria Wade, please."

"One moment please... sir, Dr. Wade checked out this morning," the woman said.

"Did she leave a forwarding address or contact number?" Anderson asked quickly.

"No, sir," she said sweetly. "Is there anything else I can help you with?"

"No. Thanks."

"Thank you for calling the Westin, your five—"

Anderson ended the call.

* * *

The cell phone rang three minutes after his head had hit the pillow. The lawyer groaned as he picked it up. He forced himself to swing his legs over the side of the bed and sit on the edge before he answered it. His recent global travel had played hell with his internal clock, and although it was early, he was finally lying down in his own bed for the first time in over a week.

"Yes, sir?" No one else had this phone number.

"You see the news?"

"No, sir."

"The loss was discovered early. That explains the delay. Dammit to hell, boy." The strong Texas accent rang with disappointment and anger.

"I see," said the lawyer noncommittally. They had discussed the possibility at their last meeting, but not seriously. His employer never considered failure as an option.

"The only good news is that advance ticket sales are through the roof, so we'll still make a hefty profit even without the arrival of the 'special item.' Still, we need to ensure this does not come back on us, son. I want you to take out two hundred thousand of insurance."

"Very good, sir. I made arrangements yesterday to cover this contingency. The agent will be on the ground later today. I will make sure the policy is activated," said the lawyer.

"See you do, boy. See you do. We need those strings cut."

The call ended. The lawyer pulled the battery out of the cell phone. He would dispose of both parts later in separate public garbage cans. He pulled out the next phone in the series, inserted the battery, and turned it on, placing it on the night table.

The lawyer pushed himself out of bed and groggily walked to the bathroom. He needed a very cold shower and some very hot coffee to wake up before he called Las Vegas. He would not call from his home, even on a 'safe' cell phone; he would have to drive to another part of the city so the call was logged on other towers. He needed to call the broker, the middleman between him and the assassin. If he was lucky, the broker would tell him to proceed, and the lawyer could be back in bed in an hour.

* * *

Anderson decided he needed some air. He walked outside to the railing at the side of the ship, holding on to the top bar. He glanced at the police barricade line. There were only a few people there, but he knew that would soon change dramatically. 'Circus' was an understatement, but unless he could solve the entire affair in less than fifteen minutes, it was unavoidable.

Anderson typically avoided the press. His hidden past made him fear exposure. He made many other excuses to others, but the truth was that he did not want to be seen by certain dangerous people from his past. In addition, he worried about the US government. Anderson was living under another man's identity, and not only was he criminally liable for that, but he could also be deported. If he were identified as a deserter, there was no doubt he would be sent back to France, where the Legion would take possession of him. In their eyes, he still owed them three years of his life, regardless of the circumstances of his departure. Having the press three deep past the barricades with telephoto lenses would be a huge problem.

His cell phone vibrated on his waistband, interrupting his train of thought.

"Anderson." He automatically turned his back to the reporters.

"Hi, Stephen. It's Masumi."

"Yes, Masumi?"

"I don't mean to disturb you. Just wanted to let you know Victoria came by this morning to get her purse, and I invited her to stay over. She had some problem with her hotel and needed somewhere to stay."

"Is she there now?" he asked. "I need to talk to her."

"Yep, one sec."

"Hello," Victoria said.

"Victoria. Have Masumi put cable news on. A man named Cahill just announced the theft in Pittsburgh. It will not be long before the press descends on the ship *en masse*."

As an educated lady, he didn't think Victoria the type to swear often, but she surprised him. "—What a stupid thing to do. I'll bet he wants to use this as advertising for the museum, but it will just cause unneeded panic. Is there anything I can do?"

"No, I don't think so. I already talked to Sid Morgan, and we were too late to stop it. He tried his best as well. Listen, if you are coming to the ship, then you had best do it soon. In an hour, there will be reporters ten deep beyond the barricades. You can ask Vinnie to drive you."

"He's gone to the hotel to pick up my bags. I'll have to take a cab," Victoria said determinedly.

"Okay, have it drop you off on the corner of Whittaker and Water streets. It is just down from here. I will make sure Bill has an agent there to escort you in."

"Thank you, Stephen. Bye."

"See you soon." Anderson was going to return his phone to his belt when two Egyptian guards walked by, speaking in Arabic. He started to turn to go talk to Bryant when he heard one say, "This is madness. We did nothing wrong, and we did our jobs correctly. Yet they treat us like criminals." Anderson took his phone, dialed a number, but did not hit *send*. He then put it to his ear and pretended to make a call as he listened to their conversation. The pair stopped about ten feet away.

The original voice continued speaking, "... Kareem, I was spoken to at length by the FBI this morning."

"As was I, for almost an hour. This is what they do. They will talk to everyone on board. We did nothing wrong, my friend."

"When they look at me it is with disbelief in their eyes. They know something! You saw them. They took a member of the crew off the ship in handcuffs."

"I heard that he was wanted for crimes in another country, and he is most probably the thief. What is there to know, Farhaan? Tell me this. What great evil did you do that resulted in the theft?"

"Nothing. Of course nothing."

"Then why fear these police? As you say, we have done nothing."

"The mask could have been stolen while we were on guard, Kareem!"

"How? We were alert the whole time."

"Not I, and you know this!"

"Yes, I was there, Farhaan. Remember? It was seasickness only."

"I don't know... I don't know..." The doubt in Farhaan's voice was obvious.

The one called Kareem looked over at Anderson, whom he saw out of his peripheral vision. Anderson laughed lightly and said to his imaginary phone call, "Of course. How are you doing today?" It was convincing, but still Kareem motioned for Farhaan to follow him further forward on the deck, and the rest of their conversation was lost.

Anderson stood there a few minutes to finish his 'call.' Then he went down to arrange for an escort for Victoria.

* * *

Victoria arrived at the corner of Whittaker and Water thirty minutes later. She was a half block away from the pier. The cab

179

dropped her off, and she found herself standing alone. She had chosen to wear her black-rimmed glasses once more and had her hobo purse strap over her shoulder. She looked around, but she saw no one near her. Victoria wanted to call Stephen, but she did not have his cell number, so she waited. She looked further down the road toward the pier. She could only see the very top of the ship's radio masts and smokestack. The rest was blocked by the large warehouses.

"Dr. Wade?" a female voice asked as it approached from behind.

Victoria turned and saw a man and woman. The man had chestnut hair, wore a dark slate gray suit, with red-and-white striped tie. The woman had a black below-the-knee skirt and matching jacket with white blouse. Her strawberry blonde hair was tied up in a tight bundle behind her head. Victoria could see that the male had a weapon holstered on his right waistband. The woman's sidearm was not obvious.

"Yes," Victoria replied.

The woman held up her black leather-bound FBI credentials with the gold seal. "I am Agent Jill Easton. Special Agent Bryant asked us to escort you to the ship. This way, please." The pair led the way, with Victoria following.

As they approached the pier entrance, she could see a half-dozen satellite transceiver booms raised into the air. The noise of many voices grew.

They turned the corner, and Victoria stopped momentarily when she saw the scene. It had been busy the night before in front of the barricades, but now it was complete gridlock. Word of the mask theft had spread like wildfire. At least four times the number of people had descended on the docks, with twice the number of press representatives. The men in the crowd wore everything from business suits to checkered shirts and hard hats. Most of the women in the crowd were dressed up, but they were holding microphones standing in front of TV video cameras. One female spectator had a baby carriage with her, her infant snoozing deeply amidst the din. A rainbow wig caught her attention, and a man stood behind one of the few male reporters, wearing jeans and a white T-shirt and holding up a cardboard sign that simply said *John 3:16*. It was controlled chaos, with everyone trying to see past everyone else. Jostling was common, and the level of excitement was gradually increasing as more people crowded into the tight space. A pair of ambulance attendants were loading a gurney into the back of their vehicle. A man, about sixty years old with an oxygen mask on his gaunt face, lay motionless as he was loaded into the back of the vehicle. Two television cameras were filming the event.

"Dr. Wade. *Dr. Wade!*" Jill said firmly to get her attention.

"Yes?" Victoria responded, tearing her attention from the scene.

"We are going to try and skirt around the right side by the warehouse. I will go first, and Doug will come up right behind you. Don't stop for anything. Understand?"

"Yes. Okay. What's going on?"

"The story broke a little while ago. The press started showing up right away, and the rest are the usual mix of people, from common to crazy."

Jill lead the way, and Victoria followed. They plunged into the mass of people at the thinnest part, right on the edge of the crowd near the warehouse. They made good progress for the first half of the trip through the crowd, but they slowed the closer they got to the police cars. The people were packed together closely there, many shouting or jostling for position. All Victoria could see was people all around her. The two agents stayed close to her, but they only reduced her exposure to the milling mass of people. She was bumped into several times. No one apologized; everyone was bumping into others. Their progress was marked by several people swearing for being moved out of their way. Eventually, Victoria could see a lot of uniformed police behind the yellow wooden crowd control barricades.

A man grabbed Victoria's forearm and squeezed. "Hey, sign my cast, beautiful!" He was on a crutch and had a large cast completely encasing his right leg. The powerful smell of a large black magic marker thrust under her nose made her recoil instinctively. Victoria stopped walking, held by the fingers were digging into her arm, but the male agent behind her shoved the man's hand away and pressed her forward, with his hand in the small of her back.

At this point, Victoria was starting to get a little scared.

A bright light flashed on in her face, and a woman with a microphone butted in. She spoke loudly and quickly. "Jennie Dougan, K-TV Action News. Are you involved with the investigation?"

The microphone was shoved into Victoria's face, and a second set of lights illuminated on her. Like a deer in the headlights, she froze. The crowd, sensing something was happening, surged forward to see what.

"Ummm," was all Victoria could get out before the agent behind pushed her past the reporter, who still yelled questions after her.

The crowd pressed around her. Someone's elbow hit her hard in the side, hard enough to almost bring tears. She winced and held her palm against her ribs to protect them. There were too many people, and all were far too close for her comfort. It was a confused, seething mass of people, and she was caught in the middle.

"I just want to ask you a few questions. Why won't you speak to us? What is your name? Where is the mask?"

In ten more steps that seemed to take forever, they were past the barricade. Jill flashed her credentials to the uniformed cops, who let them through. A couple of cops pressed toward the crowd pushing back people who tried to slip through with them.

"Are you okay?" Jill asked.

Victoria just nodded, rapidly and nervously. She was not okay. She was badly shaken, and her ribs were throbbing. As an academic used to working alone for extended periods, she was not used to unruly crowds, and she'd been roughly jostled several times. The three walked over toward the ship. More questions were yelled at her back, obviously from reporters, but she ignored them.

* * *

Anderson, waiting at the ship's railing, saw Victoria coming up the gangway between two FBI agents, Agent Jill Easton leading the way. Something was wrong with Victoria. Her shoulders were hunched, and she was looking down at the ground. He watched her climb the gangway with small halting steps.

* * *

Victoria didn't say anything as she stepped on the boat deck. She was well beyond words, teary-eyed and emotionally shattered. She walked right up to Anderson, wrapped her arms around his waist and clutched him tightly. She pressed her body close against him, mashed her face into his chest. She could smell his cologne, a subtle blend of cedar and sandalwood. His arms came up around her shoulders, and he held her. She started to shudder slightly as she broke down and cried quietly.

* * *

Anderson looked over Victoria's shoulder at Agent Jill Easton with a frown and questioning look. Jill looked back and pointed to the crowd. She rocked her hand side to side slightly like a boat in small waves to show him Victoria was a little unsteady. Then Jill smiled to reassure him that she would be okay. Anderson tightened his grip slightly to reassure Victoria, and she responded in kind.

Anderson said nothing. He simply held her. He absentmindedly brought his hand up and stroked the hair at the back of her head lightly, gently. Her hair was luxuriously smooth to him and smelled lightly of jasmine. It had been a long time since he had held a woman like that.

They stood there for a few moments. Neither one said anything. Words would not have added anything.

* * *

Agent Easton walked away, wishing she had someone to do that with her. All she had was a cat, and he only paid attention to her when he was hungry.

* * *

Victoria eased her grip and pulled back, sniffling. Anderson took a folded white handkerchief from his jacket pocket and handed it to her. She accepted it gratefully, wiped her eyes, and gently blew her nose. "I'm sorry," was all she could muster, studying the white material in her hand.

"Are you all right?" Anderson looked down at her.

She just nodded, feeling embarrassed and sniffling lightly. She stared at the handkerchief, avoiding his eyes.

"How do you feel?" he asked.

"Better, thanks." She looked up into his eyes for a half second, tried to smile, but she failed. Her gaze returned to the white material in her hand. She had stepped into Anderson's embrace without thought. She knew instinctively she would be safe in his arms. Now that it was over, she tried to analyze why she had done that and was failing. She was self-conscious and realized she must look a fright. Victoria wrung the handkerchief in her hands. *Should I say something?*

"There is a bathroom just inside the door," Anderson suggested.

Without a word she nodded, walked into the hatch, and found the head. It held a simple porcelain sink, mirror, and toilet made of stainless steel. She closed the hatch for some privacy and washed her face. She touched up her makeup from the small kit in her purse and saw her eyes were a little puffy. *Damn it, why am I acting like such a girl?*

Victoria had been alone most of her adult life, traveling through Third World nations on the way to remote digs. She actually liked a solitary lifestyle. It was so unlike her to fall apart like that. She had always considered herself independent and usually didn't need outside support, but going through the crowd had not been pleasant for her. The scrum outside combined with the overall issues to produce disaster on a scale that was unprecedented in her life. This was not a missed airplane flight, misplaced dig notepad, or something else easily manageable that she could handle in stride. This was an international crisis where she had little to no control. Her career, her standing in the academic community, and her future were all in jeopardy. There was so much to lose, and it had all hit her at the same time.

By contrast, Stephen Anderson seemed relatively unaffected by the chaos surrounding them. He was rock-steady in the maelstrom, like a pier piling deep in raging surf, and she must have instinctively sought to hold onto him. *Is that it? Is that the reason why? Am I simply looking for someone to get me out of this mess, or is there more to it?* She couldn't quite rationalize why she had melted so quickly in his arms. *His arms. So strong and welcoming.* He'd said nothing, just held her. It was exactly what she'd needed, and he had known that without prompting.

Using the mirror, she peered into her own eyes, searching for answers that would not come. Victoria tucked the soiled handkerchief into her purse. She would wash it before returning it, she decided.

Victoria took one last look in the mirror, critically examining her face. *Well, that's the best I can do for the moment.*

She opened the door and walked a few paces away from the head. Anderson greeted her with a mug of steaming coffee in a white China mug. "Here, I thought you could use this." She looked into his eyes briefly, smiled in thanks, and took a sip. It was made with half a sugar and cream, exactly how she liked it. *He remembered how I take my coffee.*

"Thank you, Stephen." She kept her gaze on the steaming liquid, afraid to look into his eyes. She thought she should say something, but he didn't give her the chance.

"Masumi said you needed a place to stay."

She looked up at him and talked rapidly. "Yes, I hope that's okay. All the hotels downtown are booked, and she offered me your spare room."

"Of course it is all right," he said gently. "It will be nice to have the company. With the press involved, things are going to be a lot more complicated from here on out."

"Any progress?" Her thoughts were still jumbled, and she was glad for the distracting conversation. She looked back at the coffee.

"A little, but nothing definitive. The crew and passengers have all been interviewed, and nothing of consequence has come up. The forensic evidence has gone to the lab, but they are saying it will take them at least a week to process it. I had a look in the hold, and nothing jumped out at me. We have no major leads, just a few minor suspicions, and honestly, there is nothing tangible. Security was tight at every stage, and the cargo was under direct observation the whole time. This was a professional job with no loose ends. The good news is the crane accident. It allowed us to discover the crime long before we should have..." His voice trailed off.

"Yes?" she asked, looking back up at him.

"What? Oh nothing, I was just saying we discovered the crime well before Pittsburgh. That is the only real break we have had this far. If the cargo had been signed for in Pittsburgh, I would not be here."

"Why's that?" she asked, brow furrowed.

"Our coverage was only for the transit on the *Costarican Trader* and subsequent trip to Pittsburgh. Once accepted by the Carnegie, it would have fallen under their insurance, which is not with Worthor."

"Oh, I see. Then we're lucky it was discovered here." She smiled with some enthusiasm.

"Do you mind if I leave you here? I need to go see the captain."

"I think I will be safe surrounded by a half-dozen FBI agents," she said with a touch of sarcasm. The brief conversation left her feeling much better.

"Okay. See you soon." And he walked to the inner stairway.

* * *

Anderson went up two levels on the interior stairs. As he passed the captain's cabin, he heard a loud voice exclaim from the bridge. "Will you tell that S.O.B. that the cargo will be released when it is released! I don't need him asking the same idiot question every half hour! If you get any further communication from him on this topic, keep it to yourself." He handed back the clipboard with the message form on it.

"Yes, Captain."

Anderson turned the corner to see the ship's radio operator scurrying away. The harried operator passed Anderson on his way to the radio room one level below. Captain Kincaid was standing by the radar screen, looking flustered to say the least.

"Permission to enter the bridge, Captain?" asked Anderson from a respectable distance away.

"Granted." Kincaid accompanied his permission with a terse nod. He turned to look at a chart of the harbor on the navigation table.

"Anything I can help you with?" Anderson asked as he approached.

"I don't think so."

Anderson kept quiet, letting the captain keep talking.

"The Director of the Jensen Museum is calling every half hour asking when we'll be getting underway. He keeps complaining about his schedule being upset. Frankly, it's getting annoying and my 'give a damn' reserve is dangerously low with this delay." The captain stopped, looked down at the deck, and took a moment to calm down a bit before continuing. "Sorry, Mr. Anderson. None of this is your fault. My apologies. What can I do for you?" He turned away from the chart table.

"Couple of quick questions, if you don't mind," said Anderson.

"Of course," replied Kincaid.

"How often did the crew check inside the forward hold?"

"Both the fore and aft holds were checked at the turn of every second watch. Did you need specific times?" Kincaid asked, reaching for a clipboard on the wall.

"It would help, yes."

"We checked during middle watch at 00:30, forenoon watch at 8:30, and first dog watch at 16:30. Realistically, you can add at least a half hour to those times before the men would reach the forward hold. They start in the engine spaces, work their way aft, then work their way forward. When in the hold, they would look for anything amiss, ensure that watertight doors were closed, and keep an eye open for any loose cargo netting," Kincaid explained, returning the clipboard.

"I see. Was anything reported from the forward hold during the voyage?"

"Nothing was mentioned to me, and if it had been serious—like an open watertight door, for example—then I would've heard about it right away and entered it into the ship's log. Anything minor—a puddle on the floor, a burned-out light bulb, that sort of thing—would've been considered housekeeping and fixed without any notification to the bridge. The crew was thoroughly questioned, so I suspect nothing major occurred. It was a fairly uneventful crossing overall."

"As I understand it, the guards have been in the forward hold for the entire duration, from loading until now, correct?" Anderson leaned against the navigation table and crossed his arms.

"Yes. It was a sore point for me initially. Safety is a big concern for my crew and passengers. Having them in the hold would normally not be allowed. However, I'm glad they were there in retrospect," stated Kincaid.

"Why is that, sir?"

Kincaid pointed at the forward hold for emphasis. "Because with them there, it tells me the mask was taken prior to it coming on board. That exonerates my crew, and there can be no black mark against my vessel."

"So you feel the mask was taken prior to loading?" Anderson posed the obvious question.

"Must've been. From what I've heard in the transit over, the guards were selected randomly from over a hundred applicants. Their schedules were also selected so they were not paired with someone they knew. Nigh on impossible to get past two alert guards in a well-lit hold. No, it had to be done before it came on board."

"Logic would tend to agree with you, Captain. However, at no point in the journey was there insufficient security. It should be impossible for the mask to disappear, but yet it is gone," Anderson pointed out.

"Then, Mr. Anderson, you must rely on the sage advice of Mr. Sherlock Holmes," Kincaid cryptically said.

"Excuse me?" asked Anderson, confused.

"You have to understand that I spend the majority of my life at sea. As a result, I read quite a bit. In the library, there's a red-leather-bound compilation of *The Adventures of Sherlock Holmes*. In one of the stories, Holmes states, 'When you have eliminated the impossible, whatever remains, however improbable, must be the truth.' It would seem as if you are in need of the same advice."

Anderson nodded his head.

"I wish you luck, Mr. Anderson. The sooner we can clear this up, the faster we can get underway. The owners are getting quite frustrated at the delay dockside. We can't make money sitting idle, and in forty-eight hours, it'll come to a head."

"Why forty-eight hours?" Anderson asked.

"We asked for an extra contingency fee for all the special preparations, and to cover any expenses not foreseen in the original contact. That fee is currently paying the expenses to sit idle dockside and cooperate with law enforcement. Things like electricity, docking fees, food, etc. are being covered by the extra. However, that'll run out in forty-eight hours. At that time, we'll either need additional funds from the Egyptian government, or we'll be forced to leave the cargo on the pier and head off. The amount of profit we make is razor thin, as we compete against the large bulk container ships three times our length. Our schedule is typically booked weeks in advance, and this delay will affect us for some time. We should have been underway at first light for Norfolk. After that, we go to South America to deliver our cotton and will not return to North America for a couple of months before returning east, probably to England."

"You can just leave the cargo on the dock?"

"Yes, sir. We have cleared customs, and the police have completed their forensics sweep. There is nothing stopping me from ordering the cargo off-loaded. I am staying because Agent Bryant feels it would aid the investigation. I am happy to cooperate until the contingency fee runs out, then I need to keep our schedule or we run the risk of severe financial hardship. In today's economy no one can afford to sit idle."

"I see. Well, we will do our best. Thank you, Captain. Do you mind if I wander the ship?" Anderson asked.

"Anywhere except engineering. Those spaces are dangerous to a lubber, even when at dockside. No offense." Kincaid grinned.

"None taken, Captain." Anderson said with a smile. He extended his hand. They shook amiably and departed company.

* * *

Anderson left the bridge by way of the port side. He descended to the 02 deck on the exterior stairway and stopped where the stairs ended in a small landing. He leaned forward, placing his forearms on the railing. He looked out over the water. He mentally measured each of his remaining theories against the facts he knew to that point.

Bill Bryant came up the stairs. "Hey Stephen, you look like you have given up. Decided to leave it up to the pros after all?"

Anderson ignored the good-natured barb. "No, just getting some air and running a few things through my mind. I may need to head out for a bit for some background information."

"Good luck getting through that mess out front. What sort of info?" Bryant asked, his 'cop' voice obvious.

"Jensen. The museum in Norfolk, Virginia," he answered immediately.

"I can save you a trip. Once we learned part of the shipment was going there, we had agents from the Richmond office do background checks on all of the current board and staff there. They are all clean. Worst thing we found was an outstanding parking violation, and that is only because the lady is fighting it in court. Nothing there."

"Okay, thanks. I still need to get off the boat for a bit, regardless. You have a helicopter on call?" Anderson asked, giving Bryant an amused glance. He already knew the answer to that question.

"Ha! Do you know how much paperwork that would result in? Hell, I can't get a helicopter for myself without the SAC's approval... still, I can see if the Coasties would give you a lift out across the harbor."

"Thanks. I am going to walk around the vessel first. Then I'll go talk to Dr. Wade before leaving, so it will be a while."

Anderson began his walk at the bow of the ship. He skipped the forward hold, because he had examined that area well, and went into the other areas. The crew, passengers, and FBI agents occupied the public spaces on the vessel. Areas like the radio room, bridge, and mess were continuously occupied by multiple people. Anderson noticed that the library seemed to be the only space on board not being used. It had a solid door, while the rest of the spaces had railed curtains, if anything at all. Other than that one observation, he saw nothing else that piqued his interest. He avoided the engineering spaces and checked out the incinerator room last. He paid particular attention to the inside of the incinerator itself and poked through the ashes with a long piece of discarded wire.

* * *

Anderson found Victoria at a table in the mess. It smelled like lunch was minutes away. The scent of corned beef and cabbage permeated the room. Anderson told her he was leaving the ship, and she wanted to go with him.

"Victoria, I cannot take you this time. The man I am going to meet does not like strangers. It took me a year to develop him as a source," Anderson explained.

"I'm doing no good here, Stephen. Until the cargo gets released, I'm in limbo. I called Sid on my cell. The board is meeting tomorrow afternoon. If there's no good news, then I'll probably be out of a job, and there's a good chance the exhibit will return to Egypt unseen. I need to do something." She sounded upset, but she kept her composure.

"Sid said you didn't have a cell phone," Anderson observed.

"I got one for emergencies. One of those prepaid models to use on the trip. I forgot to give him the number until today, since we had e-mail."

"I understand. Look, I will be back in a couple of hours, then we can leave, and I will take you out for dinner tonight so we can both relax."

"Promise?" she asked.

"I just did. Give me your cell number."

She read the number off the phone's LCD display.

"Got it." He nodded.

"Aren't you going to write it down?"

"No. I always memorize the important numbers," Anderson said with a smile. "I'll give you a call just before I head back."

"Okay. Good luck," said Victoria.

"See you soon."

CHAPTER 12 – AULD LANG SYNE

The Coast Guard picked up Anderson from the harbor side of the *Costarican Trader*. The crew winched down the sea stairs, and he walked down to the waiting boat. The Coast Guard vessel was a twenty-five-foot-long aluminum-hulled Response Boat-Medium or RB-M. There were a hundred and eighty of them in service, and the Coast Guard used them in shallow-water operations around the country. That particular one was made by Marinette Marine. They had 1650 horsepower generating a top speed of forty-two knots. It had a black hull and white superstructure, divided by a thin red line that ran along the top of the hull segmenting the colors. On the prow of the vessel, just forward of the wheelhouse, was a mount for twin .50 caliber machine guns, but no weapons were currently in place.

A Petty Officer First Class was there to help him aboard the vessel. Dressed in a blue uniform, the khaki green holster holding his .40 SIG Sauer P229R DAK pistol stood out clearly under his low-profile life vest.

"Permission to come aboard?" Anderson asked while still standing on the sea stairs.

"Granted, sir. If you'll take a seat in the cabin, we'll have you clear of here in no time," the PO1 said.

As soon as Anderson was seated, they moved off. Once clear of the pier and into the main shipping channel, they opened up the throttles. The crew only used two-thirds of the available power, but they cut through the calm water at twenty-eight knots. The trip down past the other piers only took five minutes, and they left him on a popular boardwalk near some trendy night spots that were just starting to open their doors. He luckily caught a taxi dropping off a pretty waitress at work; he held the door open for the woman and got a nice smile for his trouble. Reggae music came from the cab. The waitress stretched her long, tanned legs and walked into the restaurant. Anderson took her place in the back seat.

"Möbius Café, Foulkes Street," Anderson told the cabbie, a young white kid with red dreadlocks, three-day-old stubble with many uneven patches, and a rainbow wool cap. The smell told Anderson what the driver had been smoking.

"Right, mon. Is a fine, fine day," replied the driver. Anderson ignored him.

* * *

The cab pulled up in front of a gaudy neon-lit storefront. A painted wooden sign hung out into the street, with the name *MÖBIUS* on top, a stylized Möbius strip beneath, and *NET CAFÉ* on the bottom. Garish green, red, blue, and yellow shapes assaulted Anderson's eyes from under the store's glass front. Things like neon-lit palm trees, a bumblebee, a robot with flailing arms, a warrior with a sword, and a dragon head breathing flames took up the entire window. Above the open doorway an oval flashing neon *OPEN* sign blinked on every two seconds. The island music in the cab conflicted with the techno beat coming from hidden speakers over the business's threshold.

Anderson paid the cab driver, waited for a receipt, and then walked into the business. He paused in the doorway and took off his sunglasses; it would be darker inside. The neon shapes in the front window had matte black-painted plywood behind them, blocking most of the natural light from getting inside. In the dim interior, Anderson could see roughly thirty wide-format LCD monitors; none was smaller than twenty-four inches. Each monitor rested inside mini cubicles, painted black.

In front of each monitor were a mouse, a keyboard, and a teenager intently concentrating on some sort of computer game. Most were playing a medieval combat–themed game with over-muscled heroes and buxom underdressed female magicians or priests in robes. A few were directing multiple small-scale futuristic tanks or rockets and building empires while crushing their neighbors. A small cluster of teens in the far corner was directing soldiers through dirty streets in an urban combat simulation.

The cacophony from the explosions of modern weapons and the battle cries of ogres and trolls permeated the room. Anderson found the disparate sounds disconcerting, but the kids seemed to automatically filter out the sounds for their game alone.

There were few girls in the room, and only a few of those were playing games themselves; most watched over the shoulders of the boys or talked among themselves. Anderson was more than double the average age of the teens in the room. None looked up at his entrance; they were intently staring into their own personal virtual worlds.

Anderson walked up to the counter. A young blonde girl about seventeen years old sat behind the counter by the cash register and a small PC. Her head was down, and she was reading a *Cosmopolitan* magazine .

Several glass door refrigerators were behind her, and each refrigerator held the usual assortment of juices, caffeine drinks, and colas. Racks of potato chips, snacks, and other junk food were densely packed along the walls.

"Hey," said the young lady upon seeing him, looking up and half-smiling.

"Can you tell Nawaz that Anderson is here?" he asked.

She nodded, picked up a wall-mounted handset for the intercom, and punched a button. The sounds from the gaming did not allow him to hear what she said, but she hung up in seconds.

"In the back, third door on the left." She pointed with her thumb.

"Right, thanks." He knew the way.

Anderson went through the black hanging curtain on the back wall, walked past the bathrooms and down the short corridor to the last door on the left. He saw the video camera mounted high up at the end of the corridor and ignored it. He knocked, and a buzzer sounded. Pushing the door open, Anderson entered a small anteroom with an open doorway to his right heading further back in the building. The solid wood hat rack from the 1940s had a couple of coats hung up. Anderson closed the door behind him to stop the loud buzzing noise from the lock and headed through the open doorway. He walked up two steps onto the raised floor.

The room he entered was quite large. To Anderson's immediate left was a series of stacked PCs against the wall. Each stack was over eight feet high, and the tops were barely under the white dropped-tile ceiling. There were two workbenches with several computers disassembled on them. Tools had been left where they were last dropped, and it looked like a disaster area. One computer had several bent-tipped Kelly forceps emerging from its innards, looking like the technological equivalent of open-heart surgery.

On the far back wall was a large desk, constructed in a large arc, with ten wide-screen monitors spread evenly around the back edge of the desk. Mounted on the wall over the center monitors were eight surveillance video displays with exceptionally bright and clear pictures of the interior of the Möbius Café from various angles.

On two walls were glass-framed one-sheet movie posters from various action movies: *Aeon Flux*, *Event Horizon*, *The Matrix*, *The Fifth Element*, *Blade*, and many more. On the desk stood a framed eight-by-ten-inch black-and-white picture of Carrie-Anne Moss in her *Matrix* Trinity costume and sunglasses. Anderson knew the owner treasured it. Across the bottom of the picture was written *For Nawaz*, and it was autographed in white marker.

Anderson walked up to the man at the desk. "I would have called ahead, but—"

"You knew I don't use the phone," Nawaz Khan finished for him. He rotated his chair away from the desk to face Anderson. Nawaz was around Masumi's height; young, no more than late twenties. His large deep brown eyes, thick bushy eyebrows, and medium-length black hair advertised his eastern Pakistani origins. He looked cynical, as usual.

"This room is a lot quieter than the last time I was here," Anderson observed.

"Liquid cooling. Just finished that up last week. I got tired of wearing earplugs in here, so I piped in a series of glycol lines from the basement. After that, I just needed to get a couple of hundred CPU coolers and install them. Pain in the ass, but the good thing is I hooked the glycol lines up to a heat pump. In the winter, I should be able to heat the place just off the heat generated by the PC stacks. Helps cut down on the electricity bill. So what do you think of my Frankenstein monster?" asked Nawaz, pointing at the computer stacks.

"An impressive collection. Must have cost you a bundle," Anderson said.

"Not as much as you would think. Got them in a bulk purchase on eBay in a stock reduction sale: two hundred and seventy units for about $135 apiece. Shipping from Oakland was the bitch. 64-bit processors running at 2.8 gigs each, so nothing special. However, once hooked up in the Linux Beowulf cluster, they do all right. So what can I do for you?"

If Nawaz had spoken in classical Greek, it would have made the same amount of sense to Anderson, but he knew better than to ask for an explanation of what a 'Linux Beowulf' was. Nawaz sounded proud about it, at any rate.

"Simple inquiry. I want to know everything there is to know about the Jensen Museum in Norfolk, Virginia." Anderson specifically didn't mention that the FBI had already checked them out, because any three-letter government organization made Nawaz a very nervous man.

"Spell that," said Nawaz turning to his keyboard.

"J-E-N-S-E-N," replied Anderson while Nawaz typed it in.

"Okay. No problem. Give me forty-eight hours." Nawaz turned back to face him.

"I need it ASAP. Tonight if possible, but no later than tomorrow morning," Anderson said firmly.

"That will cost extra. Half the time means double the fee," Nawaz said pensively. "Done," Anderson agreed instantly. It was worth the extra.

"Hard copy or shall I e-mail it?"

Anderson considered. He had only started using computers in the last few years and still preferred paper over a computer screen. "Hard copy. Just courier over whatever you find to my place."

"Right. I'll include a CD-ROM with a data backup as well. Half the payment up front?"

"I assume you still prefer cash?" Anderson asked with a raised eyebrow while reaching for his wallet.

A perfect white full-toothed grin answered his question. "I'll get that done before I head off to the sci-fi convention this weekend. I won't be available until Tuesday if you need any follow-up."

* * *

Hisham was starting to feel better. For the last day he had been quite nervous around the American federal police. Their size and manner were quite intimidating. They always gave the impression of knowing more than they said. However, he had been interviewed by them, and nothing bad had happened as a result. Seeing the engineer being taken away in handcuffs had not helped his state of mind, but when he learned why, he was reassured.

He had other things to worry about. Doctor Al Dhabit had become like an old woman since the theft was discovered, and he had aged considerably since. The doctor was subject to nervous fits and screaming at random. Even though he had, for the most part, shut himself in his cabin, Al Dhabit emerged on occasion for the odd meal or to use the phone in the radio room to call back to Egypt. Rumors flew about the ship that the doctor was going to be retired and that the staff would be disciplined for the theft and national embarrassment caused by it.

The staff therefore tried to avoid Al Dhabit, and many now came to Hisham for information, which was sparse to say the least. Everyone on board was walking on eggshells. As the one responsible for the guard shifts, Hisham made sure the guards in the hold learned of the latest events when they came up off their shift. That did not take long, but they appreciated his efforts. He tried to answer their questions as best as he could. However, without concrete information, many went unanswered.

As far as the exhibition went, the schedule had been shot to pieces by the theft. Sitting dockside after almost two weeks of being on board was *not* appealing.

* * *

Victoria was sitting in the ship's mess flipping through a *National Geographic* magazine. She was starting to enjoy the photo article on Bali, with the pristine beaches, beautifully dressed dancers, palm trees, calm transparent water. It looked so inviting, so calm and peaceful. *That is what I need right now.* She had never had a real vacation to such an exotic location.

Her cell phone rang suddenly. The noise in the mess would make phone conversation difficult. She went outside onto the deck to answer it. "Hello?"

"Hi, it's Sid."

"Sid! How are you doing?" She began walking slowly down the deck as she talked.

"Good. I was gonna ask you the same question," Sid replied.

"Well, I've been better. Sitting idle is doing nothing for me right now, but I can see they're putting a maximum effort into this, so I hope for the best. Any word on the exhibit?" Victoria asked.

"We heard from the Egyptian Antiquities Council. They're very upset by the theft and are making all sorts of threats, but nothing substantial yet. We've been notified that if the theft is not solved, the exhibit will be returning to Egypt. If they do that, we'll have to start refunding money. That'll put a huge dent in our cash flow, since we've been selling advance tickets like hotcakes since we announced the exhibit. However, I can't blame them."

"No, I understand their frustration level. I'm feeling it, too. Have you spoken with Peter Cahill since the press conference?" Victoria asked, looking out at the crowd near the end of the dock.

"No, and I'm not gonna. That was a stupid thing to do, and I've got to suspect self-interest as his motivation. I'm sure he did it for promotion of the Carnegie, maybe even himself, but I know how hard it will make the investigation now," Sid said.

"You should see the press at the end of the dock. They are like a bunch of hungry piranha fighting over scraps. How is Vanessa?" Victoria asked, changing the subject and turning her back on the mass of reporters.

"She is doing fine. They rigged her up in a temporary cast. She goes back in two days for a follow up X-ray and exam. The doctor is hoping to put her in a walking cast so she's a little more mobile. She called earlier and said she was unplugging the house phones. The press has been calling continuously since the announcement, trying to find me. Clara's threatened to do the same thing in the office. I've convinced her to send all calls to voice mail for filtering instead. So if you need me, call my cell. Come to think of it, your buying a cell phone when you got there was a great idea. No one has the number, so they can't bother you. Several committee members have asked for your contact information, but they can deal with me."

"Thanks, Sid. Well, you've got my number, so feel free to give me a call if you need to talk. Say 'Hi' to Vanessa for me when you see her," she said, wandering back to the superstructure.

"Okay, kid. Take care. Bye." Sid ended the call.

"Bye." Victoria pressed the *End* button, smiling. Sid rarely called anyone *kid*.

"Doctor Wade."

She turned to see Special Agent Bryant approaching. "Agent Bryant. How are you today?" She tucked away the cell phone.

He rubbed his eyes as he stopped besides her. "Not too bad. I was able to get a few hours' sleep in the command trailer, which helped. You?"

"I'm feeling helpless. I can't do anything until this is resolved one way or the other," she replied.

"Well, hopefully we can develop some leads from the forensic evidence. However, that'll take some time, probably a week, simply because of the volume we collected. We might get lucky and find something early on in that process, but my gut tells me this was done by people who seldom make mistakes. It was done too methodically, too cleanly." Bryant crossed his arms.

Victoria said, "You don't have a week. I just spoke to my boss in Pittsburgh, and the Egyptians are threatening to pull out of the country if we don't get a resolution in a few days." She leaned against the ship's thick metal railing and folded her arms.

"Yeah, I was afraid of that. The diplomatic protection on their crates makes our job a lot harder. For all we know, other items are missing, and we cannot stop them from leaving the country. At this point, I'm hoping Stephen can pull another rabbit out of his hat." Bryant leaned against the railing as well.

"Why?" She perked up at the mention of Stephen's name.

"Stephen isn't law enforcement, so he doesn't have the same limitations we have. As a result, he has more freedom of action. That's been a huge help in the past in developing leads. He is methodical and imaginative and tends to find the solution as a result. As an FBI agent, I'm taught to look for the criminal first. Stephen's focus is primarily on the items. He is motivated to recover the property to save his company money. So right out of the gate, he has a different perspective and approach to the case than we do. He doesn't have to worry about a criminal prosecution or chain of evidence, so that does not slow him down. Of course, that is counter to what we do, so we have to be very careful, for sometimes what he finds is inadmissible in court. However, to his credit, he usually does things in a way that we can use in a prosecution." Bryant placed his hands on the railing and looked out over the dock and vehicles below them.

"So you've worked with him in the past?" she asked.

Bryant nodded. "Yes. We've worked together twice before, and I know of at least one other case where he worked with the FBI office in San Francisco. The items were recovered in all cases, and there were successful prosecutions. We got confessions thanks to the information he pulled in. He also let the local field offices take the credit, which is not typical."

"He gave you the credit. Why?" Victoria was puzzled about that.

"He said that as a private employee of Worthor, he doesn't need the publicity. Frankly, I think he likes being in the shadows. Stephen avoids all publicity. I suspect it's mostly because he deals with some fairly seedy people sometimes, and too much notoriety might drive some of them away."

"I see." Victoria had a hundred more questions, but she did not feel right in asking Bryant things she should be talking to Stephen about. "Well, let me know if I can help you."

Victoria realized Bryant was looking over her shoulder instead of at her. She turned and could see some sort of commotion on the police barricade. A tall man in a bright red nylon jacket and matching red baseball hat was talking to the police. He had a tall stack of large pizza boxes in his hands and wore a black backpack and dark sunglasses. The policeman grabbed the top box, laughed, and jerked his thumb, indicating the man could continue. The pizza man started to walk toward the boat gangway.

* * *

"What the hell?" quietly asked Bryant, mystified. No one was supposed to get past the police line unless they were on the access list, and pizza delivery guys were definitely not on the list.

Bryant left Victoria wordlessly and jogged forward to the top of the gangway.

The deliveryman got to the bottom of the ramp and handed another pizza box over to the guards at the base of the gangway before climbing up the incline. The brim of the hat and half-dozen remaining boxes hid his face as he ascended. Bryant waited until the man was a few steps from the top of the ship before saying, "And just where do you think you are goi—"

The hat's brim came up, and Anderson smiled warmly. "I thought I would bring your people some lunch. Or should I toss them in the bay?"

* * *

Anderson took the pizza into the mess and stripped off the red jacket and hat. "It is getting thick with press out there, so I thought I would make a subtle entry. The jacket, hat, and pizza boxes pretty much guaranteed they would ignore me, although I did get some hefty offers for the food coming through the crowd. I could've made quite the profit," he said, amused.

"So did you develop any new leads while you were away?" Bryant asked.

"Nothing yet." Anderson pulled his folded leather jacket out of the backpack and put in the red jacket and baseball hat. He looked for a place to hang up the backpack, but there was no place in the mess.

He walked down to the library. It was one of the few spaces not in use on the ship. He hung the backpack on a hook he had spotted earlier on the back of the library door. Anderson walked back to the mess moments later.

"I don't suppose you want to tell me who you are dealing with?" Bryant tried.

"Sorry. He does not like publicity. Don't worry. Anything of consequence, and it will come right to you," Anderson reassured him.

"Okay, I had to try," Bryant said.

Anderson saw Bryant do a double take when one of his agents cracked the lid on a box holding an all-meat pizza. Bryant held off for a whole second before grabbing a slice.

* * *

Victoria saw Anderson sidestep, so Bryant could pass, and nod to her. "There is an all-veggie pizza on the bottom if you are hungry," he said simply.

She smiled at him. It was getting easier to smile at him all the time, she noticed. "Thanks, maybe later. Giuseppe in the galley took pity on me, and I had some of his corned beef at lunch.

"The agents will appreciate the pizza. Giuseppe explained he is not feeding them. The captain only told him to feed the crew and passengers, so the agents are fending for themselves. Besides some guy I met promised me dinner, and I don't want to ruin my appetite," she said.

"He sounds like a lucky man."

"Well, maybe. I am thinking of canceling, though," she said somewhat distantly.

"Really? Why?" He took a half-step closer to her, and she had to angle her head up to keep eye contact.

"He said he would call before he came back and he didn't. Quite disappointing when a man cannot keep his word."

"Well, maybe he did call and got a busy signal. Perhaps she has no voice mail, so he could not leave a message."

"Ah. Sounds plausible, I suppose. Maybe I will give him a second chance." She smiled subtly.

"I am sure he would appreciate that," Anderson said.

Bryant turned around with a slice of partially consumed pizza in his hand. He addressed both of them. "Do you mind? Some of us are trying to eat."

They both laughed. Bryant turned away to speak to another agent.

"So what have you been up to?" Anderson asked.

She pointed to the magazine with a resigned tone. "Other than daydreaming about strolling down a beach in Bali, not much. Oh, I talked to Sid. The Egyptians are threatening to pull the exhibition. Until progress is made, I am being forced to wait patiently. There really is nothing I can do until this mess is cleared up. A dinner out does sound nice, though."

Anderson nodded and turned to Bryant. "Bill, can you arrange for us to leave via the Coast Guard again?"

"Sorry, the press has been actively trying to get to the ship via the water side, plus a few looky-lous have shown up in private boats, and the coasties are busy keeping a perimeter. If you want to leave, you will have to do so via the barricade. I can assign a couple of agents to escort you out."

Victoria did not like that prospect one tiny bit, and she could see that neither did Anderson, but there was no other option. He turned to her. "I will be with you the whole time. My Land Rover is parked just past the barricade, and once there, we can get out of here."

Thoughts of the unruly crowd and press unsettled her, but she took what he had said to heart. "Okay." She shivered, but not because she was cold.

* * *

Anderson saw that shiver and immediately peeled off his leather jacket. He dropped it around her shoulders. She noticed that it was a lot heavier than she expected. It was warm from his body heat and had his familiar cedar and sandalwood scent. It was subtle but masculine, and comforted her.

"Are you all right?" he asked.

"Yes, if we are going to go, let's go now. The more I think about it, the less I want to."

Doctor Al Dhabit stormed into the galley from an internal hatch, stopping any further conversation. His eyes were swollen, his cheeks were flushed, and he walked like a boxer who had just emerged from a brutal fight that went the full fifteen rounds. He carried a wad of papers crushed tightly in his right hand. He walked quickly towards the group containing Bryant.

He shrilly demanded, "Agent Bryant, I insist on being told of your progress. I have heard nothing from you in many hours, and my government demands results."

Bryant turned and looked at Al Dhabit's red face. "Doctor, are you feeling all right?"

"What? This is irrelevant. I want to know the state of your investiga—" Al Dhabit paused and grabbed his forehead with his hand. He swayed briefly, closed his eyes, and began to fall backwards. Anderson barely caught him in time and eased him onto a bench.

Bryant grabbed a carafe of water and poured a tall glass before offering it to the weakened man. He had to help the doctor raise the glass to his lips. Half the water disappeared. The doctor opened his eyes and stared into the glass in his hand, now resting in his lap. There was a long pause.

"Doctor?" asked Bryant.

"My wife Ghayda," Al Dhabit finally said flatly. "I just spoke with her in the radio room. My brother-in-law has been arrested, as he made the exhibit seal, and is being interrogated harshly. State security police have been to my home. They have gone through my papers, ripped open my furniture with knives, threatened my wife and children with arrest, and questioned my neighbors and colleagues at the museum. My bank accounts and credit cards have been frozen, and I am being publicly blamed by government officials for the theft in the Egyptian press. I will certainly be arrested once I step back in the country. My life is over..." The doctor's shoulders sagged as he began sobbing softly.

Anderson recognized that the doctor was exhausted and emotionally drained. "Bill, let's get him back to his cabin."

The two men helped Al Dhabit stand and escorted him out of the galley, up the stairs and into the chief engineer's cabin. They laid him on the bed. The doctor stared at the ceiling and said nothing.

As they closed the door, Hisham appeared.

"Hisham, when is the last time the doctor had anything to eat?" Anderson asked.

"I not know this. Yesterday in lunch was last, I thinks."

"Very well. Can you go get him some soup and bread from the galley? Make sure he eats it. He needs to keep his strength up," Anderson replied.

"Yes, yes. I do this." He disappeared down the stairwell.

Anderson and Bryant's gazes met. They both silently shook their heads and then headed back to the galley.

* * *

True to his word, Bryant provided two agents to escort Anderson and Victoria through the crowd. They were both large men, and their muscular shoulders and upper arms barely fit into their suit jackets. Anderson suspected a considerable amount of defensive football in both their pasts. The small group walked down the gangway, then over to the left side of the barricades where the warehouse was. By keeping the structure to their left, they halved their exposure.

* * *

Several reporters were doing broadcasts with their backs to the pier so their cameras had the *Costarican Trader* in the background. One reporter, Jen Michaels from SKY News, was in the middle of a live report. Her video feed was being sent overseas to the UK and then fed out to greater Europe via satellite.

Her British-accented voice spoke smoothly. "And so in day two of the crisis, little information has been released to the media. The American FBI has not made any public statements, and we understand from sources close to the investigation that there are no new leads at this time. The golden burial mask of Tutankhamun is a national treasure, and the Egyptian government is demanding its return." Simple red and white graphics were added on the bottom of the screen for the home audience, which said, *US Tut Exhibit in Jeopardy*, and beneath that, *Mystery theft baffles FBI*. Jen's name was in the top right corner of the screen, and a red-and-white SKY News logo was up in the top left.

Jen's segment producer supervised the shoot remotely from the SKY headquarters in Osterley, west London, five time zones away, and noticed a group approaching in the background of the shot. She recognized Victoria from her picture posted on the staff section of the exhibit web site. She keyed her headset microphone and spoke to the reporter through her concealed earpiece, interrupting the reporter in mid-sentence. "Jen, there is a group coming in behind you to your left. The woman in the leather jacket is Dr. Victoria Wade. She is the Carnegie museum representative."

Jen whipped around and made for the group instantly. Her cameraman had also heard the producer over his headset. He moved closer while framing Victoria and her companions squarely in the shot. Jen pressed between another reporter and his cameraman without apology. The startled male reporter instinctively followed along with his cameraman.

* * *

The camera lights blinded the group in an instant. More reporters, seeing the activity, rushed into the area as well, adding more illumination. The crowd pressed in, all jockeying for a better view.

"Dr. Wade! Dr. Wade... Jen Michaels, SKY News. Do you have any comment on the theft of King Tut's burial mask?" The other male reporter also shouted questions.

The group's progress was halted momentarily, but the two FBI agents pressed forward and forced a way through.

Anderson, standing at Victoria's right side, ran his forearm around the small of her back and urged her forward, trying to stay as close to the agents as possible. He tried to block the cameras with his back, but there were too many. The noise and density of the crowd was much higher than she had experienced previously.

Another female reporter from a local news station tried to get through the crowd, tripped on her microphone cord, and fell heavily. A dockworker, trying to see what all the excitement was about, stepped forward, crushing the reporter's hand between his heavy work boot and the wood of the pier. She screamed. Half the crowd tried to get closer, while the other half tried to get away. More people fell in the jostling, screams rang out, and confusion reigned.

The agents kept a slow but steady pace through the crowd. However, so did the cameras and reporters. "Do you have anything to say to the people who have bought tickets to the Tut exhibit, Doctor?" Jen asked.

"Do you know how the mask was taken?" asked the male reporter.

"Have there been any arrests?" shouted a third reporter arriving on the fringes, frantically trying to get Victoria's attention, his clawed fingers barely missing her shoulder as he reached out. Anderson used his shoulder to push it out of the way.

* * *

Victoria instinctively clung to Anderson's arm as they moved. Her head was down. As an academic who worked in quiet solitude, the loud crowd was completely alien to her. This trip through the crowd was much worse than before, and the crowd, noise, and bright lights pummeled her senses.

The agents reached the edge of the crowd and paused momentarily for the couple to catch up. Once together, they all began walking quickly to the parked Land Rover. Free of the crowd, the reporters swarmed the group, surrounding them. The cameramen walked backward to keep Victoria in the frame. The reporters yelled their questions to be heard over the others.

"Can you confirm the mask was stolen in Egypt?"

"Are you cooperating with Egyptian authorities?"

"Will this affect the exhibit schedule?"

Those and all other questions were ignored.

* * *

Anderson used his key fob to unlock the Land Rover's door when they were several steps away. He opened the passenger door and bundled Victoria inside. The door was closed, and the two agents placed their backs against the vehicle, blocking the cameras to the best of their ability.

Anderson got in the driver's side and started the vehicle. He did up his seat belt, engaged the stick shift, and slowly moved the car forward. The agents cleared a path as best they could, and when Anderson saw clear road ahead, he gunned the engine, using all 300 horsepower to escape the scene and leave the reporters in his wake.

* * *

Jen Michaels wrapped up her newscast as the cameraman turned from the fleeing vehicle and focused back on her. "Pandemonium on the docks as the investigation into the theft of the mask of King Tut continues. The public is demanding answers, and the FBI and museum staff are ignoring them. This is Jen Michaels, reporting live for SKY News."

The live SKY News video feed passed overseas to London, then was rebroadcast around Europe on the Astra 1L satellite. On the island of Tenerife in the Canary Islands, a man sat in a comfortable chair in his living room and watched the segment wind up. It was just after nine PM, the sun was setting on the horizon, and the heat of the day was just departing. The open windows let the cool evening air into the comfortable lodge. The red beams of the dying sun illuminated Mount Teide in the distance.

He had lived there for nine months, renting month to month. The name on the lease was as fake as the passport he had used to secure it.

He was shorter than average. His thick closely-cropped black hair grew down his neck and well past his collar. It was well combed and held in place with light oil. The thin mustache on his upper lip was neatly trimmed. The only sign of his fifty years of age was slightly gray temples.

He had been in reasonably good shape at one point in his life, but that had slipped considerably over the last few years. Not enough exercise and too much rich food had left him slightly pudgy. His eyes were blank and emotionless. He wore a quality open-necked white shirt that had been pressed to perfection. His slacks were black as were his leather shoes. The only jewelry he wore was a gold pinkie ring on his right hand. The ruby set in the gold band shone brilliantly. Engraved in the gold around the gem was the inscription *E.S.M. de Saint-Cyr – 1979.*

The lodge was spotless. He paid a local woman to come in daily to ensure it was kept so. *Colonel* Benoît Rochon liked to have things in order.

He had turned to the SKY News channel randomly just before the segment began. The agitated crowd had caught his attention. *Americans. So emotional. That sort of chaos would never happen under my leadership. Sidi Bel Abbès ran like clockwork because of my guiding hand. Only the desertions of undisciplined fools interrupted my otherwise efficient command. If it were not for that—*

Rochon was about to change channels when someone in the segment caught his attention, shocking him like little ever did. As the news moved on to other stories from around the globe, he sat silently, deep in thought.

On the outside, Rochon's face had a stone like façade, but internally, he raged. His thoughts solidified, and after a few seconds, he knew what needed to be done. He retrieved a small notepad from a desk drawer. He wrote down the license number of the Land Rover while it was still fresh in his mind and tucked it into his billfold.

Rochon stood and walked over to the phone. He did not have a vehicle of his own, so he called a taxi. He looked up another number in the thin local phonebook and dialed again. The airline ticket agent was most helpful, and he made reservations for two for the next day securing it with a new credit card in his false name. When done, he picked out a silk zipped jacket of dark gray from his closet.

The cab arrived five minutes later, and Rochon walked out of the lodge and down the granite steps. He got into the back and said, "*Whiskeria del Luna.*" His voice was flat and emotionless, but there was power behind it.

The driver raised his eyebrows, smiled, and gave a lascivious whistle, but when he saw the humorless dark eyes staring back at him in the rearview mirror, it was enough to cancel all further conversation for the rest of the trip.

* * *

Once they got onto the interstate, Anderson changed up into high gear. He then reached over with his right hand and offered it to her. Victoria did not say anything at all during the drive; she looked completely overwhelmed. She clutched his hand and sat quietly. Anderson squeezed a little more tightly to reassure her. She used her free hand to pull out the handkerchief and wipe her eyes. Then she held it to her stomach and looked out the passenger side window for the rest of the trip.

Anderson had to take his hand back to shift gears when they left the interstate. It was the only time he regretted buying a standard transmission.

They arrived back at Anderson's place quickly. He used the remote door opener and pulled straight into the bay for the Rover. Vinnie's van was missing; he was out doing errands. Anderson walked around to her door and opened it. She was still sitting motionless. He held out his hand. "Come on. We are home."

She took the offered hand, and they walked across the garage and upstairs. He had to let go of her to unlock the door, and they went inside.

Anderson slipped off his shoes and put on his slippers. She placed her pumps on the rack as well. "Why don't you go up to your room and unwind? We will head out for dinner around seven. It is a really nice restaurant."

* * *

Victoria's shoulders were tense and severely knotted. Her ribs still ached, and she rotated her head and massaged her neck and shoulder muscles with her fingers. "Okay, I will grab a shower, but I would kill for a hot bath instead," she said offhandedly.

"Well then, go grab your things, and meet me over there when you're ready." Anderson pointed to the room on the top floor opposite to hers. Masumi had told her it was his bedroom.

Not sure what to think, she just nodded and went upstairs to the spare room. Her suitcase was waiting for her on the bed. To one side was a jade green silk bathrobe with similar color terrycloth lining. Victoria picked it up; it was machine embroidered with flowers and a bird that looked like a sparrow. On top of her suitcase was a white nylon mesh laundry bag and a small folded note on pink paper. She read, *Hey girl! The robe should fit. If you have any laundry, drop the bag inside your door, and I will take care of it. Gab when I get back.* There was a cute smiley face with big ears, big eyes, and three hairs that made her smile, and then the initial *M* came last.

Victoria closed the door to her room, opened her suitcase, and dumped her laundry into the mesh sack. Then she stripped off all her clothes and added them to the bag, leaving it by the door. She slipped on the green robe, which came to just above her knees. She checked herself in the dressing mirror before she grabbed her toiletry bag and walked out onto the walkway. She went around the upper walkway under the glass block windows. She took her time examining some of the books on the shelves. She saw Russian, Japanese, Arabic, French, German, and English books mixed in together—arranged alphabetically by author, she realized.

She got to the door, which was open. She knocked lightly, feeling a little trampy walking into a man's bedroom dressed in just a robe. She was admiring the sparse décor and large bed when Anderson turned the corner. "Hi. This way," was all he said before walking back into the bathroom.

The standup shower and sink were quite modern, but it was the matching Jacuzzi tub that caught her attention. It was at least six feet long and big enough for two people if they liked each other. The taps and faucet were oversized and chromed. The tub itself was spotlessly clean and shiny. Blue-trimmed decorative tile outlined the tub, and the light from the glass block above was soft and diffuse. Several large candles were on the outside of the tub, but it was daytime, and they were unnecessary.

"There are some fresh towels and a face cloth on the counter, some assorted bath beads and bubble bath in the drawer there, and the water-jet controls are fairly simple to use. If you need anything, I will be downstairs." He left, shutting the door behind him.

Ten minutes later, she was up to her neck in hot water turned a gentle blue color from a couple of bath beads labeled *Serenity*. She let the heat of the water soak into her for a long time before turning on the water jets. When she did turn them on, the powerful jets swung back and forth, covering the majority of her back and legs.

When she could take no more, she shut off the jets, washed her hair, and took the opportunity to shave her legs below the knee. As she shaved, she found herself happily humming a little tune from her childhood. Victoria emerged from the water feeling like an overcooked piece of asparagus. She bent forward and wrapped her long hair in a towel and twisted it so it would stay in place. She dried off her body and slipped into the robe. Before she did up the robe tie, she looked at her ribs and could see the bruise where she had been hit. The water began to recede after she opened the drain.

She picked up her toiletry bag and started to leave the bathroom, stopping when something shiny on the counter caught her eye: an old-fashioned straight razor, sitting beside a brush and porcelain shaving bowl.

She gingerly picked it up. The razor handle was evidently high-grade silver, for it weighed more than she expected. When she unfolded the blade, she could see the edge was worn with a slight curve, indicating many years of use. It was engraved with the manufacturer's name on the blade. Victoria was tempted to feel the edge, but she resisted the urge, knowing the danger. She had never known a man who shaved in the traditional way and thought it was quaint. She folded the razor and placed it back how she found it.

She stopped in the threshold to his bedroom and took in the huge king bed, furniture, and the few decorations she could see. It was Spartan, with little—actually, nothing—in the way of pictures or anything personal. She wondered why. Her feminine curiosity wanted to open the closet and take a look at his clothes, but she understood she was a guest, so she walked to the bedroom door and out onto the elevated walkway.

Anderson was down on the couch watching television. A commercial was playing as she emerged. She descended down the stairs, and he smiled at her as she approached. "Feeling better?" he asked.

"Mmmmm. Just what the doctor ordered," she joked. She sat on the couch beside him, pulling her legs up underneath her.

The television returned to the show he had on. "Coming up next on *Mythbusters*..." said the voice-over announcer, and Victoria looked at the set with open-mouthed surprise.

"I can change the channel if you like."

"Don't you dare!" She grabbed the remote out of his hand and placed it on the coffee table beside her toiletries bag. She grabbed a large cushion and propped it up against him. Then she lay down on her back with her head on the cushion so she could watch the TV. The water-jets had done a wonderful job of massaging her sore muscles, the hot water had warmed her up thoroughly, and the relaxing experience of lying motionless had forced away the last negative emotions of the day. She watched the show's opening credits, smiled, and caught herself thinking, *If he gave me a pint of cherry ice cream, I would jump him right now...*

* * *

The cab pulled up to the gate of the Whiskeria del Luna, a classical house in the Roman style. The front of the house had several columns that made it look larger than it really was. The grounds were well taken care of, and the hedges, foliage, and lawn were immaculate. A medium fountain with a stylized fish at the edge sent a trail of water into the air. When the stream came down, a scalloped bowl caught it. A gentle breeze was blowing, bringing the smell of the sea. Rochon got out of the cab, told the driver to wait, and went inside.

Rochon walked up the hall, passing the curtained waiting room with a couple of young men on vacation dressed in ratty jeans and T-shirts. A middle-aged woman with just a touch too much makeup and a blouse one size too small sat behind the reception desk. She smiled warmly. Rochon was mature, well turned out, and from the quality of his clothing she doubtless correctly assumed that he had a few Euro in his pockets. Men like him were always welcome here.

"*Como o senhor está?*" she asked warmly in Portuguese. She leaned forward slightly to show off her low-cut top.

The word *whiskeria* meant *brothel*, and the Luna was one of the better known in the islands. Rochon had little regard for whores, and his tone communicated that. "I am looking for Antoine. Get him," he said in rough Portuguese.

"Antoine is with Michelle at the moment. Would you care to wait, and I will have Stephanie bring you a drink? Or if you prefer, I can give you some personal attention myself?" The madame leaned forward and breathed in deeply to expose a little more décolletage.

He flashed a hundred-Euro bank note and said firmly, "Get him. Now."

The sight of the dark green bill and the edge in his voice motivated her to get out of her chair. She walked down a corridor and disappeared behind a thick burgundy curtain. He stood in front of the desk. Outside he appeared calm and patient. Inside he was seething at being forced to be in that common place.

A couple of minutes passed, and a male voice shouted angrily from down the hall. The madame scurried out from the hallway and went back in behind the desk. The curtain was ripped aside, and a man walked into the lobby with his shirt hastily half-tucked and unbuttoned to the waist. A light jacket was folded over the crook of his left elbow.

"Who the fu—!" was all he said in French as he emerged before he spotted Rochon. He halted mid-sentence with a look of disbelief. His unbuttoned tropical short-sleeved shirt revealed a toned chest and stomach with multiple healed scars, characteristic of someone who led a violent lifestyle.

However, the impression of the man's stern face was that he typically gave more than he received. His alias was *Antoine*, but his real name was Hugo Rodin. He had served under Rochon in the Legion as an *Adjudant Chef.*

"Come," Rochon said in French, leaving with no further explanation. He pocketed the 100 Euro bill, ignoring the pleading look from the madame. No whore would ever get his money. The larger man followed wordlessly, tucking in his shirt and buttoning it as he left.

Rochon waited in the garden. The cab he had taken was waiting as instructed, but the driver had taken the opportunity to turn the vehicle around. He could see the surprise on the driver's face; bringing a man out was the last thing he had expected Rochon to do.

The driver noticed Rochon watching him and returned his gaze to the road. The guitar-based flamenco music on the car CD player ensured he could not overhear any conversation.

"Sir? Why are you here?" Rodin asked in French. The larger man was deferential to the smaller.

"Do you remember the deserter? The *Sergent* who was found by the Tuareg west of Daiet El Ferd after he ran?"

Rodin's eyes narrowed at the distant memory, and his voice grew distant and cold as he recalled the incident. "Yes, sir. Martin. I brought what was left of his body back from—"

"He is alive," Rochon interrupted brusquely.

This took some time to process and the larger man's face assumed a confused look. His eyes, full of disbelief, stared at Rochon looking for a hint of jest, but he knew he would see none. "He is alive? Where?"

"The United States. I saw him on the news tonight, and I know how to locate him. Are your false papers in order to travel?"

The larger man finished putting his clothing back in order as he answered, "Yes, sir. I picked up the new passport last week."

"Then we will waste no time. Pack and meet me tomorrow morning at the airport, Air Europa departures. 6AM for an 8:30AM flight. We will take the shuttle flight to Madrid and then on to the U.S. from there."

"Yes, sir."

Rochon stepped into the back of the cab and ordered the driver to return to his lodge. He never even thought to offer Rodin a lift. Officers did not share rides with the enlisted. That he was no longer an officer and the other no longer enlisted did not occur to him. The cab drove down the paved driveway and into the night.

* * *

"Martin. Alive?" Rodin said out loud. "Not for long."

He decided he needed a cab as well and began to walk back inside to call one. Then he recalled that he had paid for an hour and still had forty-five minutes left. He decided that packing luggage would come second tonight and re-entered the building to find Michelle.

* * *

Forty-three hundred kilometers to the west of the Azores, a man of common height and average features walked out of the arrivals area at the city airport. He was dressed casually in slacks, a polo shirt and a light summer jacket, carrying an overnight bag. He was of an age where he looked like a middle-management type approaching the end of his career. With salt and pepper hair and a few wrinkles, no one paid him any attention. He could blend into any North American crowd without effort. He was careful not to wear anything too flashy or noticeable, to pass unnoticed.

He had arrived on a direct flight from San Francisco a few minutes before. Traveling business class with no one sitting beside him made avoiding conversation a lot easier. The only words exchanged on board were with the stewardess, and he responded in a perfectly accented Midwest voice. The man skipped the luggage claim area as he only had his carry-on, a half-full gray gym bag. It held nothing that aroused suspicions going through security: a change of clothes, socks, underwear, small first aid kit, paperback novel, and shaving kit. The clothes and other contents of his bag were all American in origin. Yet, *he* was not.

He had begun life fifty-two years previously in the Russian city of Samara and his name was Pavel Leonidovich Kogan. He paused at an airport pay phone and called the operator to arrange for a collect call. He gave her a Las Vegas number and said his name was Darren. The female operator placed the call, but no one answered. After ten rings, she suggested he try again later. Kogan hung up. If an answering machine had picked up he was to stand by and check back later. However, a continuous ring meant his mission was a 'go.' In either case, no record or notice would be made of the call, as no one had accepted the charges.

Kogan stood at the airport curb and waited, seemingly looking for something in his bag, until three cabs had arrived and left with other passengers before he stepped forward to claim the fourth. He gave an address a block away from his real destination, and twelve minutes later, he stepped out in front of a hotel.

The cab left, and he walked down the road, continuously scanning for surveillance. Seeing nothing out of place, he stepped into a rental car storefront and selected a new white pickup truck. He used a prepaid Visa credit card to secure it and was on the road in less than fifteen minutes. Kogan stopped at a local grocery store and bought some bottled water and individual snacks. He treated himself to a couple of cans of salt and vinegar

Pringles as well. He paid cash and stowed the two plastic bags of food under the seat.

Kogan drove downtown and found a convenient multi-level concrete parking garage near his destination hotel. He parked the vehicle mid-level and walked the half block to the hotel. He checked in for one night under his assumed name, using a second credit card with that alias. He informed the desk clerk he would be leaving very early the next morning. The desk clerk saw a note on the computer and informed the guest his 'marketing materials' had been delivered earlier in the day and would be sent to his room in a few moments. Kogan refused a bellhop and made his way up to the room by himself. He opened the door with the keycard, using a handkerchief to turn the handle.

A bellhop appeared at the door of his room ten minutes later. Again, Kogan opened the door with his handkerchief. The bellhop carried a long rectangular Pelican hard case with a pair of heavy padlocks on the hasps. The case was matte black and just over five feet long. There were two other couriered packages. A small sealed cardboard box of two cubic feet and a large envelope. Kogan had shipped the long case and cardboard box from San Francisco the day before. The envelope had come from Dallas. He didn't bother looking from where; he knew it was an accommodation address. Kogan instructed the bellhop to lay the packages on the bed, while using the handkerchief to rub his nose while sniffing.

Kogan tipped the man five dollars and used the security bar to lock the door after the bellhop left. With tightened airport security and shrinking airline weight limits, many people were shipping things ahead. He knew it was routine for the hotel.

Kogan unzipped his travel bag and took the first aid kit out of the bag. He also withdrew a pair of surgical gloves and put them on. The box contained a white hard hat, a roll of yellow caution tape, a Day-Glo orange and yellow safety vest. All of those items save the hat and some miscellaneous things were transferred from the box into the gym bag. This exposed a pair of dark blue work coveralls in the bottom of the box. The coveralls were well-used and dirty, but not unusually so. They were also packed away.

The only thing left in the box was a stack of high-resolution color overhead images of Pier 23D and surrounding area taken from the Google Earth Web site. Stuck to the overhead picture was a small yellow sticky note with a phone number. The large FedEx envelope was opened last. There were two 8" x 10" black-and-white photographs. They were head and shoulder shots taken at long distance through a telephoto lens. The photos went into the bag on top of the coveralls, face down. He added the hard hat last and zipped up the bag.

He peeled off the FedEx labels from both the envelope and box and dropped them into a side pocket on the bag. Kogan folded the box flat and left it by the garbage can for housekeeping to dispose of. He removed the surgical gloves and slipped them into his pocket. He double-checked the room one last time and saw nothing had been left behind.

Kogan left the room with his bag and the long Pelican case after opening the door with his handkerchief. A quick scan showed nothing out of place in the room, and he let the light-springed door close behind him. Kogan was done with the room. He slung the bag over his shoulder and carried the long case with the centrally-mounted handle. He went through the lobby and walked outside with no one paying him any attention.

After a few minutes' walk, he reached the parking garage and ascended to the truck. Kogan placed the bag on the front seat and slipped the long case behind the seat, out of sight. He got in and drove to the nearest fast food place. He went through the drive-through and ordered a burger, fries, apple dessert, and coffee, paying cash. He pulled back around the restaurant and parked in the rear, making sure no one else parked near him.

Kogan ate, slowly memorizing the city map he'd found in the glove box. He located the pier and looked at all the roads in and out of the area. He identified three exit routes, a primary and two backups. He enjoyed the tasteless meal, as it was the only hot food he would take until the job was done. When finished, he took the FedEx labels from his bag and put them in the paper bag the food had come in, followed by the wrappers and boxes. Kogan squashed the trash as much as he could and dropped it into a trash receptacle in the parking lot. He also dropped in the electronic room key for the hotel room. Stepping to the passenger side, he opened his bag and slipped on the coveralls, safety vest and hard hat. Then he got back in the truck and started it up.

Kogan pulled out of the parking lot and drove to the docks. He stayed well within the speed limit and stopped at yellow lights. He purposely stayed well away from pier 23D so he would not be noticed by the many police he knew were in attendance. He had looked at the overhead picture in detail before coming here and made several building choices ahead of time. He drove to his first choice, but it was an active office building for a heavy construction company. The parking lot had been empty in the picture, but it must have been taken on a Sunday or holiday. Kogan drove to his second choice, which was also unsuitable. It looked like a call center, and it was also occupied.

The third building was perfect. It sat behind a chain link fence that had seen better days. The five-story red brick structure was a good distance away from the neighboring buildings. The gates were wide open, and there were no vehicles visible. A large billboard in front of the building showed a concept picture of a new office complex for a company headquarters. Kogan drove in and circled the building. It looked deserted. He saw a jag in the building where he could park the truck. He backed in, not only for a fast escape, but also to hide the rental sticker on the back bumper. The truck was behind the building, not visible from the road. Kogan locked the truck and walked through the entire building.

Everything that could be profitably salvaged from the decrepit building had already been taken out, but demolition on the main structure had not yet begun. The building was filled with discarded wood, old pallets, and broken furniture. Kogan walked from the sub-basement all the way to the roof. He counted the number of stairs in each rise so he could walk them in pitch darkness if he had to. When he was done, he had memorized all the entry and exit points and how to get to them from any point in the building. Last, he checked out the view from the top floor; it would do nicely.

Kogan went to his truck and retrieved the groceries, his zipped bag, and long case. He locked the truck and walked up to the top floor. He slipped on his surgical gloves before doing anything else. The first thing he took out of the bag was the red towel. Inside was a 9MM Beretta 92FS pistol, two spare magazines, and a matte black aluminum silencer. He assembled the weapon quickly, making sure a round was chambered and slipped it into the side painter's pocket on his coveralls. Opening his bag, he grabbed the yellow *CAUTION* tape and walked downstairs. At each major entry point, he placed a piece of tape across it at waist height. As he went upstairs, he placed more tape across every stair rise on each floor. Back on the fourth and fifth floors, he spread broken glass on the landing and the top third of the steps. Anyone stepping on that would make a lot of noise as they approached. Using the garbage bags and duct tape, he sealed up three open windows. The dark bags reduced the chance of someone seeing him, but also nicely blocked out the weather.

Kogan took some old pallets and leaned them up under the middle window, forming a rough table at sill height. He produced a plastic bag of cigarette butts and spread them carefully on the floor to the left of the pallets. Any forensic investigator finding the butts later in that position would assume a left-handed smoker. Kogan was neither a smoker nor left-handed. The butts were all from the same line of Marlboros, taken from a smoking area outside of a small office building. He had only ever observed one man smoking Marlboros there, and chances were good the smoker's DNA was not on file—and even if it was, the DNA wouldn't match Kogan's.

Now that the scene was set, he unlocked the long case and pulled out his latest acquisition: an M107 rifle built by the Barrett Firearms Manufacturing company, a model that featured a ten-round magazine and was fitted with a day/night optic scope. Originally bought by the US Army, this particular weapon had vanished from an Army Reserve base in Boise, Idaho, just over a year previously. Kogan had bought it from a trusted source for fifteen grand cash, with five hundred rounds of ammo included. He had only brought one magazine of ten rounds with him on this trip, nine more rounds than he should need.

He deployed the bipod legs in the front and the monopod in the rear butt of the weapon and let it rest on the pallets. Kogan loaded a round in the chamber. He set the weapon's barrel away from the window frame. It was ready.

From the lid of the long case, he took out a pair of Canon weatherproof field binoculars, which were held in place by a Velcro strap, leaving a small bag with several sets of replacement batteries in the case's lid. He used the binoculars to scan the target area through the window. From referencing the Google Earth overhead imagery scale, he knew the starboard side of the ship was roughly twenty-one hundred feet away. He could see the stern of the vessel clearly, but the further forward on the freighter he went, the more obstacles blocked his sight. Kogan could see halfway down the gangway before an air conditioning shroud on top of the FBI command post vehicle interfered. If the truck had been parked three more feet to the rear, the gangway would have been blocked completely. Kogan could see the upper part of the cargo loading booms, but not the deck below, which was blocked by the warehouse roof. He could also see the forward area of the superstructure and had a clear view of the bow of the ship. That was good enough for his purposes.

Kogan looked at the photos he had brought, committing them to memory. Few people were visible on the ship. Many of them were wearing blue jackets with *FBI* on the back. The white superstructure made the FBI jackets easy to spot. He ignored them. He had specific instructions and kept searching.

CHAPTER 13 – THE FONTAINEBLEAU

Victoria had gone up to her room at 6:15 to get ready. She'd spent a long time getting her hair just right. After blow drying and brushing it, she put it up using a dozen hair pins, and topped it off with a decorative sequined hair brooch shaped like a black butterfly. She took her time on her makeup, too, getting the foundation just right before adding the highlights to her cheeks, eyes, and lips. She chose a subtle natural lip gloss and light makeup elsewhere to enhance her natural lines. *Not bad for an old broad with crow's feet,* she thought lightly, examining herself critically from multiple angles in the bathroom mirror.

Walking out into the bedroom, she stripped off the robe. Victoria put on black thong underwear and one of her lacy black brassieres—the one from France. The stiff wire in the bottom of the brassiere slightly cut into her ribs, but it enhanced her breasts perfectly. On her pulse points, she applied *A La Nuit Eau de Parfum* by Serge Lutens, a light perfume with hints of Moroccan, Indian, and Egyptian jasmine, along with other subtle scents. She slipped on sheer black pantyhose and then stepped into her favorite little black dress, the one made by Ruby Rox, that had reflective faux gems mounted in a thin band of black leather just below the bust. The hemline was angled slightly so it was just below the knee in front and mid-calf in the rear. She reached in

225

behind and zipped herself up. The wide shoulder straps comfortably supported the material.

She smoothed the dress with her hands and twisted one way, then the other, critically examining herself in the mirror. Satisfied, she grabbed a pair of shoes from her luggage. They were black 'strappy' sandals with small amounts of sequins and beads along the outside edge with a T-strap that did up just below the ankle. Made by Annie Maka, they had a 2¼" high heel that looked like a stiletto heel from the side, but was actually wider, for both style and comfortable walking or dancing. The last thing she did was put on some multi-strand silver earrings that dangled to her jaw line.

Victoria eyed herself in the dressing mirror one last time, checking her hair, makeup, hose, dress, and shoes. Finding nothing out of place, she grabbed a large, thick Egyptian black cotton scarf with stitched dull red camels to wrap around her bare shoulders. It was supposed to get damp later in the evening. She reached on top of the dresser and took a small black leather clutch purse she had prepared earlier. Happy, she headed for the door. She walked to the staircase and descended slowly.

Anderson was in the living room turning off the equipment in the stereo rack with a remote control. He had changed into a dark, not quite black, Calvin Klein single breasted two-button jacket and matching pants. The lower button was undone. The wool material had subtle alternating blue and dark green stripes. It had been custom tailored to accommodate his torso and wide shoulders. His shirt was brilliantly white and offset by a charcoal tie. He wore black patent leather shoes that had been thoroughly shined.

Victoria reached the foot of the stairs. Anderson heard her and turned. "You look wonderful."

She flushed and smiled at the same time. "Thank you. You don't look so bad yourself."

"Ready to go?" he asked, offering her his arm.

"Yes, I'm starving." She enthusiastically took his forearm.

They descended to the garage, and Vinnie had prepared the 750i for them and parked it just outside the building. Anderson held the front passenger door open for her. He swung it shut the second she was inside.

In minutes they were on the interstate. Victoria stayed quiet, enjoying the scenery as it passed. The water brilliantly reflected the low sun. They pulled off the interstate and then went through the downtown core. On the outskirts of the downtown area, trees appeared on the sidewalks, and they pulled down a residential street to emerge on a commercial thoroughfare. They drove three blocks, and Anderson turned left onto what was once a residential area for people with moderate income in the 18th century, but it had been turned into business offices over the years for many doctors, lawyers, architects, consultants, and other professionals. A few buildings had been converted into restaurants and cozy bars.

Anderson pulled up in front of a magnificent brick Georgian mansion. It was two stories tall, with brown brick on the facade. Three spotlights hidden in the gardens illuminated the front of the building brightly. Two thick white-fluted columns were set into either side of the doorway. An elegant stained glass Palladium window topped small beveled glass panels just inside the columns on both sides of the door. Warm lighting glowed from inside. Authentic period white shutters stood on either side of each window on both floors. There was little decoration otherwise.

Anderson stopped the car and a red-vested valet attendant appeared to open the passenger door. Anderson turned off the car, alighted, and handed the vehicle valet key to the man, who gave him a ticket stub in return. Anderson formally offered his arm to Victoria, and she took it with a smile. The building looked warm and inviting.

They stepped up onto the granite landing, and Victoria could see a simple small eight-inch-wide brass plaque to the right of the door that said simply *The Fontainebleau*. Anderson swung the door in and allowed Victoria to enter first.

The sweeping staircase at the far end of the hallway grabbed her attention as soon as she stepped inside. It must have been original to the house, as the oak railing appeared to be cut from a single piece of wood and stood on an intricate black wrought iron balustrade. At the base of the steps was a thick red velvet rope, suspended at waist height.

The hallway itself was magnificent. Italian marble floors with darker marble inlay, off-white walls with subtle gold leaf accents on the molding, and a chandelier in the middle of the ceiling all worked together. A large oil painting of the Chateau de Fontainebleau was hung on the left wall. Concealed speakers played "Arabesque No. 1" by Claude Debussy in piano and guitar. It was loud enough to be heard, but quiet enough that it didn't interfere with any conversation.

Upon entering the hallway, Victoria saw an open doorway to their immediate right. That was a library with several high-back leather chairs paired around small round coffee tables. The walls had many old books and volumes on display. A large antique globe of the world stood in the far corner. A couple of people were in there, looking at the new arrivals. A waiter appeared, leaving the library with a tray full of empty glasses and a single coffee cup. He nodded politely to Anderson as he passed.

The next doorway on the right had a large arched entry and opened into a large dining room. On the far side of it was an oak podium. Behind that stood a small dark-haired man with mustache, in a custom-tailored black suit with white shirt and black tie. He had a miniature red rose with tightly-closed petals in his lapel. He was currently talking to a gray-haired older man with a much younger woman at his side. The older man's companion was blonde, buxom, and a testament to her plastic surgeon's abilities. The gray-haired man spoke in an impatient and agitated tone. Victoria could hear the conversation as they approached.

"… and I made the reservation over a month ago," the elder man said.

"Yes, Senator, and we have your reservation. There is a party currently occupying your table. They are dining late, and they are just finishing their coffee. So perhaps ten minutes more? If you would care to have a seat in the library, I will have the waiter take your drink order." The man had a slight French accent, but his

English was well practiced. His voice communicated disinterest at the senator's problem and gave the impression he was powerless to do anything.

Huffing, the senator and his dinner date turned. The senator looked at Anderson briefly, decided he was no one of importance, and went to go to the library. The man behind the podium then saw Anderson. While his greeting was far from effusive, it was certainly more cordial than the voice he had used with the senator. "Ahhh, *Monsieur* Anderson. It has been too long." He held his hands up and out in a combination of a greeting and a shrug.

"Good evening, Philippe. Table for two, please."

Victoria looked into the dining room as Anderson was speaking. The wooden mosaic floor had been lovingly restored by a master. Dark oak paneling went around the periphery of the room at waist height. Above that was thick textured wallpaper of cobalt blue. A seven-foot-wide formal white stone fireplace with mantel dominated one wall. A small fire snapped and crackled, surrounded by the blackened red brick of the hearth, giving the room a warm ambiance. Victoria could see a dozen dark oak tables standing in the room. They were surrounded by high-backed wooden chairs with white seat cushions, and all looked to be taken by diners. She purposely scanned the other women in the room looking at their hair, dresses, and shoes where she could see them. She was glad to see she was middle of the road in style and fashion compared to them. Victoria was worried that all of the tables appeared to be occupied. *If a senator could not get in after having a reservation for a month, then we'll be waiting a long time. I should have had something to eat for the wait*, she thought.

To her utter and complete surprise, Philippe grabbed two red leather-bound menus and a wine list from under the podium, tucked them under his arm, and said, "This way, please, *mademoiselle, monsieur.*"

They entered the dining room, and many diners discreetly turned to look over the new arrivals. The other women looked over Victoria's outfit, hair, and dress. The men looked Anderson over to see if he was anyone of note.

Philippe immediately turned right, and in a cozy corner by the fireplace, she saw a free table with a heavy brass *Reserved* sign. Philippe gallantly pulled her chair from the table, and she sat. The chair was pleasantly warm from the small fire. She dropped her scarf from her shoulders, and it landed behind her on the seat.

Anderson sat opposite her, and Philippe pulled her napkin from her balloon crystal wine glass and laid it across her lap. He did the same thing to Anderson, and then handed them menus and wine list. As he lit the tall candles on the table, he said, "Your waiter is Marcel, and he will be along momentarily. *Bon appétit.*" He retreated after taking the brass *Reserved* sign with him.

As soon as he walked away, she leaned forward and whispered, "How did we get in before the senator?"

"Oh, I know the manager quite well. Are you going to open your card?"

She was not sure what he was talking about, but she noticed that amidst the crystal wineglasses, fine white linen, and silverware was a single pink long-stemmed rose, surrounded by baby's breath in a small cut glass vase. The petals were tightly closed, telling her it was freshly cut. In a tall plastic holder beside it was a small white envelope. On the front was handwritten *Victoria.*

She looked at the other tables near them and saw no roses. Her heart skipped a beat, and she reached for the envelope. Pulling it free of the holder, she unfolded the back, and removed the card. It was a pre-printed stock card with a field of different color flowers around the outside. In the center was handwritten:

Thank you for sharing this evening with me.
— Stephen

Her hand came up to her chest, and she felt a surge of emotion. She reached over and patted his hand. "Thank you. I'm so very glad I came. How did you arrange this?"

"When I went out this afternoon, there was a flower shop near the pizza place. It seemed like a good idea at the time."

Victoria leaned forward and sniffed the rose. It had a subtle fragrance, and she smiled even more widely. She tucked the card back into the envelope and placed it beside her cutlery. She opened her menu and was immediately shocked at the prices. *A bowl of soup is $65? My word!*

"I have been here a couple of times. Everything on the menu is excellent," Anderson said.

Victoria found it hard to maneuver through the menu, for the food was all listed in French. She was used to dealing with French as it related to 18th century archeology, not cuisine. "Can you suggest something?" she asked.

"Do you prefer fish, beef, chicken, or pork?" Anderson asked.

"Fish tonight, I think." She made a spontaneous decision and folded the menu. "Stephen, please order for me. I am in your hands."

The waiter appeared as soon as the menu cover hit the table. He was wearing a formal waistcoat with long tails and a black bow tie. "Good evening, *mademoiselle*, *monsieur*. May I bring you a drink?"

"Is the *sommelier* available?" Anderson asked.

"One moment please, *monsieur*." The waiter departed.

Victoria wondered what was going on, but she said nothing. While they waited, she decided to test one of her observations. "Can I ask you something, Stephen?"

"Of course."

"Your accent. It's very subtle but reminds me of several European archeologists I used to work with in Egypt. Vinnie told me you grew up in the Midwest, but your accent does not sound like you came from there."

"Well, I spent almost ten years in North Africa as a geologist, exploring for oil. English speakers in Algeria and Morocco are rare and always viewed with suspicion, so I spoke nothing but French and Arabic during that time. You are not the first person to assume I was not American. In the desert, not speaking English was actually a good thing; some of the local tribes hated

Americans. They assumed I was Canadian when I spoke French, and I never corrected them for obvious reasons."

A man appeared at their table wearing an all-white shirt buttoned completely up to the top and notched at the neck. Around his neck, he wore a large silver chain made of round links. Suspended on the chain was a silver disk, also round, with a curve forming a slight depression or bowl.

"Good evening, *mademoiselle, monsieur*. I am Yves. How may I assist you tonight?"

Anderson spoke, "We shall be starting with *La Symphonie de Crustacés* followed by *Le Turbot* and then *La Framboise* for dessert. What can you suggest?" Victoria noted that the French easily rolled off his tongue.

"For the *crustacés*, a Muscadet would be most complimentary. *Le Turbot* would suggest an Alsace Fauvet. If you wish to be untraditional for *La Framboise*, I would suggest a Caribbean coffee."

"Excellent. That will do nicely. I will have regular coffee, though." Anderson handed the menus to the *sommelier*, and he departed.

"So what did you order?" Victoria asked, leaning forward, her forearms on the table.

"You will see," he said with a smile. Changing the subject, he continued, "I am glad we could take a break from today. I sense it was rougher on you than me, but my brain was hurting by the time we left. Too few facts and too much conjecture." He adjusted his napkin.

"The hard part for me was getting through that mob scene. I never deal with more than one or two people near me during the day. When doing research, I might not see anyone for hours. Even when in a crowded classroom, the students sit away from me in orderly rows. That was my first experience with that sort of unruly crowd, and it was not pleasant. I don't know how I would have reacted without you and the agents there to help."

"Well, that part of your day is over, and we can both take a night off now." He smiled.

"What do you think our chances are to recover the mask?" she asked, leaning forward.

"Right now? Two percent, probably less," he said flatly.

"That low?" The number depressed her a little. Her chin momentarily dropped to her chest in disappointment.

"With no solid leads to go on, I cannot be more optimistic. We would need to get a major break in the case, and time is against us." Anderson explained about the forty-eight hour deadline the captain had told him about.

She felt like she was starting to walk toward the crowd once more. "Oh, Stephen, can we change the subject? Let's not talk about this. We have this wonderful night away from all that. Let's enjoy it." She adjusted the napkin on her lap.

"Okay, tell me about yourself then. Where were you born?" Anderson asked.

"Believe it or not, Mumbai, India. My father was Consul General there at the time. Due to Dad's career, our family traveled a lot when I was a child. My mother told me that I took my first steps in Tel Aviv, spoke my first word in Dublin, and kissed my first boyfriend in Lomé, Togo. I was eight, and it only lasted a few days," she added quickly with a smile.

"It sounds like you traveled more in your childhood than most people do in a lifetime," Anderson observed.

"Yes, and I was very happy doing so. My mother tried to teach us the various languages and cultures wherever we went. Then we moved to Cairo when my father got an embassy job there. It was amazing to wake up each morning seeing the Giza pyramids through my bedroom window. The first year we were there, we traveled around the country and explored Luxor and Abu Simbal. I remember it as such a wonderful time. Well, until my mother passed away."

"I am sorry to hear that. How did that happen?" said Anderson.

"She was off in the Sinai on a bus tour with a few girlfriends from the embassy. Dad could not get away because he was working, and Michael and I—Michael is my older brother—were in school. The bus driver fell asleep, and he drove off an embankment. If the accident had happened near a city, she would probably have survived. It took an hour for the ambulance to get there, and she passed away from her injuries before it arrived." A momentary shadow of sadness passed over Victoria. She adjusted her cutlery as a distraction.

She shook off the negativity and continued, "After the accident, Dad hired a nanny to look after us. He started working long hours, probably to stop thinking of the accident. As a result, we hardly saw him anymore, and Michael and I spent most of our time together."

"So you and you brother became close as a result?" he asked.

"Well, we were always close, but that did bring us together even more. Michael was two years older than me and always popular with the other kids. After Dad's tour in Cairo ended, we returned to the States. Michael joined the military as a Marine and was accepted to the US Naval Academy in Annapolis, Maryland, as an Officer Cadet. Dad and I lived in Arlington, Virginia. When I went off to Brown University in Rhode Island, Dad retired from the government to a small fishing cottage in Maine. He never remarried and passed just after my graduation. I always felt he took the loss of my mother much harder than we did. Michael and I visited him as often as we could, but he had simply given up on life. We could see him slipping away, and there was nothing we could do to stop it."

"That must have been a very trying time for you." Anderson knew what it felt like to lose both parents. He nodded slightly.

"It was, but that is in the past. I accepted it a long time ago," she said with finality.

"So how did you get into Egyptology?" he asked.

"Growing up in Cairo influenced me greatly, and I always felt a need to learn more. After leaving Brown I had to finalize my dad's estate. When that was done, I enrolled at the American University in Cairo for my Master's degree. I was there for six years in total. I made quite a few trips to the Valley of the Kings, but it was the hieroglyphics that recorded history on the massive temple rooms and columns at Karnak that caught my attention. No one had ever done a complete translation, and I took that as a challenge. First, I photographed every panel, and then I translated them. That took almost two years, and in the end, the comprehensive listing and translation of all hieroglyphics in Karnak formed the basis of my doctorate."

"Yes, I have the book you published on the subject, but I have not gotten around to reading it yet," Anderson replied.

"Honestly, you're not missing much. It is pretty dry reading. Lots of repetitive references to royal lineages, battles, and prayers. It did let me spend a lot of time in Egypt, and Michael visited me several times. On the last trip he brought his fiancée, and we had a great time showing her around." She smiled at the memory.

The *sommelier* interrupted the conversation with a bottle of wine. He showed the label to Anderson, who reviewed it and nodded. Producing a tool from his pocket, the *sommelier* proceeded to deftly remove the wrapper. He unfolded the corkscrew and twisted it into the cork. While he was doing this, Anderson turned his wineglass over, and without skipping a beat, the *sommelier* splashed a small amount into Victoria's glass.

"You want me to try it?" she asked.

"Please. It is a Muscadet from Château-Thébaud," Anderson said simply, gesturing toward her glass.

The wine gave off a citrusy aroma. She sipped a small amount, and she noticed the temperature was halfway between room temperature and freezing. She could taste subtle green apple, peach, and almond undertones. It also had a slight salty taste. "Mmmmm, very nice. Thank you." The *sommelier* poured her a half glass. He turned to Anderson.

"May I suggest a lemonade for *monsieur*? It will complement the meal nicely," the *sommelier* prompted.

"Please," Anderson said, and the *sommelier* left.

"You are not having any? It is excellent." She indicated the wine.

"No, thank you. I don't drink," Anderson said simply.

"No? Why?" His statement surprised her.

"I stopped a few years ago. I find I am a better person without drinking; liquor tends to bring out the worst in me.

Don't worry—I am not an alcoholic, and I am in no way anti-alcohol, so enjoy your wine. Besides, with me not drinking, you are guaranteed a safe drive home." He smiled warmly.

Victoria's follow-up questions were interrupted when the senator and his buxom dinner companion entered the dining hall behind the maître d'. When he saw Anderson and Victoria, he instantly gave Anderson a long hard look. She did not need to be psychic to tell what he was thinking: *I know the power players in this town, and you are not one of them. So who are you, and how did you get seated and served ahead of me?*

The waiter returned with a tall glass of lemonade. Condensation was already forming on the outside of the glass, so the waiter deftly placed a leather coaster on the tablecloth before setting it down. The waiter picked up his upside-down wine glass and departed.

"So you were saying you finished your doctorate in Karnak," Anderson reminded her.

"Yes, I returned to the United States after publishing my second book to take a position at the University of Pittsburgh as an assistant professor. I taught a series of lectures in hieroglyphics and ancient scripts. When I wasn't in the classroom, I continued doing hieroglyph translations under Dr. Harold Baker's supervision until the Tut exhibit was organized. Dr. Baker is an amazing man, and I really enjoyed working with him. There was never any pressure or deadlines from him, and he was endlessly supportive. He always gave credit for work that was done and always encouraged his staff to take their time to do things right the first time. If you had a project that took ten years of effort, he would encourage you to see it through. An amazing man. When the Tut exhibit is finished, I hope I can get my position back there."

A pair of steaming plates arrived at the table. The appetizer was served in two blue and white ceramic bowls. Each serving was comprised of Tiger shrimp, white asparagus, Oscetra caviar, herb gelee, ginger, and mousseline sauce. The smell came off the bowl and grabbed their attention. The waiter departed.

"May I suggest something?" Anderson said.

"Of course," she replied, looking up from her appetizer. "Try a spoonful from the bowl."

She took her spoon and did just that. She scooped up a shrimp, piece of asparagus, and some caviar. Most seafood was tough, but the shrimp was sublimely cooked to a crisp texture. "Mmmmm, delicious," she said.

"Now, have a sip of wine," he instructed.

A second sip of wine tasted much different than the first. The salty note and other elements of the wine mixed with the seafood flavors and danced on her tongue. "Oh my. That is perfect!" she said, a little surprised.

"I don't know how to choose a decent wine, but I can choose a good *sommelier.*" They both laughed before eating.

"When I went for my bath, I saw the razor on the vanity. I have never met a man who uses a straight razor," Victoria said between mouthfuls.

"Yes, it is a DOVO Solingen razor, and that is the only thing I have of my father. He died when I was quite young, and my mother gave it to me as a keepsake years later. It took me a long time to get used to it, but I was glad to get it. It does a much better job than electric models and cuts much closer than disposables. You just have to be extremely careful when using it, for obvious reasons."

They chatted amiably through the appetizer. Victoria noticed several people talking or texting on cell phones throughout their dinner, their companions mostly looking bored and at their food.

"That's sad. People using their phones like that." She subtly inclined her head toward a cell phone talker.

"I know. However, some people here like to show just how important and indispensible they are to the world. I suspect they don't realize they are standing out, but for the wrong reasons."

"They are 'being social' with everyone except the person they are actually with. I must be old-fashioned, as I still prefer a good face-to-face conversation," she observed.

They finished their appetizer, and the empty bowls were quickly taken away. The *sommelier* returned after a few minutes with a second bottle of wine and a fresh glass. Again, he displayed the label to Anderson for approval before he opened the wine with a practiced hand and poured a little into the new glass for Victoria. The color reminded her of lemons. The first smell of the wine brought a floral garden to mind. She tasted it, and the full-bodied flavor and long finish were a treat. "Perfect." She placed the glass down so he could half fill it before leaving.

"So how did you learn about this place?" Victoria asked. The *maître d'* obviously knew him, and he said he had been there before.

"I came here shortly after arriving in town. I did a gentleman a favor, and he returned it by taking me out to dinner with some of his business colleagues. The next day I started work at Worthor, so it is sort of a good luck charm for me, I suppose," Anderson said.

The waiter brought two large plates and set them down in front of them. In the center of the plate was an oval bowl with a small casserole-style dish inside. "Filet of Turbot with artichoke jus, pepper, and spices," he announced before leaving.

That time, Victoria had a piece of fish, then a sip of wine without urging. "Ohhhhh my, I can see why you come back here. The chef is excellent."

"The chef does an excellent ribeye Cajun pepper steak as well. That is what I usually have when I come here, but it is nice to explore other parts of the menu." Anderson began to eat as well, and their conversation carried on in between mouthfuls. It was a relaxed and easy meal. The crackle of the fire and music added to the atmosphere in the room.

Twenty minutes later, the empty dishes were cleared. Victoria was served a Caribbean coffee, while Anderson received a regular blend. The rim of her glass cup had been dipped in lime, then sugar. Inside the glass was coffee that had been mixed with an ounce of dark rum and what tasted like crème de cacao.

Dessert arrived soon after. Two small plates holding a raspberry gelée surrounded by three small balls of yuzu ice cream and topped with meringue. Once more, the Caribbean coffee complemented the taste of the dessert, and Victoria took her time, savoring the last of the meal.

* * *

Kogan had settled into his aerie and kept the stabilized binoculars handy. Activity on the boat had decreased as the light faded, and there was no movement at all now. The white ship allowed him to see movement even without the binoculars. The clouds were descending slowly, and it looked like a damp and foggy night ahead for anyone on board.

Seeing movement, Kogan grabbed the binoculars and focused on a man leaving the side hatch of the superstructure. The man paused momentarily to light a cigarette with a match. The brief illumination of his face by the struck match was all Kogan needed to identify him.

After taking a long draw on the cigarette, the man casually walked forward, exhaling slowly. Kogan lost sight of him for a moment as he walked behind the warehouse roof. The man emerged on the other side and stopped walking near the bow. He was still and seemed to be looking east at the sea. A few minutes passed, and Kogan realized someone else was on the deck behind the smoker. He raised his binoculars for a better view.

* * *

The waiter appeared to take away the empty dishes. "Please give the *Chef de Cuisine* our compliments for a fine meal," Anderson said.

"Yes, that was wonderful. Thank you," Victoria added.

Anderson reached his hand across the table and stopped halfway. Victoria reciprocated, and he took her hand in his. His fingers slid across her smooth skin lightly. They said nothing but maintained eye contact.

Victoria broke the silence. "What are you thinking?"

Immediately he said, "Well, this is where I would try to convince you to come back to my place, but as you are already staying there, I am at a loss for words." He grinned genially.

She pulled away and swatted the back of his hand playfully, smiling broadly. She grabbed her clutch and began to stand. "I will be right back," she said and walked out of the dining room. She asked the maître d' for directions to the powder room and went to use the facilities. While there she checked her makeup and hair, which were holding up well.

When Victoria returned, the table had been cleared, and the bill folder had arrived. Anderson was handing it back to the waiter, who said, *"Merci, monsieur. Bonsoir."* The waiter held her chair for her as she sat, then withdrew. She saw her rose had been wrapped in a simple brown paper cone, with the petals and a few sprigs of baby's breath exposed. The card sat beside it. She placed the card into her clutch.

"Shall we go?" Anderson asked.

"Let's go for a nice drive," she suggested while standing and picking up the rose.

"Where to?" he asked.

"Anywhere with nice scenery where we can see the water. I love watching the water, especially at night. It reminds me of the Nile."

He knew the perfect place, in one of the city parks, and they stood. Victoria draped her scarf over her shoulders. They exited the dining room and passed the unmanned podium. Once outside, she saw that a heavy fog had rolled in, but her scarf kept the chill away. She was amazed to see their car waiting for them. The valet stood by the passenger door, ready to open it for her. As she got in, the valet handed Anderson his key, and he tipped the man with a discreet bill in return. As Anderson walked around the front of the car, she considered what would happen later. It had been a perfect evening so far. Wonderful food, exquisite wines, and just the right atmosphere. She sniffed the rose again.

Anderson got in and buckled up. He had just put the car in gear when his cell phone began vibrating. He grabbed it off his belt and turned to her with a grin. "At least I wait until *after* the meal to answer my phone." He keyed the phone on.

"Anderson... Evening, Bill." He listened for a long time, and his face became graver by the second. "Who...? How...? Any suspects...? Okay, I'll be there in forty-five minutes. Bye."

He dropped the car into gear and pressed the accelerator firmly while clipping his phone onto his waistband. "We may have just gotten our break," he said cryptically. She thought he suddenly sounded very serious.

"Oh, how?" she asked.

"That was Bill. Agent Bryant. A member of the freighter crew found a body lying on the foredeck. It looks like he was murdered."

"Who?"

"One of the Egyptian guards. I will drop you off, change clothes, then head out. I assume you don't want to go through the press again."

"You're right. I just want to relax. I don't think a press scrum topped off by a corpse would end my evening the way I had envisioned it," she said, disappointed.

"I am sorry to ruin your evening," he said.

"Oh Stephen, don't say that! Tonight was exactly what I needed. Thank you for dinner. I don't get many opportunities to dress up like this. It was very sweet of you." He looked over at her briefly, and she smiled warmly.

He did not speed on the way home, but he didn't waste time, either. They pulled up in front of his place, and he used the remote door opener to slide the access door open. Driving in, he backed it into its designated spot. The door immediately slid closed behind them—the hydrogen fuel meant they didn't have to worry about exhaust fumes.

The pair went upstairs and found Masumi relaxing in front of the TV, watching a nature documentary about a pride of lions. She was on the center couch wearing a pair of blue flannel pajamas with a clouds and angels pattern. A small bowl was on her lap, and the room smelled of popcorn.

"Hi, kids!" she said, waving her hand high in the air, before returning her attention back to the cute frolicking cubs on the Serengeti plains.

Anderson kicked off his shoes and jogged up the stairs to his room. Victoria slipped her shoes off and placed them in the rack before walking over to the couches. Victoria dropped her scarf over the side cushion and sat down beside Masumi. The second her rear hit the cushion, Masumi leaned well forward, placed her chin in both hands in a comical pose, and stared quizzically at her with her eyes as wide as they would go. "So? Good night out? Details, details!"

Masumi's overenthusiastic position on the couch made Victoria laugh. She began to describe the evening, her hands moving energetically. "Yes, it was. After we got back from the ship I had a lovely bath and—"

"A bath? Here?" Masumi looked surprised. She leaned back into her former relaxed position on the couch.

"Yes, Stephen has a wonderful giant Jacuzzi tub. Didn't you know?" Victoria asked.

"No, I have never been in his bedroom. Hmmm, you learn things every day."

"Well, you definitely missed out. The tub has three speeds. Low, medium, and 'who needs a man.'" They both giggled.

Victoria continued. "After I got dressed, we went out to the Fontainebleau, and had a wonderful meal. The atmosphere, the music, the wine was excellent. What a lovely evening. Unfortunately, it has ended on a bad note." Victoria explained about the killing on board.

"Oh my. Is that why Stephen is in such a rush?"

"Yes, he is going there right away. I am going to stay here. There is nothing I can contribute until this mess is cleared up."

"Well, sorry to hear about that, girl. Tell me about the meal. What did you have for dinner?"

Victoria gave her a description of the entire evening including the senator, his busty companion, her outfit, the *sommelier*, and the meal. She talked for several minutes and included details on the other patrons, the fireplace, the décor, music, and the food.

They were interrupted when Anderson emerged from his room wearing tan slacks. He was pulling on a white cable knit mariners sweater over a simple white T-shirt as he walked to the top of the stairs. He descended and walked over behind the couch. "Sorry to leave like this, but I am sure you and Masumi can spend the evening together. I have to go. Thanks for a wonderful evening out."

Anderson leaned down to kiss her just above her eyebrows, which took her completely by surprise. His lips were warm and soft. He paused only long enough to put on a pair of shoes before leaving.

Masumi waited until the door closed behind him and stared at Victoria. Masumi's face was emotionless except for one eyebrow, raised high. She said nothing.

"What?" Victoria said finally. Masumi turned her attention back to the TV. "Giving up the forehead after just one date, huh? Hussy," she said in a pseudo-offended tone.

Victoria stood up and assumed a look of false indignation. She grabbed her scarf and stood facing the couch with one hand on her hip, the other pointing at Masumi in an accusatory manner and her best professor voice. "I'm going to go upstairs and change, young lady. When I get back, we are going to discuss that bad attitude of yours over some Italian ice cream."

"Oh, great idea! I'll get the cookies and cream!" Masumi said with a smile, and she scampered off to the kitchen.

CHAPTER 14 – A BREAK IN THE CASE

"According to his passport, his name was Kareem Al-Asned. He was twenty-nine. Born and raised in Cairo. According to other guards, he has been employed by the El Rashim Security service for fourteen months. Former tourist policeman, with no criminal record. Well-liked by his peers. Supportive and friendly, from what we have determined. He was found just after dark by an engineer's mate who was wandering the deck while talking to his wife on a cell phone."

Anderson listened as Bryant brought him up to speed on the case. They stood on the foredeck, between the bow and the forward cargo door. The body was covered by a white sheet, which had roughly conformed to the shape beneath. It looked like the corpse was on its right side in what could be described as a fetal position, except the legs were straight out, with the left leg slightly in front of the right. A small spot of blood marred the sheet near where the back of the head was.

A small group was standing around them. Several FBI agents, uniformed police, and a city coroner with an assistant were filling in paperwork on a clipboard and waiting patiently.

Detective Murphy appeared at Anderson's elbow. He addressed Bryant. "I have the preliminary coroner's report. Death appears to have been caused by severe blunt trauma to the right rear of the head. Looks like a single blow. The initial examination shows that due to pallor and algor mortis with absence of rigor mortis, the body was found within fifteen minutes of death. This was confirmed by the captain, who stated he walked through this area about twenty minutes before the body was found. He saw nothing. We will have to wait for a full autopsy for anything more definitive, but those are the broad strokes. So Mr. Anderson, we meet again."

"I am sorry it is under these circumstances. I know rigor mortis, but what is algor mortis?" Anderson asked as they shook hands cordially.

"Simply put, that is how much heat the body has lost. A body loses heat after death at a fairly consistent rate. By taking the actual temperature of the corpse and applying a simple formula we can tell how long he has been deceased. They use a formula of 2° Celsius lost for the first hour and 1° Celsius per subsequent hour. Kareem's body temperature was close to normal, so he was not out here long."

"Thanks."

Bryant spoke. "Murder is under the local jurisdiction, so Mike will be taking the lead on this. We will provide whatever support we can."

Anderson stood silently. It wasn't the kind of break he'd wanted, but it was the one that had presented itself. "May I see him?"

Murphy walked over to the sheet and raised it so Anderson could see his face. It was one of the guards he had overheard on the deck earlier. He spotted a pack of cigarettes in a breast pocket of the uniform shirt. Anderson just nodded, and Murphy dropped the sheet.

"When was the last time anyone saw him?" Anderson asked.

"He was in the mess, watching a movie with a few other guards and passengers. One of the FBI agents saw him get up three-quarters of the way through the film. He went into the corridor, and the agent assumed he was going to his cabin. No one saw him after that point until they discovered the body. He must have made it to his cabin and left in a hurry," Murphy explained.

"Why do you say that?" asked Anderson.

Murphy walked to the opposite end of the body and raised the sheet, exposing the legs up to his hip. Kareem's legs were relatively straight, and he was wearing his uniform trousers. Anderson saw the man was only wearing black socks. Anderson stooped down and took a long careful look at the victim's feet, ignoring the foul foot odor.

He leaned forward and placed his hand on the deck, to balance himself. The deck was slick with moisture from the fog. His face was less than six inches away from the feet, but he didn't touch the body. Kareem's trousers and the side of his socks touching the deck were a darker shade, indicating they were moist.

Murphy continued as Anderson looked, "Best we can determine, he was in his cabin and rushed out here for some reason. The killer struck from behind, and he fell as you see him."

"Could this be related to the union problems we faced earlier?" Bryant asked.

"It is one of the possibilities we have to consider, but not a very probable one. There was no private security staff on board at the time of death. No one left or arrived in the forty-five minutes prior to the killing or until well after the discovery of the body. So the killer is someone on board," Murphy responded, looking at his copious notes on the case so far.

"When did it get foggy here tonight?" Anderson asked.

"Roughly 8 PM," Bryant replied.

Anderson tried to imagine where Kareem would have been standing when he was struck from behind. He must have been facing the bow, with his assailant coming from behind. If he had been hit in the right rear of the head, then the attacker was probably right-handed. Looking up in line with the body, Anderson saw a scupper. Something didn't look right, so he walked over. "Mike, there is a cigarette here, wedged up against the metal. Looks fresh."

Anderson stooped down to get a better look, but he didn't touch it. "It is a Samsun brand. Turkish. Looks relatively dry, and I would bet serious money it came from the packet in his breast pocket."

Both policemen walked over to take a look. "Good catch. I will have that photographed and bagged right away," said Bryant.

Anderson checked his watch. "Did you search his bunk and personal items?"

"Yes. Nothing of consequence was found. Everything was neat and in place. The shoes were in his locker," Murphy responded.

"I need to take a look." Anderson didn't ask; he stated it firmly. He had an idea, and he needed to check it out.

"Sure. Let's go." Murphy dropped the sheet over the feet and turned to the coroner's staff. "Okay, we are done." They moved in to take possession of the body for their autopsy downtown. Given the high profile of the theft, it would be done immediately on arrival by the head coroner.

The three men descended to the cabin used by the guards. On entering, Anderson saw the sole occupant of the room. He had his head in his hands and looked up as he came in. The dark circles under his eyes were deep and displayed moroseness. It was Farhaan, the man Kareem had been talking to on the deck. They must have been friends. Anderson simply nodded to him before turning to Murphy. Bryant was close behind. "Which one?"

"This locker here." Murphy pointed.

Anderson opened the unlocked locker. There were several pressed long-sleeved shirts with El Rashid Security patches. A pair of trousers, basic toiletries, and under-clothes, plus a few unopened packages of Samsun brand Turkish cigarettes. A ship laundry bag was on the floor. There were a few soiled items in there, but nothing out of place beyond the usual smells of old sweat and heavy foot odor.

Beside the mesh bag was a pair of black shoes. Anderson pulled them out and examined them closely. Just under the inner edge of the inside of the heel, on each shoe was *Al-Asned* written in Arabic, in blue ink. He held the shoe vertically and placed it close to his face. He examined the tip of the shoe for some time. Then he turned them over and examined the sole from one end to the other. He repeated the same exam on the other shoe. In the end, he placed the shoes back in the locker. "Okay. You might want to bag the shoes up as evidence. Also, the laundry bag."

"Okay. Why?" Murphy sounded bewildered.

"Go grab some evidence bags, and I will explain when you are done." Anderson kept his head still but subtly drifted his gaze toward the man on the bed. *We are not alone and cannot talk freely*, was the unspoken message.

"Right. Back in five. Bill, can I have a word?" Murphy and Bryant disappeared up the corridor.

"Take your time. I'll stay here."

Bryant paused, but then he nodded and left. As soon as he was out of sight, Anderson sat down beside the man on the bunk. "Your name is Farhaan?" Anderson asked mildly in English.

"Yes."

"Kareem was your friend?"

"Yes. We met only a few weeks ago, but he was a good man. He showed a lot of compassion for his friends," Farhaan replied. He had good English skills.

"Farhaan, I just looked in Kareem's locker. Do you mind if I take a quick look in yours?

"Mine is there. It is open." He pointed, sounding and looking puzzled.

Anderson opened the locker and saw exactly what he expected. He turned back to Farhaan. "Were all of the guards issued uniforms?"

"Yes. Doctor Al Dhabit was quite specific that all of the guards receive a uniform for the exhibition. We were issued four shirts, two pairs of trousers and—"

"Two pairs of shoes," interrupted Anderson.

"Indeed. Yes. Of course, Doctor Al Dhabit must have told you this already."

To Anderson, it was like the clouds parting on a dark day—it was the break he was waiting for. *Time to use some of the conversation I overheard earlier to my advantage.* "I understand from some of the others that you had problems with sea-sickness."

"Yes, this is true. I was suffering for many days. Kareem helped me with a special nutmeg soup that eased my illness," Farhaan replied.

"Did he give you this soup while you were in the hold?"

"Yes, this was the hardest time for me. In my bed, it was easier. He brought two containers of soup with the sandwiches. One for me, and one for him. We always ate our late meal in the hold," Farhaan replied.

Here we go. "How long did you sleep after eating the soup?" Anderson asked it firmly, with no doubt that Farhaan had fallen asleep.

Farhaan's look of horror as he met Anderson's eyes was unmistakable. He broke down in tears. Three minutes later, Anderson had learned all he needed to know.

* * *

Bryant, Murphy, and Anderson walked to the very stern of the ship to talk in private. No one could possibly overhear them. They spoke quietly for fifteen minutes as Anderson explained himself. "Look, Detective—"

"Call me Mike," Murphy interrupted.

"Okay, Mike. Until half an hour ago we knew nothing. Now we know 'when,' and in a few hours, I can probably give you the 'who.' All we need to find out now is the 'how.' The 'how' gives me the mask and you the thief; probably the killer, too."

"Maybe, but your logic is awfully weak," Murphy objected.

"You saw what I saw. Can you see a flaw in what I just told you?" Anderson countered.

"No, but I obviously don't have all the facts," Murphy replied.

"Neither do I. Look, it's a gamble, but based on what I saw tonight, it is the best logical guess I can make. All I am asking for is a free hand until later tonight. You will be in on anything I find. It will either confirm or deny my supposition. Yes, it is a guess. However, right now it is all we have to go on, and this could mean recovering the key piece of evidence we need."

Murphy still looked doubtful. "Look, the police have qualified people who—"

"Would be seen by the press and by the people on board the ship. You know how intense the press coverage is. They have the ship ringed with cameras. I won't be seen, and I won't be giving the press any information. Mike, we don't know what other evidence is on board. If the people involved see the police searching, they have the opportunity to get rid of any additional evidence."

Murphy was thinking it over with a furrowed brow.

"The deadline is ticking closer the longer you delay," Anderson added.

"All right. You get a free hand. I'll meet up with you later once I complete the initial investigation on board," Murphy finally demurred.

"Will you talk to the captain, Bill? I need to get moving."

"No problem." Bryant turned to leave.

* * *

Anderson got into his vehicle and immediately dialed a number from memory on his car cell. He didn't have to wait long before Vinnie picked up the phone. "Hello?"

"Vinnie, I hate to call you out at this hour, but I will need you and your van at the garage right away."

"No problem, boss. Will be there in twenty minutes."

"Right. Bye."

Anderson hung up his hands-free car cell phone and pulled onto the interstate ramp. He ran the new events through his mind as he drove. Yes, there were a few weak links in the logic chain, but it held together well enough—in his mind, at least. He now had two solid links in the chain, and he knew where to find the next one. At least he was no longer forced to be passive in his investigation, and that made him glad.

The drive home was quicker than normal. There was little traffic that late at night, and he arrived in the garage just after Vinnie.

"Hey, boss. What's the plan?" Vinnie asked.

"Back your van up to the cargo elevator, and I'll be up in a few minutes. Can you grab a towel and a half-dozen water bottles out of your fridge as well?" Anderson headed down to the basement stairs. Vinnie nodded and turned to organize things.

Anderson snapped on the basement lights as he descended. The fluorescents buzzed to life and illuminated the entire area. Anderson paused at the base of the stairs long enough to open the elevator door. Then he walked directly over to the workbench where the strange-looking contraption waited.

The unit looked like a large backpack and was mostly black with red trim on the edges. Two thick arm straps were evident, along with a series of black and green hoses. On either side of the unit was a pressurized tank, each with a valve at the bottom. On the top of the unit, red letters with a white undertone shadow said *DIVE RITE*. Anderson unlatched the cover and went through a laminated checklist that was beside the unit. It took fifteen minutes of careful preparation, checks and observations. When done, he latched up the unit backplate.

Next he grabbed a yellow camera housing from the bench. He test fired each strobe and checked the camera display before packing it away in a large green plastic tote. He added a red and black rubber dry suit that was rolled up on a rack. Lights, a small reel and other assorted gear were added to the tote before it was closed up.

He took a smaller blue tote from under the workbench, and while it was much smaller, it required a lot more effort to move. Last, he took a black plastic toolbox with a dive flag on top. It held various tools, extra batteries, and spare parts in case of issues.

Anderson loaded the totes and toolbox onto the elevator, closed the door, and hit the button for the ground floor. He found Vinnie waiting, with the van backed up and the rear doors already open. Anderson loaded the totes into the back, which easily slid along the smooth van floor. Anderson closed the rear doors, and the pair entered the van. Vinnie drove, and Anderson sat in the passenger seat. Several full plastic water bottles were on the passenger side floorboards.

"Where to, boss?" Vinnie asked.

Anderson gave specific directions.

* * *

Kogan maintained his surveillance of the vessel with the binoculars. There had been a lot of activity around the body at the bow. Then someone on board had turned on every single deck light the boat had. This brightened things up considerably and made his life a lot easier. He ate sporadically and drank water to stay hydrated. He had a bag designated for trash, and everything he disposed of went into there. Any empty water bottles were used for urine and disposed of in the garbage bag. He had mentally practiced his evasion routine several times and knew the steps he would follow to not leave a trace. Given his supplies, he could stay there for several days. The lack of sleep was the biggest challenge, but he had operated without it before. He would need to take catnaps eventually, and then he would use his wristwatch's alarm. However, that would not be necessary until at least twenty-four hours had passed. Dealing with sleep deprivation was part of his training.

* * *

The van ended up on a smaller dock directly opposite the *Costarican Trader*, which was less than six hundred feet away across the channel. Anderson could see the ship from straight on the bow.

As requested, the captain had turned on all of the deck loading lights over the cargo areas. The spotlights on the flying bridges were on, as well, set to their widest beam and pointing down at the water. The fog had withdrawn slightly, and the calm water's surface reflected the flashing red and blue police lights and white area lighting around the ship and FBI command post.

Anderson worked methodically. First, he slipped off his Bulova Marine Star watch. Even though it was a dive watch certified to 100 meters, it would interfere with the wrist seal on his dry suit. He pulled on thick red and black underwear, covering his arms and legs. He unrolled the vulcanized rubber dry suit and stepped into it via the open zipper at the back of the suit across the shoulders. He used the built-in suspenders to keep the dry suit in place around his waist. From the small blue tote, he withdrew two long blue weights, and he snapped one around each ankle. A titanium dive knife in a sheath came next, and he strapped that into place on the inside of his left calf.

Anderson pulled the black and red backpack device out of the tote and set it on the back of the van. As he began more checks, Vinnie came over without being asked to hold the back of the unit to stop it from falling over.

"Thanks, Vinnie."

"This doesn't look like any dive gear I have ever seen, boss," Vinnie observed.

Anderson ran his hands over the various parts as he spoke. "This is a rebreather. Do you know how regular SCUBA tanks work?"

"A little. You breathe in air from an air tank on your back, right?"

"Basically, yes. High-pressure air from the SCUBA tank is reduced down to breathing pressures by the regulator, then passed to the mouthpiece so you can breathe it in. When you breathe out, the mouthpiece vents the air, and you get the trail of bubbles going up. That is a very simple open-circuit system, but it is inefficient—the gas you breathe out is wasted. This Optima rebreather unit does not vent exhaled gas; instead, it recycles it."

Anderson began uncoiling the wiring attached to two electronic computers.

"I thought carbon dioxide was in your exhaled breath? How can you breathe that again?" Vinnie looked a bit confused.

Anderson pointed to a U-shaped hose with a mouthpiece attached to either side of the backpack. "It starts with this hose here. When I breathe out the gas, it goes through some filtering and sensors, and some oxygen is added. The end result is breathable. This is a very efficient closed-circuit system, and I can stay down for up to six hours."

Vinnie's confusion turned to concern. "That's a long time, boss. You think you will need that much time?"

"No need to worry. I doubt I will be down more than an hour and a half. I am using this tonight so no bubbles will be seen on the surface. If the police divers had gone in, they would not be able to hide from the press or anyone on board because they all use open-circuit SCUBA."

Anderson clipped the reel to a D-ring on the harness. On others he secured a small backup light, and other miscellaneous items. He slipped the long spike through a Velcro strap on one of the arm straps. The ball and some other smaller items were placed in a pouch with a heavy plastic zipper.

From the larger tote, Anderson produced a mask, heavy fins, and a pair of thick rubberized dry gloves. Then he slid his hands into the top of the dry suit. The tight latex seals at the wrist took some effort to get into, and he took his time to avoid tearing or damaging them. Once both hands were through the seals, he pulled his head through the neck seal and folded the material down inside around his neck.

"Can you help me with the zipper?" asked Anderson.

Vinnie helped him do up the large brass zipper across the back of his shoulder blades. When that was done, Anderson was sealed inside the watertight suit. Only his hands and head were unprotected. He pulled a heavy lead weight belt with black webbing from the blue tote, which took some effort to get into. He bent forward, carrying the weight on his hips while he did up the snap buckle. The belt and twenty-five pounds of lead weight ended up around his waist.

Anderson sat on the edge of the van, and Vinnie helped him into the rebreather harness. This took a few minutes to adjust properly. Once done, he took a hood and pulled it over his head. He turned on the rebreather gas supplies and the computers. The breathing loop came over Anderson's head, and he put the mouthpiece into his mouth, using it to breathe. He needed to do that for at least five minutes to 'warm up the loop' and get the system working properly. The heat from his exhaled breath warmed up the CO_2 absorbent in the rebreather to its proper operating temperature. As he sat there, Anderson made more adjustments to the buckles, and then added a camera and rolled-up mesh bag to his harness. The gloves had a bayonet mount and easily attached to the hard rings on his suit. He then strapped lights onto the back of his hand and one rebreather computer on each wrist. Both computers showed that the Optima was functioning properly. The cables from the computers ran up either arm and connected to the rebreather housing. Last, a compass on a retractable wire was clipped to a chest D-ring.

He was ready. Anderson put on the mask and took the fins in his hand. Vinnie helped pull him to his feet. The dock they were on had a staircase leading down to a landing that was at water level. Anderson walked down the stairs slowly, with Vinnie close behind, steadying him. The dive gear added over sixty additional pounds to be carried. Most of it was over his natural center of gravity, so it affected his balance, as well. The rubber suit and insulating underwear worked very well in the air and just the effort of walking quickly heated him up.

Once he was on the wooden landing, Anderson simply stepped out into the water with a giant stride. As he entered the water, he held his mouthpiece and mask in place with one hand, and he gripped his fins with the other. He floated up but was sitting low in the water, so he added additional air into the dry suit from a valve on his chest. The extra air kept him buoyant, and he floated easily on the surface of the calm water, the odd weight he wore being meaningless in the water. He placed the fins on his feet without problems. Once both his hands were free, he adjusted his gear slightly and tightened the harness straps. He quickly rinsed out the inside of his mask with water. He did not use any lights yet, to avoid detection. Taking his compass, he sighted a course that would take him to the bow of the *Costarican Trader*'s hull.

Anderson pinched his nose and cleared his ears. He gave Vinnie an *okay* sign, checked the computers one last time, purged the excess air from the dry suit valve located near his left bicep, and descended slowly below the surface.

Vinnie gave him a last wave and said, "*Buon viaggio!*"

As the water passed over his mask, Anderson was surrounded by total darkness. The transition to an absolutely black environment always caused him some trepidation, but repetition and training dramatically reduced this anxiety.

On the way down, Anderson had to clear his ears several times as the water pressure increased; he added small amounts of air to his dry suit to help offset the increase in water pressure. The backlights on the computers displayed his depth.

He came to rest lightly on the muddy bottom, landing gently on his knees. Anderson snapped on the lights on the back of his hands and found the visibility to be horrible. He held out his hand and could barely see his fingers. A check of his computers showed his depth was thirty-two feet, and the water temperature was 50° F, though he couldn't feel it in his dry suit.

Other information on the dive computers told him his equipment was working properly. He took the compass in his hand and held it in front of him. He turned his body until the bearing on the bezel of the compass matched the magnetic needle suspended in mineral oil. He had to turn over forty-five degrees to the right, which seemed counter-intuitive, but he had learned to trust the compass a long time ago. He kicked off in that direction and kept the compass directly in front of his eyes at all times.

Anderson had been qualified on SCUBA for many years. As a legionnaire, when based in Calvi, Corsica, he had joined the recreational SCUBA club on base. Since reaching the United

States, he had taken several specialty courses, and in time, he'd become a master SCUBA diver. His rebreather training had just been completed that spring. He had intended to use the device for extended dive times on the World War II wrecks of Chuuk Lagoon in the Pacific. He'd never imagined he would be using it in local waters, but the ability to move directly under the ship without leaving a noticeable bubble trail was exactly what was needed tonight.

As he kicked into the channel, the muddy bottom sloped down under him. Anderson followed the terrain until he got to sixty feet deep. He maintained that depth and kept kicking on the set compass heading. The featureless mud bottom dropped away until it was out of sight.

Black water surrounded Anderson in all directions. The channel was a busy one, and ships passed through at all hours. By staying at sixty feet, he ensured that he would be safe from any vessels traveling above him, and it minimized the nitrogen being continually forced into his blood by the water pressure around him.

The current through the channel was minimal, Anderson was glad to see. His kicks drove him through the water at a slow but steady pace. The compass never left his sight, and he had to make continuous minor corrections to stay on course.

Twenty minutes later, he saw the bottom coming up to greet him. The visibility was a lot clearer there, and he could see for almost ten feet. He kept at least five feet of clearance between him and the mud on the bottom so he wouldn't stir up any sediment. His depth gradually reduced to thirty feet as he swam along.

Anderson stopped every minute and looked up, but he saw nothing the first half dozen times. On the seventh glance, he saw the edge of the *Costarican Trader* dimly outlined above him. The dark hull would normally have been invisible under current conditions, but the powerful deck lights onboard backlit the hull and surrounding water. He turned off his lights, and after his eyes adjusted, found he could see well enough.

Anderson kicked over to the bow until it was directly above him. He used his compass and determined a course that was exactly perpendicular to the ships hull. He swam off on that course counting each kick with his left foot. As he moved along, he scanned the silt-covered bottom. Anderson saw many items: beer bottles, food cans, a bent front rim from a ten-speed bike, food wrappers, an empty crab shell, a broken cinder block, a length of thick rope, a couple of golf balls, and pieces of discarded marine engine parts. All of the items showed obvious signs of being in the salt water for a long time. He ignored them.

When his kick count reached fifty, he turned ninety degrees to the left and kicked ten times. Then he turned another ninety degrees to the left and kicked back toward the ship. At all times, his compass remained in front of his face for reference. After fifty more kicks, he was back under the vessel. That time he turned right ninety degrees and swam ten kicks further astern, then turned right again and swam fifty kicks out.

He repeated this procedure and methodically searched the area off the port side of the ship. As Anderson searched, he paid attention to his computers to ensure that his gear was operational and that he was in a safe dive profile. There was no dive organization in the world that would officially sanction diving solo at night on a rebreather in an active harbor with zero visibility. If anything went wrong, he would have to rely on his own training and experience to get himself out of it.

Anderson found himself a third of the way down the ship. He kicked out perpendicular to the hull and after twenty-three kicks he saw exactly what he was looking for. He approached the objects slowly, smiling as much as he could with the mouthpiece in. When he was a few feet away he paused and unclipped the camera. He turned on the camera and two strobes. He took a picture of the objects, the strobes fired to illuminate the scene, and for a few seconds, Anderson could see the resulting photo on the digital display through a small window on the back of the housing. He sculled around the items, using his fins to change position, and he took several more pictures until he had a dozen images taken from all angles. The last photo was taken from directly above looking down.

He turned off the camera and strobes, then finished by clipping the camera onto his harness. Anderson was reaching for the long spike he had brought to mark the spot when he saw a lump of rusted metal a few feet away; he went to retrieve it instead. It weighed about fifteen pounds and looked like an old cracked valve. Anderson returned to the found items and placed the metal valve directly beside them in the mud. He took his mesh bag, unfolded it, carefully picked up the items, and placed them into the bag. He closed and secured the bag before clipping the handles to a harness D-ring.

Anderson pulled out his reel and the orange ball, which was buoyant in the water. He attached the string on the reel to the ball. He released the catch on the reel, and the ball went up to the surface. He pulled off a few feet of extra line, and using a small dive knife, he cut the reel string. Anderson tied the end of the string from the ball to the rusty valve and then tied off the cut end of the reel string to the reel itself, a process that took some time due to his thick rubber gloves and the thin string.

Before leaving, Anderson put the reel into a side cargo pocket, double-checked that his gear was attached properly, and then swam back under the ship's hull. He ensured the mesh bag was in his hand and visible at all times. He did not want to lose the contents. Once directly under the *Costarican Trader* hull, he swam on a counter-bearing, 180° from the one he had originally used, and retraced his way back across the channel using his compass. Once he was clear of the freighter's hull he turned his lights back on.

After twenty minutes, he saw a wooden dock piling in front of him. His depth was thirty feet. He checked his computers and saw he had no mandatory decompression time. Still, he ascended to the surface slowly, taking over four minutes to work his way up from the bottom to allow any acquired nitrogen in his blood to be off-gassed slowly by the gradual change in pressure. He snapped off all but one light when he was ten feet down.

When his head broached the surface, he could see Vinnie, Bryant, Murphy, a uniformed cop, and two other FBI agents waiting for him. None were wearing their official jackets—nor did they have any lights turned on, he was glad to see. The fog had rolled in, and they could not see anything beyond a fifty-foot radius. Anderson winked at Bryant, but that went unseen in the darkness. Anderson turned off his last light before it left the water. He turned so he was facing the wooden landing. Using his fins and upper body strength, he kicked up onto the landing, at the last moment twisting into a sitting position on the edge of the landing. He spat out the mouthpiece, sealed it, and the two burly agents pulled him to his feet on the dock.

Anderson held up the dripping mesh bag in his hand, looked at Murphy and Bryant, and said, "A productive night's swim," with a huge white smile.

CHAPTER 15 – HARD EVIDENCE

Anderson had the rebreather off his back and secured in record time. He laid the unit inside the van, and Vinnie unzipped him from the dry suit. Fresh cool air rushed into the suit as the zipper parted. The hood and gloves came off next. Then Anderson pulled his head and hands free from the tight latex seals, and the dry suit hung down on the suspenders around his waist. His neck seal had leaked a little, and the underwear was moist around his collar. He turned to face Bryant, who had put the dripping mesh bag on the ground. The agents gathered around, and Anderson opened the top to reveal a pair of black leather shoes. The shoelaces were tied to the jaws of a well-used dull red monkey wrench about eighteen inches long.

Anderson looked at the items. "If I am not mistaken, that is the murder weapon, and those were the shoes Kareem was wearing when he died."

There was a prolonged silence, and Murphy broke it. "If I ever doubt you again, just remind me of this night." He chuckled lightly. "Good job. Did you mark the spot?"

"Yes, there is a small orange ball floating on the surface above where I found them. Plus, I took photos of the items on the bottom for evidence. I set the camera so there are times and dates on each picture. I'll give you the memory card with the pictures once I get the camera dried off."

"Great. I'll get photos of the reference ball tomorrow to document the spot where they were found." Murphy turned to the officer behind him. "Officer, bag these up and get them to the lab. I want this processed ASAP."

An FBI agent moved forward with a large plastic bag and held it open for the cop. The word *EVIDENCE* was clearly marked on the side of the bag. It was already marked with the date, time, location, and other information. The uniformed officer already had a pair of fresh surgical gloves on. He picked up the mesh bag still containing the shoes and monkey wrench and placed it carefully into the plastic bag held open by the agent. The cop took the bag, wrote several more pieces of information onto the side of the bag in black marker, then sealed the bag up.

While the cop was doing that, Anderson dried his hair and exposed skin with a large towel. Vinnie handed him a bottle of water, which he drained. Dehydration and diving did not mix peacefully. Anderson ran the towel over the surface of the camera housing to remove any excess seawater. He unlatched the case, took out the camera, and removed the SDRAM memory card. By the time he was done, an FBI agent was there with a smaller evidence bag, and Anderson dropped the small memory card into it. The agent nodded and moved off.

Anderson pulled his white-faced Bulova dive watch from the top of the toolbox and put it on. The titanium metal of the band was very light, and he barely knew he had it on after the clasp had been done up.

Murphy and Bryant came up beside him. "I don't expect the processing to take long even at this time of night. This will be a priority job. You look like hell. Go home and get some sleep. I'll see you in the morning with the results," Murphy said.

"In case you had not noticed, it *is* morning." Anderson showed the men his watch with a wry smile. He was tired and still had at least an hour's worth of work ahead of him, getting all the gear rinsed and racked.

"Okay, then let's make it 9 AM. We should be done by then," Murphy said.

"Oh, right—Stephen, one more thing. Tomorrow, don't come to the pier directly. To avoid the crowd, you can come to the back door of the adjacent pier warehouse. We arranged things with the owner, and you don't need to fight your way through the press anymore. Just be discreet," Bryant said.

"Right. Thanks."

Bryant shook Anderson's hand and patted him hard on the shoulder. "Good job." He left.

All of the wet dive gear went back into its respective totes in the back of the van. Any seawater that dripped off the gear stayed inside the formed plastic. After stripping off the underwear and putting his clothes back on he climbed into the van's passenger seat, and Vinnie drove off.

"Make sure you gas your van up and give me the receipt. I'll make sure you get reimbursed," Anderson said before draining a bottle of water.

"No problem, boss. So the stuff you found will help you solve this?" Vinnie asked, turning onto the access road.

"Until tonight, I was thinking it may not be solvable. There was not enough hard evidence. Now, I suspect we have a much better chance."

Anderson fell into silence for the rest of the trip. The discovery had opened up many possible avenues. He began to think each one through on the drive home.

When they reached the building, Vinnie used his remote door opener and pulled straight into the garage. He turned and backed the van up to the elevator.

Anderson popped out and opened the van's rear doors. He unloaded the dive gear into the elevator while Vinnie straightened out the back of the van. "Vinnie."

"*Sì*, boss?"

"Thanks for coming in. Take the day off." Anderson patted him on the shoulder.

"No problem, boss. You sleep well."

"I'm sure I will. Night."

Anderson pulled the elevator doors down and pressed the button for the basement. It only took a few seconds to descend. He spent the next hour disassembling, rinsing, and hanging the dive gear he had used. The gear slowly dripped dry on the racks. He shut off the lights and ascended to the garage level when he was done. The rest of the maintenance could wait for another time. Vinnie had turned out the overhead lights when he left, but there was enough ambient light coming in from the street to see.

Anderson walked upstairs and entered his home. He knew the layout well enough to navigate it without light. He went upstairs, undressed, and after a quick shower to get the smell of rank seawater out of his hair, he slipped into bed. He set his clock radio alarm for 7 AM and was asleep in seconds.

* * *

The buzzer of the alarm unmercifully ripped away the gentle blanket of slumber from Anderson. He sat up to shut off the noise; it felt as if he had just lain down moments before. He kept himself slightly raised off the mattress, knowing if he lay back down, there was a good chance he would fall back asleep.

Using all of his willpower, he flung back the comforter and stood. He followed his usual morning exercise routine, and after his session on the heavy bag, he went back upstairs for a shave and shower.

He put on a dark pair of Dockers and a polo shirt before going downstairs. He turned the TV screen so it was visible in the kitchen on the way by. The cable news channel was selected.

Anderson was in the kitchen grinding coffee beans when Victoria appeared wearing her green robe. She had her hair wrapped in a white towel and was covering up a yawn with the back of her hand.

"Morning, sleepy head. Coffee?" he asked.

She nodded and stepped in close to him to give him a brief hug. Anderson slid his hands across her back and shoulders before she stepped away. The scent of a freshly showered woman was quite pleasant to him.

Anderson put a filter in the top of the coffee pot. He put the fresh-ground coffee into the filter and added a pinch of salt to the top. He went to the sink, filled up the pot with water, and then used it to fill the reservoir. Putting the empty pot back in place, he turned on the switch.

He skipped his usual English muffin and decided to make Victoria an omelet. He pulled a large skillet from under the stove and put it on the gas burner to warm up. He diced up some veggies, added some leftover ham and grated some cheese in a pile.

"What can I do to help?" she asked from his side.

"Not a thing. Go have a seat, and I will bring some plates out," Anderson replied while whipping some eggs in a bowl.

"I'll set the table. Where are the dishes?"

He nodded in the direction of the cabinet. "There. Above the dishwasher."

Victoria got out the dishes. Anderson grabbed a second skillet and some turkey bacon out of the fridge. In a few minutes, that was sizzling away as well.

Masumi padded by, coming in from her morning jog wearing shorts and an armless white T-shirt with a red anarchy symbol on the front and back. She still had an MP3 player cord in her ears, and it waggled back and forth as she jogged in the front door. "Morning, kids!" she said with far too much enthusiasm as she dropped off a rolled newspaper on the pub table before heading up to her room.

Anderson grabbed two more eggs and added them to the bowl, while Victoria took out an extra plate for Masumi. She had the table set in a few minutes and sat down on one of the high chairs to read the paper. Anderson added the veggies and eggs to the skillet. The scent of coffee began soon afterward, as hot water hit the grounds.

* * *

Victoria rolled the local paper open on the table. The lead story was, of course, about the killing on board the *Costarican*

Trader. Mystery Murder in the Docks was the sensational headline, followed by *Curse of Tut Strikes Again.* Under the headlines was a large picture of the side of the ship, showing a pair of attendants from the coroner's office manhandling a gurney down the gangway. The shape of the body that was strapped down under the blanket was obvious.

The story took up the entire first page, but beyond the fact that some unidentified person had been killed on board, there was little else of any factual note. She read the entire page. The rest was a regurgitation of the theft, a brief history of the artifact and the supposed *Curse of Tutankhamun.* Victoria found her name three quarters of the way through the article, saying she was unavailable for comment. A full page of newspaper space that essentially said nothing, she decided.

Anderson interrupted her reading by slipping an omelet onto her plate right from the skillet. He had added cheese to it just before rolling it up. He was back in moments with some turkey bacon and a large cup of coffee made the way she liked it.

Victoria had never had turkey bacon before and was a little tentative trying it. He had cooked it so it was tender but not crispy. The surface grease had been patted off with a paper towel, and it certainly appeared appetizing. She tried a piece of the bacon with a forkful of omelet.

"Ummm, very nice." Victoria attacked her breakfast. She was halfway through the meal when Masumi appeared at her side and leapt into a seat, with slightly moist hair pulled back in a ponytail. She wore her usual ripped jeans and rock T-shirt—this one a black tee with a stylized Ozzy Osbourne logo in a dim reddish glitter.

Anderson wasted no time and placed a second omelet and bacon in front of Masumi. "Mmmmm, yummers," she said, picking up a fork.

Victoria looked at her, amused. "Yummers?"

Masumi replied in her gentle 'geisha' voice, "*Yummers* is Japanese for 'Damn, what a nice-looking breakfast.'" The girls both laughed.

Anderson, used to Masumi's wit, shook his head as he gave Masumi a steaming mug of green tea instead of coffee.

"Stephen, you really didn't need to go to all this trouble just for me, you know," Masumi teased.

"So he does not make you breakfast that often, I take it?" Victoria asked.

"Well, I have to admit, he is pretty good to me. Although I don't recall anything quite this fancy in a while. Thanks for the tea." Masumi took a sip while winking at Anderson.

"So what did you two get up to last night?" Anderson asked the ladies.

Masumi answered before Victoria could say anything. "Oh you know, the usual. We chatted about boys, pretty bows, and hair, mostly."

Victoria laughed. They had in fact demolished a good quantity of ice cream and a half bottle of wine between them. They had talked for several hours about a wide range of topics. Their lives, school, travel—and yes, boys, bows, and hair, as well. Victoria had enjoyed the relaxed evening.

Anderson slid his omelet onto his plate and returned the empty skillet to the stove. He returned with his coffee. "Any news in the paper?"

"Nothing worth reading. There is little information out there," Victoria responded. "How did your night go?"

"Quite productive, actually." He briefly ran through his discoveries from the night before, using little detail but bringing them both up to speed on what happened.

"How long have you been diving?" Victoria asked.

"For several years now. I found it was a great way to relax and literally get away from it all. I have taken several dive trips around the world. Cozumel, Raja Ampat, Chuuk Lagoon, Exuma, Phuket."

"I have no idea where those places are," Victoria said blankly.

"They are all dive destinations. Cozumel is in Mexico, Phuket is in Thailand, Exuma is an island in the Bahamas, and the others are in the Pacific. Masumi dives as well, but she is a WWW," he said with a grin.

"A what?" Victoria asked, looking between the two of them.

Masumi replied, "I am a self-admitted 'Warm Water Wuss.' If the water temp is not over eighty degrees Fahrenheit, I am staying on shore. Crazy boy over there goes ice diving in the winter. Imagine taking a chainsaw and cutting through eighteen inches of ice. Then when you get in the water, the temperature is only two degrees above freezing. Brrrr."

"You are nuts," Victoria said to Anderson, wide-eyed.

"See. Told you." Masumi pointed at him with a fork.

"Well, I see it didn't take long before the 'sisterhood' formed a united front. Fine, next time I go ice diving, I will not invite you two." Anderson sounded amused. He ate more of his breakfast.

"But take your camera when you go," Masumi said to Anderson before turning back to Victoria. "He takes great pictures. He has one taken in a quarry, where the sunlight is streaming down through the hole in the ice, and it looks like a cathedral. It's so beautiful. The air bubbles get caught under the ice, and they look like pools of liquid mercury.

"Oh, and the sharks from the Bahamas. You have to see those pictures, Victoria. He has one with a fifteen-foot reef shark about a foot away from his head. I will show them to you later."

"I've always wanted to take up diving, but I never got around to it. Not sure I want sharks swimming within a foot of my head, though." Victoria remembered the Shark Week commercial she had seen on the hotel TV.

"Don't worry. I didn't see a shark until my sixtieth dive. The bubbles from the regulator usually scare them off. Plus, with the amount of shark fishing, a lot of species are endangered," Masumi reassured her.

"Maybe I'll do it when I retire and have time. Who knows? That may be a lot sooner than I think if no progress is made." Victoria sighed.

"Ahhh, she of little faith. If I told you it will be solved by tomorrow morning, would you believe me?" Anderson interjected.

"You cannot mean that. What will a pair of shoes show?" Victoria asked.

"The more I think of it, the more I believe they will be the key that cracks this wide open. Speaking of which, I have to meet Bill at 9 AM. He will have the results of the forensic exam." Anderson stood, his empty breakfast plate in his hand. He drained the last of his coffee and went into the kitchen.

"Just leave them on the counter. I will do up the dishwasher," Masumi called after him. She pulled the newspaper over in front of her as Anderson and Victoria left the table.

"Right." Anderson came out of the kitchen. "Victoria, Bill told me they have arranged to use a warehouse to get in and out of the pier area. We should be able to avoid the crowds, if you want to come with me."

"Please, I would like that. Give me twenty minutes to get ready." Victoria got up and took her dishes into the kitchen. "Thanks for the nice breakfast," she told him on the way in. He got a peck on the cheek as a reward as she passed.

"What do you have planned for today, Masumi?" Anderson asked.

"Finishing a paper this morning, lecture at 11, then lunch with the girls. After that, I'll be in the campus library doing research. I don't know if I will grab dinner there and stay late yet. Depends on the quality of the music at the Student Union tonight. Better not expect me until late just to be safe."

"Okay. Have fun," he responded.

Victoria slipped past him in the kitchen doorway; she smiled up at him and went upstairs to get ready.

* * *

A half hour later, Anderson and Victoria descended to the garage level. Vinnie greeted them, dressed in coveralls. He had a small piece of rusted machinery in a workbench vice and was lightly tapping a protruding arm with a hammer to loosen it up. He had a broad smile when he saw them. Operatic strains of

Don Giovanni sounded in the background. "Morning, boss. Morning, miss."

"Didn't I give you the day off?" Anderson asked.

"*Sì*, boss. I thought I would work on the car."

"One of your sisters-in-law is visiting," Anderson stated.

"Chiara. She is staying three days." Vinnie looked mildly embarrassed.

Anderson laughed and patted him on the shoulder as he passed.

"Oh, boss. This came for you earlier." Vinnie said suddenly. He held up a thick sealed FedEx envelope, but there was no label on it. "A young kid in a beat-up Dodge dropped it off. Long blond hair in a ponytail. He didn't give me a name or want me to sign for it. He mentioned you by name, so I took it."

Anderson took the envelope. It was thick and weighed several pounds. "Thanks. I was expecting this. Have a good day."

Anderson walked over to the M6 BMW and opened the passenger door for Victoria. She slid into the passenger seat, and he closed the door. He opened the driver door and slipped the FedEx envelope behind his seat. After getting into the driver's seat, he buckled himself in and started the V10 gasoline-fueled engine. Anderson pulled out of the garage and turned down Watson Street. He let the engine temperature gauge come up into the green zone before going over 2000 RPM on the tachometer. It didn't take long, and by the time he pulled onto the interstate, the engine was purring.

The gearbox was as smooth as silk, and it was easily Anderson's favorite vehicle. The leather bucket seats conformed to his body and allowed him to take curves a lot more tightly than usual. He kept the maneuvers well inside the safe zone, due to his passenger, but the trip to the pier did not take long.

Anderson parked the car half a block away from the news vans. They exited the M6, and he grabbed the envelope before locking the doors and setting the alarm. They walked toward the pier, but they turned down a short alley in between the warehouses.

No one was present. He had to walk up a short flight of steps to the door and knocked loudly. Within a minute, the door opened and Anderson recognized an FBI agent from the night before. "Good morning, Mr. Anderson, Doctor Wade. Come on through. Detective Murphy is not back yet, but he should be soon. Special Agent Bryant is with the captain."

Anderson let Victoria go first, and then he walked in. It was dark, for there were few windows, but the far cargo doors were open slightly, and he could see the pier. The pair walked to the doors and emerged back into daylight behind the FBI Command Post. They walked around the front of the vehicle and made it to the gangway without incident. Anderson let Victoria go first, and he followed close behind. Just as he got to the top of the gangway, Hisham emerged from the front of the superstructure. Anderson stopped to talk to him.

* * *

Kogan's attention had naturally been drawn to the lithe woman who was climbing the gangway. Watching a group of male FBI agents for hours on end did nothing for him, but the shapely lady was worth a second look.

When the man entered his field of view, Kogan instantly recognized his target through the binoculars, but he made no move toward his weapon. He had specific conditions that needed to be met before firing. Instead, he studied the man closely. The way he moved, the way he talked. His face, his manner, his posture were all recorded in Kogan's memory to aid in future identification. The target was speaking to another man near the top of the gangway.

* * *

"Good morning, Hisham. I was sorry to hear about Kareem last night," Anderson began.

Hisham was his usual nervous self, and his English suffered for it. "Yes. This was for not be good."

"How is the staff doing?" Anderson asked.

"Much fear and doubt. They feel like a friend has been lost. Yes?"

"I understand. I'm sorry this had to happen," Anderson concluded. Hisham nodded. There was nothing else to be said, so he walked away.

Anderson turned with Victoria and walked to the nearest hatchway. Hisham continued his walk down the side of the vessel.

The pair headed toward the mess. As they passed the library, he could see it was unoccupied. Anderson stopped and turned to her. "Why don't you go grab a seat in the mess? I need to read over the contents of the envelope, and that will take a while. I will use the library so I can concentrate. If you see Bill, let him know where I am, okay?"

"Okay. I'll make a few calls and see you later," she said, then walked further aft toward the mess.

Anderson went into the library and closed the door. His black backpack was still hanging where he had left it on the back of the door. He took it down and placed it on the table, along with the envelope. Anderson unzipped the pack and took a black Olympus recording device out of a side pocket. It had a thin wire plugged into it, which he removed. It looked like a cell phone, but it was a little larger and thicker.

He sat down at the table and pulled out a pair of headphones from a side pocket on the pack. He plugged them into the Olympus unit, pressed the controls on the front of the device, and began to listen to it. Seven minutes later, he took the headset off and put it aside. Anderson grabbed the envelope and pulled out over four hundred sheets of letter-sized paper. The first few pages said:

Whoever runs the computers in this place, if there is anyone, has no idea what they are doing. Their servers haven't been patched in months, everyone has access to everything, and they need to invest in a new firewall. Security on their network is basically non-existent, and how they keep the servers running is beyond me. Crap systems management.

Enclosed are annual financial statements for the last five years, biographies on the staff, and some background info.

Short version: A year ago, they almost went under. Their fund-raising bombed, and they could not cover their expenses. I found many panicky e-mails among their board members from that time. They came right to the edge of not being able to meet their payroll. Nine months ago, they received a whopping half million grant from Invarco Holdings, a philanthropy organization out of Houston. More on them later. The thing is, the Jensen never applied for the grant. It was given to them out of the blue on the condition that a member from Invarco took a place on the Jensen board to 'advise them'; direct e-mail quote to the director. They took the money like a drowning man grabbing a life ring. With the grant, Jensen was able to make a decent bid for the Egypt exhibition, and it became the first stop. Their advance ticket sales have also added a lot of money to their coffers. Today they are flush with funds, and as a result they are bringing in several more high-profile exhibits over the next year.

Okay, now the interesting part. I was not the first person to take a look at this material. Someone entered their servers a few weeks before the grant money arrived. I found all sorts of tracks in the log files. Whoever did this had some skill but did not know enough to cover up their tracks. I rate his skill as four out of ten.

Anderson smiled. It was a typical thing for Nawaz to say. He kept reading.

Seeing that, I dug a little deeper into Invarco Holdings from public sources. They were legally formed three days before the grant was made. Their board of directors comprises five lawyers who all work for Harcourt, Johnson & Summerville, a Houston legal firm. The address for Invarco is a suite number in the law firm's building. Invarco has made no other investments in any other organization and ninety-five percent of their initial funding was taken up by the Jensen grant. Fairly selective investment, if you ask me.

Now getting info on Harcourt, Johnson & Summerville was a lot easier. Over ninety percent of their legal work is conducted for Sterling Thompson and his various companies—

Anderson stopped reading the summary at that point. *Sterling Thompson* was a name he knew well. Based in Texas, Thompson had made billions in domestic and foreign petro dealings.

Thompson didn't gamble with exploration or drilling. He let others do that and instead supplied the infrastructure for transporting recovered oil once it was out of the ground. His pipeline network and tankers carried the majority of crude oil from overseas fields to North America and Europe.

His reputation was gray. A lot of people suspected he was dealing in the shadows, but his name had never been publicly linked to any scandal. While he was investigated many times by several three-letter government organizations, no successful prosecution had ever taken place. He was reputed to have helped the CIA in Central America in some vague way during the Iran Contra scandal and had many friends of convenience. Thompson had enough money to intimidate anyone and was reputed not to stop at just intimidation. He bought political favor by donating to politicians who saw things his way. Thompson joined all the right clubs and had all the right connections. On the other hand, he was supposed to be one of the more generous oil men in Texas. He gave a hundred million away annually to various trusts, charities, and non-profits. That was less than three percent of what he made in a year.

What only a few people knew was that over the last fifteen years, Sterling Thompson had been rumored to be building up a massive collection of black market art. Sculptures, paintings, and other masterworks had been disappearing around the world, and his name was whispered as being responsible.

Again, there was no direct proof, and investigations trying to probe his involvement never went anywhere. However, the various insurance companies listened to the rumors. Thompson was rich, unscrupulous, and capable. If anyone could pull off a robbery of this scale, then his name would certainly be at the top of the short list.

Anderson noted Nawaz had not signed the pages, which was fine by him. He took the first few summary pages of the report, folded them up and pocketed them. No one else needed to see how the information had been gathered. Anderson then ran through the rest of the papers and saw several pages had salient facts marked with yellow highlighter. The evidence built page by page, exactly as Nawaz had outlined it.

Anderson also noted that identifying information had been redacted to hide the source of the information and the methods used to gather it.

He made it to the end of the paperwork just as Bill Bryant walked through the door. Mike Murphy followed, with a black leather bag in his hand. "We know how they did it," Bryant said happily.

"I know who did it," Anderson replied putting the paperwork down.

"The theft or the murder?" Murphy asked, coming in the room and shutting the door behind him.

"Both. One is in the employ of the other," Anderson said soberly.

"All right, let's compare notes. I'll go first. The shoes were a treasure trove." Murphy sat down beside Bryant, opened the top of the leather bag, and reached in. He pulled out three large clear evidence bags. The first held the red monkey wrench. The second had the pair of black shoes Anderson had recovered from the bottom of the harbor. The last was filled with several small items. Murphy handed that one over to Anderson.

Anderson looked inside the clear plastic bag and saw a small round metal bowl with raised hieroglyphics in it. The bowl was the same size as the red wax seals he had observed on the crates in the forward hold. There were two indentations, one on either side of the bowl.

He turned over the clear bag and looked at the underside of the bowl, which was flame-blackened. The bottom of the bowl had also been pressed down slightly, making a convex curve in the otherwise concave bowl. Beside the bowl was a short piece of stiff wire as thick as a coat hanger, bent in a V shape. The length of the wire was covered in black plastic except for the very ends, which were bare metal and bent in toward each other an eighth of an inch. The wire was roughly two inches long per side. A small tea light-style candle, wide and shallow, had a wick blackened from use. Several cubes of red wax were in a separate smaller clear bag. The only other contents were a pair of surgical gloves.

"These were in the heels of the shoes?" Anderson asked, turning the bag for an in-depth look.

Murphy nodded while referencing his notes. "Right. The techs found no fingerprints or fiber evidence on the exterior and decided to X-ray them just to be thorough. They found traces of wax, blue foam, and superglue on the gloves. The candle and wax cubes were in one heel; the mold and wire were in the other. All of the metal items were loosely wrapped in a surgical glove to stop any noise. They did get a DNA sample from the inner shoe cushion and glove interior, but they will take a while to process for a positive ID. We also got a good sample from the top of the wrench. If it turns out to be Kareem's, we have our murder weapon positively identified."

"It looks like the mold was flattened on the bottom." Anderson pointed to the item.

"Yes, I noticed that. We suspect that was due to him walking on it. The hollowed-out area had no internal support, so over time the weight from his heel would flatten the bowl bottom, which was pressed up against the underside of his foot. Same thing happened to a lesser extent to the candle in the other heel, but that did not affect it. I am not sure what the wire was for," Murphy responded.

"He placed the wire into the recesses on either side of the seal maker so he could hold it in the candle flame. You can see the holes on the bowl are the same size as the wire ends. Notice how the wire is insulated? Stops his fingers from getting burned," Anderson observed, pointing at the holes in the sides.

"Yeah, that makes sense. So how did they get a copy of the hieroglyphic seal? If Al Dhabit had his brother-in-law do the originals, then how did they copy it?" Bryant asked.

"They took one of the existing seals and used it as a positive mold. You can see here how the hieroglyphics in this one have rougher edges, because it is a copy of a copy." Anderson pointed.

"Okay, given the statements we have gotten to date, that brings the suspect list down to two people. The doctor or Hisham. No one else had access to them," Bryant concluded.

"Sorry, but you are forgetting there is one other person who had access to both the seals and cargo area. The ship's captain."

"Kincaid? I know the seals were in his safe, but the lock on the bag was not picked. We looked at that. Besides, why make a duplicate if you had access to the original?"

"Now do you want to know who?" Anderson asked.

"Dumb question," Bryant replied flatly.

Anderson took the electronic device out of the backpack. "When I came aboard dressed as Joe the pizza deliveryman, I left my pack on the back of the library door. I had previously noticed that apart from the deck outside, this room was the only publicly accessible space that was not being used. Crew quarters, radio room, the mess, passenger cabins, et cetera, were all shared or otherwise occupied. This was the only interior cabin people could have a quiet conversation without being overheard."

Anderson unplugged the earphones and pressed a few buttons on the front of the unit. It played for seven minutes on the internal speaker so all could hear. A lot of the recording was thumping or odd noises as people wordlessly took or returned books or magazines to and from the shelves. However, there were several minutes of recorded conversation between two men in Arabic. Neither Bryant or Murphy understood the language, but even they could hear that the tone of the conversation was low and conspiratorial.

After Anderson pressed the *Stop* button, Bryant asked, "How was this recorded?" His tone was deadly serious.

"I had this voice-activated digital voice recorder in the side pocket of the backpack. I guess I left it turned on by mistake." From Anderson's expression and tone of voice, the cops knew it had not been an accident.

"This is not admissible in court, no matter what was said. Recording a conversation without a court order or prior permission from the parties involved is illegal and will be thrown out," Bryant observed.

"I know, but I am not a lawyer—and as I said, it was left on accidentally. There was no way you could have gotten a court order to monitor this space, or I would have discussed the possibility with you. You cannot use this in court. At least, not directly." Anderson replied.

The conversation paused before Bryant said, "Okay, completely off the record and unofficially. Who were they, and what did they say?"

Anderson played the recording and gave the others a verbatim translation of the brief conversation as the tape played:

The library door clicked closed.

"I want more money," said Kareem in Arabic.

"How can I do this? I have none to give you. We'll not get anything until we meet him again in Pittsburgh."

"The original plan was to have the theft discovered in Pittsburgh, with the mask long gone by then. With the accident, that is no longer possible, and the danger to us is much greater. That puts us at higher risk, and I want more money to compensate me. If I need to run on short notice, I'll need that money to escape. Otherwise…" Kareem was insistent.

"Otherwise what, Kareem?"

"Otherwise I'll take the items I have and go to the police to work out a deal. There may be a considerable reward from them. The Americans have deep pockets. I'll not spend my days in a small cell for so little money."

"Going to the federal police will only land both of us in a cell that much quicker. Remember, the people who hired us are dangerous, and we may not live long if they learn of this. The man they hired for my job disappeared when they learned I was to be replaced. Killing is not hard for them." The speaker sounded terrified at the thought.

"I'm not scared of them. The police can protect me. They have a program for protecting witnesses in danger under false identities," Kareem said firmly.

There was a long pause. The nervous voice continued, "Very well. I know where I can find several thousand dollars. Meet me on the main deck near the bow in fifteen minutes, and I'll bring what I can."

The library door opened, and the recording ended.

Murphy tapped his finger on the tabletop. "That is pretty cut and dried. He lured him out onto the deck and ambushed him. That's first degree murder by any definition, and that's a gas chamber ride in this state."

"Right. So want to hear the rest?" Anderson asked.

"There is more?" Bryant asked, surprised.

Anderson handed over the financial data he had received earlier. The summary pages from Nawaz stayed in his pocket. For the next ten minutes, he took the detective and FBI agent through the raw data of the financial chain connecting the Jensen to Harcourt, Johnson & Summerville, using the supplied paperwork. He stopped the story at the legal firm for the moment.

"Where did you get this material?" Bryant looked and sounded stunned.

"It was delivered to me this morning. It came anonymously with no return address or name," Anderson answered truthfully.

"This paperwork answers a lot of questions. However, the big question is who engaged the legal firm to do this," Bryant said as he flipped through the paperwork.

"I was told that over ninety percent of Harcourt, Johnson & Summerville's work is at the behest of Sterling Thompson," Anderson said firmly.

The papers fell on the desk, and the FBI Agent let out a low whistle. "Okay, we just stepped through the looking glass. Sterling Thompson? Damn! He's been rumored to have been involved in several robberies, including the Gardner job, but no one has ever been able to make a direct link to him. He is slipperier than Gotti. We have to step lightly here, Stephen. He's got more judges, governors, and senators in his pocket than I have loose change in mine."

"Thankfully, that is your job, not mine. Look, my prime concern is recovering the burial mask. Prosecuting the man responsible is your job. I am sure you can legally reconstruct the material there." He pointed at the stack of papers.

"Yes, but it could be argued that he made a philanthropic donation and nothing more. We need a witness willing to testify if we want to go after him," Bryant concluded grimly.

"Like someone under threat of a death sentence from a first-degree murder charge, for example?" Anderson suggested.

Bryant smiled and nodded slowly as he thought about it. "Yeah. Exactly. Okay, I can get on board with that. So that solves my problem, but what about yours? Where's the mask?"

"I don't know exactly where it is, but I am sure it is still on board. Nothing of appropriate size has left the ship for it to be smuggled out in. Besides, I think the plan *was* to keep it on board. However, after seeing the shoe contents, I suspect fifteen minutes in the forward hold will show me exactly where it is." Anderson spoke with confidence.

"You think it's in the hold?" Bryant asked flatly.

"I know it is there," Anderson said firmly.

Bryant looked dubious. "Okay. Mind telling us how you know that?"

"Because once you eliminate the impossible, whatever remains, no matter how improbable, must be the truth." Anderson then explained his logic to both of them.

* * *

The three men spoke for several more minutes before leaving the library. They all agreed on what needed to be done. Anderson checked the mess, but the person he was looking for was not there.

"Be right back. I'll meet you both down in the forward hold," he said to Bryant, and he headed up the internal staircase to the bridge level. Making his way through the bridge, he nodded genially to the first officer as he passed. Anderson turned down the short corridor and stopped in front of the chief engineer's cabin. He knocked lightly.

The door jerked open and Doctor Al Dhabit appeared, looking in a frightful state. His shirt had several top buttons unfastened and looked as though he had slept in it. He had not shaved in several days, and his hair was a fright. The area under his eyes was dark and puffy, indicating listless and sporadic sleep habits. His skin was paler than usual.

"What do you want?" Al Dhabit irritably half-screamed.

"Doctor, would you please come down to the forward hold? We have something to show you."

"What? What can you possibly show me? My career is over. My reputation and family will suffer until the day I die," the doctor replied.

"Follow me, and see for yourself," Anderson said simply.

"This had better be worth my time." Al Dhabit did up his buttons. He continued grumbling under his breath.

The pair descended all the way down to the cargo deck on the internal staircase. The hatch to the forward hold was open when they got there. The white lights of the overhead fluorescent bulbs illuminated the short corridor leading up to the hatch.

Al Dhabit entered first, and Anderson came in close behind. Inside were the two Egyptian guards on duty, plus Bryant and Murphy. Anderson closed the hatch behind him. "Doctor, please tell the guards not to admit anyone through the hatch under any circumstances."

Al Dhabit almost argued the point, but seeing the FBI agent and detective present, he did as he was requested.

"Mike. Will you show the doctor the evidence bag?" Anderson said.

Murphy took out the clear evidence bag with the mold, wire handle, candle, gloves, and wax.

Al Dhabit looked at the bag intently. With shock he said, "This is a copy of the mold! How? Where?"

"Those items were found in the heels of Kareem's shoes. After drugging his partner Farhaan into unconsciousness, he broke the seal on the crate containing the burial mask, removed it, and then used the mold to seal the crate up to ensure that no one would notice the theft until the crate was opened up a day or more later in Pittsburgh. The dropping of the crane hook into the hold revealed the theft early."

"Then this was how the crime was done! But—but who is responsible and where is the mask?" Al Dhabit stammered.

"That is why you are here, Doctor," Anderson said.

CHAPTER 16 – DUPLICITY

A half hour later, Victoria entered the forward hold along with a few FBI agents, two uniformed policemen, Captain Kincaid, Farhaan, Merridew, and Hisham. She'd not been told why she was needed, only where, and the others' expressions suggested that they, too, lacked information. They all stayed on their side of the crime scene tape.

Al Dhabit, Bryant, Murphy, and Anderson stood by the crates on the opposite side of the tape. Victoria noticed that all of the cargo netting had been removed from the crate stacks and lay around the bottom of the boxes.

She met Anderson's gaze, and he winked at her subtly. She smiled back at him.

As the last person entered, Al Dhabit nodded to the Egyptian guard who was standing at the threshold, and he sealed the watertight hatch. The sound of the door latches being engaged interrupted all conversation.

* * *

"Good morning," Anderson began, his voice strong and confident. All eyes fell on him, and no one else spoke. "I asked for you this morning so I can answer the many questions that have been asked over the last few days."

Anderson started walking, emphasizing what he was saying with gestures. "Security on the exhibit was quite good at all stages—so good, in fact, that I initially could not see a flaw. At every point of the journey, there were multiple people with the crates under direct observation, twenty-four hours a day, often from multiple organizations. Dr. Al Dhabit planned the multiple layers of security from the outset to ensure that no one person could have unrestricted access to the cargo. I must commend the doctor in his efforts."

Anderson looked at Al Dhabit, who nodded back in appreciation.

"No chain has links of equal strength, however. Despite the apparently solid security, the mask was gone, and there were only four possibilities.

"First, the mask might never have been packed up in the first place, meaning the crate had left the Cairo museum empty, but I discounted this due to the heavy tourist and police presence during the packing operation. Second, the crate holding the mask might have been deliberately mislabeled at the museum—but again, the heavy oversight at that point made me doubt that. Third, it might have been removed during the convoy to Alexandria—but the heavy military police presence and museum staff throughout the convoy likewise made that unlikely. Last, the mask may have been taken while aboard the *Costarican Trader*. The vessel had the weakest security in the entire trip, making it the most probable solution, so I pursued it.

"While on board, the cargo was isolated under the direct supervision of two security guards. The hold was sealed, fully lit, day and night, and Dr. Al Dhabit performed several random checks on all guard shifts. He noticed nothing of consequence. Is that correct, Doctor?"

"Yes, this is true," Al Dhabit responded.

"For both guards on duty to be in on the theft would be statistically improbable. The guard force was randomly selected from many applicants. Not all of them could be in on the operation. So I concluded that one guard had acted alone. Could that one man steal the mask without alerting the other man on duty? No. That was clearly impossible. So for that to be practical, something had to be done to remove the second guard from the equation. Killing him would raise all sorts of suspicion. Bribery or coercion may not have worked and the approach possibly reported. So that left only one method.

"As many of you know, two guards, Farhaan and Kareem, were given the midnight shift. Of all the shifts, that one would see the least amount of traffic through the hold. Except for the crew going through every eight hours, there was no other traffic apart from Dr. Al Dhabit. Logically, it was the best time to attempt a theft."

Anderson stopped in front of the Egyptian security guard who was in front of the caution tape with Victoria and the others. "Farhaan, as many of you know, suffered from seasickness for the entire journey. Other guards suffered as well, but they took drugs from the crew. Farhaan's religious beliefs would not allow him to take anything for his symptoms, which left him weak and tired. On their shift, the day before the ship docked, Kareem gave Farhaan a thermos of soup and convinced Farhaan to lie down on the stretcher on the wall over there." Everyone turned to look at the rolled-up stretcher lashed to the wall.

"The soup Farhaan consumed was laced with what I suspect was a heavy dose of seasickness medication. This type of medicine normally causes drowsiness, and as he was already lying down and worn out from several days of illness, sleep was inevitable. Farhaan remembers falling asleep and being woken by Kareem. Kareem told him it was only for a few moments, but Farhaan recalls being surprised when he was told it was several hours later than he thought. On awaking, Farhaan recalls smelling a cigarette. We found Turkish brand cigarettes in Kareem's shirt pocket and locker, along with boxed matches. I believe he smoked one in the hold to cover the sulfur scent of the match used to light the small candle to melt the wax. With that information, we now know *when* the crime was done."

Anderson began walking back and forth again. "So we knew who probably did the crime, leaving the question of *how* it was done. Until Kareem's body was found on the deck, I had no idea. The murder was the key.

"Detective Murphy was at the murder scene when I arrived. Kareem had last been seen heading to his cabin, dressed in his uniform. The body had been found later, still wearing the uniform, but without his shoes. As a pair of shoes had been found in Kareem's locker, Detective Murphy assumed that Kareem was chasing someone onto the deck. I looked at the body carefully, and I examined his feet. The deck was wet from the fog in the air, yet only the sides of Kareem's socks were moist, where they were touching the deck. Just a few steps on the deck would have soaked the bottom of his socks, so he could not have walked there without shoes."

"Now, when people are struck in the head, it is instinctive for them to roll up into a ball. This is called a fetal position, where the arms and legs are brought up close to the body. Kareem's upper body was like this, but the legs were outstretched. Someone had pulled them straight, probably while removing his shoes.

"The other thing I noticed was that Kareem had a very bad foot odor, which was obvious when you got within a few feet of him. In his locker, he had a laundry bag, and his dirty socks smelled, as well. Yet the shoes in his locker were odorless. Obviously, these were not the shoes he was wearing when he died—and he likely did not wear his second pair at all during the entire voyage.

"So we now have a killer, who clubs Kareem to death and then takes his shoes for some unknown reason. Imagine he is now standing on the deck with the murder weapon and a pair of shoes. He cannot risk walking into the ship, or someone might see him with those items. So the logical thing for him to do would be to throw them overboard. Detective Murphy, can you show them the murder weapon, please?"

Murphy wordlessly opened the black leather bag and took out the plastic evidence bag holding the red monkey wrench and held it up so they could all see it. After a few seconds, he placed it on a nearby crate in full sight of everyone.

Anderson continued, "Now the killer also had the shoes he took off Kareem, but the shoes might have floated if he throws them into the water. So he tied the shoelaces to the wrench before throwing them overboard—killing two birds, as it were. Detective…"

Murphy produced the clear evidence bag with the shoes and held it up for a few seconds before putting it beside the wrench on the unopened crate.

Anderson looked over the people on the far side of the crime scene tape. He could see he was making a striking impression on one person in particular. "I went for a dive in the harbor just a few hours after the body had been found. I found the shoes tied to the wrench roughly thirty feet away from the side of the ship on the bottom of the harbor. Now, why would anyone want to get rid of a pair of shoes? Indeed, why would anyone be willing to kill for such a small thing? That question was answered by the crime lab, which X-rayed the heels and found… Detective?"

Once again, Murphy was briefly the center of attention as he produced a clear evidence bag, this one containing the contents found in the heels. Several people behind the crime scene tape moved a little closer for a better view. One did not move at all, Anderson noted.

"The contents of the hollow heels included surgical gloves, cubes of red wax, a small candle, a mold with the same hieroglyphic seal you can see on all the crates in this hold, and a wire handle. Not much to look at, but certainly enough for someone to kill for. The shoes' contents gave us the *how*. With the replica, Kareem was able to break the seal on crate *AJ*, remove the mask, and seal the crate up again.

"So Kareem now has the mask in his possession. Now, *how* could he get it out of the hold and complete the theft? The mask itself is quite large, at twenty-one inches high, and it weighs almost twenty-five pounds. The incoming guards would have noticed him taking anything of substance out of the hold. With Farhaan asleep, Kareem could conceivably have left the hold, but the ship always has crew active at all hours, and getting to any place outside of the forward hold unseen would have been challenging.

"At one point, I thought he might have tossed it overboard in some sort of floating or inflatable container, but this was obviously a methodical plan, well thought out, and I had no reason to believe the mask had left the ship in such a haphazard manner. The entire ship had been thoroughly searched twice, once by customs, and once by the FBI. Nothing was found. Only the pilot boats and the Egyptian frigate approached the *Trader* during the entire transit—and again, there was no way the mask could have been smuggled off the ship. I even checked the incinerator room to see if he had simply destroyed it. I found nothing there." Anderson paused.

Captain Kincaid broke the silence. "So where was the mask taken?"

"Exactly," responded Anderson, pointing at Kincaid. "*That* is the very question that originally stumped me, because the ship had been searched repeatedly. However, I soon realized the entire ship had *not* been searched. Dr. Al Dhabit had made it perfectly clear that the exhibit crates were under diplomatic protection and the FBI was not allowed to perform a search of that cargo. While the majority of the cargo was going to Pittsburgh, some crates were to go to the Jensen Museum for a smaller exhibit beginning in Norfolk, Virginia. The incident with the crane enabled the discovery of the theft well ahead of the scheduled time that the crates would be normally opened in Pittsburgh. Dr. Wade, you said it would be no less than twenty-four hours before the cargo was unpacked at the Carnegie?"

"Yes. It would've been delayed initially by the late hour of the arrival. These items are fragile, and unpacking would have required a careful and methodical process. Then, depending on the order in which the crates were unpacked, it could have been several days before the loss was discovered."

Anderson turned back to Kincaid. "Captain, how long would it take you to get to Norfolk from here?"

Kincaid answered without pausing. "A little under seventeen hours at regular cruising speed."

Anderson turned back to the group. "So if the crane incident had not occurred, the Jensen cargo would probably have been off-loaded in Norfolk before the theft had even been discovered in Pittsburgh. Even so, it would have taken at least another four to eight hours after the loss was discovered before the investigation began looking at the *Costarican Trader*, which would have been well on its way to South America by then."

Anderson turned back to Kincaid. "Captain, are you still being assailed by messages from the Jensen director asking when the cargo would be released?"

"Yes, we have received continuous requests from them, asking for updates on our arrival time."

Anderson continued to the rest of the people in the hold, "I overheard the captain say something similar to his radio operator. Why would anyone need to send such frequent inquiries for a relatively minor museum exhibit? Why the urgency? So we were left with a series of contradictory facts. The mask had been stolen from its case. It could not have left the cargo hold without a major diversion, and there had been none. Even if it had been possible to take it from the cargo hold, it would have been impossible to remove it from the ship without serious preparation and several people. The entire vessel, save the diplomatically protected crates, had been thoroughly searched by U.S. Customs and again by the FBI. Last, the Jensen was sending numerous requests to have the cargo released.

"The only single answer that fit all those situations was that the mask had been hidden in the Jensen part of the cargo, and the people responsible desperately wanted it delivered."

He paused to let that sink in.

Victoria broke the silence first. "You mean it is still here?"

Anderson continued without answering her question. "When we looked at the contents of the shoes, I noticed the bowl of the replica mold had been slightly crushed under the weight of Kareem's heel. Not surprising, as he weighed at least a hundred and seventy pounds, and the shoe heels had been weakened by being hollowed out. So any seal produced by the damaged replica would have this same flaw. Detective Murphy, Special Agent Bryant, Dr. Al Dhabit, and I took all of the netting off the cargo and checked every seal. We started by examining the top crates in the Jensen shipment. I reasoned Kareem would have found it impossible to move these heavy boxes without assistance, so it was logical to start on top. It took us under a minute, and we found this... Bill."

Bill Bryant reached into jacket and pulled a small clear evidence bag with an intact red seal in it out from his inside breast pocket. The wire embedded in the wax had been cut, allowing the seal to be taken off the box intact. Bryant held it close to the observers, letting them see the deformed surface in the seal.

Anderson spoke. "Ordinarily, this would have passed a quick inspection. Dr. Al Dhabit was through the hold several times and saw nothing out of place. The cargo netting over the boxes obscured the view of the seals to some extent. He expected to see an intact seal, and when he did, he did not look at it any closer. We found it only because we knew what unique feature to look for: the flattened bottom. Dr. Al Dhabit broke a wax seal to get into crate *AJ* after the lid was damaged. The pieces of that seal were recovered from the deck by the FBI lab techs. Special Agent Bryant placed a call to the lab. The seal fragments were reexamined and found to have the same surface flaw."

"Which other crate had the fake seal?" Victoria asked, her tone more of a prompt to continue than a question.

Anderson walked over to a crate stack. The box on top, numbered *42*, no longer had a seal. He turned to Al Dhabit. "Doctor, may we move this crate closer to everyone?"

The usually overprotective administrator acquiesced immediately. "Of course."

"Bill. Can you give me a hand?" Anderson asked.

Bryant and Anderson grabbed the rope handles on the side of the crate and moved it to the deck just in front of the crime scene tape. The two men were in decent shape, but they strained to move the thick wooden box. The small crowd pressed forward to see over the tape.

"This is crate *42*." Anderson opened the lid. It swung back on its hinges, and he placed it gently onto the deck so it was fully open. Anderson removed the thin layer of blue insulation and put it aside, exposing the tops of the several large white vases. Each was individually wrapped in see-through plastic sheeting and surrounded by blue foam that had been cut to accommodate the shape of each piece. Smaller depressions in the foam held the individual lids. "Dr. Wade, you are the local New Kingdom expert. Can you tell us what these are, please?"

Victoria leaned forward and studied them for several seconds. "They are alabaster amphorae. Many were found in the Tomb of Tutankhamun. These, I believe, were recovered in the treasury directly beside the burial chamber."

"Dr. Al Dhabit?" Anderson asked.

"Dr. Wade is correct. There were many amphorae found in the tomb. These are not the best examples and were allotted to the secondary exhibit."

"Dr. Al Dhabit. Could you remove the amphorae and their lids please?" Anderson asked.

Al Dhabit leaned forward and carefully extracted the pieces by grabbing the plastic wrapping on each. The doctor placed the pieces on a flat area of cargo netting, side by side so they would not roll. He put the lids nearby. The last amphora removed was the largest. He cradled it in his arms like a baby.

Merridew spoke up. "Wait a second. So if I follow you, Mr. Anderson, you're going to say the mask was hidden in that box. But those vases take up almost the entire height of the box, with little clearance. They are all solid and undamaged, so there is no room for the mask to be inside without massive holes being punched through it."

"Almost correct, Mr. Merridew. You are forgetting the mask already had a hole. Remember, it was shaped to fit over the head and shoulders of the Tutankhamun mummy. Think of it like an upside-down bucket. Solid all around and on top, but hollow on the bottom."

Anderson grabbed the top layer of blue foam in the box and easily pulled it up. It had the shape of a large pizza box, with holes for the amphora in several places. More rigid foam was revealed against the inner sides and bottom of the box, with spaces for the small amphora. Anderson reached in and withdrew a large piece of loose foam from the center. It had been shaped by hand and was a little smaller then the mask itself. It was set into the box upside-down. That piece had been further hollowed out to accommodate the width of the larger amphora.

"As you can see, the mask would have fit into the foam here upside-down, with the open end toward the ceiling. This loose piece of blue foam in my hand would fit inside the mask, and the hole in the inner foam would be on top, allowing the largest amphora to rest inside with ease. The larger flat piece on top only had holes for the amphora, which was glued in place, so if you looked in the holes you would only see blue foam."

Anderson reached inside the hole again and withdrew a tiny tube of instant glue that was already inside a small evidence bag. "This superglue was probably inside the shoe heels, as well. It was used to reseal the top layer of foam insulation after the mask was placed in here, so it would not move. We had to rip the foam apart when we inspected the box and found the glue tube inside."

* * *

One thing was still missing. Victoria could see the mask-sized indentation, and she could certainly imagine it being placed in there upside-down. However, all she could see in the box now that the inner core had been removed was blue insulation. There was nothing else inside. "Stephen. Where is the mask?" Victoria asked, confused and concerned.

Anderson walked over to Victoria to answer her question. "When we went through the box earlier, Dr. Al Dhabit was worried about the way it was positioned, so we returned it to the original packing." With the flourish of a master magician finishing up the last trick of the evening, Anderson opened the lid of crate *AJ*, pulled aside the upper layer of blue foam insulation, and revealed a gleaming mass of gold and semi-precious gems.

She looked down onto the face of a legend. The face of the Boy King glowed under the fluorescent lighting. Made of polished gold, it radiated warmth even in the harsh lighting. Much care had been taken by the ancient craftsmen to represent the facial features of the pharaoh so his soul could recognize his body and return for his resurrection. His nose, cheeks, and lips were all represented in gold. On either side of his face, Tutankhamun's ears stood out, with large holes. Cobalt blue lapis lazuli edging surrounded the obsidian and quartz pupils of his eyes and traced off toward the ears.

Much of the color on the mask was produced from natural juices taken from produce of the Nile River valley. Black eyebrows highlighted the eyes even more. The long braided light blue beard coming from the chin was another obvious symbol of the pharaoh. Surrounding the head and draped over the shoulders was a headdress with a series of alternating blue and gold stripes. On the forehead was the head of a cobra of black, red, and coral blue—the symbol of Upper Egypt—directly beside a vulture with a black beak—the symbol of Lower Egypt—indicating that Tutankhamun had ruled over all Egypt. The broad collar of semi-precious stones and colored glass came around the bottom of the mask ending on both shoulders with the symbol of Horus, a falcon.

Even after more than thirty-three centuries it had lost none of its power or grandeur.

Victoria looked over at Anderson, awestruck. "You found it."

Before Anderson could say anything, Kincaid asked, "So that is it? We can offload now?"

Anderson turned to him and said, "Well, that is almost it. The only question left is *who*."

"But the *who* is obvious. Kareem was the thief. He possessed the tools in his shoes; he drugged his partner and swapped the crates when he was unconscious," Kincaid stated.

Anderson nodded. "Correct, but that is all he did. He was not in a position to make the arrangements for the packaging. Nor was he capable of organizing the Jensen end of the operation. He was hired to do the swap only. All of the crates we saw today were made in Egypt, and this operation was thought out well ahead of time. This complete operation was preplanned, and everything was in place before a single item was loaded. The stacking of the crates was also a factor, and Kareem was not on duty in the hold during the loading in Alexandria. As I said, one man could not move these boxes once they were in place. So both crate *AJ* and *42* had to be on top of their respective stacks, or the plan would simply not work. Logically, others had to be involved to supervise the packing up of the items, to tell the loading crew where to put the crates, and to control the guard schedule to let Kareem have the shift with the most freedom of action. Then there is the person who used the monkey wrench and bludgeoned Kareem to death. Would you like to tell us who that person is, Hisham?"

Hisham said nothing, but as the others looked on him, he began a low-pitched wail. The tension finally became too much, and like a drowning man on the edge of going under, he panicked. Hisham screamed incoherently and lunged for the hatch. The noise echoed off the steel walls.

Anderson saw Victoria start and scrambled clear of the wild-eyed Egyptian. Several backed away, while others stepped forward to stop him. The two uniformed police officers got to him first and grabbed ahold of the flailing man. They easily took him to the steel decking, pulled his hands behind his back, and placed him in handcuffs. Then they searched his clothing thoroughly and satisfied themselves he had no weapons before they pulled him to his feet.

Tears streamed down Hisham's face. He sobbed uncontrollably, his head pressed forward, and he avoided meeting anyone's accusatory gaze. His entire body shook as he sobbed.

Detective Murphy stepped forward and addressed the two uniformed officers. "Take him up to the ship's library. Don't let anyone speak to him, and we will be up in a few minutes."

The police left with Hisham between them. An Egyptian guard opened the hatch for the officers and closed it behind them after they had passed through.

Kincaid broke the uncomfortable silence. "I can see him being a thief, but a murderer? That is hard to buy. He does not look like the type."

All further revelations would wait until they had interviewed Hisham directly. "We need to talk to him about that," was all Anderson said. "Dr. Al Dhabit, you had better call some of your staff down and arrange to have the mask and amphora repacked. There is no reason to delay the shipment any longer, assuming you still want the exhibit to go ahead."

Al Dhabit did not hesitate, a sincere smile on his face. "With the mask safely back in our possession, there is no reason to delay. I will have to communicate with my government, of course, but unless they contradict me, the exhibit goes forward to Pittsburgh." His growing smile eased the tension in the room.

Special Agent Bryant stepped forward. "Doctor, we will have to keep everyone on board until we can interview Hisham. It is possible others are involved, and we need to sort this out before anyone leaves. Plus, we will need to hold a press conference at some point to announce the recovery. I would like you there."

"Of course, but we will be able to pack the mask back up?" Al Dhabit asked.

"Yes, sir. That is still diplomatically protected material, and we cannot take it into evidence. Luckily, the murder of Kareem is the more serious of the charges, and we have enough evidence in hand to prosecute that crime instead of the theft." Bryant turned back to Anderson and Murphy. "Gentlemen, we need to talk about what to do with Hisham and how to approach this."

The three men walked across the forward hold to have a private conversation. The hatch was opened and the small crowd began to filter out, leaving the two Egyptian guards to guard the mask of the Pharaoh.

* * *

Several minutes later, Murphy, Bryant, and Anderson climbed the stairs and approached the door to the library together. A uniformed officer stood guard outside. The cop nodded at Murphy as soon as he saw him and opened the library door. The second uniformed police officer was inside the library, watching the prisoner.

Hisham sat in the chair facing the door. He raised his chin off his chest as they entered. His hands were drawn behind his back as the handcuffs were still in place. Tears streamed down his face. "I did not do this thing. I did not do this," Hisham protested immediately. The officer outside closed the door after all three had entered. Murphy sat to Hisham's left, Bryant to his right, and Anderson directly across from him. The second uniformed officer kept his place against the side wall of the library.

Murphy nodded to Bryant, who took out his recorder. Meanwhile, Murphy looked at his watch and wrote down the location of the interview, the time, and the date. Then he noted who was in the room. Murphy had to turn to see the uniformed officer's nametag.

Bryant said, "Hisham, we are recording this interview. Do you object?"

Hisham shook his head. "No, I not object," he responded weakly, his head dropping back down.

Detective Murphy pulled a printed card out of the right breast pocket on his suit and read it carefully. "Hisham. You have the right to remain silent. Anything you say can and will be used against you in a court of law. You have the right to have an attorney present during questioning. If you cannot afford an attorney, one will be appointed for you. Do you understand these rights as I have explained them to you?"

"Yes," replied the Egyptian, voice broken. There was no resistance in him.

Detective Murphy spoke. "Hisham, do you wish to give up these rights and speak to the police at this time without a lawyer being present?" His pen was suspended over his notepad ready to record the answers. Even though the interview was being recorded, he still wanted the written record, just in case.

"Yes. I speak," Hisham said weakly with his chin against his chest.

"Hisham, how long have you worked for the Cairo museum?"

"Three years."

"What is your job there?" Murphy asked, his pen moving continuously.

"I responsible for pack and unpack of museum items," he said simply.

"Were you responsible for the packaging for the Tutankhamun Egyptian Exhibit?" Murphy asked.

"Yes."

"Did you create the custom packaging for the crates in that exhibit?"

"Yes."

"Specifically, did you create the packaging for items in the two crates labeled *AJ* and *42*?"

"Yes." Hisham was completely still through the questioning. No movements at all.

"Which crate originally held the burial mask of Tutankhamun?"

"Crate *AJ*."

"Did you create the hidden hollow area inside crate *42* to accept the burial mask?"

There was a perceptible pause, and the tension was palpable. Murphy knew that if Hisham denied it, said nothing more, and asked for a lawyer, it would dramatically complicate matters.

Murphy celebrated silently when he answered. "Yes."

"Who instructed you to create the hidden area inside crate *42*?"

"I not know."

"You say you do not know the name of the person who instructed you to modify crate *42*?" Murphy asked, looking over at Bryant with a raised eyebrow.

"No, I not know," Hisham replied. His gaze lifted to the group. The detective sensed truth in the reply.

"Where did you first meet this person?" Murphy asked.

In his halting English, Hisham tried to explain. "A man come up to me on a street outside my home in Cairo. He say he have special project that pay good. We have coffee and talk. He offer hundred thousand Egypt pounds for me to do this. Yes? He also say I come to America and be live there."

"Describe this man." Murphy said.

"Very rich clothes with Mercedes and man to drive him. I see this as he leave. He American lawyer. Yes?" Hisham said.

* * *

Anderson's blood ran cold at Hisham's answer. *Could it be connected?* He had no physical description to go by, just the fact the man who tried to have him killed was a nameless 'lawyer.'

* * *

"When did you meet him?" Murphy continued after writing the last answer down.

"In Cairo, four month past," Hisham said.

"When did you first meet Kareem Al-Asned?" Murphy asked.

"Two month past in Cairo coffee house with lawyer. We talk to how this work."

"When was the last time you saw the lawyer?"

"The day ship sails from Alexandria. Doctor Al Dhabit let staff go to city for last visit. I let Kareem free of his duty to go to shore. We go different way and meet in room above cleaning place for clothes with lawyer. We talk for half hour, lawyer give Kareem shoes, then we come back to ship."

"When was the mask taken and placed in crate *42*?" Murphy asked.

"I told by Kareem he do this one day before we dock. Yes? We meet in library where no one can hear us talk."

"Just before Kareem was killed, you met him again in the library. What did you talk about?" Murphy unconsciously leaned forward in his eagerness to hear the answer.

For a moment, it looked like Hisham would deny it, but a piercing look from the detective squelched any resistance. "With broken crate *AJ* and missing mask, Kareem talk about wanting more money. He scared of police. He scared of jails. He want to run. Kareem come to me and ask for more money so he can leave, but I say I have none to give. He say he go to police and confess. Work out bargain," Hisham explained.

"And what did you do?" Murphy prodded while writing.

"I scare. I fear for jail and my life. I tell him to meet me on deck to discuss. That I bring some money." Hisham's face dropped again. "I scare of jail too. On way to Kareem, I see tool leaning against wall. I pick up and walk out. Yes? Big fog covers the ship, and I walk up back of Kareem. He no see me. I no want to go to jail. I scare he speak police and me be kill. I want to go to America." Hisham's voice was shaking.

"So you approached him from behind and had the wrench in your hand. What did you do next?" Murphy stared hard at Hisham.

"I hit Kareem one with tool. He fall. I scare. I knew bowl is in shoe so I throw into sea with tool. Then I go for my cabin and wait." Hisham began crying again.

Murphy addressed the other two men at the table. "Well, that should be enough for a preliminary interview. We can take a more detailed statement once we get him downtown. Did you have any questions, Stephen?"

"Just one. Hisham, can you describe the lawyer?"

Hisham looked at Anderson. "Sand hair with blue eye. Very cold look. Taller than me with nice clothes. Not fat, not thin."

Anderson just nodded.

Murphy said, "We can get our artist to do up a composite sketch and see if we can get a face on this guy. Anything else?"

Both Bryant and Anderson shook their heads; further questions could wait. "Very well. This is Detective Murphy, terminating the interview at 10:32 AM."

Bryant shut off the recorder and the men rose. Murphy turned to Hisham. "We will be taking you to the police station downtown in a short time. Until then, if you want anything, just ask the officer by the wall."

Hisham just sat there motionless, his head angled down again. Anderson, Bryant, and Murphy all left the library and closed the door behind them. Anderson gestured for the men to follow him. They went out on deck on the port side of the ship, where no one else was about.

Bryant was the first to speak. "Stephen, what is the matter? You turned white as a ghost halfway through."

"Remember the DC-3? Kavanagh said 'It looks like you pissed off the wrong lawyer, pal.' What if the two incidents were not isolated? What if they wanted me out of the picture? They wanted it to look like an accident, and it was almost two weeks before the ship docked."

"Their plan was to have the theft discovered in Pittsburgh, which meant you shouldn't have even been involved to begin with," Bryant objected.

"I know. However, I would have been called in to investigate the *Costarican Trader* portion of the trip once the theft had been discovered, if only to prove there was no valid claim against Worthor. Given my track record, maybe they just wanted to increase their odds of success."

Murphy spoke up. "If this ties Sterling Thompson into the picture, then Hisham is now a very important witness. If his lawyer arranged things, we can tie this directly back to Thompson. I will make sure we have extra security in place before we move Hisham.

"This also makes finding the lawyer a priority. I will get on the composite sketch as soon as I get Hisham downtown. At least we know what legal firm to begin our search at. Look, until we get this locked down, I don't want anyone to mention

Thompson's name. All sorts of obstacles will appear if this gets out."

The others nodded in agreement.

Bryant spoke. "I'd like an agent sitting in on your interviews with Hisham, Mike. If this generates a definitive link to Thompson we can pursue that end of things. I'll make sure they speak Arabic as well, which may help."

"No problem. I'll keep you in the loop. Okay, I'll see you two in a few minutes. I have to make some calls." Murphy walked away a few steps to use his cell phone.

* * *

Anderson was so preoccupied with his thoughts that he was surprised when Bryant reached out for a handshake. "Congratulations, Stephen. You figured that out nicely. With Hisham's confession, we don't need to rely on your dubious recording. Catching Hisham and Kareem talking in there did help to understand who was involved. His statement matches what you recorded. That makes it a clean case."

Anderson shook his hand. "Thanks. Do me a favor. I know Doctor Wade has been having a hard time with Carnegie management. She has been telling me there are rumors of replacing her flitting around. When you have the press conference announcing this, anything you can say on her behalf would be appreciated. You might also want to have a word with Al Dhabit and fill him in on the Jensen connection. No need to mention Thompson, but he needs to know they were at least unknowing participants in this."

"Done. By the way, I am happy to give you the credit you are due as well. You certainly earned it." Bryant smiled.

"You know my policy on that, Bill. You get the credit in full. As far as the press is concerned, I don't exist." Anderson smiled back. Keeping his past hidden was the real motivator, but Anderson could not admit even to his friend. Too many questions would be asked.

"No, but you do get the paycheck," Bryant observed, laughing.

"That reminds me. I need to make a call," Anderson said, grabbing his cell phone and dialing.

"Mr. Worthor's office," a formal female voice said.

"Good morning, Galina. It is Stephen Anderson. Is Warren available, please?"

"Mr. Worthor is at home, but he instructed me to route your calls to him. One moment, please, Mr. Anderson."

After a few moments of classical music, Warren Worthor's easily-identifiable voice came on the line. "Stephen, good morning."

"Good morning, Warren. I have good news for you. We located the mask, and it is unharmed. It was secreted in the forward hold inside another crate. The police have one man in custody, a member of the Cairo museum staff. The other man involved is dead. He was an Egyptian guard. I will forward you a written report as soon as I get back to my place."

Victoria came out on deck. She walked over, smiling at him.

"Nonsense, Stephen. I want you over here this evening. I owe you a night out for this one. You saved us a lot of money once again. Well, apart from your hefty fee, of course." Warren laughed.

"I have been thinking about that. With an insured value of $80 million, my twelve percent commission works out to 9.6 million."

Victoria's eyebrows skyrocketed.

Anderson continued, "What would you say to just five million and a first-class trip for two to Bali, instead?" Anderson looked down into her amber eyes as he spoke; Victoria beamed and slowly nodded at him.

Worthor didn't hesitate. "That is what they call a no-brainer, mister. Deal! I'll call Janet and make arrangements. Call me around 3 PM, and I will fill you in on the details."

"Thanks, Warren. I'll be bringing a guest as well. Talk to you in a couple of hours."

"Right. Bye." Worthor hung up.

* * *

Victoria couldn't smile more widely if she tried.

"So. I take it you would like to go to Bali with me?" Anderson asked simply while clipping the phone back to his belt holster.

"I think so." Victoria moved closer to him. The closer she got, the more she had to tilt her head up to look into his gray eyes. *The mask is safely recovered, the exhibition will move ahead, my career is back on track, and now he is offering to take me to Bali. Kiss me, kiss me, kiss me...* went through her mind.

Anderson leaned down and wrapped his arms around her waist. She moved closer, placed her palms and forearms on his chest, and their lips touched for the first time in a gentle kiss that lasted only a few seconds. They backed off and looked into each other's eyes for a moment.

She felt Anderson's fingertips caress her lower back. Victoria slid her hands up around his neck, and they kissed more intensely. The space between their bodies completely disappeared.

CHAPTER 17 – CUTTING THE STRINGS

Victoria stood in Anderson's embrace for a long time. They spoke quietly. Others who came along seemed to recognize the intimacy and avoided the area.

"I have to leave soon. The exhibit will be heading out as soon as we can arrange for the trucks again," Victoria said softly.

"Yes. How long will the exhibit keep you in Pittsburgh?" Anderson asked.

"Three weeks, but there's at least a week on either side of that to unpack and repack. Once the shipment is received by the next museum, I'm free as a bird."

"Sounds like you will need a nice vacation after all that work. At least you know you have something waiting for you at the end. Besides, Pittsburgh is not that far away, and I do have some extra 'mad money' to spend on some out-of-town trips now. Mind if I drop by? I have some frequent flyer miles to burn," Anderson asked gently. His fingers stroked the side of her face and upper cheek.

"I'll take you to a fish restaurant I have been dying to try, on the top floor of an apartment building overlooking the junction of the Allegheny and Monongahela Rivers. I cannot imagine a more romantic spot for dinner," Victoria gushed.

Anderson spoke softly. "Well, I don't know about tomorrow, but I know we have tonight. We are going out for dinner with the Worthors."

Bryant approached them. "Sorry to interrupt, but we are taking Hisham off the vessel now. Thought you would want to know."

Victoria and Anderson separated and followed Bryant around the front of the superstructure. Victoria walked close to Anderson, but as they passed the rounded superstructure, she fell slightly behind. Uniformed police began exiting the starboard hatch. A pair of officers came ahead, followed close behind by Hisham. Hisham had his hands handcuffed in front. The police had placed him in a thick bulletproof vest. The light blue color of the vest contrasted against Hisham's white shirt. Two more uniformed officers walked immediately behind him. Anderson began walking toward the railing.

* * *

Kogan saw the target come into view. He squeezed earplugs into his ears as he confirmed the man on deck was the same as in the photograph. He instantly swapped from his binoculars to the rifle and cradled the butt into his shoulder. The optical sight was not as powerful as the binoculars, but he could easily spot the target. His instructions on when he could act were simple, and those conditions were now met. The rifle's safety switch was flipped off, and he lined the sights up ahead of where the target was walking. Kogan's finger rested on the trigger guard while he waited, assessing wind and other factors that could affect the shot.

* * *

As he walked to the railing, Anderson watched Hisham descend the walkway. The railing was only waist high. Victoria was a half step behind to his right. As he moved forward,

Anderson felt the hair begin to rise on his neck; something was wrong.

He scanned the dock below, but he only saw a few police cars with rotating lights parked at the foot of the gangway, ready to receive the prisoner. The adjoining warehouses had a few security personnel standing on the roof. Their weapons were down, and they were all relaxed.

Still, something was wrong. He could sense it. During his Legion days, he would have taken cover instantly upon having this sensation while in a combat zone. It was something he had learned not to ignore.

Mike Murphy was standing at the foot of the gangway, talking to one of the police drivers. Anderson moved sideways toward the gangway, trying to get his attention. "Mike!"

* * *

Kogan saw the target would walk directly into his sights. His fingertip left the trigger guard and lightly landed on the trigger. The wind was minimal, and even at twenty-one hundred feet, the effects were easily adjusted for. With a muzzle velocity of twenty-eight hundred feet per second, it would take almost a second for the bullet to travel the required distance. Kogan made sure he led the target by a sufficient amount to compensate for the motion. He squeezed the trigger just as the target's side touched the second ring of the cross hairs in the scope so the man would walk right into the bullet's path. The ignition of the two hundred and ninety grains of propellant rocked the weapon back into Kogan's shoulder. The spent shell casing was ejected, and a new round was automatically chambered. It sounded more like a cannon than a rifle going off and left his ears ringing even with the earplugs.

An unexpected gust of wind forced the bullet up slightly as it traveled, but the effects were negligible, and it still struck the intended target.

Hisham was a third of the way down the gangway when he was hit. His type IIIA bulletproof vest was designed to stop up to a 7.62 rifle round, but there was no body armor in existence that could stop a .50 caliber round.

The police would later determine that the bullet came at him at roughly a fifteen-degree angle, thereby avoiding the policemen. It struck him in the upper right chest, passed through the vest, nicked the top of his heart, carried on to sever his spine, and then passed through the back of the vest, impacting on the inch-thick hull plating of the *Costarican Trader*. Even then, the bullet still pushed through six more interior walls, and it finally stopped, flattened, on the inside of the opposite steel hull.

The only positive thing the vest did was to contain the majority of the gore and bone that exploded from the victim's back, preventing it from spraying the policemen behind.

Hisham collapsed on the gangway and had just started to roll when the report of the rifle reached the ship. Several loud echoes came almost immediately from many directions. Victoria screamed, and Anderson grabbed her, shoving her to the decking. He instinctively placed his body between her and the danger.

Hisham, already dead, rolled off the gangway under the lower rope balustrade. He rotated as he fell, and his chest impacted on the side of the pier. His hips were on the edge of the dock, and his legs hung over the side. It looked like he might fall, but against the odds, he hung motionless.

Police, FBI, and the private security agents all drew their sidearms and looked for a target. They scanned the top of the warehouse and buildings within a few blocks, waiting for a second shot, but they saw nothing. The suddenness of the attack shocked everyone. Both the police and FBI began making radio calls.

* * *

Kogan was on the move the second he saw the bullet strike. He applied the rifle safety switch and collapsed the bipod and monopod. The rifle and binoculars went into the long case, and he snapped it shut. Kogan turned and recovered the ejected shell casing off the floor. Having practiced with this weapon in the Nevada desert, he knew exactly where to find it. The shell case was hot, and he quickly wrapped it up in a fast food napkin before dropping it in his designated 'garbage' grocery food bag. Kogan pulled out the earplugs and dropped them into the garbage as well. The photos of Hisham and Kareem, plus the two plastic bags, went into the zippered bag. He put on the hard hat. Then, with long case in one hand and the zippered bag in the other, he stepped toward the door. He paused, turned back, and scanned the room for anything he had forgotten. Seeing nothing out of place, he rapidly descended the stairs, breaking the caution tape with his body as he moved through it.

He was at his pickup truck within twenty seconds and loaded the bags behind the seat. Within a minute and fifteen seconds of taking the shot, he was driving out the front gates. He took his primary exfiltration route. Kogan stripped off the surgical gloves and slipped them into the bag beside him.

Driving below the speed limit, he went three blocks north before turning left and going west for six more blocks. He looked in the rearview mirror and was glad to see red and blue police lights pulling into the intersection and stopping traffic two blocks behind him. He drove for another fifteen minutes into a busy commercial area with several strip malls. He pulled into a random fast food restaurant and went to the very rear of the parking lot. Seeing a pair of garbage cans, he pulled into an empty parking spot near them. Kogan kept the truck between him and the restaurant to avoid any surveillance cameras. Reaching behind the seat, he grabbed the plastic garbage bag, tied the top of the bag up, and put it in the trash. He reached for the silenced pistol next. The silencer was unscrewed, and the disassembled weapon went into his bag. He slid the coveralls off and placed them in the second plastic grocery bag that held the rest of his unconsumed water and snacks. The hard hat went on top.

Kogan got back in the truck and drove another block before pulling into a second fast food place. Again, in the rear parking lot, he placed the hard hat and second bag into separate trash receptacles before driving away.

He needed to call the number given to him then arrange to have the rifle and pistol couriered back to an accommodation address in California. Afterward, he would make his way back to the car rental business to return the truck, after wiping down all the areas he had touched with alcohol wipes. Kogan knew he had more than enough time to make the west coast flight to L.A. in six hours. Then a shuttle flight to San Francisco to pick up the weapon and finally pick up his car for the nine-hour drive home. He would be back in Las Vegas by the following afternoon.

He had been told that neither of the men in the photographs could be taken into custody. Watching one kill the other had been unexpected, but it made his job a lot easier. He still completed one contract, and confirmation of his payment would doubtless be waiting for him in his designated Grand Cayman account when he got home.

* * *

Bryant jogged up to Anderson and Victoria, who were prone on the deck. The FBI agent holstered his sidearm as he approached. "They got Hisham. He's dead. Looks clear."

Anderson released Victoria and began to stand. He assisted her to her feet, and she instantly was in his arms, shaking. Anderson held her close.

Bryant spoke while patting beads of sweat from his forehead with his jacket sleeve. The day wasn't hot. "We've locked down a five-block radius and are searching everyone leaving the area. However, we just lost our only witness."

Anderson just nodded. Bryant saw Victoria's state and withdrew. Anderson was glad he had recovered the mask, but he regretted the price that had to be paid for it.

At least his job was over. The police and FBI had to take the investigation from there, so it was out of his hands. That was fine with him, as he had more important things to take care of.

While he had known Victoria only a short time, it was nice to have her in his arms, and she seemed to share that sentiment. He took her around the back side of the superstructure to the port side of the ship. There were all alone there, and he let her calm down while in his embrace.

* * *

"Good afternoon. I am Special Agent William Bryant of the FBI. Thank you for coming on such short notice. We have some background information sheets being handed out now for your reference. To my right is Detective Michael Murphy, Robbery-Homicide. To my left is Doctor Mohammed Al Dhabit, Deputy Administrator of the Cairo Museum and coordinator of the Tutankhamun National Exhibit. I have a brief statement, and then we would be happy to take your questions."

"At approximately nine thirty this morning, the funerary mask of King Tutankhamun was recovered intact by agents of the FBI in cooperation with the local police commanded by Detective Murphy."

Many brilliant camera flashes went off almost simultaneously. With the already bright lights of the many video cameras, it was almost unbearable. Bryant had to avert his eyes to avoid the bulk of the illumination. He ignored the yelled questions and continued speaking when the flashes slowed. "I would like to thank Doctor Victoria Wade, who was the local exhibit representative of the Carnegie Museum of Natural History. She was unable to be here due to other commitments. Doctor Wade's expertise as an Egyptologist played a key role in the recovery of the pharaoh's mask, and her participation in the investigation sped things up considerably.

"As it has already been reported, a member of the Egyptian private security force on board the *Costarican Trader* was murdered late yesterday evening. His family has been notified, and I've been authorized to release his name. It is Kareem Al-Asned from Banha, Egypt, which is a suburb of Cairo. There is more information on him in the handout. His killer was arrested

THE LEGIONNAIRE: MASK OF THE PHARAOH

this morning and subsequently confessed to the murder of Al-Asned during questioning on board. As the suspect was being taken off the ship, he was gunned down by a sniper who has so far eluded police."

More flashes went off as more questions were shouted. Video taken from the barricade of Hisham being shot and falling off the gangway had made all of the major cable news outlets. Again, Bryant ignored the shouted inquiries. "The sniper fired from the top floor of an abandoned building several streets away from the docks. That location is currently being subjected to a thorough examination by a forensic team. The shooting victim's name cannot be released until his next of kin have been notified. A coordinated manhunt for the killer, involving city, state, and federal law enforcement, is underway."

More shouted questions and strobe flashes conspired to interrupt him. He carried on over the din. "Doctor Al Dhabit has asked to make a statement about the exhibit. Doctor."

Bryant stood aside and Al Dhabit took the podium, his 'grandfather' smile evident. More flashes went off.

"Please, please. My old eyes are not as good as they once were," Al Dhabit said with feigned good humor, producing a few smiles among the press, but it only intensified the flashes. He waited until they had abated somewhat before continuing. "I have just finished consulting with the Egyptian Antiquities Council. The Council along with the government of Egypt is very happy the mask of the pharaoh was located. We wish to thank the FBI and local police forces who assisted in this effort. Given that the mask was recovered without damage, I am pleased to announce the National Tutankhamun Exhibit will proceed. Advance ticket sales have encouraged us to not disappoint the tens of thousands of people who are expecting to see this exhibit. There will be one unfortunate amendment to the secondary tour. Due to the delay caused by the theft, we will be unable to accommodate the Jensen Museum in our revised schedule. Instead, I have been in touch with the next museum stop in Charlotte, North Carolina, and they will be extending their original exhibit schedule by eleven days to accommodate us.

We apologize to the staff and patrons of the Jensen, but this schedule change is simply unavoidable because of the delay."

"*Doctor, can we see the mask!*" screamed a reporter in the rear of the crowd. It was so loud that he could not ignore it.

"You may. In exactly six days, the doors will open at the Carnegie Museum of Natural History in Pittsburgh, and you will be able to see the mask and several hundred other artifacts from the New Kingdom. We look forward to working with Doctor Victoria Wade to coordinate the Pittsburgh portion of the tour. I understand she has gone ahead to coordinate the new schedule."

Now that the one shouted question had been answered, more followed. The news conference descended into the usual anarchy.

* * *

Anderson turned off the television. Victoria lay on the couch under his left arm. Her back and shoulders rested against him.

"Just before we left, Bill said he was going to fill Al Dhabit in on the Jensen museum finances. Having the mask found hidden in their shipment did nothing to help. Sounds like he came up with an elegant solution. The Jensen will have to refund the advance ticket money now," Anderson said.

She looked up at him. "I called Sid. He said he'd handle the next couple of days for me. He also heard from Cahill. Ticket sales for the exhibition have sold out, and they are considering printing a few thousand more. I also have universal and unreserved support from the board. Surprise, surprise. Thank you, Stephen."

"You are welcome. I dislike bureaucracy as much as you do. They won't be able to take you off the job now." He smiled.

"What time do we meet Mr. Worthor?" She looked at her watch.

"Seven-thirty. He is sending his driver to pick us up here. We will meet Warren and his wife Janet at their house. You sure you want to go?" Anderson replied.

"I didn't at first, but I think a night out will do me some good. Seeing that poor man shot right in front of me. That'll take some time to forget. I need something to take my mind off it. Well, I need to get ready. Looks like my 'little black dress' gets another evening out. It's too bad I didn't pack more, but I only thought I'd be here for a few days."

"Well, I won't be offended by seeing it again. As I recall it was rather a nice outfit. Of course, that might have just been the lady underneath."

Victoria smiled and walked away. She ascended the stairs to her room and closed the door behind her. She had stripped off her clothes and was just in underwear when there was a polite knock at the door.

"Who is it?" Victoria asked as she pulled on her green robe.

"It's the plumber. I've come to fix the sink," said Masumi, several octaves lower than normal.

Victoria opened the door, and Masumi forced her way in with three large flat cardboard boxes in her hands. Masumi pressed Victoria back into the room with the boxes and closed the door behind her with her backside. Both women smiled.

"I just got back with Vinnie. Stephen called ahead and said you were heading out with Mr. Worthor." Masumi dropped the packages on the bed. "He also said you might need something appropriate for dinner, so I went shopping!" Masumi excitedly clapped her hands. She flipped the top box open, revealing a bold red slip dress with spaghetti straps, surrounded by white tissue paper. The labels were still attached.

Victoria picked it up; the side slit in the skirt went almost to the hip.

"Oh my God, I can't wear that." The traditional and conservative woman in Victoria recoiled from the red material and sexy slit. "Besides, I don't have shoes to match."

Masumi put one hand on her hip and bent her other hand at the wrist. "I just *knew* you would say that." She closed the top box and pushed it aside. Inside the second box was a similar dress to the first, but in black and a little more conservative. Victoria reached in and pulled it out by the straps. It was long, sheer, and made out of fine polyester fabric that flowed when it moved. Victoria held it up against her and looked in the mirror. "I don't know…"

"Well, try it on. That's the only way you'll know," Masumi prompted.

Victoria dropped the robe on the bed and pulled the dress on. The upper half of the dress was shaped in an X, both in front and back. The hem went down to mid-calf, which was fine, but when she leaned forward the dress fell away from her body. "I can't wear a bra with this, and if I lean forward you can see everything," she said embarrassed.

"I just *knew* you would say that," Masumi repeated, with the exact tone and mannerism as before. Victoria removed the dress. Masumi put it away and opened the third box. This dress was flat black, but Victoria could see a decorative design with sequins. "I know you will like this one. It is a Herve Leger bandage dress. Just put it straight on," Masumi commanded.

The dress was a lot heavier than it looked, but it fit well. It was sleeveless with broad shoulder straps to support the weight. Masumi helped her zip it up. Across the bust was an X-shaped overlay of black sequins. The pattern sparkled in the light of the room. The material was snug, but not tight. *Not a bad fit overall.* Victoria only had one observation. "The hem is a little north of the knee, isn't it?"

"Well, Stephen said you were going to 'dress up' for tonight, and that is as far 'up' as current fashion will let you go." Masumi laughed. "Come on, girl. You have the legs for it. Live a little. Plus, you won't flash half the restaurant in that little number," she finished impishly.

"It is really sparkly." Victoria turned and looked at herself from all angles in the mirror. The short hemline was only a few inches above her knee, but she still thought it decent, and she decided she liked it.

"Oh, one sec. I almost forgot." Masumi ran out of the room. She was back in a minute carrying a black silk handbag with sequins sewn onto the surface. A long black shoulder cord was attached to both ends of the purse. "I got this years ago. It's a Makki. You can borrow it if you like."

Victoria looked in the mirror and saw the handbag went perfectly with the dress. Over the last few days, she had dealt with the theft of the mask, the threat of losing her position, a murder, and finally seeing a man shot a few feet away from her. After all of that, she was not expecting Masumi's kindness, and the thoughtfulness made her tear up a little. She hugged the younger woman.

Victoria pulled away after a few seconds and wiped her eyes. "Sold. How much do I owe you for this?"

"Come on, Victoria. You don't owe me a thing. It is a gift!" Masumi had her hands on her hips and looked terribly insulted.

"I can't have you buying me a dress," Victoria said defiantly.

"Oh don't worry, I didn't. Stephen had me put it on his credit card." Both women laughed and hugged again.

"Now you go get ready while I go try on the red dress. It is way too small for you anyway." Masumi said, retreating with a devilish grin.

CHAPTER 18 – A REUNION OF OLD FRIENDS

Worthor's driver called Anderson on his car phone to announce his arrival time. Victoria and Anderson were both ready and made it downstairs just as the white stretch limousine pulled up to the door.

Anderson wore a conservative ash gray single-breasted Brooks Brothers suit. Custom tailored, it fit perfectly. A thin-banded tie of several different red shades was around his neck. The bands were slanted at a forty-five degree angle.

He noticed that Victoria had again put her hair up with the black butterfly, and she'd added black silk hose, a choker of pearls, and a different set of silver dangle earrings. She wore the same sandals and scarf around her shoulders as the evening before.

The driver of the limousine hopped out exactly at seven-thirty and made it to the rear door in time to open it for them. Victoria entered first.

Anderson knew the driver. He was a former college football player who had aspirations of the major leagues before a knee injury removed that option. He was at least six-foot-four, and his muscular frame was barely contained in the simple black suit he wore. Apart from being Warren Worthor's driver, he was also one of his 'minders'—a polite term for *bodyguard*. Worthor had several minders working around the clock. "Good evening, Kenneth," Anderson said.

"Good evening, sir," was the response as Kenneth tipped his chauffeur hat.

Anderson climbed into the back when Victoria was clear of the door.

The Lincoln stretch limousine was decked out in the finest materials. The white leather seats were plush and soft. Mahogany-grained wood cabinetry stood out directly behind the driver's seat with built-in entertainment center, small fridge, mini-bar with several liquor bottles, crystal glassware, a television, and a CD/DVD player. An opaque power privacy window was between the rear passenger compartment and the driver's seat. Six people could comfortably sit in the rear.

As the door closed behind Anderson, he watched Victoria take in the back compartment. "Wow, I wish my apartment was this nice."

"Warren has a Maybach stretch he uses for entertaining foreign businessmen which is even nicer. However, this will certainly do for tonight," Anderson responded.

The limo moved off, and the ride was very comfortable. With its dynamic suspension, efficient sound insulation, and comfortable seats the journey was quite pleasant.

The car wound westward, taking the interstate in the opposite direction from the city. An interchange put them on a northern four-lane expressway, and in a short time they found themselves driving with forest on either side of the highway. Kenneth took an off ramp and turned east. A few more turns later, and both the quality of the homes and the spacing between them increased dramatically.

* * *

Kenneth turned down a private paved road, and they drove for at least two miles through a healthy forest. Birch, elm, poplar, and spruce trees were their only companions. Victoria saw no manmade items for the entire distance. The trees ended without warning, transitioning to a perfectly flat and green lawn that any country club would kill for. Victoria saw a large putting green off to her right. They turned a corner, and she gasped as she saw Worthor's home. It was at least six thousand square feet. Spotlights in the grounds and under the eaves highlighted every feature. The house was an L shape, with a wide circular driveway running around the inner courtyard. Inside the area defined by the driveway was a large Japanese Zen stone garden. Raked lines in the quartz-rich gravel surrounded large stones, making the space look like a sea frozen in time. A single seven-son flower tree emerged from the center of the white rock, clusters of white flowers present on the tips of the branches. A four-car garage comprised one side of the L, while the other was a modern three-story structure.

Unadorned concrete garden walls held small shrubs on both sides of the entryway. The rough stucco exterior walls were Spartan; adornments would have detracted from the appearance of the massive building. The top two floors were accommodated under a sloped red tile roof and several cut-outs had been made in the roofline to allow windows and verandahs. The roof had several large skylights and two unusually large white chimneys, one at either end of the building. The house was obviously modern, but it had several classic elements like pillared arches in the design that hinted at Spanish influences.

The limo pulled up and parked in front of the entryway, and Kenneth promptly opened the door for the couple to alight. Anderson went first and held out a hand to assist Victoria out the door. Arm in arm, they climbed up the cut granite steps to the front entry. The door opened when they were several steps away, and a plump balding man of about forty greeted them. He was dressed as a traditional English butler with a black tail coat, a slate gray vest, and a white shirt with a high collar and wide matching tie. "Good evening, Doctor Wade, Mr. Anderson."

"Good evening, Sherman," Anderson replied.

"Mr. and Mrs. Worthor will join you in the great room momentarily. May I take your wrap, Doctor?"

"Thank you, Sherman." Victoria slipped the scarf off her shoulders, unused to this kind of treatment.

"This way, please." Sherman led the way, and the couple followed. Victoria watched the butler; she had never seen a man dressed in a formal coat with tails outside of movies.

The entryway had an Italian marble inlay floor and ornate crystal chandelier above. They immediately turned left into a large great room that was at least forty feet long. The natural stone fireplace at one end soared to the ceiling. The warm hardwood floors welcomed them.

Three couches were arranged in a sunken area before the fire, putting occupants at eye height with the flames. The wall to the back of the house was a series of large glass windows overlooking the ocean. Victoria walked over to them and could see the house was near the edge of a cliff.

The room was so large that Victoria did not even notice the grand piano in the far corner until she was close enough to touch it. A pair of closed double glass doors led into a dining room, and she saw an exquisitely set table waiting for them.

"May I get anything for you, sir, Doctor?" asked the butler.

"No, thank you, Sherman," answered Anderson. Victoria was speechless.

"Very good, sir." Sherman withdrew from the room.

"What do you think?" Anderson asked her.

She looked at him over her shoulder and mouthed *Wow*. Anderson laughed and went over to her. "I know. I had the same reaction the first couple of times I was here. Don't worry. Warren and Janet are regular people. A lot of this is for entertaining business acquaintances, and—"

"Stephen! Glad you could make it." Warren Worthor strode into the room, wearing a Brioni black pinstripe suit and red striped tie with a regal-looking lady at his side. Sherman followed behind the owners and stopped in the doorway.

Worthor vigorously shook Anderson's hand while Victoria examined the other woman's outfit. Mrs. Worthor wore a royal blue silk halter dress with asymmetrical overlays with a conservative hemline just under her knees. T-strap pumps, a solitary sapphire pendant, and matching earrings completed the outfit. Her long hair was also up and had a natural strawberry blonde hue. She was in excellent shape, at least ten years younger than Warren, and had an ethereal quality. Her oval face and emerald eyes could have proudly adorned the cover of any women's magazine.

"Good evening. Warren, Janet, may I introduce Doctor Victoria Wade? Victoria, this is Warren and Janet Worthor."

The women shook hands. "Pleased to meet you, Victoria. Welcome to our home," Janet said warmly, with an Irish accent.

"Thank you. It is lovely. I was just looking out at your view of the ocean."

"We decided to build it on this site because of the view. The only thing missing is the sun setting in the evening, but we are on the wrong coast for that. We do have dazzling sunrises, however. Did you notice the gardens out back?" Janet asked.

"No. I didn't." Victoria had missed them completely.

"Let's go take a look. Warren, would you mind entertaining Stephen? This way, please. Now Victoria, where did you get those darling earrings?" Janet led her off to the windows.

* * *

Worthor turned to Anderson and spoke immediately—not harshly, but not as gregarious as usual. "Okay, Stephen; something I need to know. Contractually, I'm obliged to give you twelve percent, but you are willing to settle for half that. Why?"

"Well, Warren it is quite simple. First, you have been a good boss and friend to me since I came here. Second, 9.6 million is a ridiculous amount of money, and I simply don't need it. Five is more than fair. Besides, taking less will make you look good in front of the board. You can tell them you negotiated with me for a few hours."

Worthor slapped him lightly on the bicep. "The day I hired you was a great one for both of us, I think. We are going to be eating here tonight. I wanted to get out to the Cheshire Country Club, but Herb Waxman rented the whole place for his

daughter's wedding reception. Carl has been working on some traditional German cooking for us, so I suspect we are in for a treat. Like a drink?"

"Ginger ale, please."

Worthor turned to the butler. "Sherman, a ginger ale for Stephen. Champagne for the rest."

"Yes, sir," Sherman said before retreating.

"Come on, lad; sit down. You need to tell me all about this little adventure of yours." The men made their way to the couches. They each sat on the near ends of different couches. A gentle crackle of burning hard wood added to the atmosphere. Anderson briefly recounted the events of the last few days before concluding, "...And that is why I feel Sterling Thompson is not only responsible for this theft and murder, but also for the Augusta break-in."

"Augusta? Oh, you mean because of the stamp that was used to lure you to the hangar. I see. Well, without evidence, there's nothing we can do. If the FBI is aware of this, then they will pick up the investigation from here. Do you think he'll come after you again?" Worthor asked, concerned.

"I doubt it, at least in the short term. He is a businessman, and there's no profit in revenge. With the FBI alerted, it would be foolish to try."

Sherman returned with a silver tray that held a glass of ginger ale, three fluted crystal glasses, and a sterling silver bucket filled with ice. A bottle of champagne stuck out from the bucket. Sherman handed the ginger ale to Anderson, then picked up the bottle and showed it to Worthor. "I thought a 1990 Bollinger, Grand Année, would be suitable for a celebration, sir."

"Excellent. Thank you, Sherman."

With deft fingers, Sherman removed the wire harness from the cork. He applied pressure with his thumbs, and the cork flew out with a traditional pop of expanding gas. The cork landed right in back of the fireplace.

The women appeared just in time to take a glass full of champagne. The men stood as the ladies approached.

Warren took his glass and raised it. "If I may make a toast? Stephen, I would have to work very hard to find a gentleman as honorable and hardworking as you. To your health and continued success. Cheers."

"Cheers," said everyone else, smiling while they clinked glasses. Anderson looked uncharacteristically subdued and mildly embarrassed.

The champagne was excellent, and everyone relaxed back on the couches. Anderson sipped his ginger ale.

"Stephen, Victoria told me a little of this affair. If I may ask, what was the first thing that aroused your suspicions?" Janet asked, leaning forward.

"Well, the first thing that really got my notice was the guard schedule. In the interview with Doctor Al Dhabit, he mentioned that Hisham had arranged the guard schedule to coincide with Eastern Standard Time. However, when we spoke with Hisham, he said he had never before been out of Egypt. It seemed unlikely that a man who had never traveled outside of Egypt could take such a thing into account, especially when he was considered to be a fairly simple man. I suspect the person who planned this thought that up to make sure the late night guard shift stayed in the early hours and did not shift six hours earlier as the ship progressed westward. It did not fit Hisham's character at all to think to that depth."

"So it's just like what you experienced with the missing Picasso last year," Janet observed.

"Exactly. It was something very small that did not feel right. I often feel like a man in an unfamiliar darkened house when I start an investigation. You spend a long time finding the first light switch, but once it is on, it makes it easier to find the next switch, and so on."

"I like that analogy." Warren said. "I need to use that at the next board meeting. Some of the financial reports they are sending us lately are cryptic. Mind if I use it?"

"Feel free." Anderson smiled.

322

"Victoria was also saying she lived in Egypt for several years, and... Yes, Sherman?" Janet asked the butler, who was hovering at a polite distance.

"Pardon the intrusion, madame. Dinner is served in the blue room."

Everyone stood and followed the butler down the room. Sherman turned at the grand piano and opened the pair of double doors with beveled glass leading into the formal dining room.

The carpet was a Prussian blue, thick and a dream to walk on. The walls were an ice blue, and white wood accents broke it up nicely. The room could accommodate perhaps a dozen people, but the minimized table could amply seat four. A light wood sideboard took up a lot of the far wall.

Sherman entered the dining room and stood behind a chair. "Mrs. Worthor." She sat down. Sherman then grabbed the chair to Janet's left and said, "Doctor Wade."

Warren indicated that Anderson should sit opposite Victoria, and he himself sat at the head of the table.

* * *

Victoria looked around. The chandelier scattered the light through multicolored glass, adding a subtle texture to the simply decorated room. The windows looking out over the sea were hard to ignore, and she could see whitecaps further out. Opposite the windows, an open door led to a large butler's pantry and wet bar.

The table itself was perfectly set with shining silver utensils, candleholders, and trays, all etched with the same ornate floral theme. The thick off-white linens and the tablecloth were made of the same material. The centerpiece was an arrangement of fresh-cut flowers low enough that Victoria could clearly see Stephen over the top. White china dishes sat on blue chargers, which matched the theme of the room. Victoria studied the salad plate already set before her. She recognized lettuce, shaved carrot, and Spanish onion, but there were a few other things she couldn't identify. The thin dressing had spice and pepper flakes.

Sherman lit the candles and went to the sideboard. He returned with a bottle of wine and stood beside Warren. "I thought a Riesling for tonight's meal, sir."

"Excellent," said Warren, and Sherman opened the wine.

Janet turned to Victoria. "We were lucky to pick up Carl. He's a Cordon Bleu–trained chef, and until last year, he worked for the president of Germany."

Victoria was impressed. "Why did he leave such a good job?"

"The president lost the election and could no longer afford to keep him," Janet explained. "Being German, he likes to cook his native dishes, but I often ask him for Irish meals, and Warren does enjoy his roast beef or chicken. Carl was excited to give us a full German menu tonight."

Sherman poured the wine, and Warren took several minutes to assess the wine's color, aroma, and taste. When done, he nodded, and Sherman filled his and the ladies' glasses.

"Anyway, the salad is getting cold. Dig in," Warren joked. He picked up his fork, and the rest followed suit. They began to eat. Victoria was pleasantly surprised.

Janet saw Victoria's reaction. "Good dressing?"

"Lovely. I thought it would be watery, but the flavor is wonderful."

Janet smiled. "Carl told us he's not the chef for those on a diet."

Warren spoke up. "Stephen, I was thinking. The *Mary Rose* is currently in Singapore. If you wanted to use her instead of staying in a resort, I can have the crew sail her to Bali with a week's warning. From there, they would take you anywhere you wanted to go. At least then you would not be stuck in one place."

"Very kind of you, Warren, but I am only fifty percent of the decision-making process for that trip." Anderson glanced over at Victoria.

"I'm sorry. What is the *Mary Rose*?" she asked.

Warren answered with a gleam in his eye, "It's a hundred and ninety foot, three-mast sailboat. I bought it in a tax sale. The

Silicon Valley millionaire who owned it forgot to pay the IRS their due. It has a huge master's cabin and eight smaller guest quarters. There's a formal dining salon, library—all the comforts of home. A crew of twelve mans her. You just point and tell them where to sail, and off you go. It has all the latest gadgets, and I just had a decent dive platform and a pair of Jet Skis added."

"We just got back from Singapore, and we stayed on board while Warren was negotiating some contracts. It really is a wonderfully relaxing place to stay," Janet added.

"Sounds wonderful. I don't know how to say no to that." Victoria looked over at Anderson.

"You can't. I never take *no* for an answer, young lady. Then it is settled." Warren gave a satisfied smile.

Janet turned to Warren. "The wine is perfect, darling."

Sherman took the empty salad plates to the kitchen. He then returned with four plates on a silver tray. He served the Worthors first and then the guests.

"Potato pancake with sautéed spinach and Swiss cheese for your appetizer," Sherman announced. He topped up the wine glasses before leaving.

Warren picked up his utensils. "I hope our meager city is measuring up to your standards, Victoria."

"I must admit, I have not seen a lot of it since arriving. I was tied up in the various exhibit negotiations for a couple of days, and that time was spent in office after office. We did get out to the Fontainebleau last night, which was a wonderful meal."

"Yes, decent food, but an impossible place to get into. Takes weeks to get a reservation. I saw Senator Golding this morning, and he was telling me he made reservations a month in advance and still had to wait for a table." Warren shook his head.

Victoria wondered again how Stephen had gotten into the restaurant. "Well, maybe we hit them on a good night. We had no trouble at all." The Worthors laughed. Victoria smiled politely, unsure why they laughed so hard. Anderson looked more than a little uncomfortable.

Janet diplomatically changed the subject, and they conversed on several other topics.

"… And that was how I went into construction," Warren finished up.

Sherman removed the empty dishes. He returned with four larger blue-on-white dishes. Again, he served the Worthors first, then the others. "Breaded pork tenderloin stuffed with Black Forest ham, Munster cheese, and German mustard. Served with red cabbage and spätzle," Sherman informed them before leaving.

Victoria thought the tenderloin looked wonderful with the thick gravy around and over it, but there was a pile of what looked like very short spaghetti strands. The color and shape were wrong for pasta. She turned to Janet. "What is this?"

"It is called spätzle. It is essentially an egg noodle. Have some with the pork gravy," Janet suggested.

Victoria took a little and rolled some spätzle around her fork. She dipped the noodles into the gravy and ate it. "*Mmmmm…*" was all she needed to say.

"Making spätzle is incredibly easy. It is just eggs, flour, milk, and salt. It is a traditional side dish instead of French fries. Not that the German version of French fries are bad, by the way. Carl is a traditional cook in many senses. I suspect his mother made it this way for him. Do you like garlic?" Janet explained.

"Yes, I love it. Why?" Victoria wondered between mouthfuls.

"Carl makes a dish called Graf Dracula. It is a thick sauce that has six full cloves of garlic per serving. You serve it over a thick tenderloin steak." said Janet

"*Six* cloves?" Victoria was shocked.

"It is a meal everyone has to have at the same time, obviously. It is a very good meal if you are coming down with a cold, too." Janet chuckled.

"How did you and Warren meet?" Victoria asked.

"Oh, not a very exciting story, I am afraid. I came here from County Carlow and trained as a hairdresser, but after ten years I got tired of being in a salon. I woke up one morning wanting a complete change of career. So I took some night courses and became a computer technician. It was a good career change and nice pay raise, plus I found I was pretty good at it. I ended up in a firm that Warren bought out soon after, and I was kept on after the merger. I was called into his office to fix a problematic laptop, and a year later, he proposed." Janet looked at Warren with happy eyes.

"Love at first kilobyte," said Anderson, and they all laughed.

"Quite so, Stephen," Warren said jovially.

Janet turned to Victoria. "Tell us of your experiences in Egypt. Warren and I have always spoken about going to Cairo, but that's one destination we have missed so far. He has little business centered in the Middle East, and that is his usual excuse for going somewhere."

"Well, I—"

"Now darling, we have to pay for those trips. We may as well make some income while traveling. That way we kill two birds, as they say," Warren interrupted.

"Please finish what you were saying," Janet told Victoria, ignoring the interruption.

For the next several minutes, Victoria recounted her experiences in Cairo and Luxor, telling mostly good, some bad, and a few amusing stories along the way.

* * *

Anderson looked at Victoria as she spoke to the Worthors. It had been a long time since he had let a woman into his life, over a year and a half. He'd thought that the wound from the last time would never heal. Now, in a matter of days, he had someone who had gracefully danced past all his barriers and defenses. She was intelligent, warm, feminine, and very attractive. Anderson realized he had been missing a lot in his life over the previous months.

By the time Victoria was done speaking, the main course was finished, and the plates were cleared.

* * *

327

Sherman returned with moderately thick slices of cake topped with cherries and drizzled with a red sauce. "Black Forest cake with cherry glaze," said Sherman after the plates were put in front of them. He then produced medium-sized brandy glasses for the three alcohol drinkers and poured a small amount in each.

Victoria saw there were seven individual layers of cake, each separated by either cream or cherry filling. It lay on a small plate that had been dusted with confectioner's sugar and a chocolate drizzle pattern. "It looks too good to eat," she said finally to Janet, dessert fork in hand.

"Carl does take pride in his presentations. He will be happy to hear you were impressed."

Sherman went round the table, serving coffee and clearing the empty wine glasses. She noted that they had gone through the better part of two bottles.

Victoria pressed the side of her fork into it and met no resistance at all. She took the smallest piece with a cherry and cream layer, and it melted on her tongue. The traditional German Black Forest cake had a completely different taste and texture than the North American–style cake she was accustomed to. It was heavenly.

Conversation lagged while they consumed the cake and brandy. After they were finished, Sherman returned to clear the table. "Shall I serve coffee in the great room, sir?"

"I think so, Sherman. Thank you. Shall we retire to the other room?"

Everyone rose and moved back to the couches. The fire had been built up with fresh pieces of oak, and it crackled and popped as the flames slowly consumed it.

Sherman appeared with a large silver tray, carafe of coffee, silver bowls, and fresh cups.

"Thank you, Sherman. I will attend to the coffee," Warren said.

"Yes, sir." Sherman bowed slightly before leaving.

Warren poured coffee and handed it out to everyone. "So the exhibition will be going forward, I hear."

Victoria nodded. "Yes, that's good news for the Carnegie. The public has really thrown their support behind us. This single three-week exhibit will generate enough funds to finance at least two years of operations. There's talk of approaching the Smithsonian to take some of their items on loan. Fewer than fifteen percent of their artifacts are on display at any one time. The rest are stuck in storage. We hope to make a deal to bring several seldom-seen items to Pittsburgh."

"Excellent. I'm sure you will do well." Warren said.

"Well, to be honest, I may not be with the Carnegie once the Tutankhamun exhibit moves on. As an Egyptologist, my value to them more or less disappears with the pharaoh's items. I'll probably be back teaching at the university before too long."

"Their loss, I'm sure. Victoria, tell me a little more about Luxor. I would really like to visit the temples there. Which is the best, in your opinion?" Janet asked.

Warren began talking to Anderson about golf, and over time, they conversed on a multitude of topics, consuming several cups of coffee.

Sherman cleared the coffee table, and the evening was drawing to an end.

"Janet, thank you for having us over. You have a wonderful home," Victoria said.

Janet smiled. "I'll have to have you over some afternoon for tea and give you the full tour."

Victoria smiled back. "I'd like that."

"Bring your bathing suit. We just finished the glass roof over the seawater pool, and that is something you cannot miss out on. The view of the ocean from there is very nice."

"I will, thank you," Victoria responded.

"Well, I think we should be going," Anderson said. "Warren, Janet, it was very good of you to have us over."

Everyone stood, and Sherman appeared in the door with Victoria's scarf as if by magic.

"Thank you, Stephen. An informal dinner is so much more rewarding than entertaining businessmen. We need to do this more often," Warren said.

They began walking to the door, and Victoria decided she had drunk too much coffee and wine. "Excuse me. Is there a powder room handy?"

"Of course. Down the corridor, first door on the right." Janet pointed.

Victoria disappeared, leaving Stephen with the Worthors.

* * *

"Stephen, she is a treasure," Janet said quietly. "I can see why you like her. Do me a favor: Don't keep her in the dark about your owning the Fontainebleau for too much longer. It would not be right."

Anderson could only smile and nod slightly.

"Now that you have such a charming dinner companion, you need to come by more often, young man," Warren said.

"I shall try," he said noncommittally.

"I mean it. You need to be more sociable and get out of that rambling old bottling plant more often. You can start by being at the Sunny Brook tournament on the 23rd. I will not take no for an answer. I have not seen a driver in your hand for a while, and let's face it; I enjoy making my money back on the 19th hole." Warren wore a sly grin.

Anderson laughed heartily. Warren slapped him on the shoulder and laughed as well. Warren continued talking about golf.

* * *

Victoria appeared soon after, and Sherman helped her into her scarf. "Thank you, Sherman."

The men shook hands while Janet closed on Victoria for a pseudo-hug and pressed cheek to cheek with her. "You found a wonderful man," Janet said softly for her ear alone before withdrawing. Victoria nodded and smiled.

"Thank you for having us over," Victoria said to the Worthors, shaking hands with Warren before leaving.

"Good night," said Warren, and Janet slid under his arm in the doorway.

The limousine was waiting for them, with Kenneth standing at the open rear door. Victoria slipped in first, followed by Anderson. The door closed behind them, and they sank into the rear bench seat. Victoria slipped up against him, and his arm went around her shoulders. They said nothing.

The trip back to Watson Street was quick; at that time of night, there was little traffic. They pulled up in front of the building, and Kenneth made his way around to the rear of the car to open the door for them. Anderson emerged first and offered Victoria his hand to assist her out. She emerged, with her smile beaming to the world.

"Thank you, Kenneth." Anderson unlocked the access door with his key.

"Good night, sir."

Victoria entered the garage first, and Anderson followed. The lights were off, but there was enough light from the stairwell to see properly. Anderson locked the door behind him and found Victoria waiting for him. They walked upstairs with their arms wrapped around each other.

Once inside the foyer, the only light was from a single overhead miniature fluorescent bulb. They kicked off their shoes, and Victoria turned to him wordlessly. She melted into him and her hands began to wander across his chest. He kissed her, lightly at first, but then with passion as she reciprocated.

Wordlessly, effortlessly he scooped her up into his arms and began to walk to the stairs to his room. Her arms snaked around his neck, and she smiled. "Why are you carrying me?"

"Because you need to conserve your strength for other things tonight. If you want me to put you down, just say so." Anderson looked deeply into her eyes.

She said nothing. The rest of the night did not require words.

CHAPTER 19 – IN CAUDA VENENUM

Kenneth pulled away from the front of the red brick building. The white limousine accelerated easily as he pulled down Watson Street. Two hundred feet down the street he passed a bus stop. He saw the two men talking under the bus shelter, but thought nothing of it. He was tired and had an early start the next morning. He passed them without taking any additional notice.

He didn't know the buses had stopped coming to that street four hours ago.

* * *

The taller man tucked away the mini-binoculars he had hidden under his coat seconds before. He also produced a Walther PK380 pistol which he cocked and held in his hand. He spoke in French. "It was definitely Martin. You were right, *Colonel*. Let's go." He took a step toward the former bottling plant with the weapon against his thigh.

"Wait." *Colonel* Benoît Rochon ordered calmly, still standing in the bus shelter.

Adjudant Chef Rodin stopped and turned. "Why wait, sir? That is his home. He is right there. Let's go pay him a visit."

"Put the weapon away. It may be seen." The *colonel* ordered firmly. The larger man did so, reluctantly walking back to the shelter. "*Adjudant Chef,* I admire you. You are a man of action. You fear nothing, and I cannot imagine a more formidable soldier."

The larger man took the praise to heart; it was seldom given. The colonel continued, "However, we need to do this correctly. He is on familiar territory; we do not know what awaits us inside. So we need to plan this properly. How much did he cost us?"

That question was easily answered. "Hundreds of thousands of Euros, our careers, our country, our freedom." Rodin could barely contain his anger.

"Exactly. If you wish to balance the books, then we need to do this correctly. A quick bullet does not do this," the *colonel* said calmly.

Adjudant Chef Hugo Rodin knew his limitations. He was a man of action, not words, not imagination. The colonel was the opposite. Continuously plotting and planning, but with little physical prowess, the colonel was the brains of the pair. They needed each other to succeed and always had. Rodin was now certain that Martin had instigated the investigation against them that had them hounded out of the Legion. They were now deserters themselves and had been found guilty of several serious crimes *in absentia*. They could no longer return to France or any French territory, even with false papers. The risk of being recognized by former comrades or the *Gendarmerie Nationale* was simply too great. They had to endure a life of exile.

The *colonel* was right. A bullet would not give him the satisfaction.

"What shall we do, then, *Colonel?*" asked Rodin.

"We shall take our time, and we bring him down by degrees. Systematically take everything he holds dear from him. Strip it away layer by layer. Let him feel what he put us through. After he has lost everything, when he begs for mercy, you may end his life, but not before," Rochon said calmly.

Rodin nodded slowly as he comprehended what was in store for their former comrade. The evil grin that emerged on his face told Rochon he had his support. "Where do we start, sir?"

"I am sure the private detective who provided us with his address from the license plate number can give us more information on him and his new life. Come. We need to make arrangements," ordered Rochon.

The pair disappeared into the darkness.

AUTHOR'S AFTERWORD

When researching the French Foreign Legion, one fact becomes obvious very quickly: Much of the information about the Legion in the public domain is incomplete, exaggerated, or just plain inaccurate. One of the few accurate references I found in my research was *Life in the French Foreign Legion* by Evan McGorman. Evan spent five years in the Legion and wrote about his experiences in detail. Not only did that book provide a wealth of background information, but Evan proved to be a valuable correspondent and assisted me in shaping the careers of the characters. Anyone interested in a career with the Legion should definitely read his book first (available on Amazon.com).

In using the French Foreign Legion as a backdrop for Anderson's character, I wanted it to be realistic. That being said, Sidi Bel Abbès was indeed a Legion base, but was closed down in 1961 soon after the War of Algerian Independence. The setting of a base in the middle of a desert was too good to pass up, and I kept it open a little longer than history dictated.

Geordie Millar—the well-known nature artist, voice-over actor, musician, and my frequent dive buddy—was also a driving

force behind this novel. His motivation, encouragement, and friendship through very difficult times cannot be understated.
http://geordiemillar.com/

My friend and fellow author Keith C. Blackmore also provided support and advice. He began his writing career well before I did and was gracious enough to assist me. Keith provided me with answers to my many questions and gave me excellent feedback on this manuscript.
http://keithcblackmore.com

Several people assisted to improve this manuscript by reading early drafts and providing feedback on the characters and story. The feedback from Mark Crouse, Jan Lee, Joanne Harvey, and Ethan Jones was helpful and very much appreciated. In addition, I cannot say enough positive things about the staff at Red Adept Publishing for their support and efforts on my behalf.
http://redadeptpublishing.com

From what I can determine, the Mask of King Tutankhamun took its last trip outside of Egypt in 1979, with its final display at the American National Gallery of Art. (Multiple inquiries to the Cairo Museum to clarify this have gone unanswered.) It has been determined that the mask of King Tutankhamun is too 'fragile' for any future trips and is currently on permanent display in a dedicated room of the Cairo Museum, which I visited in 2006. Several thousand magnificent artifacts and personal items from the late pharaoh are also on display. No pictures can do that exhibit justice, and I would encourage you to see it for yourself.

If you are in Egypt, a side trip to the Giza, Saqqara, and Dahshur pyramid complexes are definitely worth your time. Saqqara and Dahshur are a short drive south of Giza. Their distance from Cairo make them less convenient to tourists, and they are therefore much less crowded and much more accessible.

Today, only three hundred tourists are permitted to enter the pyramids at Giza each day. Given the many thousands who go to Giza daily, your chances of getting inside are slim. The Red Pyramid at Dahshur barely has any visitors. It has no visitation limits and can be explored at a leisurely pace. Be warned that entry into the burial chamber is challenging. After walking up a third of the pyramid on the outside, there is a small but very long sloping tunnel that needs to be navigated to get down into the interior. Ancient Egyptians were quite small, but even they would have issues in such an enclosed space. The inconvenience is worth it once you get to see the massive corbel-vaulted ceiling of the main burial chamber.

The Valleys of the Kings, Queens, and Artisans—along with the Temples of Hatchepsut, Luxor, and Karnak are all located in or near Luxor—are also worthy to be experienced firsthand. Spending several days in Luxor is recommended.

I could not find any monetary value for the mask and the determination of eighty million dollars is purely from my imagination. Truly, it must be considered priceless, for Tutankhamun has the only tomb ever found to be completely intact, and the burial mask is therefore unique. In conducting my research, I found many variations on how to spell Tutankhamun / Nebkheprure, but I chose to use the spelling as presented on the Cairo Museum web pages. The Cairo Museum website is unreliable and often down, but it can be found at:

http://egyptianmuseumcairo.org

The Jensen Museum of Norfolk, Virginia; the Harcourt, Johnson & Summerville law firm; the Worthor Corporation; Credence Security; El Rashim Security; and Invarco Holdings are fictitious and not based on any actual institutions. The Carnegie Institution for Science was established in Washington, D.C., by Andrew Carnegie in 1902 with a ten million dollar grant. Two million dollars more was granted in 1907, and a further ten million in 1911. The Institution was established as an organization for scientific discovery. The Carnegie Museum of Natural History is one of four Carnegie museums run by the Carnegie Institution for Science. If there was a short list of museums that could afford to bring Tutankhamun's mask to North America, the Carnegie Museum of Natural History would certainly be on it. It is located at 4400 Forbes Avenue, Pittsburgh, PA.

http://www.carnegiemnh.org/

The Federal Bureau of Investigation has a dedicated Art Crime Team. It comprises fourteen special agents, each responsible for art crimes in their respective geographical areas. The Art Crime Team receives specialized training in art and cultural property investigations. They take on cases around the world, cooperating with foreign law enforcement agencies and FBI legal attachés. Three special trial attorneys from the U.S. Department of Justice are assigned to the Art Crime Team for supporting prosecutions. As I write this, the Art Crime Team has recovered over 2,650 items of art and cultural property with a value exceeding 150 million dollars. I purposely opted to not use this team in the novel so I could use the more generalized character of Special Agent Bryant, who will be seen again. The FBI has their Web site at:

http://www.fbi.gov

The *Costarican Trader* (named *Costa Rican Trader* in some references) exists, but its days of hauling cargo are long past. It was a Liberian-registered steel-hulled freighter that ran into high winds and heavy seas on April 28th, 1967. It lost maneuvering and drifted stern-first into the rocks north of Halibut Bay, near Halifax, Nova Scotia. The crew was able to walk directly onto the shore, and the grounded ship was so accessible that RCMP officers had to be posted to keep looters off her. The vessel was 376.5′ long, with a beam of 51.6′, draft of 21.7′, and was either

2650 or 4141 tons displacement (records conflict, but I am inclined to believe the larger amount given her length).

The vessel currently lies in eighty-five feet of very cold water, and I saw her when taking my wreck diving course in October of 2007. It has suffered terrible damage over the years. I was taken aback when I saw inch-thick steel plating torn and peeled back like paper in places. The bow was ripped off by years of wave action and currently points straight up at the surface. It has formed an artificial reef and is the home for many species of fish, anemone, and invertebrates. When I found the need for a traditional Atlantic general cargo freighter, the *Trader* fit the bill perfectly. The description of the ship is based on photographs, registry records, and my own direct observations of the wreck inside and out.

The tug *Rozi* is also a wreck sitting at 118 feet down and is located northwest of Malta in the Mediterranean. I reasoned that if Clive Cussler can raise the *Titanic* from 12,600 feet for one of his novels, then surely bringing up a small freighter and harbor tug from shallow coastal waters was within my meager powers.

FedEx, UPS, DHL, and the other courier services routinely X-ray and otherwise inspect packages in their possession. Evidence of this can be found on the various courier websites under their "Conditions of Carriage" pages. Why? Many couriered shipments go on the same aircraft that you and I travel on daily, and they have to make sure there is nothing nefarious on board. I ignored this fact in the novel for the purposes of dramatization. Anyone who sends illicit weaponry or any other contraband through a courier is probably going to get caught.

Finally, the techniques used by Kogan and 'the lawyer' to throw off investigators are also inherently flawed. There are ways, remarkably simple methods actually, for police investigators to get around them. Forgive me if I don't explain what or how. It was never my intent to make a criminal's life easier, and I would never publish anything that could flaw an investigation. Don't say you have not been warned. If you do choose to use any of the described techniques for masking criminal activity, don't write me from your cell block to complain they didn't work.

I am a Divemaster with several hundred dives under my weight belt. This made writing the underwater sequences very easy, as I simply drew from my own experiences. Unfortunately, I do not have a rebreather qualification. Rebreathers are considered 'technical' diving, and proper training is considered so important that some rebreather electronics come locked when shipped from the factory. They have to be unlocked by a qualified instructor before use. Not wanting to misrepresent the use of a rebreather in this novel, I had to rely on feedback from Rebreather and Technical Diving Instructor Howard Packer of CCR Dive Training LLC in Miami Beach, Florida. Howard is an enthusiastic advocate of rebreather technology and its safe use in diving.

http://www.ccrdivetraining.com

As an amateur student of history, I try to keep things historically accurate wherever possible. Luckily, I can fall back on the fact that this is, in the end, a novel of fiction. Any 'errors' you may have come across were either unintentional or necessary for dramatic effect.

Thank you for supporting my work! I hope you enjoyed the first book of the three currently planned for the Legionnaire series. Please feel free to leave a review to let other readers know what you think.

http://sjparkinson.com